The Ten Commandments of our Fake Marriage

J. M. Brinson

ISBN –

Paperback: 979-8-9857294-6-7

eBook: 979-8-9857294-7-4

This is a work of fiction. Names, characters, incidents, and dialogues are products of the author's imagination and are not to be construed as real. Any resemblance to actual events or persons, living or dead, is entirely coincidental.

Cover Design by: Meghan Mcculough

Interior formatting by: Victoria Lynn with The Glory Writers

First Printing

Contents

For the Natalie to my Kit and the Harry to my Declan, I love you to the
moon and back.
And for Aunt Peggy, who has always encouraged my love of words.

First Commandment: Thou Shalt Not Drinketh From The Carton

Anna Katherine slouched in the stool at the bar top of Declan's kitchen. "If we're going to do this, we need a set of rules."

Declan nodded thoughtfully. "Yeah, totally. I'm with you on that."

She was confused when he disappeared from the kitchen, but when he came back with a pen and a notebook full of paper, she understood his plan and started laughing when she saw him write The Ten Commandments of Our Fake Marriage *at the top in his loopy handwriting.*

"I'm coming up with the first one, and don't even try to argue with me or I'm taking back my agreement." Anna Katherine expected Declan to complain, but he simply smiled, and his eyes shone with amusement as he watched her. She thought for a moment, but when she saw him go to the fridge and grab the milk, she knew exactly what the first 'commandment' was going to be.

"You can't drink straight from the carton."

Declan's eyes slowly met Anna Katherine's over the rim of the milk jug before carefully placing it on the counter without taking a sip.

"It's easier and more time efficient than getting a glass," he argued.

"It's gross. If I'm going to be forced to live with and marry you, we will both at least act civilized.*"*

He groaned, rolled his eyes, and trudged to the cabinet for a glass for his milk.

Anna Katherine smiled. "This is such a beautiful start to our marriage."

1

"Carson is a really nice young man, Anna Katherine." Patricia's voice filled the car through the speaker of Anna Katherine's phone.

Anna Katherine was on her way to her best friend's house. She had received a frightening letter that demanded Nat's involvement, and her mother, who had impeccably horrible timing, chose that moment to call for a nice catchup.

Of course, by catching up, she meant trying to bully Anna Katherine into another blind date.

"I'm sure he is, Mom." Anna Katherine did her best to keep her irritation at bay.

"His mother works with your father, and he comes from a respectable family. He went to the private Christian school in town, graduated top in his class at Millsaps, and regularly attends church."

"He sounds perfect for you. Why don't you dump your husband and go on a date with Carson?"

"Anna Katherine Tran!"

"I'm just saying, Mom…" She trailed off, her shoulders tensing as someone pulled out in front of her, forcing her to hold in the road rage. "He seems perfectly decent for someone who has your taste in men."

"My taste." Patricia's voice had gone flat, clearly unimpressed with Anna Katherine's joke.

"Yes."

Patricia Tran meant well, Anna Katherine knew this. Her mom was simply acting out of concern and love for her. Anna Katherine just wished good ol' Patty would maybe be concerned for her a little less than she was currently. Anna Katherine, much to her mother's dismay, was perfectly fine being single at the ripe young age of twenty-five. She had all the time in the world to settle down. She wanted to spend her twenties exploring who she was, what her role in this world was going to be, and well, *not* spending these years settling down and immediately having children like her mother had.

The world was consistently changing, and what was once expected of young twenty-somethings wasn't what Anna Katherine saw for herself. She never felt led in any direction other than where she currently sat.

Which was in a run down vehicle that she could barely afford as a full-time barista at Hattie's Cafe. Sure, she made some extra money with her photography side-hustle. But that hadn't really taken off yet, and baristas only did so well with tips.

Her mother thought Anna Katharine could do more with herself, and maybe Patricia was right. But Anna Katherine felt content where she was, and until she felt the pull from somewhere much more demanding than

Patricia, she was going to stay right where she was.

"If you're implying that I don't have good taste—"

"That is not at all what I am implying, Mother. And you know that. What I am simply saying is that what you wanted in a husband and what I want are two completely different things. Dad is great for you, but I don't need a carbon copy of him for myself."

"You're quite impossible. Have I told you that lately?"

Anna Katherine smiled. "Not lately, no."

There was a deep sigh on the other end of the phone. But it was not the sigh of defeat. Anna Katherine knew it would take a lot more than her refusing to go on a blind date to stop her mother from further meddling. "Alright then. I will tell Carson's mother to call off the date."

"Thank you."

"You're still coming to family dinner this week, aren't you?"

Anna Katherine nearly snorted before she said, "As if you'd let me miss."

"Hush now. You make me sound like I'm the impossible one."

"You are!"

"Goodbye, daughter! Love you!"

And with that, Patty hung up right as Anna Katherine pulled into Nat's complex.

Serenity Grove was a small city, big town that was nestled in the heart of the deep south in Mississippi. Anna Katherine had only ever lived in Serenity Grove along with most occupants of her home. Few ever left, and if they did, they usually came back. There was something about Serenity Grove that drew people in. The only reason Patricia met Anna Katherine's father, Timothy, was because he moved to Serenity Grove to attend their local college.

As far as hometowns go, Anna Katherine figured she could have landed in a much worse place. The residents were friendly and genuinely kind. The pine trees that hovered over the streets always made her feel safe in her little southern cocoon. That is, until the evergreen pines turned yellow, causing her body to betray her as allergies wrecked her life.

The only thing she didn't love was the humidity and heat, which she was reminded of the minute she stepped out of her car and was hit with the sticky wall of wet air. Her hair was already sticking to the back of her neck by the time she made it into Nat's apartment.

Nat's house always seemed to smell like cinnamon. No matter what season they were in or if she had just burned a strawberry Pop-Tart in the toaster again, it never failed to smell the same. Welcoming and cinnamon-y. It was just one of the reasons Anna Katherine loved visiting.

Another reason was because it was Nat's home. Nat, her constant and forever best friend. And best friends are supposed to be comforting during a time of crisis. Which worked out well as Anna Katherine seemed to live in a constant state of crisis.

"You knew prices were going to go up."

Nat was sitting on the floor by her coffee table. School had just started back, and her coffee table reflected that. It was no longer clear of all papers, notebooks, and planners like it had been during the summer. Now there was not an inch where Anna Katherine could see the stained wood beneath the organized mess.

"But I didn't know it was going to be so significant!"

Anna Katherine snatched the letter from where it had fluttered to the floor when it fell out of her pocket. The new price for her rent stared her in the face. That, plus the rising prices for WiFi, gas, and the basic foods she lived off of—there was no way she was going to make ends meet without finding a new place to live.

Nat looked up from what appeared to be a scribbled picture of poop. "We talked about this. You agreed to start budgeting and to put some extra cash away so you wouldn't be put in a bind."

"Is that a poop emoji drawing?"

Nat, to her credit, didn't seem shocked by the question and knew exactly what Anna Katherine was referring to. "No, they were told to draw and color a square."

"That is a triangle at best."

"And poop at worst."

Anna Katherine let out a half-hearted laugh, "Exactly."

She watched as Nat wrote something on the paper and set it aside on one of the many piles of paper on the table.

"So?"

Nat's voice startled her, but Anna Katherine was still able to feign ignorance. "So what?"

"What are you going to do?"

Anna Katharine pulled her knees up to her chest and rested her chin on top. "I have no idea."

There was a pause, and then Nat sighed and finally got up from the papers. "You're waiting for me to offer for you to stay here."

Anna Katherine gasped, "I am doing no such thing!"

"You have exactly two friends: Declan and myself. You could potentially stay with Alex, but I have a feeling neither of you would want that unless it was truly a life or death situation. You could also move out of the city and back with your parents, but I'm sure both you and Mrs. Patty wouldn't be able to survive that. So that leaves Declan and myself." She paused again, and gave Anna Katherine a pointed look. "In a way, Declan makes more sense. He does have an extra bedroom. But—"

"My parents would have a fit."

Nat nodded, "As would I. That's a hot mess express just waiting to take off."

"It could work."

"No it couldn't. For so many reasons. And I would be an awful friend to say otherwise."

Anna Katherine couldn't help but smile when she said, "Well, we both know he won't turn me away."

"Which is exactly why it would be a bad idea. Neither of you can say no to each other."

"It's not like I'm not exactly getting any other offers."

Nat laughed, but there was little humor in it. She stared off in space for a moment, and Anna Katherine could almost see the wheels turning in her friend's brain as she thought things over. Nat was a woman of habit, and she liked her space. But she also had a heart the size of Texas. If there was someone in need and she could do something about it, then she would. No matter how much she cringed at the thought.

"You can stay with me."

Anna Katherine grinned, and not even Nat's hands lifting in a halt in front of her chest could make it go away.

"But only temporarily. We need a time limit."

"Six months?"

"I was thinking two."

"Four?"

"Three."

Anna Katherine's smile widened. "Three it is."

Declan wasn't surprised when he unlocked his door and saw shoes that weren't his by his entryway table. He also wasn't surprised by the blue rain jacket hanging on the hooks near his entryway closet or by the sleeping woman on his couch. The only thing he could see of her was a tuft of black hair peeking out from underneath the blanket. He had long since grown accustomed to and accepted the fact that Kit seemed to make herself at home in his apartment.

He hung up his bag and jacket on the spare hooks and took off his shoes as quietly as he could. He peeked over the couch to check on Kit while rolling up his sleeves to start cooking himself - and apparently Kit - dinner.

It was nothing extravagant. Just soup and sandwiches. It was the end of the month, and Declan desperately needed to go to the grocery. He made do with what was left in his pantry.

He was pouring the soup into two bowls when there was movement from the couch, and soft feet padded their way into the kitchen.

"Hey, sleepyhead." He greeted his best friend without turning around as he finished up the plates and bowls.

There was a short moment of silence before she answered, and when she did, he could still hear the sleep in her voice. "When did you get home?"

He turned around then, and found her already sitting on the bar stool, black hair all askew, her hazel, almond-shaped eyes still heavy with sleep, and what he was pretty sure was dried drool on the side of her mouth and chin.

"Not too long ago. Didn't want to wake you up."

"I 'preciate that." She took the plate and bowl from him and immediately started eating.

"What do you want to drink?"

She shrugged, and when he still didn't get an answer after a few beats, he filled up a glass with water. When she chugged it as soon as he placed it in front of her, he eyed her.

"Have you drunk anything other than coffee today?"

"I had an iced coffee for lunch."

"That is not..." He stopped and shook his head, trying not to roll his eyes. "You know what? I'm not even going to start. It's not like you listen anyway."

In response, she just smiled as she took a bite of her sandwich.

After that, they ate together in silence. Neither one of them felt the need to fill it with small talk. Declan thought that might be one of the reasons he preferred her company to that of many others. Doing life with her wasn't awkward, and in the rare moments where it was, they just kept going, rarely allowing it to interfere with their friendship.

Once she had completely finished her sandwich and licked the last drops of soup from her spoon, she pushed her plate and bowl away and rested her arms on the counter.

"So. Declan."

He eyed her carefully. "Yes?"

"I need a favor."

He sighed and acted like he was put out when he asked: "What is it this time?"

"As we all know, my rent has gone up. Exponentially."

He nodded and took the last bite of his soup. "And you and Nat came up with a very great plan for you to budget so you wouldn't panic."

"Exactly. The thing is..." She trailed off and refused to look him in the eye. "I may have forgotten to put that money into savings."

"Anna Katherine."

"Don't *Anna Katherine* me!"

"I will when you make stupid mistakes!"

"It was an innocent mistake!"

He gave her a flat, unimpressed look. "An innocent mistake can also be a stupid mistake."

She groaned. "It just... happened so fast."

"It didn't. But what is the favor you need?"

"I'm moving out. I'll be staying with Nat while looking for a new, cheap place to stay. The thing is, Nat's apartment is small, and all my stuff won't fit. Even if it could, I don't think she'd allow it. But you..." She trailed off and gave him a hopeful look.

"But I have a spare bedroom." He stated flatly, eyeing her carefully.

"You never use it! Right now the only thing in there is your Christmas tree! And it's August!"

He ignored the dig about the Christmas tree. "So you want to use that bedroom as storage until you find a new apartment?"

She nodded. Her bun was falling even more to the side with each nod, and she looked so endearing and hopeful. He couldn't have denied her even if he wanted to. Which he very much wanted to. He liked his things organized. And, yes, there was a Christmas tree in the spare bedroom, but it was put away nicely in the corner. All he had to do was pull it out for the holidays. Everything had a place. He knew that when Kit was finished with his place, he would be lucky if he was able to find the bed. But, this was *Kit*.

He sighed. "Fine. When is this happening?"

He had barely managed to get the question out when she squealed, leapt out of the stool, and came running around the counter to give him a rib-crushing hug.

"Thank you, thank you, thank you!"

With a laugh, he hugged her back.

Anna Katherine met Declan during their sophomore year of college. She was introduced to him through her then boyfriend, Jonah, and when her and Jonah had a messy breakup, she was able to keep Declan. Jonah kept most everything else, including but not limited to her dignity, but she felt like she came out as the winner because of Declan. He'd been by her side through thick and thin ever since.

And since graduation, they had been through more "thin" than "thick."

Another thing in her life that was just as constant as Declan—other than Nat, of course—was her job.

Opening Hattie's Cafe in the wee hours of the morning and having to get there before the crack of dawn was not necessarily one of Anna Katherine's favorite parts of being a barista—she definitely wasn't a morning person naturally—but the beautiful sun rises were definitely a plus. As was her boss.

Martin, the owner of the small cafe, was the main reason she had never gone in search of a new or different job. He was good to his employees, and she was loyal. Plus, every major and minor holiday, he gave them all bonuses. The job also allowed her the time and flexibility to work on building her reputation as a freelance photographer. Her life wasn't traditional by any means, but it allowed her the freedom to do what she loved.

As much as Anna Katherine hated waking up early, the opening shifts were her favorite. There was typically a morning rush filled with regulars whose orders she knew by heart, a fact that helped the first hours go by relatively quickly. After her "lunch" break (because who really eats lunch at 9:30?), she typically only had a few hours left. Unless, of course, she decided to work a double. Which happened more often than not as of late, especially with the rising prices of, well, everything in her life it seemed.

Before Declan started his "big boy" job, he would come visit Anna Katherine at work during lunch. It was one of the things adulthood had stripped of them that she missed. So she was a little surprised when she spotted him walking down the sidewalk headed toward the coffee shop. Since the weather was still warm enough to fry an egg on the asphalt, he had ditched his cardigan and rolled up his sleeves. It was a look that Anna Katherine preferred on him. However, she did not prefer the deep scowl on his face. She much favored his "cheeky" smile and eyes that seemed to shine whenever they bickered.

"Kit."

Upon walking through the store doors, he marched—there was really no other word that fit his walk—to the counter and, in a much more dramatic sense than his usual calm demeanor usually demanded, slammed the palms of his hand on the counter.

She paused and took in his mess of honey-tinged brown hair. It was always slightly disheveled. He somehow managed to make it work even when wearing his professional attire. Not for the first time, she was tempted to run her hands through it. She shook away the thought. She cleared her throat before she asked, "What's wrong?"

Drawing a deep breath, he stared at his hands a moment, seeming to realize how dramatic he was being. Removing his hands from the counter in order to cross his arms and lean across the bar toward her. "So you know Harry and I had to get visas, right?"

She nodded. "Yeah. You got student visas for school, and Harry has been reminding you to update yours."

"Right." He glanced away from her and scratched his chin. "About that..."

"Declan." She moved into his line of sight, "What did you do?"

He grimaced. "It's more a matter of what I did *not* do."

"Declan Anthony Mullins, I swear if you don't start talking and tell me what happened..."

"Okay, okay, okay. Sheesh." There was a beat where he watched her carefully and then continued, "I'm being deported."

Anna Katherine's eyes went wide, and she found herself unable to do anything but stare at him.

Declan, finally finding his words again, continued. "I never renewed my visa after graduation. Harry kept reminding me, but I kept procrastinating."

"That's not procrastinating, Declan! That's flat out ignoring it!"

The few customers that were in the shop glanced over at them, and Anna Katherine lowered her voice. "What the heck, Dec? What were you thinking? You're supposed to be the logical one out of the two of us! I get evicted, but you have your life sorted! You're not supposed to be on this trainwreck with me!"

He scratched his chin again, his eyes downcast and refusing to meet hers. "I just... I thought I had time, and then I kept forgetting." He smiled, something that seemed so out of place in this ridiculous conversation. "You didn't get evicted, though. Stop exaggerating to the point of lying."

"This isn't something that you forget!" She slammed the rag that was in her hand onto the counter and stormed to the espresso machine. She chose to ignore his comment about her exaggerations as well as his stares as she dumped out the old grounds, hammering it against the rod on top of the trash. She slammed it a few more times before measuring and tamping out fresh espresso.

Declan was watching her, eyes narrowed in either concern or confusion. Anna Katherine couldn't quite figure it out. Nor did she want to at this moment.

"You're mad."

She gave him a look that clearly portrayed what she was thinking before going back to the espresso and steaming half-and-half. She hated the smell of steamed half-and-half. It had a tendency to smell like spoiled cheese. Once the milk was done—extra, extra hot—she dumped it into a cup. Some of it splattered on the counter, and she huffed but otherwise ignored it. She started the espresso and stared as the piping hot black liquid poured into the small silver cup. She could feel Declan's eyes on her, but she was refusing to look at him. Dumping the two shots of espresso into the cup, she sprinkled raw sugar and cinnamon on top, before placing the lid on and slamming it down in front of Declan. Milk and espresso squirted out the small hole from the force of her anger.

Declan stared.

"Here. Maybe a breve will wake up some of those brain cells if they're not already fully dead."

"Why are you so upset about this?"

Her eyes went wide, and she wished she could slap him. She held it in though. As much as her brother could argue the point, she wasn't one for physical violence. Mainly because she was at work, only slightly because he was her friend.

"Maybe because my friend is an idiot and now the government is kicking him out." She took a steadying breath, but it didn't do much to calm her rampant heart.

"Okay." Declan sighed and nodded. "I am an idiot. But maybe we can fix this."

Anna Katherine looked at him incredulously. "There's no fixing this! You forgot. The government saw. You're getting kicked out. And I'm losing my best friend!"

Anna Katherine hated how his eyes softened when she let that last part slip out. She also hated how his hand covered hers, but she didn't move it away.

"Oh, Kit..." He gave her hand a squeeze.

"Don't do that."

A small smile appeared. "Do what?"

"Pity me."

He let out a hollow laugh. "I feel the farthest thing from pity toward you."

She ignored him. "If anything, I should be pitying you."

"See, this is the Kit I know and love."

She glared at him and yanked her hand away. "You know nothing."

He nodded as if he was agreeing with her.

"It's just empty space up there isn't it?" She leaned forward and tapped between his eyes. "Just air and cobwebs."

"You're right. That's how I win trivia every week. The cobwebs are really pulling their weight."

She glared. "I hate you."

He smiled. A real smile this time. One that reached his eyes and made them crinkle. "The feeling is mutual, Kit-Kat."

That night when Anna Katherine got back to her apartment, Declan was there. He was lounging on the old, possibly moldy couch, feet propped on her rickety coffee table, and scrolling through Netflix on her computer. Her TV was one of the first things she got rid of when she was trying to save money for her rent going up.

It was hard to believe she only had two weeks left in this apartment.

She dumped her keys in the bowl on the coffee table and slipped her shoes off. "Why are you not at your apartment?"

He looked away from the screen and watched her. "So I might've panicked earlier today. I'm not for-sure getting deported. There's a way around that. I am, however, getting fined."

She gawked at him.

"But," he raised a finger in her direction and a wicked smile appeared, "I have an idea."

"Oh?" She was only partially listening as she went to her kitchen to find a snack. There wasn't much there, but she found popcorn she had popped last week saved in a baggy and grabbed it along with a glass of water.

"There's a way for me to stay and to attain my citizenship here," Declan called from his spot in the living room.

She scoffed as she joined him on the couch. "And what's that?"

He repositioned himself so that he was facing her. "I can get married to someone who is already a citizen."

She laughed, "What? Are you just going to find someone off the street? Declan, that's ridiculous, not to mention *illegal*."

"It wouldn't be someone random. It would have to be someone I know very well."

"Mhm." She took the computer from him and started scrolling through Netflix herself.

"And someone who knows me really well."

She nodded. "Right. So, who's the lucky lady? You haven't been on a date in ages, and the only person who *might* know you well enough is our beloved Harry."

"You're forgetting one very important person."

"Who?" She glanced at him briefly before going back to her search on Netflix. "I know all of your friends—not that you have that many—and no one knows you as well as him. You don't even have many friends who are women. I mean, there is Nat, but I think she would rather kill you than marry you."

He nodded. "Yeah, Nat is definitely out of the question."

"And I mean unless you're thinking about getting back together with—"

"No."

She froze, realizing what she had been about to say. "Right. Not her."

Finally she put the computer on the table and turned to face Declan. "So who will it be?"

Declan stared at her, and there was something there in his eyes. It was the same look he gave her during trivia when he knew she had the answer, but her brain wasn't cooperating with her. This time, though, it made her stomach tickle. She ignored it and mentally went through all of the people, specifically women, that he knew. Well, that he knew and would be willing to marry. There was no one that she could think of. No one else in his life knew him better than Harry and herself.

Her heart stopped. She felt her eyes go wide. Her mouth went dry.

"Declan Mullins. You are *not* thinking what I think you're thinking."

Seeming pleased that she had pieced it together, he smiled wide and spread his arms out. "You make the most sense!"

"Exactly what a girl wants to hear when being proposed to."

"You know me already. We're best friends. It is totally believable that we start dating and get married quickly!"

"Declan, no!"

"Think about it, Kit! It solves both of our problems! I won't get deported, and if we get married, you can move in with me. You won't have to move in with Nat or your parents or Alex. You said it earlier, I have a spare bedroom!"

She couldn't take her eyes off of him. Surely this wasn't the same logical friend she's had for years. Slowly, she shook her head in disbelief. "This is crazy."

"It will get your mom off your back. I know she's still hounding you to get married."

"I'm twenty-five. There is no rush for me to get married. I don't know why she's pushing so hard. It's not like I'm on a death sentence."

"You pay what you can for rent. Or just buy the groceries or something. I don't know. We can work out payments and who buys what later. But we can get married, and you can move in with me. Mum will be ecstatic, you won't be homeless, and I won't move back to Ireland. Everyone wins!"

"And what happens if we get caught?"

"Well, I'm pretty sure we will get fined and/or go to prison." His voice dripped with sarcasm.

"Declan!"

He was entirely too calm for her liking. "Look." He placed his hand on her knee. "Just think about it, okay? I'll do some research and figure everything else out. But just... don't dismiss it just yet."

She felt herself softening, and she hated it. She never could say no to him. "Fine. I'll think on it."

He leaned back, lifting his arms above his head like he was cheering while watching one of those soccer matches he loved so much.

"That isn't a yes, Declan."

He smirked. "But it isn't a no either."

She shoved the computer toward him. "Shut up and find us something to watch."

2

Declan graduated with an accounting degree, something that went completely over Anna Katherine's head. She *barely* graduated with a degree in general social sciences. Her parents had told her that the degree she had chosen would make it difficult to find a job, but she hadn't cared at the time. Now she made a living as a barista, and if Declan hadn't found her a very cheap apartment years ago, she would be living out her worst nightmare—living in her childhood home with her parents. She shivered just thinking about it.

"I'm going to need you to start from the beginning. I really do not understand what is happening right now." Nat was speaking slowly and carefully and in a tone that Anna Katherine had come to learn was her teacher-voice.

They were both in Nat's classroom. There was a pleasant scene of woodland animals frolicking painted on the one wall that didn't have doors or windows. Anna Katherine's brother had sketched it on the wall, and Anna Katherine and Nat had painted it the summer after Nat's first year of teaching. Underneath it was the classroom library filled with picture and story books that her kindergarteners loved along with a couple of bean bag chairs. That's where Anna Katherine sat beside a chubby little chipmunk who sat on a tree branch on the wall staring at her.

She sighed. "To be completely honest, I'm not entirely sure either."

"Kit."

She let out a long whine that her mother would have scolded her for. But she didn't feel like finding the words to explain this situation. Unfortunately, Nat wasn't a mind-reader. That was truly the only downfall of their friendship. "What are you confused about? I'm homeless. Declan is about to get deported. Marriage solves all of our problems."

Nat gaped at her, "Marriage is *sacred*."

Anna Katharine looked up at the painting. "Did you hear that, Chipmunk? Little-Miss-Angry-at-the-World says marriage is sacred. Do you remember when she swore to never get married?"

Nat threw a red crayon at her. "Do not talk to the woodland creatures. My children do it enough. One day I'm scared they are going to talk back."

"The point is, you have no room to call me out on this."

"True." She opened her desk drawer and pulled out another red crayon to finish whatever she was working on. "But Mother Dearest does."

"What Patricia doesn't know won't kill her."

"I think hiding the fact that you are *married* is going to be a hard thing to do."

"Obviously." Anna Katherine sat up with a huff. "We won't hide that from her. Just the fact that it's, you know, a sham."

There was silence for a moment before Nat spoke up again. "Did he at least ask properly or did he just... say it?"

"He obviously asked. He didn't come into my work demanding that I marry him."

"That's not... What I meant was, did he propose properly?"

"With a ring and a huge romantic gesture? Heck no. He looked panicked and could barely get it out."

"If my best friend is getting married, I demand a proposal."

"It's *my* life," Kit argued back.

Another beat of silence, and then, "You're not really thinking of marrying him, are you? If they find out it's not legit, there are fines and charges."

Anna Katherine shrugged. "What else am I supposed to do? He's going to be shipped off if I don't do this for him."

"Anna Katherine Marie Tran."

Anna Katherine gasped, "Do not call me by my full name!"

Nat ignored her. "It is not your job to clean up his messes. He messed up with his visa, not you. This is his problem to fix."

"Yeah, but if I can help him..."

"No but's, Kit. I'm serious. This is a *felony*."

Anna Katherine stared at the fluffy carpet that laid between two small bookshelves instead of looking at her friend. If Nat saw her, she'd know she was nearly already set on doing this. After all, it was *Declan*. She couldn't say no to him. Even if she could say no, he had done so much for her during their friendship. Maybe this was the one thing she could do for him in return.

If someone off the street asked Declan who his best friend was, he wouldn't hesitate before saying Anna Katherine. However, if someone from his friend group asked, he'd say Harry Whitlock. Mainly because he didn't want to listen to his friend whine if he said anyone other than him. And it was true— Harry was a close friend and one of the best, but nobody compared to Kit. Which was why it made complete sense for him to marry her in order for him to get out of this mess he found himself in.

When Harry came over to hang out after Declan had met with Kit the previous night, the first thing out of Declan's mouth was, "Apparently I forgot to renew my visa."

Harry froze and then very carefully placed the food he had brought with him on the counter. "What do you mean? I reminded you every day for a month."

"It wasn't every day."

Harry just stared.

"Yeah, well, y'know…" Declan trailed off before walking over and putting the beer in the fridge. "It's all a real mess right now. Unless I figure something out, which I think I have, I'm getting fined and possibly deported."

As if in slow motion, Harry blinked. "And what mad plan have you come up with this time?"

Declan turned around to face him so he could see whatever reaction Harry was sure to have. "I asked Kit to marry me."

Another blink. "Mate."

Somehow Harry was able to encapsulate all of his thoughts and feelings into that one word. Maybe it was a talent that all Australians had, but Declan was pretty sure it was a talent reserved for his friend.

The two of them had met early on in their first year at university. The school made it fairly easy for students from abroad to meet and get to know one another, and since the school's football team was well known globally, there were many international students to get to know. However, it was a curly, auburn-haired, green-eyed Aussie that found him and decided to stick around. Back then, Harry had been more like a golden retriever than a human.

"Don't look at me like that." Declan rolled his eyes and grabbed the plastic-ware in the drawer Kit always shoved them into.

"Are we sure this is a good idea?" Harry asked while looking through the menus Declan had dumped in front of him.

"Why wouldn't it be? Better than the alternative, innit?"

Harry didn't miss a beat. "You're already fully in love with the girl."

Declan shot him a glare. "I am not in love with Anna Katherine."

Harry chuckled. "Right. And I'm not Australian. Either way, you're definitely keen on her."

Declan began divvying up the Thai food that Harry had brought over. "Being keen on someone and being in love with someone are two different things. We've known each other for ages. She's fit and makes me laugh. Of course I'm attracted to her on some level, but she's my friend. It'll go away. We've been friends for too long for it not to."

Declan ignored the disbelief on Harry's face as he walked back to the couch with his plate full of food. Thankfully, Harry didn't bring it up for the rest of the night.

The next day at work all Declan could think about was that he had all but gotten down on one knee and proposed to his best friend.

He was mad.

He was a fool.

He was a mad fool.

And he was an idiot for forgetting about his visa.

He was in a daze all morning, and the first chance he got, he left for lunch. He had just gotten off the elevator when his phone vibrated.

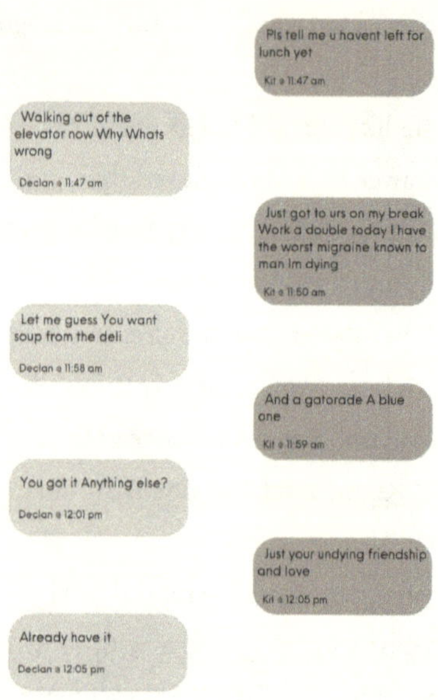

He was a mad fool.

And he was an idiot for thinking he *wasn't* infatuated with this girl.

If Anna Katherine hadn't been sure she had been about to die from the pain behind her eyes, she'd send a flurry of heart emojis. Instead, she turned off all the lights in the apartment, closed the blinds, and curled up on the couch under the blanket Declan's mom knitted last Christmas, and it didn't take long for her to fall asleep.

She woke up to bags rustling, something falling off the counter, and Declan muttering under his breath.

"You're awful at being quiet, Dec."

She caught him grimacing when she opened her eyes to mere slits. He looked apologetic when he said, "I really was trying to be quiet."

Anna Katherine sat up, and when she noticed the small carton in his hands, she smiled. "What's that you got there?"

Declan looked down at the ice cream in his hands, almost as if he had forgotten about it. "Oh. I got you some mint chocolate chip. I know it's your favorite."

Anna Katherine made grabby-hands at it, making him laugh.

He was still laughing as he shook his head and said, "You're going to ruin your appetite, Kit-Kat."

She huffed. "I'm the one with the migraine. Just give me what I want before I decide not to keep you from being deported."

He laughed again, but grabbed a spoon and brought her the ice cream. He went back for his sandwich and her soup, and when he joined her on the couch, he lifted her feet up to make room for himself before letting them fall on his lap. For a moment he watched as she shoveled the ice cream in her mouth, and then he asked, "So does this mean you've decided?"

She gave him a side-eye. "You knew I wouldn't be able to say no to you, not even for something as ridiculous and outlandish as this. Which should make me upset. But, yeah, I've decided."

He beamed at her, and she rolled her eyes.

"I promise you won't regret this!"

"Pretty sure I already do."

He gave her legs a pat. "Don't worry that pretty little head of yours. This will all work out. I know it."

She took another bite of ice cream before saying, "I already told Nat about your mad idea."

His lips lifted in a smirk. "Yeah, I already told Harry, too. I guess we need to come up with a game plan, huh?"

She nodded, "Yeah. Get our story straight and all."

He took a bite of his sandwich, and around his mouthful of food, he asked, "What time do you get off?"

"Five, but I'm meeting with some friends."

"Oh, yeah. I forgot. What about tomorrow night?"

She nodded. "Free as a bird. I'll be all yours."

"Music to my ears."

Second Commandment: Thou Shalt Not Tell Anyone Past, Present, or Future That Our Marriage is a Sham

"No one can know the truth of why we're getting married. Not even Alex."

Anna Katherine pulled at her bottom lip. "Except for H and Nat."

Declan's eyes crinkled. "Right. Other than them."

She was quiet for a moment as she thought about all the people they were about to lie to.

"I'm awful at lying to my brother."

"Well, between now and whenever you talk to him next, you better get good at it."

Anna Katherine stuck her tongue out at him, but he ignored it and handed her a cookie.

3

Two nights after she had agreed to help keep Declan in the country by any means necessary, Anna Katherine was walking to the college library to meet up with her brother for a Saturday night church service and dinner, while Nat lectured her through the speaker of her phone.

"This is just..." She huffed. "You and that boy have had a lot of stupid ideas, I'm not going to lie. But this one really takes the cake! None of this is going to end well." Not for the first time, Anna Katherine felt pity for Nat's student's. She had been on the receiving end of Nat's disapproval and lectures for more years than Anna Katherine could count. She would hate to be a five year old who had to see that look of disappointment or the flat, exasperated tone Nat was using with her now.

Anna Katherine looked both ways before jogging across the street. "I don't know why you're so against this."

There was a pause and then she heard Nat sigh. "I don't want you to get hurt, Kit."

Anna Katherine laughed. "It's Declan. He's the last person on this cursed planet that would ever hurt me."

There was another bout of silence, and Anna Katherine knew her friend was overthinking everything that could possibly go wrong with this plan. It probably didn't help that Nat came from a broken home. In her eyes, all relationships were doomed from the start, and no one could truly be trusted. Anna Katherine was always so honored to be the exception to that rule in her relationship to Nat.

"I'm sure Harry supports this plan wholeheartedly. It sounds like just the right amount of stupid for him to be a part of."

"Actually, Declan said he's pretty against it as well."

"And yet the two of you are still going to ignore your best friends." Despite not being able to see Nat's physical reaction, Kit, if she was a betting woman, would have put money on the fact that her friend just rolled her eyes. "This is crazy, Kit!"

Anna Katherine let out another soft laugh. "Look, as much as I am enjoying you lecturing me and calling me crazy, I'm at the library and Alex is walking out. I'll talk to you later."

"Don't get married between now and tomorrow."

"No promises."

"Anna Katherine Tran!"

"Bye, Natalie!"

She jogged the rest of the way to her older brother and leaned into him when he spread his arms out for a hug. "How's the thesis coming along?"

Alex was three years older and their parents' pride and joy. He thrived in college and followed their father's footsteps in biomedical engineering. He had an internship position at the university's hospital, graduated top in his class, and was now furthering his education. He was everything their parents wished she had been. From an outside perspective, she had every right to feel bitter toward him because of it, too, but fortunately for both of them, he was one of her favorite people in the entire world.

Alex grunted. "It's not. Let's talk about anything else."

"Well…" She pulled away from Alex and started twisting her fingers so much so that they popped, an awful nervous habit she had started back in middle school that her mother hated. She couldn't pin-point exactly when it happened, but she blamed the pressure of state testing. "I have some news."

He cocked an eyebrow as they started walking away from the library. "Oh?"

"Mhm."

Alex smirked. "Are you going to tell me or am I going to have to guess?"

She let out a nervous laugh. "I don't think you'd ever be able to guess this one."

He glanced at her. "Yeah, well, out with it then. Your reticence has me thinking you got knocked up or eloped."

She choked on air, and he stopped walking to stare at her wide-eyed.

He looked a little pale when he said, "Please tell me I'm not an uncle, Kit!"

She slapped his arm. "I am not pregnant! It's just… I, um… Well, you see…"

"Anna Katherine Marie Tran."

"Declan-and-I-are-getting-married-so-he-won't-get-deport-ed-and-I-won't-be-homeless," she mumbled in one long breath.

Technically, she wasn't supposed to tell him that it was a sham of a wedding, but she had always been terrible at lying to her brother. Declan should've expected this and not enforced the secrecy so strictly.

Alex went still. In the calmest voice she had ever heard him use, he said, "I must have misunderstood you, because there is no way on this green earth that you just said what I think you just said."

She stared up at him. "You can't tell Mom and Dad!"

"Obviously!" He threw his hands up in the air. "They'd skin you alive if they knew you were breaking the law! Because that's what you're doing. You know that, right?"

"Yes. Nat has repeated that several times."

"At least one of your friends has some sense." He eyed her like he had never truly seen her until now. "What are you going to tell Mom and Dad?"

She shrugged. "The truth. Kinda. That Declan asked me to marry him. We'll tell them that we've been dating a little while, but wanted to keep it lowkey."

He shook his head. "If I go home and see gray hair, it's on you."

"You tell me that nearly weekly anyway. I keep telling you to just name them after me."

He ruffled her hair and smiled when she glared at him. Despite his efforts to hide it, Anna Katherine knew it was forced. His eyes still held worry in them. As they started walking again, he gave her another glance. "There's no talking you out of this?"

She shook her head. "I gotta help my friend out."

He mumbled something unintelligible under his breath and draped his arm over her shoulders. "I'm accepting this. For now. But you're paying for dinner tonight."

Anna Katherine gently nudged him in his side with her elbow, but he doubled over as if she had knocked the air out of him. "Stop being so dramatic. You know I don't have the money to pay for dinner!"

He straightened up, and she knew what was coming by his mischievous smirk before he said it. "Not my fault you chose a career that barely pays the cost of living!"

"You're no longer my favorite brother."

"I'm your only brother."

"Which means you can also be my least favorite. Congratulations."

He reached out to shove her shoulder, but she dodged it and skipped a few feet in front of him. "Missed me!" She shouted over her shoulder, and like the true adult she was, stuck her tongue out at him. Her brother, always in good spirits, chuckled and jogged a few steps to catch up with her.

Alex dug his keys out of his front pocket. "Come on, slow poke. We don't want to be late to church."

Anna Katherine brought her brother to Declan's apartment after dinner. Her friends and by extension, Alex's friends, were there and waiting. Declan, Harry, and Nat were all together on the couch watching a documentary.

Nat twisted around at the sound of the door shutting, and when she saw Alex she smiled at him. "Surely you talked some sense into your sister!"

He shook his head, "Unfortunately, I knew it was a losing battle."

At that, Declan spun around, eyes wide. "You told him?!"

Harry punched him in the arm. "Of course she did. She tells Alex everything. You should've seen this coming, mate."

Declan glared at him, but when he turned back to Anna Katherine, his eyes softened. "No one else can know. I'm serious, Kit."

"Yeah, yeah. I know." Making a beeline across the room, she squeezed herself between Harry and Declan, only for Harry to unceremoniously shove her off the couch.

"The only Tran sibling that has the honor of sitting that close to me, is

Alexander, Kit."

Anna Katherine smiled, unbothered by his teasing. However, his playful tone was missed by Nat. "Don't be a jerk." Nat rolled her eyes and slid onto the floor to sit beside Kit, who had positioned herself in front of Declan's legs.

Alex went to join the boys on the couch, and as they finished watching the documentary about a serial killer from the 70's and bickered between themselves, Anna Katherine ignored them. She tilted her head back to look at Declan.

"Hi."

He smiled. "Hi back."

"How was your day?"

He ran his fingers through her hair and twisted it off to the side. "Not too bad. Bit lazy, if I'm honest."

"Lucky you."

"How was work?"

She gave a small shrug. "Alright. Tips were crap though."

He hummed sympathetically. "You work the closing shift tomorrow, yeah? Maybe that will make up for it."

"Yeah, maybe." Although she knew closing shifts had nothing on opening shifts when it came to tips. She closed her eyes and leaned her head back. Her early morning was catching up with her, and exhaustion wasn't far off. If it wasn't for the fact she could have a sleep in tomorrow, she would be attempting to ease out of the door to go home.

"Hey, Anna Katherine?"

"Hm?"

"Thank you."

That caused her to open her eyes. She instantly smiled up at him. "Anything for my favorite human.

Harry was surprised when Nat agreed to let him walk her home after the documentary came to an end. It wasn't often the two were by themselves without Declan or Kit as a buffer. They had never gotten along, not even in college. They knew exactly how to push each other's buttons, and there were times where Declan and Kit banned them from even looking at each other. On this night, however, they were getting along just fine. If only because they shared a common anxiety.

"You know this is going to ruin them, right?"

Nat nodded. "Can't say I'm not worried about them."

Harry guided her across the street with a gentle hand to her back. "We should try to stop them, right?"

She snorted in a very unladylike manner. "You really think either of those two would listen to us? They'd die for each other."

"So we're just supposed to sit on the sidelines and watch them implode?"

She cut her eyes at him. "At least we'll be around to pick up the pieces in the aftermath."

Harry sighed. "I'm going to have to ask my doctor for an increase in my anxiety meds, aren't I?"

Surprising even herself, Nat laughed. "Yeah, probably. You might have to start sharing with me, though."

"How do you think the parents are going to react?"

"Her mom is going to freak."

Harry tried to smile, but his worry was preventing a full-blown grin. "Móirín will be over the moon, probably."

"At least watching this trainwreck happen will be entertaining."

This time, Harry laughed. "Yeah, at least there's that."

4

Anna Katherine had few mornings she could sleep in. Sundays were the main day of the week she knew without a doubt she would have the morning off. Early in her employment at Hattie's Cafe, she learned how fun the Sunday brunch crowd was, and while the tips didn't make up for the weekday morning rush, they were still a nice addition to her paycheck. Of course, this meant she missed Sunday morning church services, which drove her mom crazy. Patricia wanted church to be a family affair, and letting go of her adult children to make their own choices was still something she was working on. Anna Katherine still went, of course, just to the Saturday night service instead.

Since they had discussed and agreed on their plan of action to keep Declan state-side, he and Anna Katherine hadn't seen each other as often as she would have liked. It had gotten so bad that Anna Katherine even thought about bringing him lunch to his work, and she hated going to his work while all of his coworkers were there. It caused her to feel in the way and awkward.

With Declan's deportation looming over them, they needed to get the ball rolling. After shutting everything down and cleaning the machines and dishes, Anna Katherine made her way to Martin's office in the back.

The door was open, but she still knocked to get his attention.

He glanced up from whatever he was doing—probably working on the schedule—and gave her a smile. "What's up?"

"Is there any way I can have next Sunday off?"

Martin didn't hesitate in saying yes. "I'll get the new kid to fill in for you. You have big, exciting plans for next weekend?"

Anna Katherine groaned. "Just lunch with the family. Declan will be joining us."

"Ah, Declan. And how is our Irish lad doing?"

She shrugged, "Well enough I guess."

He nodded. "Is everything shut down?"

"Yes, sir. Doors locked and floors mopped."

"Excellent. Now get out of here before I have to pay you overtime."

She smiled but did as she was told. On her way out, she hung her apron on one of the hooks and grabbed her leftover containers from lunch. She went out the back and walked to where her car was parked. Leaning against the car, she took a steadying breath before she called her mom.

It took several rings before Patricia answered. "Hello?"

"Hey, Mom."

There was rustling in the background as Patricia responded. "What have you been up to today?"

"Just got off work." There was more rustling and Kit was finding it distracting. "What's that noise in the background?"

"Oh, your father and I went to the store after church. We're just now getting home." There was a pause before she made the dreaded statement. "We missed having you with us at service this morning."

"We've been over this, Mom. I can't because of work."

"You and I both know that there are other shifts you could work if you only prioritize your time with family."

"Mother."

"Anna Katherine."

She sighed, trying to rein in all the frustration and anger at her mother's relentless pestering over her church attendance.

"Well, you'll be pleased to know that I took next Sunday off."

There was a pause, and Patricia sounded suspicious when she asked, "How come?"

"I was thinking I could attend church with you and Dad, and afterward we could have a family lunch. Declan could join us."

"And why would Declan be joining our *family* lunch?"

"Because he doesn't have one of his own over here. You know this."

"Fine. I'll inform your father. Maybe we can even get Alexander away from his thesis long enough to join us as well." She still sounded suspicious, but she was at least going along with it. For now.

"Sounds good."

"Church starts at nine."

"I know."

"Don't be late."

"I promise I won't be late."

Anna Katherine could feel her mother's eyes boring into hers through the phone. "Don't lie. Making promises you can't keep is lying."

"Mother. I won't be late," she reiterated through clenched teeth.

Patricia huffed, "We'll see."

"Tell Dad I love him."

"I will." Another pause. "I love you, dear."

Anna Katherine sighed, releasing some of the tension that always showed up when she talks to her mother. "Love you too, Mom."

Anna Katherine sat on the bed feeling utterly defeated and looked toward her friend with a hopeless expression.

Nat stood in Anna Katherine's small bedroom and looked around. Her hands were on her hips, and she had a very serious expression. She had brought cardboard boxes over to help Anna Katherine start packing.

"You don't have too much stuff, Kit. This shouldn't take very long to pack up, and between our two cars we should be able to get a good bit of it to Declan's in a few hours."

Anna Katherine fell back on the bed, and it was barely a few seconds before Nat joined her. "I know you have to be exhausted after work. It means a lot that you came over to help."

"Well, I figured if I didn't help tonight, we might be panic packing the night before your lease is up."

Anna Katherine grabbed her pillow and slapped Nat with it. "I don't procrastinate *that* badly."

Nat laughed, "Maybe, but it's very close." She shoved the pillow off of her. "First things first. We need to make a list of everything you absolutely need for the next few weeks while you stay with me. Then we'll make a pile of things that go to Declan's and a pile of things that will be coming with you to my place."

"I'll also need a small pile to keep here while we move things around."

"Good point. You obviously need to keep your toiletries here. So we'll pack up your bathroom last. You barely eat here as is, so we could probably go ahead and pack up your kitchen things and anything in the living room."

"The clothes are going to be a nightmare."

"Yes. That's why we'll have a list."

"You and your lists."

"They're helpful!" Nat sat up and pulled out her phone. "Okay. Off the top of your head, what things do you need to keep in this apartment?"

Anna Katherine thought for a minute. "My work uniform, definitely. My sneakers. A few dresses for church. My unmentionables."

"Unmentionables?"

"That's what Patty calls undies and bras."

"How have I not heard this before?"

Anna Katherine shrugged. "Do you have many conversations with my mom about underwear?"

"No, you're right."

The two of them spent the next several minutes making Nat's list. They both decided the bedroom was too overwhelming to do much of anything with right now, but they did get a lot of the kitchen and living room packed away and put in their cars. After they had moved all the things into the vehicles, they took a quick break by watching an episode of a sitcom they both enjoyed and eating the oreos they found in the back of one of the cupboards. Neither of them felt the need to mention how stale they tasted.

After the break, they drove to Declan's where he and Harry were waiting for them. Thankfully the girls didn't have to carry the boxes upstairs themselves. The guys insisted on having them sit down and eat a bite—Declan made a point to clarify it must be healthy and nutritious—while Declan and Harry carried all the boxes up and put them in what would eventually be Anna Katherine's bedroom.

Neither Anna Katherine or Nat made a move to try to convince the guys they were able and willing to help out.

The following Friday, she was scheduled to close the shop. The sun had already gone down, and it wasn't that she was *scared* to walk by herself, but she definitely wasn't one hundred percent confident she'd make it home unscathed, either.

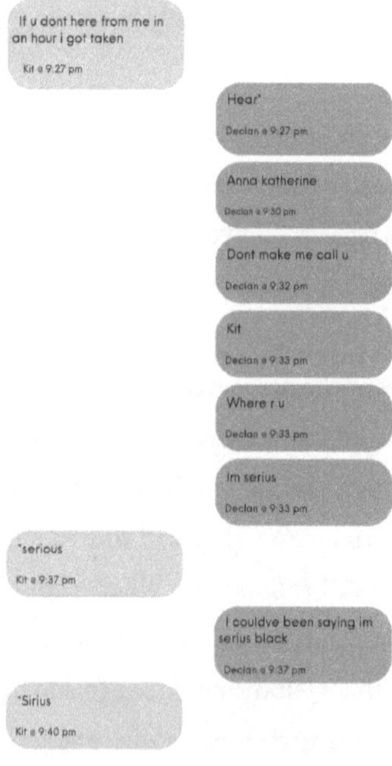

Anna Katherine smiled when her phone started buzzing with an incoming FaceTime call from Declan. She pressed the green button, and when his blurry face came into focus, she saw that he was frowning.

"Why the frown?"

"Oh, maybe because you're trying to give me a heart attack?"

She rummaged in her bag until she found her headphones. Once she had them connected, she moved her phone back so she could see him. "Killing you was not my intent. Apologies."

"What took you so long to answer?" And then as if just now noticing she was in the dark, he added, "Where even are you?"

"I had an issue with the alarm system and had to call Martin, but all is well now. And I'm walking to the bus stop. I just got off work."

Declan's eyebrow ticked up. "And where is your car?"

"Alex told me it needed to be serviced."

"You could've called me. I would've picked you up."

"I didn't want to disturb your Friday night."

"Kit-Kat, you and I both know my Friday nights involve sitting on the couch and eating pizza. Usually with you. Disturbing me in that state isn't possible."

"I thought you might've been with Harry."

"Harry is out on a date."

"Ah, so that's the reason you're all alone."

"That and you're a loser who has to work."

"Excuse me for trying to make a living," Anna Katherine grumbled.

Declan chuckled. "You're excused. Are you at the bus stop yet?"

"Nearly. I see it just ahead."

"Good. I can't have my fiancé taken from me before I'm given my citizenship."

"Declan Anthony Mullins! I sincerely hope that was a joke."

"Obviously it was a joke. I need you for more than just that."

"I feel the love."

"Ditto."

"Hey, Dec?"

"Hey, Kit?"

She ignored the teasing tone in his voice. "Are you ready for Sunday?"

"Yep," Declan said with a pop of his lips.

Despite the nerves causing an eruption of butterflies in her stomach, she smiled. "Good."

There was a pause. She noticed he repositioned himself on the couch and brought the phone closer to his face. She could see the freckles that sprinkled across his nose on the pixelated screen. "Are you ready?"

She had made it to the bus stop, and she propped her back up against a pole, resting her head on the cold metal. "Not in the slightest."

She knew that Declan stayed quiet because he knew her well enough to know she would say more if given time.

"I just can't believe I'm about to lie to my parents about what is possibly one of the most important things of my life."

He watched her carefully through the phone. She was grateful that he didn't have a platitude for an immediate answer. He clearly knew those wouldn't help her at this moment.

"We can cancel the entire thing at any time, Kit-Kat." He rested his head against the couch cushions, and she had the sudden need to be there with him, snuggled up on the couch with a blanket and a warm drink.

"I'm not going to back out."

"But you can if you want to. I wouldn't be upset."

"But I won't."

"Good."

"Great."

"Perfect."

"Wonderful."

He smiled, finally. "I promise it's all going to be okay."

She straightened and pushed her hair out of her face. "You keep saying that, and it's beginning to lose meaning."

"You gotta look at the positive, mate! Sure, we might be lying to everyone we care about, but we're about to get tax benefits. I'm not getting deported, and you won't have to go find a new place to live!"

"Somehow that doesn't make me feel any better."

Declan ignored her and kept going. "I took a Psych class with Harry once, and that professor said that people who were married lived longer. I'm basically giving you extra years. You're welcome."

"I'm pretty sure there was more to it than that. Maybe even being in love. Who knows. Maybe it's that healthier people are more likely to get married than sickly people. Either way, you are not gifting me a longer life."

"Are you saying you don't love me? I'm hurt, Kit."

"Of course I love you. I'm just not in love with you."

"Fair enough." The phone moved and lost focus as he stood up. "I'm going out with H tomorrow morning. You wanna come?"

"No, but thanks. I need to pack and clean."

"Want me to come over after and help?"

"You don't have to. I'll see you on Sunday."

"Right. And we'll have to act in love and such."

She scrunched up her face. "Ugh, gross. Why did I agree to this?"

"Because I'm your best friend."

She groaned, rolling her eyes. "Lucky me."

Looking up, she saw her bus coming. "The bus is here, and I'm safe and sound. Thanks for being my knight in shining armor."

"Anything for you, Kit."

"Bye, Dec."

The screen went black as the call ended, and she wasn't entirely sure why

her heart was beating a little faster than normal as she stepped onto the bus
to go home.

48

5

Declan, though he would have rather stayed home, agreed to go with Harry to the animal shelter. Harry had a reputation of going through dates with women the same way Kit went through cups of coffee—quickly and without much thought. Declan knew the truth though, and the truth was that his friend had one of the most genuine hearts and whenever he fell for a girl, he fell hard. There were times Declan thought the reason Harry went on so many dates was simply to protect that soft heart of his. So when Harry asked Declan to go with him with the intention of finding the girl he met at Hattie's Cafe the week before, Declan happily agreed.

"Thanks for coming with me today."

Declan took a break from staring out the window to look at Harry. "Yeah, it's no problem."

Harry glanced at him. "You nervous?"

Declan sent him a questioning look.

"Kit's parents can be intense."

He shrugged. "Not really. It's not like it's real."

"But her parents need to think that it's real. Or did you forget that already?" Harry drummed his fingers on his steering wheel along with a Fleetwood Mac song that was playing from one of his many playlists.

"Of course I didn't forget." As an afterthought, he muttered, "How could I?"

"Well, you did forget to renew your visa, so I just needed to make sure."

"Forget you, Whitlock." Declan watched Harry drive as he turned off the main street and onto a road that led out of town. "Why are we going to the animal shelter anyway?"

"I already told you. I met a girl at the coffee shop and—"

"Yeah, I got that part. But why not just wait to run into her again at Hattie's Cafe? This is borderline stalking."

Harry looked affronted. "I am many things, Mullins, but a stalker is not one of them. I waited a week. She hasn't shown back up. This is my plan to speed things up a little."

"It's an awful plan."

"Not as awful of a plan as illegally marrying your best friend who you might be in love with just so you won't have to go back to Ireland."

"I am not in love with her."

"Okay. Sure." Sarcasm dripped from Harry's voice.

"Didn't you just go on a date last night?"

Harry shrugged. "It didn't end well."

Declan snickered. "They never do, it seems."

"Declan?"

"Yes?"

"Shut up."

Declan and Harry had been roommates for three of their four years of college, so Declan was mostly used to his—as Nat would say—'not well thought out plans to get the girl'. Declan had never seen himself going to an animal shelter to help Harry get a date. But he also never thought he would be threatened with deportation, so he didn't have much ground to stand on there.

When they arrived, Declan went straight to the dogs. Harry might have wanted him to be a wingman, but he would much rather see the four-legged, tail-wagging, smiling dogs that started yipping and barking as soon as they saw the car pull up. That was a mistake.

His second mistake was spotting a mutt a few kennels down who was sitting in the corner staring at him. He ended up in front of her and read the info sheet.

"Hi! My name is Fox! I'm a coonhound mix who likes barking at thunder, befriending smaller dogs, and even though I am much too large, I still think I'm a lap dog! I love cuddles, treats, and playing fetch, but only with people I trust! I think cats are chew toys, and other big dogs scare me. If you take me home, I will love you forever!" Declan glanced at the dog again. "Well, Fox, don't you just sound adorable."

"Pet shopping today?"

The voice from behind startled him, and he nearly jumped out of his skin. When he turned around, he saw one of the workers in their blue polo and khaki cargo pants. "Oh, uh, no. Just here with a friend."

He felt something wet against his fingers, and when he looked down, he saw Fox licking them through the fence wire and slowly wagging her tail.

"That's a shame. She doesn't warm up to a lot of people right away, and it seems like she's already fond of you."

Declan knelt down. "You're a picky one, aren't ya? I can relate to that." He reached through the gate and scratched her chin. "You really are a cutie."

Ten minutes later, Declan was in the shelter's office signing papers and handing them his card for the adoption fee. Harry still hadn't reappeared, and Declan definitely hadn't called Kit before signing the papers. Which had been his third mistake.

When he walked out of the office, he had his new pet ownership papers, a new pet parent pamphlet, and Fox who was leading him away on the leash that the shelter had given him.

He reached down and rubbed her ears. "Your new mum is going to be so excited when she sees you. I can't wait to see her face."

They walked to Harry's car, and it was then when Declan spotted Harry leaning against it.

When Declan got close enough, his friend called out, "Where'd you disappear off to?"

Harry looked up from his phone. "Went looking for the girl. She's not here today, so this was a useless trip. I tried to call to see where you were but—" It was only then that Harry seemed to notice the dog that was with Declan. "And what do we have here?"

"This," Declan said proudly, "is Fox."

Harry just shook his head with a slowly growing grin and muttered, "Kit is going to kill you."

Anna Katherine had spent her morning scrubbing every inch of her kitchen and throwing out anything they hadn't already moved to Declan's. She was determined to leave the apartment spotless enough to get back her deposit.

She was obsessively scrubbing the baseboards when her phone rang.

"What do you want, Alex?"

"Wow, don't sound so thrilled to hear from me."

She puffed out a breath and stood up. "It's not that."

"You're cleaning, aren't you? I can hear it in your voice."

Anna Katherine sometimes hated how well her brother could read her, even over the phone. "It's none of your business."

He laughed, "Okay, sure."

"Did you call to play mind reader or was there another reason?" She put the phone on speaker so she could kneel down and start cleaning again.

"Sheesh. You're really stressed about something."

"Alex!" she barked.

"Right, I was just calling to say that I'm coming tomorrow. Something tells me that you and our parents are going to need a buffer."

She took her frustration out on the poor baseboards. "Gee, thanks for the vote of confidence."

"You're being absolutely impossible today."

"Mom would say I'm impossible every day."

"I see this conversation is going nowhere."

She stopped scrubbing again to glare at the phone. "You could've at least told me you were coming before I talked to mom yesterday. Now I'm going to have to call her again and tell her that her golden child is coming."

"I am not the golden child, but on that note, I'm hanging up. I love you! And for the sanity of everyone in your life, please take a break and do some breathing exercises."

"Bye, Alex."

"Bye, Kit! Love you!"

She hung up without another response.

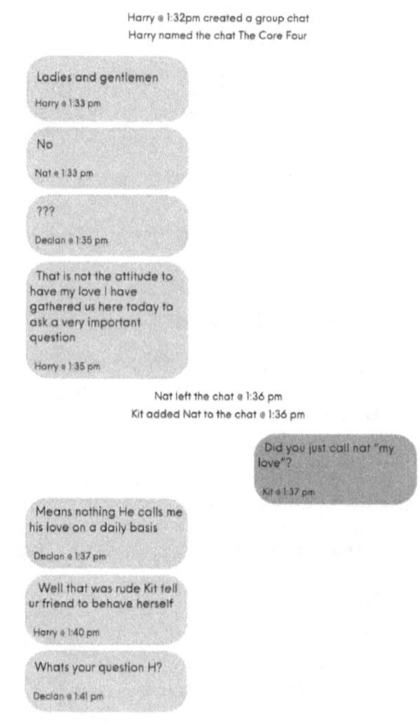

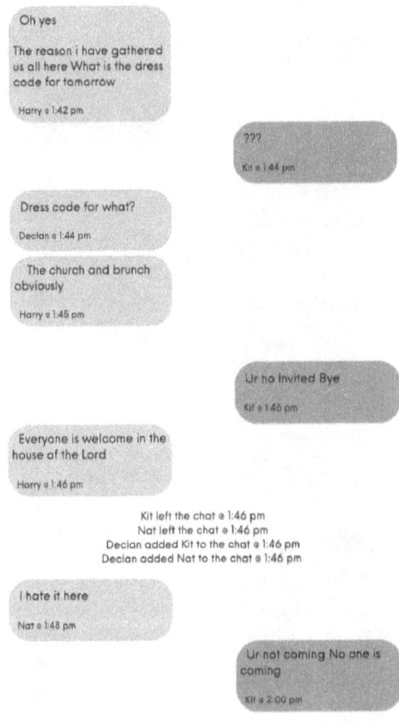
Oh yes
The reason i have gathered us all here What is the dress code for tomorrow
Harry @ 1:42 pm
???
Kit @ 1:44 pm
Dress code for what?
Declan @ 1:44 pm
The church and brunch obviously
Harry @ 1:45 pm
Ur no Invited Bye
Kit @ 1:46 pm
Everyone is welcome in the house of the Lord
Harry @ 1:46 pm
Kit left the chat @ 1:46 pm
Nat left the chat @ 1:46 pm
Declan added Kit to the chat @ 1:46 pm
Declan added Nat to the chat @ 1:46 pm
I hate it here
Nat @ 1:48 pm
Ur not coming No one is coming
Kit @ 2:00 pm

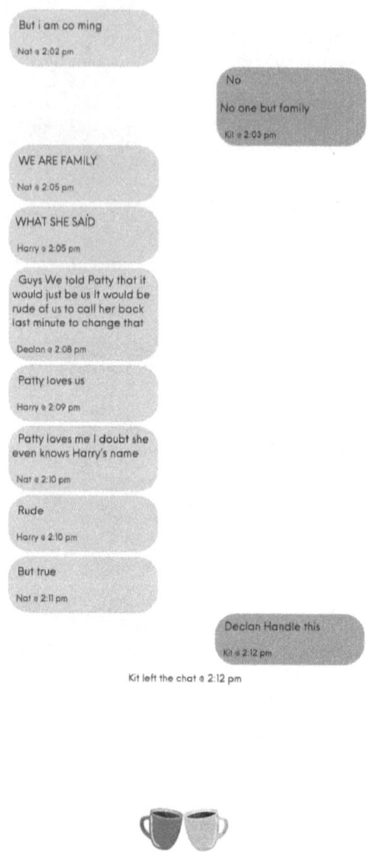

Declan and Fox made their way up the stairs and to Kit's apartment door. Part of him thought maybe he should call or send a text outside the group, but instead he found himself on his way to her.

The door, which was covered in chipped paint and he was fairly certain was rotting, was unlocked. He had told her a thousand times to keep her doors locked, but Kit only followed her own rules. He was pretty sure she kept them unlocked simply to spite him. He definitely wouldn't put it past her.

While the kitchen was spotless, the living room was a complete wreck. There were boxes everywhere. Some of them were only half put together. Others were overflowing with clothes. Two were marked as "stupid stuff" but had shoes in them. He grimaced. He should've come by sooner to help her pack.

He set Fox up beside the couch with a few treats, a toy, and a blanket for her to sleep on, and then went to find Kit. It wasn't hard. She was lying flat out on the bathroom floor, headphones in with music blasting, and her arms crossed over her face.

He called her name, but she didn't hear. He gently kicked her foot, and she jumped up. Her eyes were wide and bloodshot.

"Declan! Warn a girl! You scared me."

"I called your name, and I wasn't exactly quiet coming in."

She glared at him.

"Why was your door unlocked?'

Instead of answering his question, she asked, "Why are you here?"

He crouched down so he was more eye level with her. "Well, you dramatically left our group chat. I figured you were stressed and needed a friend."

"I'm never stressed."

That made him smile. "Never ever."

"Nope."

"Then you certainly don't need me."

She smiled back. "Never needed you."

"In that case, I'll just take my organizational skills and leave you to packing."

He acted as if he was about to stand, but before he could, she grabbed his hand. "I mean, I don't *need* your help, but I would be very grateful for it."

They both grinned. A strand of hair had come out of Kit's bun, and was falling in front of her face. He went to brush it behind her ear, but before he could, something tackled him. As he fell forward onto Kit, she screeched in his ear. A blur of paws, fur, hair, and tongue was all that could be discerned as Fox started licking them. Kit continued to screech as the dog wallered and stepped all over them.

Declan was finally able to sit up and grabbed Fox by her new collar. "Fox! Sit."

Surprising everyone in the small bathroom, Fox did exactly what Declan said. Declan stared at the dog that now sat between him and Kit.

Kit, on the other hand, scooted back against the tub and looked in shock at the dog, then at Declan, and then back at the dog.

"Declan."

"Yeah?"

"What," She looked at him again, eyes hard and unamused, "is this?"

"This is Fox."

"That is not a fox. That is a dog."

"Fox is her name."

"Fox is a stupid name for a dog."

"It was her name at the kennel."

"And why do we know that?"

"I went with Harry to the kennel to help him get a date."

Kit didn't say anything, she just looked at Declan and then pointedly looked back at Fox.

Declan sighed. "We went for a date for Harry, but came out with a dog for us."

"Us?"

"Yeah, you've been saying you wanted a dog!"

"I did not."

"You did. We were in the park playing ultimate frisbee, and you said..."

"THAT WAS LAST SUMMER!"

Declan was half certain that if Kit had been a cartoon at that moment, smoke would have been billowing out of her nose and ears.

"Declan, please tell me you did not adopt a dog the day before we have to tell my parents that we're engaged. Please tell me you thought that through and realized what a horrendous idea that was. Please tell me she's just here for the ride, and you'll take her back in a bit."

Declan rubbed the back of his neck, hesitant to respond to Kit. "Well, I would since you asked so nicely, but I'd be lying."

"Declan!"

"What?! You wanted a dog! I wanted a dog! We now have a dog!"

"But you didn't even discuss this with me beforehand!"

"I thought you'd be happy!"

She rubbed her hands over her face and groaned. When she spoke again, it was softer and more controlled. "Any other day, Dec, and I would be. But I have to pack up this entire apartment by the end of the week. We have to tell both of our parents that we're getting married and somehow convince them that we've been in love this whole time. And now you just waltz in here with... with..."

"Fox."

"You just waltz in here with Fox, and you didn't even think to talk to me before you made this huge decision."

Declan winced. "Okay, but..."

"Who is even going to take care of her? You work all day, and I work all day with early mornings and usually don't have the weekends off. This poor girl is going to be locked up all day long. Did you even think about that?"

"I'll come home for lunch and go on a walk with her."

She sounded skeptical when she asked, "Every day?"

"Well, maybe not every day. You'll be home some days...."

"See. It's already starting. You're already signing me up for responsibilities I didn't ask for."

"Anna Katherine." He sounded miffed even to himself. "You're being impossible."

"Not the first time I heard that today."

"Can't say I'm surprised."

They stared at each other in silence. The only sound was that of Fox panting between them. Declan reached out and scratched her ears, and the dog leaned into it with closed eyes.

"Okay." Declan started as he still scratched the dog. "I'll make a deal with you. We keep the dog."

"That doesn't seem to be much of a deal."

He nudged her foot. "I wasn't finished. We'll keep Fox, but if at any point you begin to feel overwhelmed, I will return her to the pound or find her a better home."

"I feel overwhelmed right now."

"Yes, but that's Patty's doing, not Fox's."

"It's your doing for not renewing your visa, you jerk."

He chuckled. "That's fair. But..." He trailed off and stared at Fox for a moment. "But, she chose me at the shelter. I couldn't say no once she immediately warmed up to me. She needs a good home."

Kit scowled, and after watching the dog carefully, she scooted closer. Another moment and she was reaching out to pet Fox with a smile on her face. "She chose you, huh?"

He grinned. "Yeah."

"Well, we can't very well turn her away."

His smile grew. "Certainly not."

With a huff, she relented. "Fine. We can keep her. But until I move in, she is one hundred and twenty percent your responsibility. We'll revisit things once I move in."

His eyes crinkled. "You are the absolute best, Kit-Kat."

"I know." She sighed.

Anna Katherine knocked on Declan's door. He had already put an autumn wreath up despite Anna Katherine telling him dozens of times that it was still too early for it. But when he came from a place that actually experienced the seasons only to move to a place that had a grand total of one and a half seasons, she didn't completely blame him for silently encouraging the cooler weather to hurry up.

When no one answered, she tried to open the door, but it was locked. She knocked again, this time louder, and waited again.

Several moments later, the door opened. Anna Katherine had been expecting a Declan that was dressed and ready to go. Instead, the version of her friend that stood in front of her was one she rarely ever saw. She nearly couldn't believe it, but there he was. Declan was as disheveled as her mother the night before every Thanksgiving as she tried to make the house spotless and perfect.

He was still in his pajamas. The checkered pants had a rip in one knee. The slippers he had on were caked in what looked to be mud, and he reeked of chemicals and cleaning products.

"Declan Mullins, my dear and lovely friend, why the heck are you not dressed and ready to go meet my parents at church?"

There was a bark, and Declan grimaced. "There has been a terrible accident."

Anna Katherine shoved past Declan and looked around the apartment. Everything seemed fine and in its place, but then she noticed all the cleaning supplies on the floor on the couch. And then the trash bag. And the giant wet spot on the couch. And then the smell hit her.

She covered her mouth and nose with her shirt and hands. "What in the world is that terrible smell?"

"Fox got in the trash last night. She had accidents all throughout the apartment."

She raised an eyebrow. "More than one?"

"Thankfully the poop was on the floor and was easy to clean up. The vomit on the other hand…"

Anna Katherine made a face of disgust. "Where is she now?"

"Your bedroom."

"Why?!" she screeched. "Why not in the bathroom?"

He dragged his hands down his face. When he was able to look at her again, he muttered, "I tried to flush her accident and now the toilet is overflowing. She got it all over her. I tried to take her outside to wipe her down, but she got away from me."

He pointed to the rip in his pants as if that explained everything. Which it didn't.

"When we came back up, I put her in her bedroom to keep from getting into any more messes. I'm trying to clean the couch before it sets in and permanently stains it, but the bathroom is still a wreck."

"We have thirty minutes, Declan."

"I know."

"It takes twenty to get to the church."

"I know."

"That means we only have…"

"I *know*."

Anna Katherine took a deep breath, which she immediately regretted when the smell hit her again. She coughed and groaned, but finally squeaked out, "Okay, here's the plan."

Anna Katherine took over cleaning the couch cushion while Declan went to the bathroom to mop up the mess in there. After what felt like an eternity of scrubbing, it looked good enough to her, and she walked back to check on Declan's progress. Other than a wad of paper towels and a foul stench, the bathroom looked as good as new.

"I told you getting a dog right now was a bad idea."

As if on cue, Fox barked again.

Declan ignored them both, placing the mop in the tub to clean later and picking up the trash. "How's my couch?"

"As good as it's going to get."

He groaned, but said nothing else.

"Do you want me to call and cancel today?"

He gave her a startled look. "Why would we do that?"

"We're going to be late and you've had a bad morning. I doubt you feel like dealing with my hectic family after all of this."

He waved her concerns off. "Of course we're not going to cancel. We need to tell them we're engaged, and it's better to do that now than to do it later. Let me just change and then we'll leave."

He gave her hand a squeeze as he passed her, as if she was the one that needed comforting, not him. "I'll be sure Patty knows that this was my doing and not yours."

6

Of course they hit not only traffic, but what seemed like every red light between Declan's house and the church. The closer they got, the more frequently Anna Katherine checked the time. And the more she checked the time, the faster she bounced her leg up and down.

"We're so late." Even her voice was rattled by her nervous jostling.

"I'm surprised your mom hasn't called yet."

Anna Katherine bit her lip. "She probably has. I turned my phone off."

Declan didn't respond, but instead reached over and rested his hand on Anna Katherine's knee.

Slowly, the bouncing stopped.

The parking lot was full when they pulled in, and the presence of her childhood church being so close did little to ease her tension.

"She's going to kill me."

Once the car was parked, Declan unfastened his seatbelt and turned in his seat to give her a proper look. He tried to seem calm, but she could see that even he was a little nervous. "She's not going to kill you, Kit."

She shook her head vigorously, "No, she will. Not only am I late, but I'm engaged. I haven't even properly introduced you to my family."

"Your family loves me."

"They love best-friend Declan. They haven't met boyfriend and fiance and soon-to-be-husband Declan."

"Best-friend Declan is the same as husband Declan."

Anna Katherine leaned forward and covered her face in her hands. She shook her head. "I can't do this. I can't walk into that church and sit with my family knowing that I'm about to lie to their faces."

"How are we lying to them?"

She shot upright and waved her hands hysterically between them. "What do you mean how are we lying to them? Declan! We're telling them we're engaged!"

"And we are engaged! We are getting married!"

"But they're going to think we're in love! We're lying!"

"The action we're doing is true, but the reasoning is just a little—embellished."

"A little?" She sounded out of control even to her own ears.

Declan took her hands in his and placed them in his lap. "Anna Katherine, I need you to breathe and to listen." Once she took a deep breath and let it out, he gave her hands another squeeze and continued. "We don't have to follow through with this. We can find you a cheaper apartment. I can take out a loan to pay the fines. We can make you an online dating profile to get your mom off your back."

She groaned. "That sounds worse than marrying you."

He chuckled. "The point is, we don't have to do this."

"But if we do this, it can speed up the process for you to get citizenship, and it will help us both financially."

"Yes, but it isn't the only way forward. You have a choice."

Anna Katherine drew a deep breath and took a moment to take in all what he had said. To take *him* in.

His eyes were clear with genuine concern. In the morning sunlight, they were bright blue. Darker than most blue eyes, but somehow all the more beautiful.

She had always been envious of his eyes. "Are you still willing to go through with this?"

His eyes softened, and he let go of her hands only to reach out and brush a strand of her hair out of her face. "That shouldn't matter when it comes to your decision."

She took another deep breath. "Yeah, let's do it."

"One word and it's over. If you change your mind at any point, just say the word and we'll stop the whole thing."

She nodded and grabbed her purse, drawing another steadying breath. "Right back at ya."

The first worship set was just ending as they walked in, and the rows were filled with people. She and Declan stood in the back, scanning the pews for her family. It took them a moment because, of course, they were sitting in the second row from the front.

"I swear they sat there just to make my life more difficult," she muttered in a whisper to Declan.

Declan didn't say anything. Instead, he took her hand in his and led her down the aisle to where her parents and Alex were sitting. Anna Katherine could feel people's eyes on them as they continued to walk all the way to the front. She kept her eyes on her and Declan's hands and not on the eyes watching them.

"Stop freaking out," Declan whispered as they neared the row where Patty and her dad sat.

"I'm not freaking out."

"Don't lie in church. He'll strike you down." His lips ticked up in a half grin.

"I don't think either of us are in a place morally to call the other out on lying."

"Touché."

When they got to the row where her family sat, she led the way past a couple that sat nearer the aisle than her brother Alexander. He looked half asleep when he smiled up at her as she squeezed by him. Her father was listening to the pastor who was on the stage, greeting everyone and making announcements. He caught her gaze briefly to give her a smile and a pat on the back. Her mother's piercing gaze seemed to see right through Anna Katherine and Declan. More importantly, fixating on their still intertwined hands.

Instinctively, Anna Katherine loosened her grip, but Declan held tight. He led her with a hand gently on her back past her mother and positioned himself between the two women. Anna Katherine let out a sigh of relief from not having to sit beside or answer all of her mother's whispered questions.

Declan leaned toward her mom. "Sorry we're late. This morning didn't go as planned."

Her grin was tight, but she gave Declan a reassuring pat on the shoulder. "Don't you worry about that, dear."

Anna Katherine tried to catch her mom's eyes, but Patricia was doing a wonderful job of avoiding eye contact. With a sigh, Anna Katherine settled in beside Declan, eyes straight ahead, and did her best to focus on the sermon.

Anna Katherine stood close to Declan while the family gathered together by the main entrance once the service was over. Other families and friends were gathered in groups throughout the room. Some were drinking coffee silently together waiting for the next service. Others were talking about their week or, like the Trans, their plans for brunch.

Patricia hitched her purse higher on her shoulder. Her brunette hair was perfectly styled and, for once, her hazel eyes were not staring judgingly at Anna Katherine.

"I made reservations at a place downtown. They close early on Saturdays so I was unable to call back and adjust the number of seats we needed after Declan called me, but I'm sure adjusting the number once we're there won't be an issue. I think it's so great that your friends wanted to join us, Anna Katherine."

Kit glanced at Declan. "I thought you handled that."

"The best I could do was get them to skip the service."

"I would've preferred them to come to the service and not brunch!" she hissed under her breath.

"Dear, what could you possibly be complaining about now?"

Anna Katherine gave Declan a piercing look before trying to control her face enough to give her mother a gentle smile. "Nothing, Mom. I just didn't realize Harry and Nat were still joining us for brunch."

Surprisingly, that seemed to placate Patty.

"Oh." Patty smiled and clasped her hands in front of her. "I don't know about you four, but I'm starving. I had a very small breakfast."

"Dear, you had coffee. Did you even eat anything?"

"Coffee is breakfast."

Declan elbowed Anna Katherine. "I see where you get it from."

Patty cleared her throat to get their attention. "I'm assuming you all will meet us there?"

Alex, Declan, and Anna Katherine all nodded. "We'll follow behind you guys."

"Excellent! Let's get going. Our reservation is in fifteen minutes." Patricia led the way out of the church building, and the rest of their group followed close behind.

Declan was surprised that somehow he and Kit were the first to arrive at the restaurant.

As Kit unfastened her seatbelt, she gave him a side-eye. "You're a speed demon."

"I barely went over the speed limit."

"We were all but flying down the road!"

Declan shook his head. "Whatever you say, love."

As he turned the car off, he leaned over and reached into the glove compartment in front of Kit.

"What are you doing?"

He rummaged around for a moment before he found the small box wrapped in velveteen. For reasons he didn't want to look too deep into, his heart was pounding. "Looking for something."

"Your wallet is in the cup holder."

He pulled his arm back with the box hidden in his grasp. "It's not my wallet I was looking for."

Kit eyed him suspiciously. "Declan Mullins, what is going on?"

He stared at the small box in his hand for a moment. With a steadying breath, he opened it and gingerly took the ring out. Reaching toward her, he offered the ring to her in the palm of her hand.

"If we're engaged, you need a ring."

Kit all but forced herself out the car as she scooted back and looked at it as if it might bite her.

"You look like I'm trying to poison you."

She ignored him. "What is this?"

"It's a ring, Kit."

She glanced up at him, and her eyes looked absolutely petrified. "Why?"

"Have you listened to anything I've said?"

"Where did you get this?"

The truth of it nearly slipped out, but he held it in. "Found it. It's basically worthless."

She reached out and took it between two of her fingers. "You just... found it?"

He nodded.

"Suspicious timing."

"Just take the ring before I tell your mom that you sent Nat on the last blind date she set you up on."

She gasped. "You wouldn't!"

"Try me."

She glared at him, but slid it on her finger anyway. And just in time, too, because Timmy and Patty pulled up on one side while Alex pulled up on the other.

Frantically she pulled the ring back off, and Declan groaned.

"I'm just... I'm just going to keep it in my purse until we tell them." She twirled it around her fingers. "It's a beautiful ring. It would definitely catch my mom's eye before we're ready to tell them."

Declan didn't argue. She did have a point. "Fine. Here's the box."

Thankfully, the restaurant was able to change their reservations, and they were given a round table on the patio that had enough seats for all seven of them. Even more surprisingly, Harry and Nat showed up not only on time, but together.

Nat looked absolutely done with Harry.

"He called at the last minute for a ride." She rolled her eyes. "It's like he's incapable of doing anything by himself."

"I just enjoy your company, Natalie."

She ignored him and went to sit on the other side of Kit, which positioned her between the two Tran siblings. Harry sat on the other side of Alex and beside Kit's dad. That left Declan sitting between Patty and Kit.

The waitress came to take their drink, and when Kit ordered a mimosa, Patty made a clicking sound with her tongue, but otherwise stayed silent. Still, that little non-comment alone made Kit tense up. Declan placed his hand on her knee in an attempt to remind her to relax.

He and Kit had agreed to tell her parents the news once everyone had finished the main course. That way, they reasoned, they could go through most of the morning without her parents freaking out. Even with that knowledge, Declan felt Kit tense up once more when he took her hand and cleared his throat.

"Mr. Timmy, Mrs. Patty." Declan made sure to look her dad in the eye while he spoke. "Kit and I have some news we need to share with you."

He went to move his hand away, but she tightened her grip and pulled his hand onto her lap. The action made him smile, and it almost distracted him from the task at hand.

Timmy placed his utensils and napkin beside his plate. "And what's that?"

Patty, who was carefully watching the two of them, raised an eyebrow. "Good news, I hope?"

The Tran siblings glanced at each other, and Declan was tempted to smile again when he saw Alex trying to hide his laughter by shoving a piece of toast in his mouth.

He cleared his throat again, afraid that he would laugh at the older Tran. "Well, I think we'll just come out and say it."

"Yes," Timmy nodded, his tone a little gruff. "I think that's an excellent idea."

"Kit and I have been dating for a couple of months now. We wanted to tell both of you, but it was so new for the two of us. Going from friendship to dating can be difficult to navigate. We didn't want any outside pressure, so we kept it to ourselves for a while. But, well..."

He trailed off, something keeping him from going on.

This time, it was Kit who reassuringly squeezed his hand.

"Mom, Dad..." She glanced around the table, a well-practiced brilliant, yet fake, smile on her face. "Declan and I are engaged."

7

Silence engulfed the table, and Anna Katherine could barely find her breath. Either too scared to stop talking or too stupid to shut up, she kept going. "I really hope you support us. I know it's not how you imagined all of this would go, but Declan and I are really happy with the direction of our relationship. We love each other and—"

"Declan." Her dad's voice stopped her rambling cold. Her dad's typically smiling face morphed into one of anger. An emotion that shocked Anna Katherine enough to stop talking all together.

"Yes?"

"You spend a lot of time with my daughter."

"I do."

"A lot of time alone with my daughter."

"Well, yes."

"If I recall correctly, when I first realized how close the two of you were becoming all those years ago, I sat you down and we had a very important conversation. Did we not?"

"We did, sir. But you see—"

"And I asked you if you felt any romantic feelings toward my daughter."

"You did, and at the time I—"

"And you told me that you didn't. You assured me that I could trust you with her. You said the two of you were just friends. That's what you said, was it not?"

Anna Katherine watched in horror. Out of the two of them, she had expected her mom to react negatively. She hadn't even thought of her dad.

"It was, but that was years ago, and a lot can change—"

He cut Declan off again. "I also asked that if any of that happened to change at any point, you would be honest with me. Hiding your relationship with my daughter from me is far from being honest, Declan."

"I understand that, but—"

This time, it was Patricia who interrupted him. "Timothy, that's enough. Leave Declan alone. He's done nothing wrong."

Anna Katherine let out a sigh of relief, but when her mom turned to look at her, she realized she had felt relief too soon.

"You," Patricia pointed to her. "How could you do this to us?"

She tried to respond, but no words came out. Thankfully, Declan came to the rescue. "It was hardly her doing, Mrs. Patty. I was the one who asked her to keep it a secret and who proposed."

Patricia smiled at him, "Sweetie, we know you're innocent in all of this."

"Innocent?!" His voice rose several octaves.

"Mom! That's—"

And then the entire table went silent again till Alex blurted out, "I'm dating Natalie!"

Anna Katherine, who was still looking at her brother, saw the confusion and surprise on his face at his own words, but he quickly managed to hide it.

Natalie choked on the sip of coffee she had just taken, "Excuse me?"

He chuckled, but it sounded forced. "Well, that was hardly the way I had planned on telling my parents, but…" He trailed off, unsure of how to continue.

Harry glanced at the two of them. There was an emotion on his face that would have interested Anna Katherine had all hell not broken loose around the table.

Timothy groaned and Patricia gazed wide-eyed around the table. Before anyone could say anything else, Harry jumped up, spreading his hands wide, and managed to spill Timothy's iced coffee all over Patricia's dress. A hush enveloped the table.

Natalie coughed, "Well, I think this is an excellent time to ask for our checks. I'll go find our waitress."

Alex leaned over to whisper to Harry. "What was that?"

"I was going to give a toast!"

Alex snorted. "That worked out really well, didn't it?"

No one said much of anything else as they gathered up their things and prepared to leave.

Declan reached for the handle to the passenger door of his car for Kit when Patty blocked her path to his car. "Why didn't you tell us, Anna

Katherine?"

Declan wondered if Kit discerned the hurt in her mother's voice.

"Mom, you're so invested in my dating and love life. It's suffocating. I had no idea how you were going to react to me dating Declan. Is it impossible for you to understand that I just wanted some time to enjoy a new relationship with him before it was dissected by my family?" Kit sounded tired but more genuine than she had all day. Declan knew that at the core of it, there was truth behind her words.

She seemed to take in Kit's words and process them slowly. After what felt like a few minutes, she nodded, and when she spoke, she sounded hurt. "I'm sorry I ever made you feel like you couldn't come to me."

As Patty slid into the car, Timmy confronted Declan and Kit once more. "This conversation isn't over, you two." Turning, he entered the driver door of his own car, and they drove off.

Harry, Alex, and Nat gathered around Kit and Declan by their cars.

No one was surprised when it was Harry who decided to break the silence. "Well, that was something."

Declan groaned.

Kit patted his arm, and tried to smile to their friends. "You all are coming over to Declan's, right?"

Everyone nodded in agreement and then headed to the apartment where they would rehash the entire disaster of a brunch.

Anna Katherine collapsed on the couch when Harry, Alex, and Natalie had finally left while Declan cleaned up the last signs of the dog's accident from that morning. Fox was asleep on the floor in front of her, and Anna Katherine draped her arm over her face while letting out a groan.

She heard Declan's footsteps toward her, and let out a whine when he shoved her legs off the couch so he could sit. She kicked him grumpily before resting her legs in his lap. She wanted to glare at him when he only chuckled in response, but moving her arm to look at him seemed like too much effort. Instead, she gave a halfhearted attempt to kick him again, but he saw its coming and caught her foot before she could make contact.

"This morning was fun." He gave her leg a pat.

Lifting her arm off her face she peered beneath it at him., "I think we need to Google the definition of 'fun' because it definitely was not *fun*."

"You're just being a Pessimistic Perry." He gave her another pat, "Hey, Wesley called and wanted us to meet up for drinks tonight before he leaves for that interview."

"Definitely not."

"Figured. Told him we could hang out later this week when he gets back from Dublin." He reached over and grabbed the remote that was resting on the arm of the couch by her head. "Wanna watch something?"

Anna Katherine let out another groan. "Something mindless. My brain can't follow any sort of an actual plot."

"Alex and Harry started a show last week. Pretty entertaining. Wanna give it a go?"

"Sure. Why not."

"Speaking of your brother," Declan chuckled as he said, "I can't believe he lied to your parents just to get the heat off of us."

She tried to smile, but it felt more like a grimace. "I guess he isn't too bad after all."

He gave her one more comforting pat on the leg before starting the show.

Halfway through the first episode, both of them were fully into the drama, but when Declan's phone went off, it pulled them both out of the trance they had been in.

"I think we have officially transformed into an old married couple, Kit-Kat." Declan twisted his phone around so she could see the picture he had received from Wesley. "They're all off having fun, and we're sitting on the couch, drinking cheap wine, and watching reality TV."

Anna Katherine giggled, relieved to feel a bit more lighthearted. "I think you're right. When did this happen?"I'm going to take a wild guess and say when we got engaged."

"As if this wasn't exactly what we were doing weeks ago before you nearly got deported."

Declan hummed. "It was more of a fine than a deportation, love."

She ignored him. "We're probably going to forget how to date by the time our divorce comes around."

"As if you know how to date now." He scoffed. "When was the last time you went on one?"

She shoved him in the shoulder. "That's rude."

He managed to look a little apologetic. "It's true though. You haven't been in a relationship since Jonah."

He wasn't wrong, but that didn't mean Anna Katherine enjoyed it being pointed out. "Okay, yeah, but I have been on dates."

He snorted. "You've barely given any of those guys a chance. You nitpick them to death."

"I do not! I just know what I want."

"Well, I think you're just not over Jonah." When she gave him an incredulous look, he simply shrugged.

"I *am* over him. He was just my first love, and that was a messy breakup."

"Yeah, I was there for most of it. You don't have to remind me."

She pulled her legs up, creating space between them and turned to face him. "Yeah, I know you were. I don't think I would've survived it without you."

He rolled his eyes as he said, "Of course you would've. You had Nat, and even if you didn't have her, you would have survived on your own. You're stronger than you give yourself credit for."

"You literally had to drag me out of my bed and convince me to shower, Declan."

"Okay, so you would've smelled like an overflowing sewer, but you still would've survived."

She stuck her bottom lip out. "You're a jerk."

"What happened to you loving me and not surviving without me? Let's go back to that."

When he grabbed her feet and placed them in his lap, she let him. "What about you? I don't think I've ever known you to have a girlfriend since we've been out of college."

"I've had plenty of girlfriends."

"Serious ones? That lasted more than a month?"

He had the decency to look bashful at that. "Okay, fine. You might have a point."

"Those are not girlfriends. They are flings." She poked his side. "First love. C'mon. Tell me."

"Her name is Vivian. Completely thought I was going to marry her. She stayed in Dublin for uni, but we did the long distance thing for a while. She ended it right before I met you, actually. I just haven't met anyone I wanted to endure that kind of heartbreak for since then."

"Was it bad?"

He shrugged. "It was a pretty clean break, but I was still torn up about it."

"Which great friend of Declan helped you through it?"

He paused, and then let out an awkward chuckle. "Jonah, actually."

"Oof." She grimaced.

"I know." He reached out and pulled her to him. "You know, at least we got those messy first loves out of the way. Heartbreak and all. I mean, if we're going to lose this many of our single years, at least we got it out of the way early."

She leaned against his side. "And now we're also going to be divorcees in our twenties as well."

"Overachievers. That's what we are," he joked.

She reached up for a high five. "Heck yeah we are."

Declan started to stand up. "C'mon. Let's take Fox out so we can end this night and put this day behind us."

Third Commandment: Thou (Declan) Shalt Always Put the Toilet Seat Down

*A*nna Katherine came back from using the bathroom, a grimace on her face. "I know the third commandment. You have to put the toilet seat down after you use it."

"I always do that!"

"Then explain to me why I just fell in."

Anna Katherine was in the midst of breaking down boxes in the back of the shop when she heard the bell over the door jingle. A few moments later, her coworker and friend Mackenzie called for her. As she walked back to the front of the shop, she knew it was either a large order or...

"Nat." She smiled. "What are you doing here?"

"Harry and I were talking, and we've come up with a plan to help you guys really sell the whole thing."

Anna Katherine gave a sharp look to her friend before motioning toward Mack, but thankfully she was busy cleaning the espresso machine, and the hissing noises it was making were too loud for her to hear Nat.

"Careful what you say around people," Anna Katerine whispered with raised eyebrows.

"Sorry." Nat didn't look the least bit sorry. "Anyway, like I said, Harry and I were talking and—"

"I'm sorry, back up. You and Harry were willingly talking to each other?"

Nat rolled her eyes and went to where the bar stools were at the other end of the counter. "I know. Desperate times call for desperate measures. You're welcome."

"I'm not sure if I should be thankful or not since I don't know what the plan is."

"Stop acting like I don't ever have your best interest at heart. So there I was, scrolling through Instagram at work."

"As any responsible teacher does."

"The kids were at recess."

"I stand by what I said."

"Anyway," Nat huffed and rolled her eyes again. "As I was saying. Instagram. Scrolling. I saw a friend from college post something about her engagement party. The pictures were adorable and everyone looked so happy for them. It was perfect."

"Mhm."

"So then I saw Harry—"

"Why did you see Harry?"

"We were at the grocery store."

"I thought you were at work."

"I was, but this was after that! Keep up, Kit. I was at the grocery store and I ran into Harry. Literally. Our carts collided. It was his fault. He wasn't paying attention to where he was going. Did you know that he just recently moved closer to my apartment? Anyway, Harry also knows this friend and..."

"Imagine that. A friend from college also knowing another friend from college."

"Can you please stop interrupting me? So we were chatting about this girl and the engagement party, and for once, Harry had an absolutely brilliant idea."

Nat stopped talking, eyes wide, and stared at Anna Katherine.

"Am I supposed to guess? You told me to stop interrupting, and I hate guessing."

Nat giggled, like she couldn't hold in her joy any longer. "Harry and I are throwing you and Declan a surprise engagement party!"

Before Anna Katherine could say anything, there was a gasp behind her. "You and Declan are engaged?!"

The smile dropped off of Nat's face, and Anna Katherine slowly turned around. Mack was behind them, no longer cleaning the espresso machine, with a pile of dirty milk towels in her hands.

"Oops." Nat had the decency to react.

Anna Katherine grimaced. "Surprise?"

"Wait until Martin finds out! We've been thinking something was going on between the two of you, but you've been in such denial and so secretive! And now you're *engaged*?!"

Anna Katherine turned back around to glare at Nat. Under her breath so Mack couldn't hear, she whispered, "I hate you."

"Tell me everything! When did this happen? How did he propose?" Mack was positively giddy.

"Well..."

"And when did the two of you even start dating? Kit! I have so many questions!"

Anna Katherine glared even harder at Nat. Thankfully, her friend took the hint and commandeered the conversation.

"And we will answer all of your questions, I'm sure, just after we give the bride-to-be a moment to breathe. It's still all a bit new for her."

"Yeah, I feel like it all just happened last week," Kit added.

"Have you told your parents yet? Who all knows about the engagement? Is the wedding going to be here or back in Ireland? And wait, if it's a surprise, why are you telling Anna Katherine, Nat?"

"I hate surprises. The thing is, we're keeping our engagement hush-hush for right now," Anna Katherine finally managed to say. "I'd appreciate it if you didn't tell anyone just yet. We just told my parents, and we still have others to tell before we want the news traveling."

Mack nodded in understanding. "Of course. You don't need to worry. I won't tell a soul."

The bell over the entrance rang, and Martin walked in as Mack was ending her sentence.

"What aren't we telling a soul?" he asked, catching only the tail end of the conversation.

Mack, full of energy and excitement, spat out, "Declan and Kit are engaged!"

Both Anna Katherine and Nat glared at her before she realized what she had just done. "Oops. I won't tell a soul... starting now."

Anna Katherine covered her face with her hands, and Nat reached out to pat her shoulder comfortingly.

Martin looked around the shop and took in the mood. He chuckled as he walked around the corner and toward the back of the shop where his office was. "I didn't hear a thing. Consider me deaf until you want to tell me yourself, Anna Katherine."

The three of them watched in silence as Martin disappeared in the back.

Nat ended the somewhat awkward silence and said, "That man is truly one in a million. Can he be my boss too?"

"You'll have to quit teaching and become a barista."

Nat scrunched up her face in disgust. "No thank you. I like my little humans a lot better than I like the average population."

Declan had been expecting a quiet night alone at his place. Harry had a FaceTime date with his family who was back in Australia, and he hadn't made plans with any of his other mates since this whole madness with marrying Kit had begun. Kit herself was taking a break from packing and cleaning her apartment to go see some superhero movie with her older brother. It was supposed to just be Declan and Fox, until, that is, there was a knock on his door.

He glanced at his watch. It was only six, and the food he had ordered wasn't scheduled to arrive for another forty minutes. Fox, useless as a guard dog, stayed sound asleep as he went to see who was at the door.

He was a little taken aback to see Nat.

"Hello." He took a moment to examine her after opening the door. She didn't seem panicked, which was a good sign. "What are you doing here?"

"Can I come in?"

Declan stepped to the side, ushering her in. "We didn't have plans, did we?"

He, of course, knew the answer to that question. As much as he loved Nat, and as much as she tolerated him, they almost never saw each other without Kit or Harry in tow, and it was usually Kit, more often than Harry.

For whatever reason, Nat seemed to have a horrible taste in her mouth when it came to his best friend.

Making her way inside his apartment, she sat in one of the chairs across from the couch. "No, but I was in the area and decided I needed to talk to you."

He went back to where he had been reclining on the couch beside Fox, who was still sound asleep. "You do know we have phones. You could've just called."

"Stop being difficult." He waited for her to say more, but she just watched Fox for a moment.

Declan was itching to know what she wanted to discuss, but if being friends with Kit had taught him anything, it's that if he stayed quiet long enough, the women in his life would speak up eventually.

After another moment, Nat leaned forward, resting her elbows on her knees. "You know my thoughts on this sham of a marriage plan."

He opened his mouth to respond, but she shook her head. "No need to respond. Surprisingly, I'm not here to call you an idiot for coming up with such a plan." There was another pause, and Declan remained silent. "Kit is my best friend."

He nodded. "She's mine, too."

"She's a lot to handle. She's loud and passionate and likes to go down her own path, regardless of what anyone in her life advises her to do. A lot of people view it as too much. View *her* as too much. Jonah did. A lot of our friends from high school did."

Declan did not view Kit as too much of anything. She was Kit, and she was the perfect amount of herself—even when she did give him a headache from time to time.

"And because of this *too-muchness* of hers, people forget or don't realize that she's actually a person who feels her emotions very strongly. So whatever emotion she feels, it's all-consuming for her." She gave him a warning glare. "When she's hurt or in pain, she feels it just as deeply as when she's on top of the world."

A part of Declan was offended that Nat felt the need to have this conversation with him. Of course he knew all of this about Kit. He had all but studied the psychology of one Anna Katherine Marie Tran in uni. He knew her ins and outs better than he sometimes even knew himself, and he prided himself on being self-aware. But another part of him was thankful Kit had someone that cared enough to sit down and have this awkward conversation with him on her behalf.

Still, he wasn't necessarily happy to be on the receiving end. "What are you saying, Natalie?"

She straightened. "If you hurt her, I will murder you. We're in the deep south, Declan. Just because we live in a town called Serenity Grove doesn't mean we're all pure and innocent. Don't think I can't get away with it either. I know plenty of people who have pigs or chickens or meat grinders."

The thing was, Declan knew how serious Nat was being. Never in his dreams would he dare to get on her bad side. He wasn't as stupid as Harry in that regard. He wasn't sure if it was the absurdity of the very idea of him hurting Kit, the mention of the farm animals, or what he was sure Nat thought was her use of an intimidating glare, but whatever it was, it caused a laugh to explode out of him.

"Declan!" She groaned and crossed her arms. "I'm being serious! This is not a laughing matter!"

That just made him laugh harder. Fox lazily opened one eye to look at him, huffed, and curled tighter into a ball, as if to try to get away from his ruckus. Finally, his laughter subdued. "I know you're serious," he said between lingering breaths of laughter.

"Then why on earth did you find it so funny?"

"It's just..." His smile faltered. There was a truth in the pit of his stomach that seemed to be attempting escape. Drawing a deep breath, he swallowed. "I'd never intentionally hurt her."

"I'm not concerned about the intentionality. It's the unintentional hurt I'm worried about." She bit her lip, hesitating before she went on. "She cares about you, deeply."

"And I her." His stomach churned.

She squinted her eyes at him. "What are *you* saying?"

He stood up and went to the kitchen. He needed a glass of water. He was suddenly feeling nauseous. "What I'm saying is that she's my best friend and soon to be my wife, whether it's a marriage of love or of convenience doesn't change that fact. I give you full permission to hurt me in whatever crazed, medieval ways you have up your sleeves if I hurt her beyond repair."

When he turned around with his fresh glass of water, what he had said seemed to have pleased her. "Good. I'll hold you to that."

He motioned toward the door. "I ordered food. You want to stay?"

Shaking her head, she stood. "Thanks, but no. I need to get home and prepare for my little humans tomorrow."

"Right. Well, be safe driving home."

A smile finally lit her face for the first time during her visit. "Always am."

If anyone told Harry that every grocery store was the same, he would like for them to go from his old grocery store to the one he had to shop at now. It was not that it was terribly different. Every layout is the same, he'd give them that. But everything else? What was on each specific aisle? That was all a complete toss up!

He had been shopping here for about a month since moving into his new flat, and he was still having difficulty finding what he needed at the grocery.

The spices were all in a different aisle, the breakfast food was not where he was used to it being, and don't get him started on the chips. He had nearly run over a terribly fragile looking elderly lady with his trolley because he was searching for things on his list instead of looking where he was going. Shopping was so much easier when you just knew where everything was, like a muscle memory.

He was looking for hummus—which was not near the eggs and cheese like it was at the other store—when he heard a familiar voice.

He peeked around the corner and smiled to himself when he saw her standing there with a shopping basket in her hand. .

"Natalie Thompson. We meet again."

If he didn't know any better, he would've sworn she groaned before turning around to face him. She was on the phone, but the conversation must have come to an end because she was muttering a goodbye before slipping her phone back into her purse.

"Harry Whitlock. We have got to stop meeting like this."

He rested his arms on the trolley. "I don't know. I quite like it."

"At least you didn't attempt to run me over this time."

His face fell. "No, but I nearly ran over an elderly woman earlier."

To his surprise, and maybe even her own if the widening of her eyes meant anything, she laughed. "They're going to end up banning you from this store."

The trolley rolled closer to Nat under his weight, and it was only after stumbling a few steps that he gained his balance again. "Nah, I'm too charming."

She rolled her eyes. "Sure. You're too *something*."

"Delightful? Pleasant? Lovable?"

"No. Absolutely not."

He laughed. "Well, since I have you here, can you please inform me where the hummus is?"

She nodded her head down the aisle. "At the end of this aisle."

"Thanks." He glanced at his list. "And, uh, what about the rest?"

He handed her his phone where his list was, and watched her as she took it from him. "You telling me you don't know where any of this is?" she asked with a raised brow.

"I'm telling you that this is completely different from the store near my old apartment, and I am going to end up running someone over if someone—if you, don't help me find the rest of the items on my list."

She shook her head. "You're helpless."

"But you'll help. You can't help yourself."

She shoved the phone back to him. "C'mon. Let's go."

He followed closely behind her as they went to find the rest of the items on his list. Occasionally, she would grab something from the shelves and place it in her own basket. They were standing in front of the ice cream as she debated whether or not to buy a pint, when Harry remembered his conversation with Declan earlier.

"So, I hear that you are throwing threats around this week."

She grabbed a pint of 'cookies and cream' and glanced over her shoulder at him, "What do you mean?"

"I talked to Declan."

Her face paled, and he couldn't help but smile. "I know you think that the meat grinder was probably too much, but—"

He interrupted her with a laugh and, "I'm sorry, did you just say meat grinder?"

She nodded.

His laughter only grew louder. "There is no way you threatened Declan with a meat grinder!"

"This isn't funny!" she hissed, looking around.

He was laughing so hard, he couldn't respond.

She stood there, arms crossed with her basket dangling beside her, and a fierce frown etched on her features. "Henrison Whitlock."

The wrong name made him laugh even more, which, in turn, only made her frown deepen. Finally, after a moment, he was able to reel himself back in and gain some composure.

"I can't believe you threatened to kill my best friend. You're a mad-woman, Nat!"

She huffed. "My role is to protect Kit."

He nodded. "So does this mean my role is to protect Declan? In that case, maybe I need to threaten Kit with all the poisonous animals we have back home."

"Threaten her and die." She was still not smiling, but there was a touch of humor in her eyes.

"You couldn't hurt me if you tried, Thompson."

She narrowed her eyes at him. "Oh, and why's that?"

"You find me too endearing." He turned his trolley around to go to the cashier. But before he took his eyes off of Nat, he winked. His back was to her before he could see her reaction, but her silence told him he had won this round.

<h1 style="text-align:center">9</h1>

Declan's computer was set up on the table, when Kit had stumbled through his door still in her pajamas and her hair looking more knotted than not. Her work uniform was half stuffed in her purse, half dangling out and threatening to drag on the floor. As soon as she was close enough, he handed her a cup of coffee. She nodded in thanks.

They had planned on FaceTiming Móirín, and due to the time difference and their work schedules, it had been hard to find a time that would work for all of them. But he knew they needed to tell his mom about the engagement sooner rather than later. Thankfully, Kit hadn't put too much of a fuss when he mentioned an early morning where she didn't have to open Hattie's.

They sat next to each other at the table, and Declan took a moment to position the computer before calling his mom.

"I need another cup of coffee for this," Kit mumbled as she took the last sip of coffee from her travel mug.

"Here." Taking the cup from her, he stepped to the counter to refill it. As he was doctoring up her brew, Móirín answered.

She gasped when she saw Kit. "Anna Katherine! Oh how nice it is to see you mo mhuirnín."

Kit glanced at Declan for help when she didn't understand the word his mum had said. He smiled at the endearment and whispered, "It means, *beloved*."

Kit's smile grew when she heard the translation. "It's nice to see you too, Móirín! How is it over there?"

"Oh, the same as always. Missing my sweet boy."

Declan sat down then and gave his mum a quick smile. "Don't start laying the guilt trip on me already, Mum. I told you, I'm going to come home for Christmas this year."

She scoffed. "Mar dhea."

Kit threw him a questioning look again. Instead of translating for her, he bit the bullet and dove right in.

"Mum, Kit and I have some news." Bracing himself for what he was about to tell her, he hoped that she would have a more positive reaction than Kit's parents, but there was always a chance this would not end well.

Apparently, he had taken too long to say anything, because Kit exclaimed, "Declan and I are engaged!"

Móirín's face froze, and he wasn't entirely sure if it was because of the poor connection or because she was mentally processing what was just said.

"Oh, that's wonderful news, my loves!"

He drew a breath. It was definitely the connection then, because her face was still frozen and becoming pixelated.

His mother continued congratulating them, and Declan thought he might've seen a tear or two when the connection finally decided to cooperate.

"Oh, your father would've loved to see this day, Declan."

He smiled. "I know, Mum."

Tears really were making an appearance then, and Móirín started dabbing at her face with a tissue.

"Don't get all mushy on me now."

She clicked her tongue at him. "Hush now. You're my baby and you're getting married. I think I have a right to get a little mushy."

"Yeah, Declan." Kit elbowed him in the side. "Let your mom have this one."

He smiled, but before he could defend himself, his mother screeched and he jumped.

"Oh! Does this mean that you're both coming for Christmas?" Móirín was grinning ear to ear with her hands on her cheeks. She looked so hopeful, that Declan didn't think he'd be able to deny her this.

He and Kit hadn't discussed what their union would do to their plans for their families over the holidays. But when he glanced at Kit before answering, she smiled and nodded. Apparently the Tran family would just have to do without Kit this year. He cringed. Patricia would have a fit.

"Yes, Mum. We're both coming. The wedding is in November, so we will both be there."

Móirín began asking about the details of the where and when, and after a few more minutes, Declan had to interrupt her gushing.

"I'm sorry to cut you off, Mum, but I need to get to work."

"Oh, of course you do! And I'm sure Kit does as well. I'll call you both later this week and we can work out the details of when I'll fly in."

"Sounds great, Mum."

"Stay safe, my loves!"

Once the call ended, he stood and went to the bathroom to finish getting ready for work.

"You don't talk about him much."

His toothbrush was dangling from his mouth when Declan stuck his head out of the bathroom door sending her a questioning glance. "Who?"

"Your dad." He shrugged. "He passed away when I was younger. I don't remember a whole lot, but I do remember how well he loved Mum and me." "What do you mean?" He finished brushing his teeth before he answered. "He used to surprise Mum with a basket of her favorite treats. It was never planned. Never expected. He worked long hours, so he wasn't home to cook us meals often, but he never went to bed with a dirty dish in the sink, and he never expected Mum to do it." He squeezed past where she stood in the hallway as he headed to his bedroom to grab a button up. "Whether they talked about it beforehand or not, I'm not sure, but he always did the clean up no matter how late he got home. And he never complained. He always made sure her car was filled with petrol. Little things like that." Kit was standing in his bedroom doorway watching him finish off the buttons. "He sounds like he was a good man." Declan smiled. "He was one of the best." Walking up to him, she wrapped her arms around his waist. "Good thing you take after him."

10

Harry created a group
Harry added Timothy (Kit's dad) to the group
Harry added Patty (Kit's mom) to the group
Harry added Nat to the group

Good afternoon everyone!

Harry @ 4:00 pm

Who is this?

Timothy (Kit's dad) @ 4:00 pm

That's Harry, dear.

Patty (Kit's mom) @ 4:01 pm

Do we know a harry?

Timothy (Kit's dad) @ 4:05 pm

Yes, yes. Declan's foreign friend

Patty (Kit's mom) @ 4:06 pm

Sorry about my friend. I told him to introduce himself but he must've forgotten

Nat @ 4:06 pm

Natalie! How's my future daughter-in-law?

Timothy (Kit's dad) @ 4:10 pm

Timmy, don't be ridiculous They only just started dating

Patty (Kit's mom) @ 4:10 pm

Well What a way to start off the conversation

Harry @ 4:11 pm

Harry and I are planning an engagement party for Declan and KitIt's a surprise. The owner of G'Day Latte has agreed to have it at the shop after hours We were wondering what nights work best for the two of you?I'm sure Kit would want you both there.

Nat @ 4:11 pm

OH WHAT A WONDERFUL IDEA Let me look at my calendar, dear. I'll give you a call with a few dates once i know

Patty (Kit's mom) @ 4:15 pm

Do you need any help with the planning? What about the decorations? Who is catering it? Will there be music? Timmy has a wonderful mix CD we could use...

Patty (Kit's mom) @ 4:17 pm

I think we have it all under control, Patty But if we need ANYTHING you will be the first we call

Harry @ 4:20 pm

What he said.

Nat @ 4:21 pm

Anna Katherine quickly realized that living with Nat was interesting at best. It reminded her of being back home, only because she was once again hyper-aware of how loud she was being or how much space she was taking up. She hadn't expected living with her best friend to be anything less than perfect, but it definitely wasn't the best situation.

Since moving in with Nat, Anna Katherine had made sure she had woken up in enough time to put away the sofa bed where she was sleeping, clean her coffee mug, and pick up whatever else she needed to from getting ready. She had done a really good job of it, too. She was proud of herself. It felt as though she were creating new rhythms in her life and it was becoming easier with each morning.

Of course, all good things must come to an end.

She overslept, waking up an entire hour late.

Nat's apartment was about twenty minutes from the shop, which wasn't terrible, but it wasn't the greatest, either. Having to be at the shop by 5:00, she'd have to leave Nat's by 4:30, which meant she had to wake up no later than 3:30 in order to be ready on time.

Waking up at 4:30 was far from ideal. As a result, she did not have time to pick up her towel from the rushed shower she took, throw away the empty PopTart box as she took the last one, or put the sofa bed back into the sofa.

As she sped-walked to her car, she sent a message to Nat.

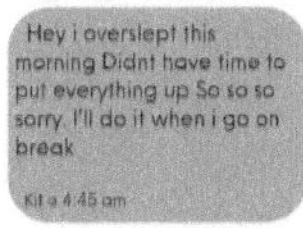

As she slid into her car, she sent another text to her boss.

She sent him a thumbs up, her pounding heart slowing just barely.

After the morning rush, one of the new hires showed up, and Anna Katherine trained him for a few hours before going on break. She was about to go outside to eat her lunch when Martin called her into the office.

When she stepped in the small, crowded room, he asked, "How did Lance do?"

She lifted a shoulder in a shrug. "He seems to be doing well enough on the register, and the customers love him." She paused before smiling and adding, "Especially the moms."

"Ah," Martin chuckled. "Glad to hear that he's doing well. Do you think he's ready to move to drink making?"

"Should be. I don't see why not."

"Wonderful. Are you up for training him?"

Anna Katherine straightened her spine, and her arms that were crossed fell to her sides. "Training is reserved for managers."

Martin watched her for a moment, a gentle smile playing at his lips. "You're the best shift lead I have, Kit. We just lost a manager. I can rearrange a few things, and I'd love for you to be the opening shift manager."

She blinked. "What?"

"Or..." He smiled and leaned back in his chair, "I could give it to Mack?"

"No!" The word left her mouth before she could overthink it. She cleared her throat. "I mean, no way. I'd love to be a manager. I just... I didn't know we were looking for a new one."

They talked for a few more minutes about what her new duties would entail and when they would start, but before she left to officially start her break, she paused in the doorway.

"So, Nat and Harry, my friends, are planning an engagement party."

He tried to hide his smile, but failed miserably. "And who's engagement are we celebrating?"

She groaned. "I know that you know. You know that I know that you know. There is no need for us to act like we don't know."

"I believe what I said was that I hadn't heard anything."

She gave him an annoyed look and rolled her eyes. "Hey, Martin?"

"Yes, favorite barista?"

"Declan and I are engaged and are getting married in November."

"What! That's wonderful."

"Thanks." Sarcasm dripped from her one word response.

"Would you like to host an engagement party—that I haven't heard a thing about—here?"

She stomped over to his desk and grabbed a sticky note. She scribbled down Nat's number. "Call Nat. She's the planner. I refuse to plan my own engagement party."

He laughed. "I'll call her today."

She didn't respond as she walked out of the office, pretending she didn't hear him when he called out, "Congrats on making opening manager *and* your engagement! Big things!"

Once she was outside sitting at the saggy, old picnic table, she pulled her phone out of her apron pocket.

She was relieved to see that Nat didn't seem too upset about it, but the emoji did cause worry since Nat wasn't one to usually use them. It might mean she was overcompensating. However, she ignored the worry for now in favor of messaging Declan.

Before she could respond and make plans with Declan, Nat messaged her again.

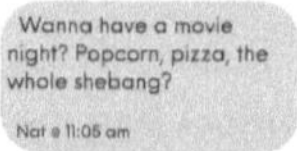

She was torn between Nat and Declan, but sent Nat a thumbs up before she found herself overthinking it too much.

Anna Katherine and Nat were piled on top of Nat's bed like a couple of cats with the computer between them. Surrounded by pillows, blankets, popcorn, drinks, and a smorgasbord of snacks, it was looking like it was going to be a good night.

Nat pulled up one of the only movies they could always agree on, *While You Were Sleeping*, and started rearranging all the pillows around her to get comfortable.

Anna Katherine stayed where she was, already quite comfortable and only a short reach away from her favorite snacks.

She had just shoved a handful of popcorn in her mouth when Nat said, "I can't believe you're finally manager! It only took over five years!"

She finished chewing before attempting to respond.. "I feel like it came out of nowhere."

"You've been telling him you're interested in the position for years now," Nat pointed out.

Sandra Bullock started talking over the opening credits, and together, both of them quoted one of their favorite lines from the movie with perfect timing. *"I just don't remember it being this orange."*

Without missing a beat, Anna Katherine continued the conversation, "Yeah, but he hadn't asked, and I wasn't aware we were looking for a new one! It came from left field."

"I don't understand that saying. What does left field have to do with anything?"

Anna Katherine shrugged. *"It's raining cats and dogs* doesn't make much sense either."

"I'm about to fly off the handle." Nat moved her hands in front of her, "What handle! Why are we flying?"

"I'm full as a tick. I mean, I get it, but it's gross. Can we stop saying it?"

"That one is gross." Nat scrunched up her face and mocked a shiver. "I also don't understand *fixin'*. How did saying I'm about to do something become I'm fixin' to do something?"

"Same with *reckon*."

"Huh. Reckon I might could since I'm fixin' to go to town."

They both giggled at their exaggerated southern accents and sayings. Once the giggles calmed down, Nat bumped shoulders with her. "Real proud of you, though."

She smiled. "Thanks."

The next morning, Anna Katherine got up the first time her alarm went off, which was nearly unheard of. She didn't want to disturb Nat since they both ended up sleeping in her bed last night after the movie. Taking quick shower, she whizzed through getting ready for work, having a nice warm cup of coffee out in the living room before heading to open up the shop. Of course, she lost track of time and ended up rushing out the door of the apartment, leaving her mug and blanket at the end of the couch without a second thought.

Harry was, once again, at the grocery store. It was sheer luck he noticed Nat calling him since his phone was still on silent from work.

"And what have I done to deserve a call from Natalie Thompson?"

"I can't last another week of this."

"Mhm. I'm sorry to hear that." He grabbed a rotisserie chicken and placed it carefully in his trolley. "And what are we referring to?"

"Anna Katherine Marie Tran living in my apartment!" she all but screeched her best friend's name into the phone. Harry had to pull the speaker away from his ear so he wouldn't lose hearing.

"You two are best friends. I highly doubt that there is truly trouble in paradise."

"This," she seethed, "is not paradise. It's hell."

"And what does this hell look like?"

"She left her towel on the floor this morning. I nearly tripped on it."

Harry gasped dramatically. "Oh my goodness."

"And there are not one, not two, not three, but *four* mugs by the couch that she has been neglecting to bring to the kitchen. I'm not even expecting her to wash them. Just put them in the kitchen!"

Harry waited a moment to be sure Nat was finished with her rant before he said, "Breathe, Nat. You only have a handful of weeks left. You can make it."

"Can I though?"

"I have full faith in you."

She harrumphed.

"Don't do that."

"I told her this was a bad idea."

"You tell her all her ideas are bad ideas."

"Well, this one was exceptionally bad."

"It's just your control issues flaring up." Harry wished she was in front of him rather than on the phone. "Relax. It's fine. Clean up after her for a little while. It's not forever."

"But if I do it for her, she won't learn!"

"Natalie."

"What?"

"You are not her teacher. You are her friend. Act like it."

Nat sounded a little defeated when she finally said, "I don't like it when you make sense."

"I often make sense. You just choose to ignore it."

She sighed. "Thanks for listening to me rant."

"Anytime, Nat. I'm always here for you."

She was quiet for a moment, and Harry thought she might just hang up without saying bye. But then she said, "You're picking me up for the engagement party."

"Oh, am I?"

"Yes. I'll be ready at five thirty. Don't be late."

And with that, she did hang up.

Harry chuckled and shook his head before sliding his phone back into his pocket and carrying on with his grocery shopping.

The night of the engagement party snuck up on Anna Katherine, and before she knew it, they were headed to their "surprise" party. Anna Katherine thought she and Declan did a pretty good job of acting surprised when they walked through the door with their friends. She was thankful that the crowd wasn't too big. Nat and Harry had kept their promise and it was just a few close friends, coworkers, and of course, her parents and Alex.

Martin was talking with her dad, and while Timmy was busy, Patty came over to speak with Anna Katherine.

"Your friends did a great job," Patty enthused.

Anna Katerine smiled. "I know. They really outdid themselves."

She gave her daughter an unimpressed look. "You could've done a better job at acting surprised."

For a moment, Anna Katherine thought about playing dumb, but there was no way she was going to pull this one over on her mom. "How did you know?"

"You mean other than your terrible acting skills? You and Nat tell each other everything, and with the two of you living in the same apartment, she was bound to blab."

She wanted to argue with Patty, but it was the absolute truth. There was nothing she could deny.

"Declan did a much better job pretending to be surprised. Very believable. You should ask him for notes on how to be a better actress." Patty's tone was dry, and a bit too judgy for Anna Katherine's liking.

"Well, I won't be doing that. I have no plans on acting anytime soon or ever. But thank you for your opinions."

Declan, who had been thanking a few friends off to the side, joined them with a warm smile. He gave Patty a quick hug. "Thank you so much for coming,"

"Oh, of course we wanted to come support our favorite Irish boy."

"Not to mention your daughter," Anna Katherine mumbled.

"Stop mumbling, dear. It's unbecoming."

Timmy, having finished his conversation with Martin, joined them. He smiled at Anna Katherine, but didn't acknowledge Declan. "How's my beautiful daughter?"

She leaned into a hug but said, "She would be better if you'd greet her fiance."

When she stepped away from her dad, she was not at all surprised to see him scowling. "I did acknowledge him. Then I decided to greet you."

Patty elbowed her husband. "Behave, Timothy."

Timmy deflated slightly and put his focus on Declan. "Good evening, Declan."

Declan greeted him with a handshake and a smile, but didn't get one in return. Declan turned toward her. "I'm going to go say hey to William. I'll be right back."

She nodded, still focused on her parents.

"I need you two to get it together."

Patty and Timmy both looked confused. As one, they asked, "What do you mean?"

"I was on Mom's bad list when I was as single as they come. All she wanted was for me to get married. Well, now I'm getting married! And guess what! My father, who I thought was a gentle and understanding man, is treating my best friend and future husband like dirt."

Her bluntness seemed to have ruffled Timmy's feathers. He went to speak, but stuttered and stumbled over his words.

Patty placed a hand on his arm and spoke up for both of them. "Now that's not exactly fair, dear."

"What's not fair is you acting like I don't exist when I'm beside Alex or Declan, and you," she pointed her finger at her dad, "acting like Declan doesn't exist just because we're getting married!" She took a deep breath before continuing. "Declan is a good man. He's the best I've ever met, and more than that, he treats me better than anyone else in my life. He's gracious and forgiving and trustworthy. And you're treating him like something the raccoons would dig out!"

She stopped, taking a steadying breath and waiting for her parents to say something. Anything. But for once in her life, they both stayed silent, just staring at her.

"Well, as much joy as this conversation has brought me, I think it's time that I go make the rounds."

Patty looked like she was about to argue, so Anna Katherine added, "You did a great job of teaching me to be a grateful host."

With that, Patty's mouth snapped shut, and Timmy placed his arm around his wife's shoulder.

Anna Katherine started mingling, saying hello and thanks to a small group of friends from high school that Nat had invited. They were gushing over her ring and the engagement and, of course, Declan himself. They kept telling Anna Katherine how lucky she was.

One of the girls, the one with more sense it seemed, asked, "Does he make you happy?"

Declan caught Anna Katherine's eye from the other side of the room and her stomach flipped. She smiled. "Yeah, he definitely makes me happy."

Declan had somehow been roped into another conversation with Patty and Timmy. Thankfully they seemed to be trying to win their daughter's favor back. This conversation was much more polite than the one he had engaged in with Timmy when they had first walked in.

Timmy was staring off somewhere. Declan looked to see what he was watching and saw Nat in the corner of the room with their friends. Timmy asked, "Why are Nat and Alex not spending much time together? Did they break up?"

Declan was confused for a moment before he remembered the brunch. He wasn't sure what their plan was for that little lie, or if Alex and Nat had one at all, so he shrugged. "I'm not sure."

Just then, Alex walked by. Declan grabbed his arm.

"Alex! Perfect timing. Your dad was just asking about your relationship with Nat!"

Alex froze, and a little color drained from his face before he shook himself out of it. "Right. Nat. My girlfriend."

Declan watched as Alex glanced around before he found her with Harry and William. He lifted his arm in a wave. "Nat! Natalie, babe, come here."

Nat and Harry both spun around, and Declan thought it was curious that Harry's face was unreadably a blank slate.

Nat wove her way to their small group, looking only slightly startled when Alex wrapped his arm around her shoulders. "Nat and I are doing just fine."

Nat glanced around. "We are?"

Alex cleared his throat. "We sure are. Dad was asking how our relationship was going."

Finally, a light bulb seemed to have flicked on and Nat's eyes widened in understanding. "Right. Well, it certainly isn't as great as the couple we're celebrating tonight, but I can't complain."

Declan was about to take the opportunity to leave and go find his friends, but Kit came up and slid under his arm. She smiled up at him, "Hey."

He gently flicked her nose and smiled when she scrunched it up. "Enjoying yourself?"

"Always."

Before either of them could say anything else, William started shouting excitedly, and all Declan could make out was his and Kit's names. It took him a moment to realize what William was shouting and why everyone started looking at him and Kit.

Harry and Nat had told Declan and Kit that they needed to sell being in love with PDA, so it shouldn't have come as a shock to him when people cheered for them to kiss, thanks to William's encouragement. Somehow, he still wasn't prepared for it.

He had his arm around her, which was normal enough for the two of them, but when William and his other mates started chanting for him to kiss her, he tensed up. Looking down at Kit, he saw that she was surprised too, but when she just smirked and gave him a small shrug, he knew that she was giving him the okay.

He leaned down and kissed her cheek, ignoring the boos that erupted around them. "Last chance, Kit-Kat."

She rolled her eyes. "Just kiss me already, Mullins."

Who was he to deny her? He cupped her face in his hands, rubbing her cheek with his thumb before obeying her. At first, the kiss was innocent enough, but then she kissed him back and let out a soft gasp. That sound made him want to kiss her more.

When he pulled away, she looked dazed, and he had to look away. He tried to focus on the cheers of their friends instead of the way he wanted to kiss her again.

He failed.

The party didn't last too long, and even if it was for a sham engagement, Anna Katherine enjoyed having everyone they loved and cared about in one place. After an hour or two, people started trickling out, saying their goodbyes and happy wishes to the engaged couple, and heading home to rest up for work the next day.

Nat stood up and yawned,\. "As much as I love you guys, I gotta get home. I have to be at work early tomorrow."

Harry seemed surprised. "But I drove you here."

"Yeah." She shrugged. "I'll just take an Uber."

"You're more stupid than I thought you were if you think I'm going to let you take an Uber alone when I can just drive you back myself."

Nat's face turned red. *"Let me?"*

Harry nodded, grabbing his keys and wallet from the table, and following Nat to the door.

"You hardly have any ground to *let* me do anything, Harry."

He held the door open for her, the look on his face showing pure irritation. "Geez, woman. Just let me drive you home."

Declan and Anna Katherine laughed at their friends, and when Declan's phone started vibrating with a call, she slid it over to him. "Think Wesley is calling."

Declan saw it was a FaceTime and answered it. "Hey, mate."

Wesley looked as irritated as Harry had moments ago, "Don't 'mate' me, Declan Anthony Mullins."

"Middle and surname? What did I do now?"

Wesley's eyes widened in mock surprise. "Oh, you don't know? Maybe the small fact that I wasn't invited to the engagement party!"

"You're in Dublin for an interview!"

"That's hardly the point," he huffed out. "After all that whinging about Kit I had to listen to all these years, you don't even tell me that you asked her out! And now you're *engaged*!"

Anna Katherine cut her eyes at Declan, and a blush started to creep up his neck. "She's sitting right beside me, you dingbat."

"Oh." Wesley had at least enough sense to look sorry. "Pretend you didn't hear that, love! Declan, mate, I don't think I can get you a wedding present after this."

"Oh shove it, Thatch. You're more of a tantrum thrower than Harry."

"Speaking of, remind me to give him a good lecture when I get back for not inviting me."

Once Declan was off the phone with Wesley, Anna Katherine gave him a playful nudge. "So you *whinge* about me, huh?"

He groaned and covered his face with his hands. "Please don't start, Kit."

She poked him where she knew he was ticklish, and when he let out a high-pitched squeal, she laughed. "C'mon, tell me what you tell all your friends about me."

"Not a chance." When she went to poke him again, he grabbed her wrists. "You're a complete menace, Anna Katherine."

She just smirked up at him. "Yeah, and now you're stuck with me for better or for worse."

When he let out another groan, she couldn't help but laugh again.

That night, Harry and Natalie once again found themselves without their best friends as Harry drove Nat home. It was only once they had gotten inside his car that they had stopped arguing and bickering. They had stopped talking all together, actually.

Harry kept glancing at her out of the corner of his eyes, and finally Nat had enough of it.

"What, Harry?"

"Nothing."

"Clearly it's not nothing. You keep looking over at me."

He stayed silent until they turned onto her street. It was only then that he spoke up. "You still think this is going to end with us picking up their pieces?"

"There's no other way."

He pulled at his bottom lip before responding, "Yeah, I was afraid you'd say that."

When they were in front of her building, he put the car in park. "Home sweet home."

For once, Nat shared a small smile with him. "Thanks for the ride."

"I'd believe you were actually thankful if you hadn't fought me all the way to my car."

She opened the car door. "Goodnight, Harrison."

"Not my name." The door slammed shut, and he rolled down the window as she started up the stairs. "G'night, Nat!"

She gave him a wave, but he stayed parked in front of her building until he saw the lights flicker on in her apartment.

Fourth Commandment: Thou Shalt (Declan—Again) Buy Anna Katherine Tran Mint Chocolate Chip Ice Cream Once A Month

"*I*'ll take the trash out every week."

Anna Katherine thought for a minute before saying, "No, I don't like that one."

"Only because you know I'll do it anyway, and you want to get something out of these rules."

She smiled. "You have to buy me mint chocolate chip ice cream once a month."

"You're ridiculous."

"And you're more ridiculous than I am because you asked me to marry you."

12

Anna Katherine was curled up around Fox on Declan's bed while he sat at his desk filling out forms for his marriage green card. She was trying to fit in a nap, but Declan kept asking questions and keeping her up.

"Who's the sponsor?" Declan squinted at his computer. "Oh, wait. I'm the beneficiary, right? That would make you the sponsor?"

Anna Katherine wrapped her arms around Fox, who sighed as if she had the entire world on her shoulders. Apparently it was a tough life being a dog. "I don't know, Declan. Which has been my answer to the past ten questions and will probably be my answer to any other future questions. I don't know why you didn't hire a lawyer for this."

"Because," his tone heavily implied that she should know this, "immigration lawyers are hella expensive, and I refuse."

"Whatever. Just Google these things. Don't ask me."

He glared at her. "You know, you don't have to be here with me if I'm being such a bother." His glare turned to a look of confusion. "Why are you here and not at Nat's? Didn't you say you were going to clean up the apartment before your shift today?"

She ignored his glare. "I haven't seen you all week. Of course I'm going to be here."

"Then stop acting like I'm annoying you."

"You *are* annoying."

Declan was either too focused on the form to listen to her or he was simply ignoring her. Anna Katherine would bet on the latter of the two.

"Hey, we need photos of the two of us together. Like, from college and stuff," he interjected.

She cracked an eye open. "Why?"

"To prove the legitimacy of our relationship."

"Oh, right. I can email them to you tonight after work."

"You're a lifesaver." He didn't even bother to look away from the form on the screen. "Oh, just put them in our shared Google Drive."

"Yep, sure. Now be quiet so I can get a quick snooze before I have to go to work."

"Kit, you need to leave in twenty minutes."

"Shush..."

Sunday nights were for the boys. It was the one day of the week that Declan blocked off as a no Kit or Nat zone. Only Harry and his mates were welcomed. He needed it for his sanity.

"How did Móirín take it?" Wesley was sitting at Harry's table with his feet propped up on the top. William was glaring at Wesley's feet with disgust but didn't say anything. "Also, don't think I've forgotten that I wasn't told about you and your Kit dating."

Declan had met Wesley in college. They both were on the university's soccer team and were both international students. Declan from Ireland, and Wesley from Manchester. It had always been interesting to Declan how, even if they were from different countries, the international students always flocked together. He had met many people from all over the world during his college years, but it was Harry and Wesley that stuck close even after their time in college came to an end.

William stopped looking disgusted long enough to ask, "Yeah, why was it so hush-hush?"

William had come into their life a little later, not until Declan started his current job, but he fit right in with Harry, Wesley, and Declan.

Declan glanced at Harry who just smirked and gave him a shrug.

"Oh, uh, Kit was just nervous about her parents finding out, but Móirín was thrilled of course. She's going to be here the entire week of the wedding."

Wesley finally pulled his feet off the table, and William looked relieved. "When is the wedding?"

"Second weekend of November."

William looked surprised. "And how long have you two been dating?"

"A couple of months."

"Wow, never pegged you to be the type of guy to jump right in after a handful of weeks, mate."

"Well," Harry spoke up, finally coming to Declan's assistance. "They've known each other for over five years. It's not as fast as it actually seems."

"I saw it coming a mile away," Wesley proclaimed proudly.

Declan threw a rolled up napkin at him. "Oh, shut up, Wesley Thatcher. You didn't see anything."

"I had 20/20 vision for the love life of Declan and his Kit." He sighed dramatically. "I feel like it was just yesterday Declan was nursing the heart Vivian shattered, and he was swearing off all women. Now look at him willing to commit his entire life to our sweet and beautiful Kit."

If Declan had something else to throw at him, he would have. "You act like this has been such an epic slowburn."

Declan startled when all three of them said in unison, "It has."

"Jerks," Declan snarked. "Did Harry here tell you he's currently jealous of Alex for dating Nat?"

Their voices mixed together as they all shouted at once.

"Natalie?! I knew there was something there!"

"Once again, we're in the dark! How did we not know!"

"Declan, I'm going to kill you."

Declan laughed. "Alex tried to take the heat off of Kit and me when we told her parents. Apparently, that was the best he could come up with at the moment. You guys should've seen Harry's face. Completely priceless."

Laughter erupted around the table, and Declan was glad to have the attention off of him and Kit again. He didn't miss the rude gesture Harry flashed his way, however.

Anna Katherine took Fox for one last bathroom outing while Nat was finishing up making the buffalo dip before Mack came over. Once finished, she let the dog off the leash inside and joined Nat in the kitchen. Her friend wasn't thrilled at the idea of having the dog over to join their girl's night, but she didn't put up too much of a fight against it.

Nat didn't bother looking up at her when she said, "I still think this is a bad idea, ya know."

Anna Katherine knew she was talking about Declan, but she was tired of this lecture. "What? The buffalo dip? It's always delicious."

Nat gave her a flat look. "I'm serious, Kit."

"Yeah, I didn't get that the first hundred times you told me."

"I just don't understand why you're doing this."

"Declan will have to go back to Ireland if I don't."

"Once again," Nat finally looked up and pointed a spoon at her. "Not your problem."

"I can't very well live without him." Anna Katherine ignored the disbelieving look that crossed Nat's face. "He's giving me a place to live. Plus, now there's Fox."

"I just think there's more to it than that."

"Don't even start, Natalie," She gave her friend a glare, warning in her tone.

"What?"

"I know where you're going with this, and it's truly outlandish."

"It's not exactly unheard of to fall for your best friend. Besides, Declan is one of the good ones."

Anna Katherine stared at Nat but was saved from any response when Mack came through the door shouting, "I am here, and I am ready for all the food and all the gossip about one Declan Anthony Mullins!"

Declan had only been to the country club once before when Kit had locked her keys in her car and he had to drive her there to get the spare set from her parents. It had been a month after first meeting her and had also been the first time he had met Timmy.

He had never been intimidated by Kit's family. Jonah had always complained about Alex being too overprotective of her and her parents being too judgmental. When he had been just her friend, he had never seen that side of her family, and it didn't take long for her parents to love him. But now, he was sitting in front of Timmy and had no idea what to say, because if looks could kill, he'd definitely be dead by now.

"Patricia and I have done a lot of thinking since the dinner."

Declan really wanted to grimace, but he did his best to keep his face neutral. "Yeah, I imagine so."

"You can probably also imagine we weren't exactly thrilled with how this all has played out." Timmy leaned back in his chair.

Declan stayed quiet, not knowing what to say and wondering if there was a way he could make this situation less awful.

Thankfully, Timmy spoke up again. "Alex sat us down for a chat. He explained to us the situation."

Declan felt the blood drain from his face.

Crap.

Anna Katherine sped all the way downtown and to the only parking lot she knew that would have parking. She didn't double check to see if she was inside the lines of the parking space and ran down the sidewalk to the restaurant where her mother told her to meet. She had ten minutes until she was late, but according to Patricia Tran, you were late if you were on time.

By the time the restaurant met her gaze, her back was coated in a nice layer of sweat, and she had to wipe her upper lip where more was gathering. It might have just turned October, but that southern humidity didn't relieve in autumn. It made Anna Katherine regret ever leaving the comfort of Nat's air-conditioned apartment

Seeing the scowl on her mother's face made her regret it even more.

"Anna Katherine." Patricia checked the time. "You're nearly late."

She smiled. "Ah, but I'm not. I feel like this calls for a celebratory round of mimosas."

Hell must've frozen over because Anna Katherine was sure she saw a microscopic smile on her mom's face. "You would've ordered bottomless mimosas anyway."

"Yeah, but they mean more this way."

Patricia shook her head with a smile. "Sometimes I wonder if you're really my daughter."

Anna Katherine laughed and headed into the restaurant. "Yeah, I question it, too."

The hostess at the entrance greeted them with a warm smile and led them to a small table near the back window. It gave them a beautiful view of the garden behind the building.

"I think I'm going to get the triple chocolate pancakes." Anna Katherine's mouth was watering just picturing them.

"Oh, honey, that's too much sugar first thing in the morning. How about you get the breakfast bowl?"

If she wasn't trying to convince her mom that yes, she was a mature enough adult to get married and please help with the wedding costs, she would have argued with her. But, for once, she kept her thoughts to herself.

"Yeah, you're probably right."

Patricia laid the menu down. "Before the waitress comes back, I just want to say..."

Anna Katherine braced herself.

"Your father and I understand, and we want to pay for your wedding dress and your honeymoon."

Anna Katherine choked on air.

"Sir," Declan gulped. "I can explain."

Timmy looked confused. "Explain? There's nothing to explain, son. You're in love with our daughter. You were both nervous about how we would react, and after that Sunday brunch, it seems your concerns might have been warranted."

"What?"

"I don't fully understand why you both were so adamant about keeping it a secret, but Alex convinced us your intentions are pure." Timmy gave him a piercing look. "Your intentions are pure, aren't they?"

Declan choked on nothing. Once he calmed down, he managed to say, "Of course."

"Now, let's eat some breakfast so we can go golf, yeah?"

For once in his life, Declan was dreading golfing.

Patricia looked offended. "Honestly, Anna Katherine. There's no need to be so dramatic."

She looked at her mom incredulously. "I'm over here struggling to breathe, and you think I'm being dramatic?"

Patricia made a show of smoothing out her napkin that sat on her lap. "Well, you are."

"Mother!" Anna Katherine's eyes went even wider.

"Just pull yourself together, won't you? We need to get through this brunch so we won't miss our first appointment."

"What appointment?"

"I scheduled some time for us to go look at wedding dresses. Nat is going to meet us there, and she'll FaceTime Móirín."

"*Today?*"

"Of course today. We don't have long since the two of you don't want a long engagement. And don't worry, we'll be finished in time for you to make it to your shift."

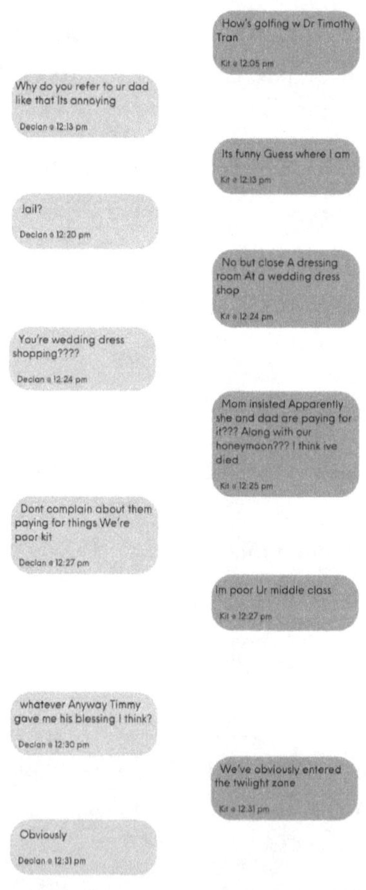

Anna Katherine had lost count of how many dresses she had tried on. Her heart wasn't really in it, for obvious reasons. She didn't see herself falling in love with one specific dress, but when the woman came back with the last one Nat had picked out, that might've changed. It had an empire waist with an off-the-shoulder neckline and quarter-length lace sleeves.

She stepped out of the dressing room, fully intending to tell her mom and Nat that this was the one, but the words disappeared when she saw a familiar curly-haired idiot sitting between her mom and Nat.

"Harold."

"Not my name."

"What are you doing here?"

He looked up from his phone, and whatever response he had never saw the light of day when his jaw dropped open as he stared at her. "Wow." He stared a moment longer before adding, "Declan isn't going to know what hit him. You look gorgeous, Kit."

She blinked. "Uh. Thanks. But you never answered my question."

"Well, since you failed to invite me, Nat told me what you all were doing, and here I am."

Nat looked annoyed. "I didn't tell him so that he would come."

"I needed to be here!"

"Harry," Anna Katherine started, "Typically the best man does not come to these things."

"*Typically.*" Harry mocked. "Nothing about this arrangement is typical."

Patricia laughed. "You can say that again. Now, Anna Katherine, the dress?"

"I think this is the one."

Harry and Nat whooped and hollered, her mom actually looked pleased, and somewhere in the store, someone rang a bell.

When Anna Katherine went to Declan's after her closing shift that day, he was on the couch with his feet propped up on the coffee table, Fox asleep under his legs.

"We're going to have to do a couple of interviews, but it looks like the last one is the most intense," Declan called out from the couch. "I Googled some of the questions that they ask, and I don't think we should have much trouble with them. Still, I was thinking we could get Nat and Harry to help us out with them. You know, do a mock interview or something."

She scoffed and jumped over the back of the couch, landing beside him. "Can we please talk about something other than your green card? Like, it's important, but my brain is mush after today." She snuggled against him and pushed his computer out of her way.

"You're like a darn cat." He acted put out, but he did nothing to stop her.

She ignored him. "Wanna see pictures of my wedding dress?"

He glanced down at her. "You serious? That's bad luck."

"Yeah, but it's not like this is a real wedding." Kit pulled her phone out and tapped to her camera roll.

"Anna Katherine!" He snatched her phone away and turned the screen off. "I'm not taking any chances!"

She pouted. "You're no fun."

"And you're ridiculous."

She snatched her phone back. "Whatever." She adjusted herself so that her head was in his lap. "I feel like we never see each other anymore, Dec."

He started brushing her hair with his fingers. "It's not like we saw each other much before."

"Yeah, but now when we would've had lazy days together, you're being whisked away to the country club by my dad. My mom is demanding I do weekly brunches with her, and apparently wedding planning is not as easy as I thought."

"We could schedule a time just for us. No one would think it's weird since we're supposed to be in love anyway. We can tell everyone it's our designated date night or something. No one would question it."

Kit sat up. "Actually, that's a good idea. We *are* supposed to be in love. We need to be comfortable acting like a couple. PDA, handholding, you know. The whole shebang. Gotta keep the illusion strong."

"Yeah." He nodded again.

"This is a great idea, but I don't want to tell Harry or Nat."

He raised his eyebrows. "What? Why?"

She laid back down and looked up at him. "Because when it comes to this whole marriage thing, they're being overbearing. If we tell them we're having date nights or practicing being a couple, they'll want to be a part of it."

"A secret date night?" Declan laughed. "Fine, what's another secret in the midst of this entire lie anyway?"

She smirked. "Exactly."

They fell into a comfortable silence for a few minutes, and he nearly jumped when she blurted out, "Our honeymoon is going to be in New Orleans by the way."

He looked down at her again. "Really? And when is that again? Fleetwood Mac is having a show there. It'll be sick if it's at the same time and we can get tickets."

Anna Katherine shrugged. "Not sure, but I'll let you know."

13

Anna Katherine woke up bright and early. For once, she was grateful that she had grown used to waking up with the sun. It made these early mornings easier. She showered, dressed, and shot Declan a text, but she wasn't expecting a reply. Surely he would still be asleep.

There wasn't a need to rush, but the excitement was causing her to hurry. Shoving the pullout mattress back where it belonged in the sofa, she didn't take the time to fold the blankets or put her pillow where Nat always liked to keep it during the day.

But it was only just this once. Anna Katherine was sure Nat wouldn't find an issue with it.

On the way to his apartment, she stopped by the bakery to get a few of their favorite pastries. Once at Declan's, she was careful going in so Fox didn't get spooked and cause a ruckus.

Tiptoeing to his bedroom, she eased the door open, noticing Fox curled up at the end of the bed. The pup barely lifted her head to acknowledge or look at Anna Katherine.

"Some guard dog you are."

She opened the door the rest of the way and went to sit on the edge of his bed.

"Declan…"

He swatted her hand away.

"C'mon. Up and at 'em! It's Saturday morning. The sun is up and the coffee is being made. It's a beautiful day!" She poked his cheek with her finger again and smiled when he cracked an eye open.

When he saw her, he buried his face under the pillow and mumbled something that sounded awfully like he disliked her.

"What was that? I couldn't hear you since you're trying to suffocate yourself." She pulled the pillow off of his face.

He gave her a very not so friendly look. "I said that I didn't like you."

She nodded. "Yeah, that's fair. But, come on! We've got things to do!"

Declan pushed himself up so that he was leaning against his headboard. "It's Saturday, Kit. We don't have any plans."

"Incorrect. Mom called me last night. She and her friends want to throw us a bridal shower."

"I'm coming?"

"No, of course not. They gave me a choice between the couple shower and the bridal shower. This is my time to shine, Declan. Of course I chose the bridal shower."

He pinched the bridge of his nose dramatically. "I still don't understand what that has to do with me."

"Our *registry*. We need to go and make it! I want that standing mixer!"

He gave her a blank look, but when she didn't go on, he sighed. "Can't you do that on your own?"

She shook her head. "Nuh-uh. You have to come with me. Come on! You can finally get dinnerware so that we can serve more than two people at once! With matching bowls and no more plastic cups from restaurants!"

She could see him breaking, but slowly. "Can't we go once I've had a bit more sleep?"

"I have work, Declan! I have a photography gig at one and a shift at four!" She poked his chest. "Listen, you're getting *citizenship* from this deal. The least you can do is come with me so I can get those shiny presents from family and friends."

He was almost there. She could see it in his eyes. "Kit-Kat..."

"You can finally get that knife set you've been eyeing..."

That was the final straw. "Fine. I'll come, but you're driving."

She didn't stop smiling even when he shoved her off his bed and stomped off toward the shower.

When the nice man who was helping them with their registry said they could add to it or change it at any time by going on their website, Declan could have killed Kit.

If only his citizenship wasn't in the palm of her hands.

"Online, Kit?"

She avoided looking at him.

"You knew, didn't you?"

She shrugged.

"Anna Katherine Tran, I swear if you woke me up during my Saturday sleep-in for nothing—"

She spun around to look at him, "It wasn't for nothing! We get to use the scan-gun thingies, and this way is so much more fun and organic!"

"But my sleep."

"But nothing. You can sleep when you're dead."

"Something tells me that marrying you is going to bring that day a lot sooner than I had planned."

"I'm ignoring that, and now we're going to go look at the towels. Big and fluffy. That's the goal here."

They spent two hours in the store, and it was only after forty-five minutes that Declan stopped complaining. Anna Katherine declared it a win.

In between all she had to do that day, Anna Katherine went back to Nat's apartment for a quick change of clothes. Nat was on the couch going through a stack of papers from work.

"Have fun today?"

Anna Katherine looked up from digging around her suitcase and saw Nat watching her. "Yeah! And we have a lot of cool things on our registry."

"Standing mixer?"

"Obviously." She grabbed the clothes she wanted and rushed to the bathroom to do a quick change.

"Hey," Nat called out. "Do you think you can do a load of laundry or dishes today?"

Anna Katherine stuck her head out. "Yeah! I'm super busy today, but I'll do it when I get home from work."

Nat smiled. "That's perfect. Thanks Kit!"

As she ran out the door, she shouted, "You're welcome!"

She left her pile of dirty clothes on the bathroom floor, but she figured if she was doing a load of laundry tonight, that was fine. Nat definitely wouldn't mind.

14

The shower was the following week, and Declan was thankful Kit had chosen the bridal over the couple shower. This meant he was able to sleep in and stay in his pajamas all morning while she was getting ready and rushing around before Patty came to pick her up. He wasn't at all surprised when after half an hour, Kit was already texting him.

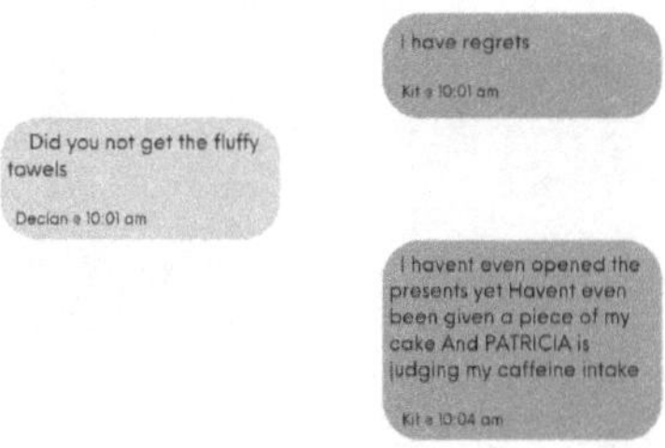

To be fair U do drink a lot of coffee

Declan @ 10:05 am

Watch it, Mullins Now shes judging me for being on my phone

Kit @ 10:05 am

Well it is rude to not be mingling Those people did buy you all those fancy presents

Declan @ 10:05 am

Pls come.

Kit @ 10:06 am

What happened to this being ur time to shine?

Declan @ 10:06 am

I can shine another time This wont be my only chance Declan. Please.

Kit @ 10:07 am

Ur mother will shoot me

Declan @ 10:08 am

She would not She doesnt own a gun Actually she might i wouldnt be surprised tbh But that doesnt matter Every old woman in this town is in love with you

Kit @ 10:10 am

I do have a charm that they cant seem to resist

Declan @ 10:11 am

She would not She doesnt own a gun Actually she might I wouldnt be surprised tbh But that doesnt matter Every old woman in this town is in love with you

Kit @ 10:10 am

I do have a charm that they cant seem to resist

Declan @ 10:11 am

Declan Does this mean ur coming Declan Please III stop complaining about the toilet seat III always restock the toilet paper Delcan!!!

Kit @ 10:11 am

Geez woman Have you no patience? I was in the shower Send me the address

Declan @ 10:20 am

The room grew quiet when Declan walked in. He didn't mind, though. His attention was on Kit sitting at the other end of the room surrounded by gifts and at least three empty cups of coffee. He wouldn't be surprised if there were more cups with her name on them scattered throughout the room. When she spotted him, she smiled, and Declan started walking toward her.

"Hello, Princess. Your knight in shining armor is here with your carriage."

Her smile immediately fell. "Why are you like this?"

He gave her a small shrug and leaned down to kiss her cheek. Before he pulled away, he whispered, "Just doing what the lady asked, love."

He turned to face the room full of women, his hand resting on Kit's shoulder. "Sorry for the interruption, ladies."

Patricia was watching both of them, already suspicious of whatever was going on. "What are you doing here, Declan? Not that it isn't lovely to see you."

He gave her his best smile. "Well, the plan was to stay home and give my bride-to-be her moment to shine. I definitely wasn't complaining since that meant I could have a quiet Saturday morning to myself for once, but..." He trailed off and gave Kit a sympathetic look. "Kit was texting me complaining about an awful migraine. You know how bad those can get for her, Mrs. Patty. I decided I might as well come to at least help her pack everything in the car."

"A migraine?" one of the other ladies asked. "Why didn't you tell us, dear? We would have wrapped this party up."

"Oh, you know our Kit. She didn't want to come off as rude or ungrateful. She didn't even want me to come, but I insisted."

"Putting it on a little thick, don't you think?" Kit muttered under her breath in an aside to him.

He gave her shoulder a gentle squeeze. "I'll just start packing up these presents and let you ladies visit a little longer." He bent down to kiss her forehead and whispered, "You need to trust me more."

She rolled her eyes. "Sure thing, sweetheart."

And then for the room to hear, "Just let me know if you need anything, love."

On his way to the car with his first load, Patricia stopped him. "You handle her well, Declan."

He gave her a smile. "Thank you. I certainly try my best."

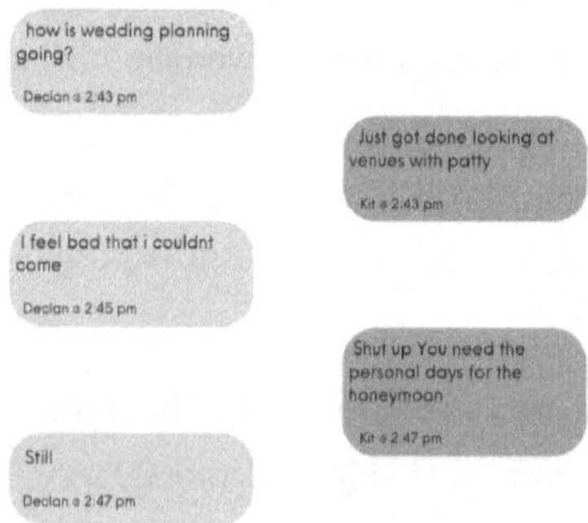

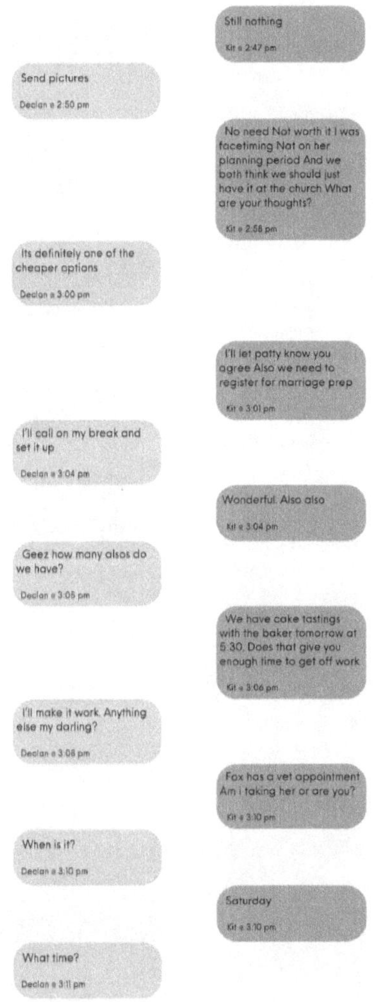
Still nothing
Kit • 2:47 pm
Send pictures
Declan • 2:50 pm
No need Not worth it I was facetiming Nat on her planning period And we both think we should just have it at the church What are your thoughts?
Kit • 2:56 pm
Its definitely one of the cheaper options
Declan • 3:00 pm
I'll let patty know you agree Also we need to register for marriage prep
Kit • 3:01 pm
I'll call on my break and set it up
Declan • 3:04 pm
Wonderful. Also also
Kit • 3:04 pm
Geez how many alsos do we have?
Declan • 3:05 pm
We have cake tastings with the baker tomorrow at 5:30. Does that give you enough time to get off work
Kit • 3:06 pm
I'll make it work. Anything else my darling?
Declan • 3:08 pm
Fox has a vet appointment Am i taking her or are you?
Kit • 3:10 pm
When is it?
Declan • 3:10 pm
Saturday
Kit • 3:10 pm
What time?
Declan • 3:11 pm

I don't remember
Kit • 3:12 pm

Lol of course you dont I'll take her You work dont you?
Declan • 3:19 pm

Opening shift, yeah
Kit • 3:120pm

Then i'll take care of our dog Want tacos tonight?
Declan • 3:21 pm

I will never say no to tacos You bringing them to Nat's?
Kit • 3:21 pm

As long as she won't kill us
Declan • 3:22 pm

She's my bestie. We're fine.
Kit • 3:24 pm

I'll see you after work
Declan • 3:25 pm

Sounds good!
Kit • 3:25 pm

What are you doing?
Nat • 5:02 pm

About to fix dinner
Harry • 5:02 pm

Stop everything We're going to grab a bite to eat If i stay here i will be arrested for murder
Nat • 5:03 pm

???
Harry • 5:06 pm

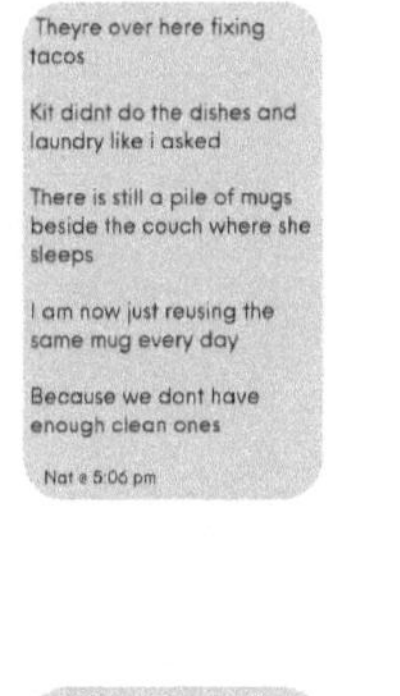
Theyre over here fixing tacos

Kit didnt do the dishes and laundry like i asked

There is still a pile of mugs beside the couch where she sleeps

I am now just reusing the same mug every day

Because we dont have enough clean ones

Nat e 5:06 pm

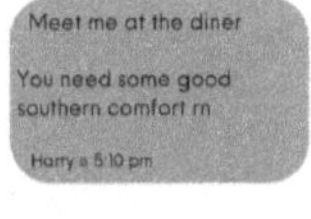
Meet me at the diner

You need some good southern comfort rn

Harry e 5:10 pm

Thanks

Nat e 5:10 pm

15

They had the bachelor and bachelorette party on the same night. Anna Katherine didn't know where or what the guys were planning, but she, Mack, and Nat ended up going to a new cocktail bar that had recently opened downtown. They took pictures of each other out on the balcony as they waited for their drinks. They each ordered just one, none of them wanting to drink too much. After they finished, they walked to a restaurant nearby for dinner.

Anna Katherine spent most of her nights in, and most of the time when she hung out with her friends it was at one of their apartments. They rarely went out, but it was nice to do it every once in a while. Especially since it came with seeing her friends so happy.

Phones weren't allowed, as proclaimed by Nat, but when Nat and Mack went to the bathroom and Anna Katherine stayed behind, she took her phone out to check her messages.

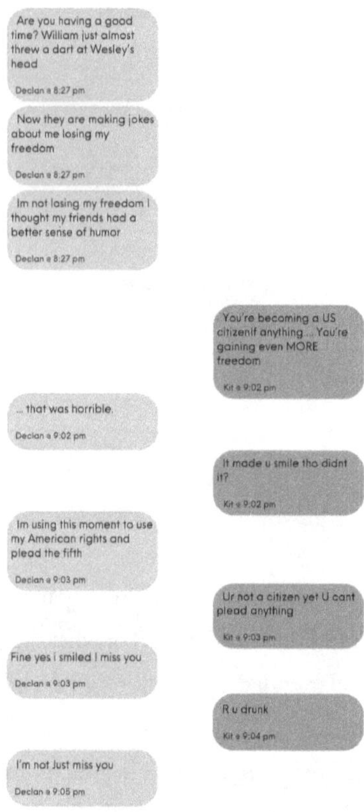

Anna Katherine smiled at her phone and sent a heart emoji right before Mack and Nat reappeared and took her phone away.

"No phones!"

"No texting the groom!"

"But I wasn't—"

"Nuhuh!" Nat pocketed Anna Katherine's phone. "No boys allowed tonight. Now, come take photos with us in front of the photo wall. We'll head home after!"

Nat was true to her word, and after the pictures, they called an Uber and headed home. It was only when their faces were covered in clay face masks and their nails wet with polish that she gave Anna Katherine her phone back.

Anna Katherine smiled and took a selfie of her with the mud mask on and sent it to him.

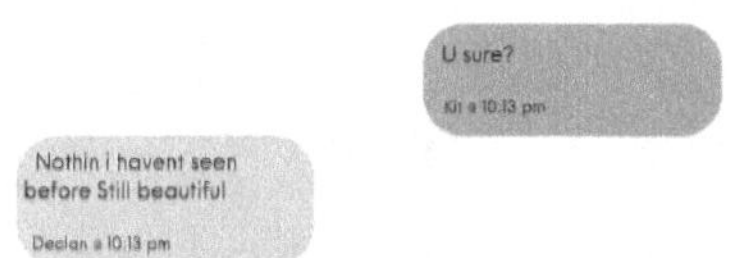

Anna Katherine hid her smile with a blanket, those pesky butterflies making an appearance again, and slid her phone under her pillow after she hearted the message. She was curled up in her bed. Nat snored softly beside her, and Mack was sound asleep on an air mattress on the floor.

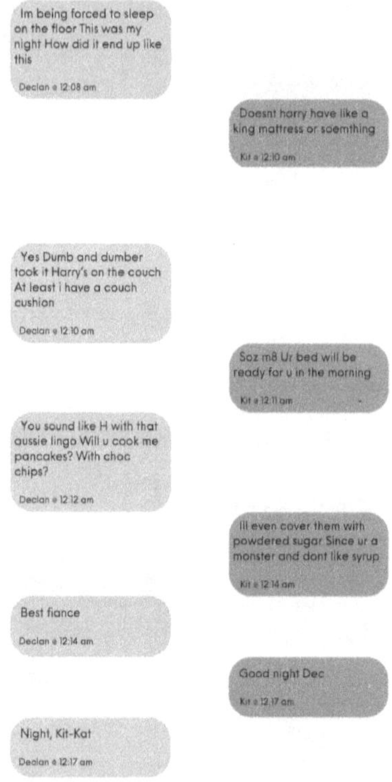

Anna Katherine continued to hide her smile and squeezed her eyes shut.

Natalie opened the door to find Harry on the other side. He told her he was coming over, but she hadn't actually believed him.

"You came."

He didn't wait to be invited in, just moved between her and the door, and made his way to the bedroom where the dresser she had texted him about was scattered around the floor in pieces.

"Of course I came," he said. "I said I would, didn't I?"

"Yeah, but we're all tired from last night, and I think I would die if I walked outside right now."

He walked to her bedroom and looked over his shoulder to ask, "Why? I thought you girls didn't drink?"

"We each had one. But I'm not hungover. We just stayed up entirely too late. My teacher body needs to be in bed early in order to function the next day."

She followed him into the bedroom and perched on the side of the bed, watching as he shrugged out of his flannel and knelt down on the floor where the instruction manual was. She kept watching as he slowly put it together, and when he was almost finished, she realized she needed to thank him.

"Thanks for helping."

Harry glanced at her and smirked. "Well, when you asked for help, I didn't think I'd be doing it all on my own."

"Should've known better," she snarked. "Besides, I've given you wonderful moral support this whole time."

He let out a laugh. "Okay, sure."

She was quiet for a moment as she watched him screw in the last piece. Her mind wandered to the night before and to her two best friends. "How long do you think they can go without falling for each other?"

He didn't hesitate when he said, "I'm pretty sure it's already happened."

Harry paused to glance at Nat, one side of his lips ticking up in a smile and showing off a dimple. "I really did ask my doctor for a higher dosage of anxiety meds."

Nat fell back on her bed and laughed, "I can't believe this is our lives."

Harry sat beside her. "Yeah, me neither." He patted her knee. "C'mon. You owe me pizza."

For once, Natalie didn't argue, and she found herself quite enjoying her time with him as they shared a pizza at a dingy shop downtown.

Fifth Commandment: Thou Shalt Not Fall In Love With Each Other

*D*eclan *popped a cookie in his mouth. He thought for a moment and then, "One obviously needs to be that we can't fall in love with each other."*

"Ha!" Anna Katherine laughed. "That's not going to be a problem."

16

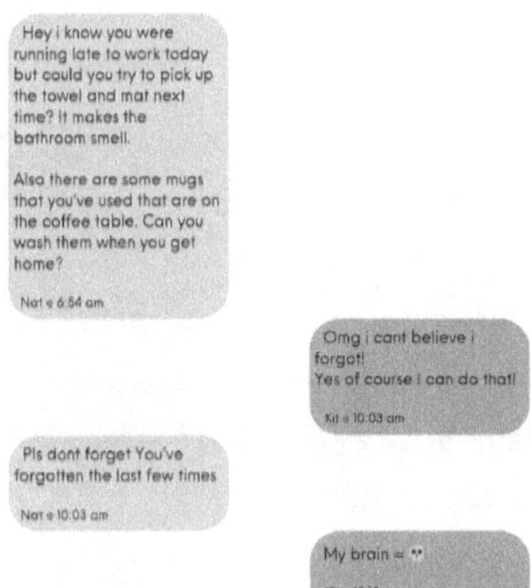

Kit got to Nat's expecting all to be well. The towels, mugs, and everything else had long escaped her train of thought. She had a good shift at work where tips had been great, and she was excited to spend the night hanging out with her best friend.

Unlocking the door, she stepped into Nat's apartment and threw her purse over the chair that sat by the door while she slipped off her shoes, flinging them against the wall. "Natalie! I'm here! Have you ordered pizza yet?"

When there was no answer, she walked deeper into the apartment. The living room was crowded with all of her things, and there were mugs littering the table beside the couch that was bed.

"I was thinking we could watch *Leap Year* or maybe something with Julia Roberts. I love her."

Nat sat on her bed in silence, aggressively folding her clothes. Anna Katherine didn't think folding clothes could be done aggressively, but Nat was proving her wrong.

"What's the matter?"

Nat pressed her lips together and continued her attack on the innocent, freshly washed clothes.

"Natalie?"

Her full name seemed to have gotten her attention, but the scowl stayed as she turned her stare to Anna Katherine.

Who was completely lost. "Are you mad? What's wrong?"

"You! You are what's wrong!" Nat seethed. "I know you're going through a lot, and I know you're stressing about the wedding, but you did this to yourself! And it doesn't take much thought or energy to take your used coffee mugs to the kitchen!"

Anna Katherine, taken aback, asked the only thing that came to her mind. "Is this really about the mugs? I'll wash them before the movie if it's bothering you that much. You never said—"

Nat interrupted her. "I shouldn't have to say! It's common sense! Common decency to clean up after yourself!" She flung the shirt she was folding back on the bed. "It's common decency to do things like refill the toilet paper!"

Anna Katherine shrunk back further against the door frame. "I meant to do that before I left..."

"But you forgot. You ran out of time. You meant to, but you didn't. It's the story of this entire living arrangement!" Nat's voice was becoming shrill. "I thought I could handle you for a few weeks. A few months. For however long I needed to before you and Declan went through with this stupid idea, but apparently I was just as stupid as the two of you! Because I can't! It's too much."

Anna Kathering couldn't move, so she simply stood there, staring at Nat in shocked silence. In all of their years of friendship, Nat had never gone off on her like this.

"Maybe someone else could handle you, though I doubt it."

Anna Katherine slowly nodded. "Right."

As she turned to leave, Nat called out, "Where are you going?"

Anna Katherine didn't bother to answer as she grabbed her purse from the floor—it had apparently missed the chair— slipped back into her shoes, and walked out the door.

Nat was fuming. The wet towels that started all of this stared at her on the coffee table. Normally when she felt this wound up, there was only one person she wanted to talk to. But in this situation, that one person was the other half of this mess she found herself in.

Pulling out her phone, she opened her contacts, but she just stared at them. Her finger hovered over Mack's name, but Mack wouldn't fully understand the situation. In fact, no one would fully understand the situation other than the people involved. She scrolled up to Declan's name, but huffed instead, dropping her phone on the sofa bed. When Kit stormed out, there was only one place she would've gone, and that was to Declan.

Nat stood and stomped to the kitchen. She opened the fridge—looking for what, she wasn't sure—only to slam it shut and glower at the closed door. There, pinned with a magnet one of her students gave her in her first year of teaching, was the silly drawing that Harry had done the other night with a ridiculous poem.

Harry is so much better than I.

I don't know why. Chicken fry.

By: Harry M. Whitlock

Before she could think better of it, she hurried back to her phone on the unmade sofa bed and called Harry.

He answered almost immediately.

"Natalie! To what do I owe this surprising pleasure?"

He was smiling, and she hated that she could tell simply by the sound of his voice.

Just as suddenly as his smile appeared in her mind, so did the chilling realization of what she was doing.

She felt like stomping like her students did when they didn't get their way.

"What are you doing?" she asked.

"Oh, you sound like you're in an absolutely *pleasant* mood."

"Harold!"

"Not my name. But I'm at my apartment."

"Good. I'll be there in ten minutes."

And without another word, she hung up.

Harry rented a place downtown. It was a newly renovated loft with a beautiful view of the park. Nat was only a little jealous that he could afford it.

Once she was off the elevator and on his floor, she hesitated in front of the door. For a moment, she had the fleeting thought to turn around and just talk this out with, well, herself. As insane as that sounded, going to Harry for assistance sounded just as insane, if not more so.

She was in the middle of thinking her actions through when the door swung open.

"I thought I heard the elevator." He pushed the door open wider to allow her to come in. "You made good time."

"Kit tells me I have a habit of speeding when I'm angry." At the mention of her name, Nat could feel her anger start to rebuild.

The door shut behind her, as Harry ushered her in. "And what caused this anger?"

He continued to guide her through the loft until she was at the counter, where she slid onto a stool.

"You know, there is a reason Kit and I never roomed together in college."

Harry walked around her to the fridge and grabbed a bottle of water. Placing it in front of her, he strode to the stove where he stirred whatever was in the pan simmering on the burner.

"You mean it wasn't you getting a better scholarship than her?"

"Harry!"

He chuckled. "Sorry. But it's true."

She took a sip of water before she continued. "No, it was more than that. We just aren't compatible as roommates. Kit and Nat as best friends is one thing, but Kit and Nat as anything more is something else entirely. Something terrible!"

"I highly doubt that. Two beautiful women like Kit and yourself could hardly be anything terrible."

For once, Nat didn't have a response. She was too busy blinking away the unwanted tears building up. Frustration gnawed at her insides.

When she didn't respond, Harry turned around. If he noticed the un-shed tears, he didn't say anything.

She looked away from his prying eyes. "Kit and I got into a fight."

"I kinda put that much together."

"She's a mess. She doesn't clean up after herself like she's some kind of child! I mean, look at you!" She waved her hands at him. "Even you're capable of keeping a clean place! Not a dirty dish in sight!"

"I'm not sure if I should be flattered or offended right now."

She ignored him. "I only agreed to this arrangement because it was temporary, but it has dragged by and is so much harder than I imagined! The first few weeks were fine. She made up the bed and the sofa went back to being something we could use instead of her unmade bed. But then she was running late one morning and didn't have time. She sent me a text explaining, and I said I understood—which I did! It was one time! Everyone runs late. I get it! But then she never made the sofa up again!"

Harry hummed in response. He was leaning against the counter while whatever was in the pan sizzled behind him.

"And, once again, if that was the only thing I had to deal with, I could suck it up! And I tried! But she leaves her coffee cups literally all over the place. There were two," she raised her fingers to emphasize. "Two! Mugs in the bathroom! What was she doing with her coffee in the bathroom? And the grossest part is, half the time the mugs aren't even empty! I found one with mold in it. Harry! There was mold in one of my cups!"

He nodded as if he understood. Part of Nat was alarmed at how good of a listener he was being, but the larger, louder part of her didn't care in the moment.

"At first, I would just take them to the kitchen myself, but it kept happening. I didn't want to cause any tension. I know how stressed she is about everything, and she hates change and this entire season for her is one big change after another. But then, I don't know. I just got tired. So I started gathering the mugs and putting them beside the table by the couch. I thought that would be enough of a sign for her to get the hint."

"But it wasn't, I'm guessing."

"It wasn't."

"How long have you been putting the mugs on that table?"

"Weeks? Months? Eventually it would get so bad that I would take them to the kitchen myself again, and the entire process would start over."

"Ah." Harry nodded as if he understood and this all made perfect sense to him. It made her feel a little less crazy. "And what else happened?"

"She would leave her wet towels on the floor of the bathroom along with the bath mat. It would cause it to smell all musty, and it is one of my biggest pet peeves! I finally tried talking to her about it, but she blamed her brain! Like, what?! She didn't even say she would try to do better! She just used some excuse and that was that!"

"Was this in person or over text?"

"I texted her because she was already gone for work."

"What was her reaction?"

"I don't know. Some emoji or something."

"Which is her tactic to avoid good communication."

Nat threw her hands up. "Exactly! You get it!" She took another sip of her water, and for a reason she didn't quite understand, Harry smiled. "The short of it is that when she got home from work today, we kind of went at it."

"What was the tipping point?"

"Well," Nat started to say, but then sighed. "It doesn't sound like that big of a deal, I guess. But she didn't replace the toilet paper, and I had an emergency today." She groaned. "I know how petty it sounds, but it really was one of those moments where toilet paper was completely necessary!"

Harry chuckled, but quickly stopped. He became serious again. "That is an important thing to keep up on."

"She's my best friend, H. But I can't live with her. I was so hoping we could make it to the wedding, but here I am making things worse the week before the wedding!"

He turned back to the stove, but he glanced over his shoulder when he said, "Tell me about the argument. What was said?"

Whatever was cooking was beginning to smell delicious. "That smells really good."

He smiled at her. "Thanks. Hope you're hungry. There's more than enough for two." He motioned for her to keep talking. "The argument."

"Right. So I may have just kinda let my anger boil throughout the day, so I wasn't in the best place when she finally came home."

He was looking at whatever was on the stove now, but she could hear him plainly when he said, "Which is understandable."

"I might have asked her where her brain was when she used the last of the toilet paper this morning without replacing it."

He scooped the contents of the pot onto two different plates. "That doesn't seem too harsh."

"I'm sure my tone wasn't what it should've been. I've been told my teacher-voice comes out when I'm irritated."

"Once again," he said as he turned around with a plate in each hand, "you're a teacher, so that is understandable."

She huffed out an unamused laugh as he slid the plate in front of her. "Thanks. What is this?"

He flitted to the oven and took out warm tortillas. "It's fajitas!"

He presented the tortillas with a flourish, and all Nat could do was stare. Something told her that it wasn't a coincidence that he cooked her favorite, but that wasn't a path she had time to explore right now.

"Mm," She rubbed her hands together. "Sounds delicious."

He handed her a napkin and fork. "Dig in. And keep talking. I might be moving around the kitchen, but I'll be listening."

She hid a smile by taking a huge bite. After she swallowed, she continued with the story. "She told me she just forgot, but she also *just forgot* to put up her towel again and to put her mug in the sink. At this point, I'm not even asking for her to clean it, just put it in the sink and I'll do it!"

"And I'm guessing you said that?"

"Of course I did. Anyway, it all ended with a screaming match and me telling her she needed to either get medicated or find a different friend."

Harry stopped where he was at and turned to face her. "Whoa."

Nat covered her face with her hands, embarrassment from her harsh words washing over her. "I know! I was awful, and I see that now!"

He took the stool next to her, but sat so he was facing her. "How did she take that?"

"Obviously not well. She ended up leaving. I'm sure she went to Declan's."

"Not surprising."

"Right."

For a moment, both of them were quiet as they ate their fajitas. It was almost startling when Harry broke the silence. "So I am acutely aware that you are only here because I am your last option. That being said, what is my role here?"

"You're fulfilling your role just fine, Harry."

"My role as a handsome substitute best friend who cooked you a delicious meal?"

She bumped her knee against his, "Knock that ego down a few pegs before I change my mind."

17

When Declan arrived back to his apartment from his afternoon with Timmy, he was expecting Fox to greet him at the door with a toy dangling from her mouth. As far as excitement went, that's as far as it was going to get that night.

What he wasn't expecting was to find Anna Katherine on his couch looking very sullen and Fox in her lap.

"Kit?"

She barely gave him a glance when he said her name. "Hi."

"I thought you were staying in with Nat tonight?"

She shrugged.

"What's wrong?"

Fox slid off of her and went to sit at his feet. She whined and pawed at his thighs. If Declan had to bet, he would say that Kit did not take Fox out before getting comfortable on the couch.

"Who said anything was wrong?"

He watched her for a moment. She turned on her side and held a pillow to her chest.

"Stop staring at me like that and go walk the dog. I know you want to." Her voice cracked at the end, and it was then that he noticed that she had been crying, her eyes red and swollen.

So many responses were at the tip of his tongue, but none of them managed to come out. He sighed. "Right. Well, I'll be back."

Outside on the sidewalk, Fox looked up at him and whined. "I know, girl. What do you think? A movie and cuddles when we get back?"

Fox barked.

"You're right. This calls for all the stops. We need to walk to the store and get you-know-what for your mom."

When Declan made it back to the apartment with Fox and a half-gallon of mint chocolate chip ice cream in tow, Kit seemingly hadn't moved an inch. And in all honesty, she looked absolutely pathetic.

"What took you so long?"

He swung the bag in front of him once he got Fox off the leash. "Just had to stop by the store."

"Thought you went running for the hills."

The usual hint of humor in her voice was gone, and when Declan took a break from scooping Kit ice cream and glanced at her, she looked serious.

"We've been over this, Anna Katherine. You aren't going to get rid of me."

She hadn't looked at him. She hadn't even paid any attention to what he was doing. So when he came over with a mug filled with ice cream and handed her a spoon, she just stared at him.

"What's this?"

"How about you take it and find out?"

"That would involve moving."

He stood there, holding out the mug between them, and waited for her curiosity to get the best of her. Finally, she heaved out a sigh and sat up. He took the opportunity to squeeze in between her and the end of the couch. She looked at him like he was insane.

"What are you doing?"

"Scooch on over, love. And take your ice cream, please."

She took her ice cream but still stared at him with an incredulous look. "Declan."

"You are obviously in need of some cuddling. So make room for me so we can watch a show, cuddle, and you can eat your mint chocolate chip."

She glanced down at her cup. "You were out of it."

He laughed as he continued to rearrange them into a comfortable position. "Of course you already checked."

"Is that what took you so long with Fox?"

"Yes, Kit-Kat. Now, c'mere."

For once in her life, she did as she was told, collapsing into him with a heavy sigh. He draped an arm around her before turning on the TV and searched for a show for them to watch. He finally landed on one they had both been watching and started it. It was more background noise than anything. Neither one of them were paying much attention to it.

"So I went to the country club with Timmy today," he started, hoping to distract her.

She hummed, but that was the only acknowledgment that she had heard him.

"It went fine. We played golf, which I know you're shocked by, and I beat him. I was afraid that would upset him, but he took it all in good stride. You obviously don't get your competitive streak from him."

"Ha."

"Speaking of your competitive streak, I went to the coffee shop before-hand and saw Mack there. She was asking about our next game night. She was right when she said we hadn't had one in a while. I told her our next one would obviously have to wait until after the wedding, but we'd make sure it would happen."

"Good call." She took a small bite of the ice cream, the first bite since he'd given it to her. Her delay in devouring the icecream was more concerning than anything else.

"What's wrong?"

She snuggled deeper into his embrace. "Nothing."

He watched her for a moment, but he knew she wouldn't give him anything else until she was ready. She was like a cat. Everything had to be on her terms, or at least what she believed was her terms.

He pressed a soft kiss on top of her head, and then snuggled them both deeper into the couch. For several minutes they silently watched the show. It wasn't until it had ended and the next episode started playing that she spoke up.

"What if you end up hating me?"

He tensed. "What?"

"What if through all of this, you just end up resenting and hating me?"

"Kit, if anyone has the potential to hate anyone in this relationship, it's you hating me. I'm the one who convinced you to marry me."

She sat up and pulled away from him. He followed suit and watched as she put the ice cream on the table.

"That's not it. What if..." She sighed and brushed her hair out of her face. "What if I'm too much for you? What if living together proves to be too much? I mean, you have your routines and I, well, I'm a mess."

He chuckled and some of the tension left his body. "You are a mess. That's true." When she gave him a disgruntled look, he went on. "What is bringing all this on?"

"Nat and I got into it."

"Ah."

"You and her are so similar. You both have clean places. She can't go to bed with dirty dishes in the sink. It drives her crazy. But it takes so much mental energy for me. I know it doesn't make sense. You don't have to tell me that it doesn't. I know."

"I do love a good, clean house."

"Exactly. You do. Nat does. My mom does. Two out of the three of those people already are exasperated with me. Nat might truly hate me at this moment. What if, after the wedding when we move in together, you just can't stand it?"

"Has Nat ever had a roommate?"

She gave him a questioning look, but answered. "Not since the end of sophomore year of college."

"Did she ever do well with the roommates she did have?"

"Not exceptionally."

"Have I had roommates?"

"For nearly as long as I've known you. It's just been recently that you haven't."

"So who do you think is going to handle someone living in their space better?"

She didn't answer right away. "You?"

"Right." He nodded. "We all love Nat. But we also all know that she has a slight issue when it comes to letting go of control. You and her living together is just temporary. By the end of the week, you'll be moved out."

"But she's my best friend."

"I'm not following."

"If my own mother *and* my best friend can get tired of me, who's to say that you won't?"

"I'm going to get irritated and annoyed by you, but you're going to get irritated and annoyed by me. It's what happens when people move in together. I know a lot of your weaknesses already, though. And you know mine. That's not to say that there won't be surprises along the way, because there most definitely will be, but we got this."

She didn't look like she believed him.

"Besides. I already deal with a lot from you. You're over here more than you're over at Nat's."

"What if you hate the way my shampoo smells?"

"I'll suck it up because that's ridiculous." He didn't say that he already knew that he loved the smell of her shampoo.

"What if all of my toiletries clutter up your bathroom counter?"

"Then we will go to the store and buy organization compartments."

"And what if I don't use them?"

"Then I will put them up for you."

"Every morning?"

"When I feel like it."

"What if you don't like the way I load the dishwasher?"

"That's assuming that you actually load it, which I'll believe when I see it."

She laughed, but immediately stopped herself. "I sometimes hate it when you can make me laugh even when I don't feel like it."

"Personally, I love that I have that ability."

"What if I leave my socks all over the place and you trip on them and get a concussion?"

"That is a lot of what if's, but thankfully, I have medical insurance."

"Declan. I'm serious."

"So am I, Kit."

She groaned. "But what if—"

He cut her off. "Enough what if's." He reached for her hand and pulled her toward him again. "You are genuinely my favorite person. If I can't handle living with you and make changes in my own life to make it work, then I don't have high hopes for myself."

She collapsed against him. "I just don't think you're taking this seriously enough."

"And I just think you're taking it too seriously." He held her close. "Trust me when I say we're going to be okay."

<h1 style="text-align:center">18</h1>

The last thing Anna Katherine wanted to do was leave the apartment. The past few days felt like Satan himself had crawled out of hell and wrote a script for her life to make it her own personal misery. First she had to go with her mother to pick out centerpieces and wedding colors. She'd begged Declan to take a personal day from work in order to come with her, but he needed to save up his days for when they went on their honeymoon and the holidays that were fast approaching. Anna Katherine didn't understand why she even had to go in the first place since her mother seemed to make all the final decisions.

That same day, she opened Declan's apartment door to a destroyed room courtesy of Fox Tran-Mullins. The espresso machine broke down at the shop yesterday when she was by herself because Mack got sick. She and Nat had still not made up or spoken since their little spat. She was pretty sure she was about to start her period, and all she really wanted to do was sit on the couch, watch a movie from her childhood, and eat ice cream. Also, sleep. She really, really wanted to sleep.

After Anna Katherine spent the morning cleaning up Nat's place, she had every intention of going through with that plan until Declan came barging into Nat's apartment, looking a bit too peppy for her liking, and asked her if she was ready to go.

She glared at him, even though he really hadn't done anything to earn that look from her. Thankfully, Declan seemed to be used to her moods and misplaced anger by now.

"And where are we going?"

He shrugged out of his blazer. "We have our date tonight, remember? We said we'd go out this week. Practice being a couple in public and whatnot."

He went rummaging through the fridge for a drink, and when she let out a groan, he looked over his shoulder at her. "Have you talked to Nat since last night?"

Instead of answering the obvious question, she said, "Patricia called. She wants to know if we want a live band or a DJ."

Declan finally decided on a water and came to join her on the couch. "And what did you decide?"

"You know I have zero power when it comes to these decisions. She decided on a live band."

"She's paying for it, I hope."

"Of course she is. By the time she's done with it, you'll barely have to pay a dime."

He screwed off the top of his water and took a swig. "Which is perfectly fine with me."

"Only because you don't have to deal with her!"

He offered her some water, but she pushed it away. "Alright then. What else happened?"

She didn't look at him. "Nothing."

"Kit." She didn't appreciate the soft smile he added to his prodding.

Another glare. "What?"

"I know something else happened."

She didn't like how well he knew her, either.

When he refused to remove his soft and concerned gaze from her face with that ridiculous soft smile dimpling his chin, she sighed in defeat. "I might have cried over the fact that I don't have any mint chocolate chip left."

She fully expected him to laugh or mock her, but he didn't. Instead he said in the softest voice she'd heard him use, "Oh, Kit-Kat."

When she squinted her eyes at him and he wrinkled his nose, she wondered when he had become so unbearably adorable.

"Go on this date with me like we had planned, and on our way home, we'll stop to get you all the ice cream your heart desires. I'm pretty sure that's in our contract anyway."

That finally made her chuckle. "Yeah, I think so."

"Alrighty then. It's settled!" He clapped his hands together and motioned for her to get up. "Go get changed so we can head out. I'm starving."

Anna Katherine looked down at her clothes. "What's wrong with what I have on?"

"It's a date, love. We gotta look the part. I'll be wearing my work blazer, so you won't look out of place. That dress you wore at Nat's birthday dinner would be fine."

She stood up with a grunt. "You're awfully bossy today, Mr. Mullins."

He smiled and said, "Someone's gotta wear the pants in this relationship."

"I just let you *think* you're in charge," she said when she patted his head on her way to her bedroom.

Anna Katherine thought about not wearing the dress just to spite Declan, but it was one of her favorites and the most comfortable dress she owned. In the end, she slipped it on, but told herself that it was for her, not Declan.

When they got in his car, they immediately started arguing about where to go.

"I thought you said you didn't care?" Declan pulled out of the parking lot, and by the look on his face, he was clearly frustrated with her.

"I don't! I'm just not in the mood for a steak."

"Or pizza or street tacos."

"All of that sounds gross right now."

"What about that old country diner out by Harry's?"

Her mouth watered. "Oh, fried chicken? Yes, please."

He shook his head. "Why didn't you just say you wanted that?"

"I didn't know that's what I wanted!"

"That's not the same thing as not caring."

"Okay, but you get more annoyed with me when I say I don't know."

"I cannot believe I'm stuck with you for the foreseeable future." He rolled his eyes, but the grin belied his words.

"If I'm so unbearable, you could've asked someone else to be your illegal wife" she huffed out. "Besides, you would've been stuck with me either way. We're best friends, dingbat."

"And who else am I going to ask? Nat? No thank you. She'd be worse than you."

"I'm sure there are people at your work that would be more than willing."

He rolled his eyes. "Anyway. At least if we were only best friends without a legally binding commitment, I could get food wherever I wanted to."

She snorted. "As if I'd let you."

To her surprise, he laughed. "That's true. Remember when I was thinking about taking that job in New York? You were about ready to chain me up and throw away the key."

"I still can't believe you even considered it! Leaving all of us behind, as if!"

He looked at her again, and she was annoyed that he wore that soft smile again. "I'm still here, aren't I?"

Even if she was peeved, she couldn't help but smile back. "Yeah, you're here."

Once they got to the restaurant, Kit immediately ran to the bathroom. Declan always teased her for having such a tiny bladder. When she came back, he had already ordered the fried chicken blue plate, a root beer float, and water for her. Because they were supposed to be on a date as an engaged couple, she gave him a peck on the cheek before sitting down in the booth across from him.

"Thanks for ordering for me, *sweetheart*."

Declan winked. "Anything for my bride-to-be."

She laughed, a blush rushing to her cheeks, and Declan was mesmerized by how beautiful she looked in that moment.

Kit was still giggling when the waitress came with their food.

They laughed and talked, and Declan made her snort out her rootbeer float when he reached over the table to take her hand, being over dramatic with the pet nicknames and the heart eyes.

Declan couldn't complain when she took food off his plate. He was simply happy to be here after a long day at work. And when he kept eyeing her float, she slid it over to him without a word.

When they got in the car, he turned up the music and found himself laughing once more as she sang loudly and proudly off-key. When he parked by the store, they sat there with the car still running as they sang along to two more songs.

He could get used to nights like these with Kit.

When Declan took her hand in the grocery store, he half expected another burst of laughter or for her to pull away. Instead she gave his hand a quick squeeze and a smile, pulling him along as she made her way to the freezer section. He teased her when she briefly wondered out loud if she should get something other than mint chocolate chip. As if she would ever choose something different.

He was reaching for his own pint of cookies and cream when he heard an almost forgotten voice come up behind them.

"Well, what are the chances of us running into each other here?"

Declan and Kit both spun around, and Declan wasn't sure which one of them was more surprised to see Jonah standing in front of them.

"Jonah?" Declan cut his eyes to Kit, a little worried about how she would react.

But she sounded calm enough when she asked, "What are you doing here? You moved."

Jonah eyed the both of them, and his eyes lingered on where Declan's hand rested on Kit's back. He flicked his eyes back to Kit. "Just moved back recently. There was a job opening, and I decided I wanted to be closer to family."

Once more, Jonah's eyes roamed across Kit and landed on her left hand. He nodded toward the ring that was on her finger. "I guess congratulations are in order."

"Oh, yeah." Kit nodded. "Uh, thanks."

Declan rubbed her back, hoping to communicate to Kit that he was with her in this. "Thanks, man."

Jonah didn't look at all like he wanted to give them congratulations. "When did it happen?"

"I asked her back in September."

Jonah hummed. "And when is the big day?"

"Next week."

He raised his eyebrows, "Pretty soon, isn't it?"

She shrugged. "Not when you think about how long we've been friends. Besides," Declan heard her tone go cold. "I trust him."

Jonah heard the underlying message. "Yeah, I guess you do." He looked between the two of them again, then nodded. "Well, it was good to see you guys. I guess I'll see you around."

Declan lifted his hand in a half-hearted wave. "Yeah, sure."

"Bye, Jonah."

Declan's hand dropped to his side when Jonah turned to walk away from them. When Kit took his hand back in hers, he looked over at her. "You good?"

She smiled up at him. "Peachy. C'mon, let's get out of here before my ice cream melts."

Once they got back in the car, Anna Katherine watched as Declan reached over her and opened the glove compartment. After a moment of digging around, he smiled and pulled out two packets of plastic utensils.

"Ah-ha!" He grinned, handing one to Anna Katherine. "A spoon for my beloved lady."

She looked at the plastic spoon and then at him. "As much as I love ice cream, I do have enough self restraint to wait until we get home."

"Yeah. but we're not going home. Our night isn't over yet, Kit-Kat."

She asked where they were going, but he refused to tell her. So she sat there listening to his playlist while they drove around the city. Eventually, she tore open the packet that held her spoon, and dug into the ice cream. When they arrived at a park and he stopped the car, she glanced at him. Her mouth was full of ice cream, but luckily she didn't need to voice her question aloud. He knew her well enough to see the question written on her face.

"We're never too old for a good swing," he said with a quick shrug.

She couldn't seem to help the laugh that bubbled out of her. Nor could she help the smile as they raced all the way to the swings, each with a carton of ice cream in their hands.

The nights were finally beginning to feel like autumn, and with the cool breeze and ice cream, Anna Katherine started getting goosebumps. Her chattering teeth didn't get past Declan, and when he noticed, he shrugged out of his blazer and draped it over her shoulders.

"You didn't have to," she tried to argue, but it didn't do much good since she was already pushing her arms through the sleeves.

A smile tugged at the corner of his mouth and his eyes softened, making her heart flutter. "I pride myself in being the perfect date, Kit. And if I just let you sit there shivering, perfect I would not be."

"Now I know how you get all those women to swoon at your feet. You trick them into thinking you are the perfect gentleman."

"Aw, shucks." He acted as if he was disappointed. "You figured out my secret."

She laughed, "Don't worry. I'll keep it safe with all the other secrets of yours I'm keeping."

They stayed there on the swings until Anna Katherine finished her pint of ice cream. She threw her empty carton at Declan when he made fun of her for eating the entire thing, but he just laughed and went to throw both of the containers away. When he came back, he stood in front of her, his hands holding onto the chains above her, head bent down to look her in the eye.

"Tonight wasn't as bad as you thought, eh?"

"If I tell you that, will it go to your head?"

"Undoubtedly."

"Then tonight was definitely the worst date I've ever been on."

He laughed again, his head thrown back and the sound echoing in the empty park. When he stopped laughing, he looked at her again, and Anna Katherine really did begin to understand why all the girls seemed to fall for him.

"Okay, on a serious note." Declan started pushing her in the swing, and Anna Katherine watched him carefully, wondering what he was about to say. "Jonah."

"What about him?"

"That was unexpected. Was this the first time you've seen him since—?"

"Since he shattered my heart and fed it to the sharks? Yes."

Declan nodded and hummed. "Thought so."

She smiled. "It really didn't bother me. Promise."

"Are you just telling me that so I'll stop worrying?"

"Yeah, but it's also true."

He gave her another push. "Well, since you trust me, I guess I gotta trust you, too."

"That is what makes a great marriage work."

There was a lull in conversation before he spoke up again. "You need to talk to Nat."

She slouched at the mention of her bestie. "I know."

"Tonight."

She slouched even further. "Can't I just text her?"

"Anna Katherine."

She turned around to look at him, and he was looking very unimpressed with her. She took a deep breath. "Fine."

He smiled. "Good."

The lights were all off in the apartment when Anna Katherine slid out of Declan's car, but she could hear Nat watching something in her bedroom. Anna Katherine took her time changing clothes and getting ready for bed before she gently knocked on the bedroom door.

When Nat called out for her to come in, she took a steadying breath before doing just that.

Nat seemed surprised to see Anna Katherine from her place curled up beneath the covers on her bed. "I thought you were with Declan?"

Anna Katherine went to sit on the edge of the bed. "I was. He dropped me off here."

"I'm surprised y'all didn't go back to his place for a bit."

She shrugged. "Yeah, that was the plan, but he insisted it was time I came and apologized to you for, well, everything."

Nat's face dropped. "I'm sorry, too. I wasn't communicating well at all during this time, and I wasn't giving you enough grace."

Anna Katherine laughed. "I think you gave me an abundance of grace that I definitely took for granted. I should've been more aware and considerate that this is your safe place and should be respected a bit more."

Nat reached out and tugged her further on the bed to wrap her up in a hug. "We were both jerks. Good thing you're my person and best friend."

She laughed and got under the covers with Nat.

19

Móirín arrived Saturday night, and Anna Katherine couldn't help noticing after a few mere moments how different she was to her own mother when she went with Declan to pick her up from the airport. She had met Declan's mom plenty of times over FaceTime, but this was the first time she had engaged with her in person. That didn't stop Móirín from hugging her as soon as she laid eyes on her, though.

"It is so good to finally meet you, Kit! Declan hasn't stopped blabbering about you since the two of you met back in uni. I told him back then that he was going to marry you, whether or not you were currently dating that idiot he called his best friend. Thank goodness you both got rid of him when you did."

Declan looked as embarrassed as Anna Katherine had ever seen him, and she couldn't help but laugh at him when he whined, "*Muuuum.* Please!"

"Is that so?" Anna Katherine all but preened. "Please, tell me more,

Móirín."

The two women huddled together and ignored Declan's protests while he waited for his mom's luggage. "Well, Kit, it all started when he came home for the winter holidays after meeting you."

She glanced over Móirín's shoulder to look at Declan who was downright glaring at his mother. Another laugh escaped her, and when he heard it, he directed his glare toward her.

"He wouldn't stop talking about this mysterious Kit. Went on and on and on. It was a miracle any of us got a word in edgewise during that holiday. I genuinely thought the two of you were already dating, so I was shocked when he finally said that the two of you were *just* best friends."

"My best friend is Harry, Mum."

Móirín ignored him. "You can imagine my shock when he told me you were dating Jonah. I was heartbroken for him, really. I'm just glad you both came to your senses and he finally told you how he felt."

Kit locked eyes with him again and giggled, "Yeah, lucky for us that we figured it out."

Declan finally saw his mom's luggage and broke the two of them up as soon as he grabbed the suitcase off the carousel. "Alright, you two, that's enough of that. Let's go grab some food. I'm sure you're starving, Mum."

On the way back to the car, Kit nudged him. "You were obsessed with me."

Declan continued to glare straight ahead. "I liked you a normal amount for a friend."

"Mhm, sounds like it." Anna Katherine nudged him again, and when she saw his scowl, she decided to give him a break. She shrugged. "I was a little obsessed with you, too."

He finally met her gaze then. "Yeah?"

"Yeah." She shrugged. "I blame the accent. Thought it was sexy at the time."

Declan smiled so wide that he looked like a kid on Christmas morning. She rolled her eyes. "Shut up. I've obviously changed my mind since then. You and your accent both are annoying."

Declan laughed. "Of course."

He wrapped his arm around her, and she leaned into his side. It was beginning to get cold, and she welcomed the warmth that he gave her. They were almost back to the car when he leaned over to whisper, "I still think your southern accent is sexy."

Thankfully, he didn't look at her, because Anna Katherine could feel her cheeks burn a bright shade of pink.

Anna Katherine was woken up in the very rude manner of Declan barging into Nat's apartment and yelling, "Time to get up, love!"

She yanked a pillow over her head when he opened the blinds. Before he could do anything else to disrupt her peace, she yelled back, "It's Sunday! I want to sleep in!"

She felt the sofa bed dip down and Declan gently tug the pillow off of her. "Did you forget Patty is requesting we all go to church this morning as a family?"

She let out a long groan, and he patted her shoulder sympathetically. "I know, I know. But it's going to be fine. Plus, we get free brunch out of it."

"There is nothing free when it comes to Patricia Tran. She'll make me pay for it somehow, just not in the typical way."

"You give her too much credit for being manipulative."

"No, you don't give her enough." She glared at him when he stood up. "Where are you going?"

"I'm going to go make sure we have enough coffee, because I am not dealing with a grumpy Kit all morning long."

"*Dealing with.* You make me sound impossible."

"You are."

She threw the pillow at him, and he ran out to Nat's kitchen while ducking to miss the pillow and laughing all too loudly for her liking. She really did not appreciate him this morning.

The church service flew by, and Anna Katherine thought it might have had to do with her and Declan whispering and giggling with each other all throughout the service. She knew her mom was constantly cutting a glare their way, but sitting next to her best friend while drinking her third cup of coffee, all while knowing they couldn't and shouldn't be laughing and talking, made it all that much harder not to.

It reminded her of the Sunday mornings of her childhood with Nat sitting beside her until Patty or Timmy were forced to separate them. It was inevitable that if Anna Katherine was sitting beside a friend during a time she was supposed to be quiet, the quiet would not last for long. She just couldn't help herself.

Alex, having missed the service for what he claimed was a much needed sleep in, met them for brunch, and once there, talked Móirín's ear off the entire time, telling her stories of Declan and Anna Katherine and all the mischief they caused during their last two years of college. Móirín, of course, ate up every bit of it. Patricia looked less than thrilled.

The week sped by with work shifts, last minute wedding arrangements, lunches with the moms, dinners with her dad and Alex—where both she and her brother were uncomfortable when their dad started getting emotional—and shopping with Móirín.

"I had a nice day with Patty yesterday."

Móirín and Anna Katherine were walking the length of the mall, stopping at whichever store had caught Declan's mom's attention. Anna Katherine knew Móirín and Patty had spent the day together yesterday, but she didn't expect to have a conversation about it.

"Yeah? That's good."

Móirín watched her, and Anna Katherine wondered what it was about the Mullins' that made her feel so *seen*. "Declan tells me you don't get on well with her."

She shrugged. "I guess you could say that. She's just so overbearing. I feel like I can never live up to the unreasonable expectations she has for me."

Móirín nodded but didn't respond right away. It wasn't until they went into another home decor store that she said, "As a mother myself, I can see Patty's perspective maybe a little easier than you can."

Anna Katherine shot her a glance but stayed quiet.

"She's proud of you, you know. But as parents, we stay worried about our kids. From the moment we see and hold you in our arms until we take our last breath, we worry. She just wants you to be the best you can possibly be."

"But she thinks my best is far more than what it actually is. She criticizes every aspect of my life."

Móirín hummed thoughtfully. "Not every aspect, I think. She wants you to be prepared and ready for the day she's no longer around. I think that's why she's so excited about you and Declan."

"Excited? I doubt that."

"Oh, she's definitely happy and excited about it. She shows it in her own way, but I can see it in the way she talks about the two of you."

"Yeah?" Anna Katherine was honestly surprised.

Móirín nodded. "She and I both have been waiting for the two of you to get your act together longer than we'd like, but we're both just happy you finally found your way there."

Anna Katherine wondered why her mother continued to set her up on blind dates if she thought that Declan really was the one for her, and then she wondered how she would have reacted if Patty *had* mentioned she thought Declan and Anna Katherine would be a perfect match. She probably would have laughed it off, but then... It wouldn't be the first time people said she and Declan belonged together. What did they see that Anna Katherine didn't?

Móirín turned to face Anna Katherine. "Now, enough home decor shopping. Let's go find you some lingerie for your wedding night."

Anna Katherine choked on the bite of pretzel she just took.

<h1 style="text-align:center">20</h1>

On the day of the wedding, Declan was in the groom's area with Harry, Wesley, and William when Nat came in, not bothering to knock. "Hello, glad to see you all are dressed." She frantically looked around the room, but her gaze settled on Declan. "We might have a crisis."

Declan shot up. "Is it Kit? Is she okay?"

Nat took a deep breath and shook her head. "Yeah, uh, she's definitely not okay."

Anna Katherine was lying on her back on the floor. She was only wearing her slip, her hair and makeup done—well, they had been done. After this,

Nat would have to touch it up again. Her heart was pounding, and she felt like the world was about to swallow her whole. She'd prefer that, actually, to what was about to happen. There was a tentative knock on the door, and Anna Katherine knew it was Declan even before she heard his voice.

"You decent?" He cracked the door open and stuck his head in.

"What do you want, Declan?"

Spotting her on the floor, he squeezed in through the door, gently closing it behind him. She blinked and he was lying there beside her on the floor.

"What're we looking at?"

"The ceiling."

"It's a nice ceiling. Very aesthetically pleasing."

"Declan. Why are you here?"

"Nat thinks you're having a crisis. I heard there was hysterical crying."

"Maybe something like that."

"Wanna tell me what's going on in that pretty head of yours?"

She was quiet for a moment, and then turned to look at Declan, only to see him already looking at her. "We're about to lie to everyone. I mean, I know we were already doing that, but it's about to be, like... legit."

He nodded, and she noticed his eyes dance over her face. Was he as nervous as she was? "We don't have to go through with it."

She was unable to keep the surprise off her face, and he kept going. "You're doing this for me, Kit. And, as much as I love you for it, it doesn't have to happen. Going back to Ireland wouldn't be the worst thing in the world. I'll still love you just as much if you tell me you want out."

She pondered for a moment. Thought about having to go out there and tell her friends and family that the wedding was off. Thought about how she'd have to sit and watch Declan pack up his life and board a plane for a place far, far away from her. Thought about how empty the apartment would be without him, how Fox would miss him, and how her friend group would seem so much smaller without him.

She shook her head. "Marrying my best friend isn't the worst thing in the world."

When Anna Katherine turned her head to look at Declan, he was already watching her. She took a moment to take in his appearance. His hair was slicked back, a look she didn't necessarily like on him, and his white button down looked perfectly snug around his shoulder. When he grinned at her, she smiled. They both sat up. Declan reached out and pushed a curled strand of hair behind her ear. "You're beautiful, you know."

She snorted. "I'm a mess."

"But a very beautiful mess."

She shifted so she could lean against him. "Thanks for coming."

"Of course." He smoothed her hair down. "But I should get back if you're okay now."

"No." She tightened her hold on him. "Stay for a little bit longer."

"Whatever you need, love."

Declan wasn't nervous. He wasn't nervous when his mum had kicked him out of his own apartment. He wasn't nervous when he and the lads had gone for a round of golf in the morning. He wasn't nervous when he had to go calm Kit down—he was definitely concerned, but not nervous. He wasn't nervous when Timmy came and gave him a talk or when Nat, even knowing it was a fake marriage, threatened him if he ever hurt her best friend. He wasn't nervous for any of it until he was standing at the end of the aisle with Harry by his side waiting for Kit to walk down the aisle toward him.

"You look constipated, mate," Harry whispered.

He glanced over his shoulder at Harry, "What the hell am I doing, H?"

"Marrying your best friend. Now shut up, smile, and look like you're in love."

When the music started, the guests stood, Kit was walking toward him, and Declan forgot how to breathe.

When she finally stopped and stood near him, he didn't hear a word the preacher said. Kit had his undivided attention.

When she smiled at him, it was like a punch in the gut. "I look good, don't I?"

"You have no bloody—" Declan snapped his mouth shut and swallowed. "You have no idea."

They went to stand in front of the preacher, and Kit handed the bouquet to Nat who looked like she was about to start crying at any moment. And then, somehow, they were already saying their vows to each other.

Declan repeated the lines after the preacher. "I, Declan, take thee, Anna Katherine, to be my lawfully wedded wife." They kept smiling at each other, and Declan really wished her smile didn't cause him so much pain. "To have and to hold, from this day forward."

Kit stuck her tongue out at him, and he nearly choked on his laugh. "For better, for worse, for richer, for poorer."

Quite unhelpfully, his mind forced him to remember a time when he was jobless, angry, and depressed. He took it out on Kit for weeks, but she didn't shy away. She called him out on his crap and helped him apply for other jobs. It was because of her that he had the job he had now.

"In sickness and in health."

Kit was the biggest baby when she was sick, and she got sick with the flu nearly every year. And Declan never failed to bring her to the doctor, get her prescriptions from the pharmacy, cook her favorite soup, and take all the sass and insults she threw his way when she wasn't feeling well.

Then, when Declan would inevitably get the same thing she had, she would do it all in return, even though she complained the entire time.

She was a pain and a nuisance, and yet...

"To love and to cherish, till death do us part."

Declan swallowed, realizing too late what he was doing.

"According to God's holy ordinance; and thereto I pledge thee my faith."

He was royally and completely screwed. *Crap,* he thought to himself.

He was so in his head that he was completely taken by surprise when the pastor said, "You may now kiss your bride."

Every muscle in Declan tensed. Of course he was going to have to kiss her. Why hadn't he thought of that? And why was he just now realizing how truly in love he was with his best friend?

Kit raised her eyebrow at the hesitation. He tried to smile as he intertwined their fingers together, and when he finally kissed her, his entire world shifted.

Declan did his best to act normal during their first dance, but Kit saw right through him. "What's up with you? You're acting like you're constipated."

He shrugged and tried to smile. "Just thinking."

"I have it under great authority that as my husband you can no longer be vague."

"Is that so?" He laughed.

She nodded, all serious. "Yes, one hundred percent factual."

He glanced around at all their friends and family watching them. "It's just. We actually did it. We're married now."

"Technically, we were already married when we got our license earlier this week."

He pinched her. "You know what I mean."

"Yeah." She smiled. "I do. But we're good, right?"

"Of course we are."

She rested her head against his chest with a sigh.

As soon as the dance was over, Declan rushed to find Harry who was already at the nacho bar, stuffing his face.

"Harry! There you are!"

Harry spread his arms wide, dripping cheese down his shirt. "Here I am!"

"I need to talk to you." He tried to grab Harry's arm to pull him away from prying eyes, but Harry pulled back.

"No way, mate. This is your night. You and Kit, in love! Tying the knot. Committing yourself to each other forever. It's quite sweet even, given the circumstances."

Declan stared at him in disbelief. "This is important, H."

"Nope." He turned Declan around. "What's important is that your bride is over there by herself when you should be over there with her." Harry gave him a shove. "Now off you go."

Declan really wanted and needed to talk to his friend, but Harry had a point. He looked over at Kit who was smiling and watching the two of them. When she saw him watching and gave a little wave, his stomach twisted.

"Okay, fine. But we have to have a talk as soon as the wedding is over."

Harry wiggled his eyebrows. "No can do, mate. After this, you're off to your honeymoon."

Before Declan could argue anymore, Harry disappeared into the crowd.

21

The drive to New Orleans the next day started well enough. Anna Katherine had a bag full of snacks, a mug full of coffee, and the perfect road trip playlist. Declan was quiet, but she put that off to him being tired after a week of wedding activities and a long night of watching Netflix. It started going downhill thirty minutes in.

Declan glanced at the radio and then at her. "What even is this music?"

She looked down at the phone. "It's nineties pop. What do you have against that?"

"Kit..." He tried not to smile, but she could see through him, "Please don't make me listen to this the entire way to New Orleans."

She skipped the song. "I'll put on a playlist of your choice if you take the next exit so I can pee."

He gave her a disbelieving look. "Already? Really? How much coffee did you drink this morning?"

"The normal amount." She shrugged.

As they grew closer to the city, Anna Katherine plugged in the bed and breakfast's address into her phone.

"It says you need to take the second exit that's coming up."

Declan shook his head. "That would take us into traffic."

"But it's Sunday. It shouldn't be busy."

"Trust me. I know what I'm doing."

Anna Katherine thought she knew what she was doing, too, but she stayed quiet and let Declan do it his way. Fifteen minutes later, they were stuck in traffic and barely moving.

When she gave him a look that clearly relayed that she had told him so, he just shook his head. "Don't even start."

"All I'm saying is, if I pee on myself, I'm blaming you."

"Really? Again?"

She shrugged. "Small bladder."

He couldn't help but chuckle and shake his head in disbelief.

Eventually Anna Katherine was following Declan into the B&B while staring at her phone, and it wasn't until she looked at the email from her mom that she remembered she forgot to change the type of room for them.

She looked up from her phone and was about to tell Declan, but when she saw him, he was already talking to what seemed to be one of the owners.

"Oh, yes. The Mullins! We have a beautiful room with one of our queen beds for the two of you. Is this your first time staying with us?"

"Queen sized? I thought we had two..." He turned around, and she knew the moment he saw her he realized she had forgotten to change the room. After a moment, he muttered, "You're going to be the death of me."

The woman looked worried. "Is there a problem?"

He shook his head. "Just a misunderstanding. It's fine. Our room?"

"Yes! Your room is on the second floor to the left, and it has a balcony that the two of you can enjoy your morning coffee on. It's really one of our better rooms. I hear this is for your honeymoon?"

Anna Katherine noticed the muscles in his back tense up. "Yeah, Anna Katherine and I were just married last night."

The woman seemed pleased for them. "That's wonderful! I'm sure you two will enjoy your time here. How long have the two of you been dating?"

"A few months, but we've known each other for five years."

"Oh, that sounds like a wonderful and romantic story. You both will have to be sure to share it with me before you head off!"

"We'll be sure to do that, ma'am."

Declan placed their bags in the middle of the room and took a deep breath when the door slammed shut behind them. "What do you want to do today?"

She clasped her hands together. "Well, dear husband—" she tried not to be hurt by the scowl that appeared when she said husband "—I'm so glad you asked. Cafe Du Monde is the first on the list. I need beignets and a cafe au lait STAT."

"More coffee? Geez, woman."

"And then," she said with a pointed look, "we can go to the zoo and the aquarium before dinner."

"And where do you want to go for dinner?"

She shrugged. "I'll let you decide that."

"How gracious of you."

She patted his shoulder as she stood up. "Now I'm going to go pee before my bladder explodes."

They took an Uber to Decatur Street and walked with the crowds to Cafe Du Monde. Declan ordered a cafe au lait for her, a black coffee with two sugars for himself, and two orders of beignets. Anna Katherine ended up eating all three of hers and one of Declan's, who only rolled his eyes when she snatched it off his plate. She sneezed then, causing powdered sugar to fly up around them, which then made them both start coughing.

Declan, who was more amused than she thought he should be by her coughing fit, grabbed his phone to snap a picture. When he flipped it around to show her, she couldn't deny that it was a cute—if not funny—photo of her.

Anna Katherine took his phone from him and grabbed his hand. "C'mon. Selfie time. We gotta post all these pictures on Instagram. That's what people in love do."

Declan rolled his eyes at her again but complied with her wishes.

She took pictures of him on the steps in front Cafe Du Monde and in front of St. Louis Cathedral. She laughed when he grabbed her sides and tickled her, telling her that if she was going to take pictures of him the entire trip, they would have to take more selfies together. They did, and when an older couple saw them, they offered to take their pictures for them. As they were leaving, the couple told them how good they looked together.

Even though they didn't have to put on a show for anyone, Anna Katherine still took his hand as they walked around the aquarium. They took their time walking through it, and Declan let her stop and stare at every jellyfish, every seahorse, and any other marine life she found slightly fascinating without a single complaint.

They walked through the Garden District to the Audubon Zoo where Declan bought her a popsicle without her even asking, and kept his arm around her waist as they looked at all the animals. She took his picture in front of the elephant fountain, and he took hers when she got on the back of the lion statue. As they were leaving, he bought her a giant giraffe that was taller than she was.

Declan carried it back to the B&B for her. "I don't think I would've bought this if I had known I was going to be the one carrying it all the way back."

"You were stupid to think I was ever going to."

He cut his eyes at her and then let out a laugh. "The things I do for you."

That night was when Anna Katherine finally allowed herself to truly realize the sleeping arrangement. Declan was still in the bathroom changing and getting ready for bed, while she stood in her pajamas and stared at the bed like it might bite.

She'd seen the movies. She'd read the books. She knew how this was about to go down. He would offer to sleep on the floor. She wouldn't let him. They'd both end up in the bed, and sometime during the night, they'd end up cuddling. The cuddling, of course, would then invoke *feelings,* and she very well couldn't allow that to happen.

She thought back to when she and Alex were still young enough to share a bed when their family went on trips. Alex would build a wall of pillows down the middle of the bed and threaten her if she dared cross it in the middle of the night.

They didn't have enough pillows for an entire wall, but—Anna Katherine smiled and walked to the small closet on the other side of the room. There on the shelf was an extra blanket. She grabbed it and rolled it up long ways so she could place it down the middle of the bed.

She was smiling at her own brilliance when Declan finally emerged from the bathroom. He stood beside her and glanced between her and the bed. Finally, he asked, "And what do we have here?"

"The solution to our one bed problem. That's your side. This is mine. Cross the line and die."

He chuckled. "Death seems like a severe punishment for just crossing a border. Especially for a married couple."

When he wiggled his eyebrows, she laughed and gave him a gentle nudge. "Stop that."

As she laid in the bed, Declan only inches away from her, she was surprised by how comfortable she felt.

The next morning, Anna Katherine woke up to Declan bringing her coffee in bed and immediately launching into their itinerary.

He headed to the restroom, but that didn't stop him from talking. "I know you want to go on a swamp tour, which I don't understand. But Diana, you met her yesterday, remember?" He stuck his head out the door to make sure she was listening. "She said there was a good combo deal where we could go on a swamp tour *and* a cemetery tour."

"Declan, can I at least take a sip of coffee before you start talking?" She took a sip with a sigh. "Also, why are we going on a cemetery tour?"

"Because I think it would be cool. There's also a ghost tour we can go on after. It's a bundle deal."

"What about that Fleetwood Mac concert? You didn't want to see if we could grab some tickets?"

Declan came out of the bathroom with his toothbrush dangling out of his mouth. "Nah. It's already sold out. I'm bummed, but it'll be fine."

Anna Katherine smiled to herself when he turned to go back to the bathroom. "I figured we can just grab dinner somewhere that looks good after the ghost tour."

"Or we can come back here?"

"Or that."

All the tours they went on were fun and exciting, but all Anna Katherine really wanted to do was go back to their room to give Declan the surprise she'd been hiding from him all week. She rarely hid anything from him, and doing so for something this exciting was eating her up.

She convinced him to come straight back to the room after the ghost tour, and when Declan decided to take a shower before dinner, she grabbed the Fleetwood Mac tickets that were hidden in her suitcase, and placed them under his wallet.

While he was taking a shower, she changed into a dress Nat had helped her pick out and touched up her makeup. When he came back out, she was sitting in one of the chairs by the window and did her best not to act as giddy as she felt. She watched as he walked to where his wallet was to slide it in his pocket, but when he picked it up, he paused.

His brows knitted together. "What's this?"

She watched as he read the print on the tickets and realization hit him. But, still, he was quiet. She stood up and walked closer to him. "I, uh, had some help from Harry. I know seeing them live is like a dream for you or something. And I couldn't let you be here on the same night as their show and not see them. You can think of it as a wedding present or—"

She was shocked into silence when he turned around and kissed her. And she was kissing him back, wrapping her arms around his neck, feeling his damp hair between her fingers and his hands gripping her hips.

It was like someone dumped ice water on her when he pulled away, running a hand through his hair. "Kit, these are amazing! How did you even pay for these?"

She tried to process what had just happened. Declan had kissed her, and she had definitely kissed him back, when there wasn't any audience or need to. She shook her head. "I, uh... What? What was that?"

Declan tore his eyes away from the tickets and blinked down at her, as if just now realizing what he had done. He blinked again. "Oh, sorry. I just got caught up in the moment. It's not like we haven't kissed before, and…" He looked at the tickets again. "Oh my gosh, Kit, these are seriously good seats!"

Anna Katherine was still reeling from the kiss and was trying to catch up. She felt like she was still stuck in their embrace, the way his lips melded against hers and…

"Thank Harry for that, not me."

Declan shook his head. "No way. Don't pass the credit to someone else. Seriously." He looked at her again, and she could feel the joy radiating off of him. "How did you afford these?"

She shrugged. "I saved my tips for a while."

The way he was looking at her, like she was his favorite thing in the entire world, made her stomach swoop low. "You're amazing, Kit."

She laughed. "Yeah, well we need to get going before we miss it."

Declan grabbed their jackets and all but dragged her out of the building.

Declan was still riding the high from the night before when they woke up the next morning. They had slept in and missed breakfast, but they went to a restaurant the owner had recommended for lunch and walked around the Garden District and the French Quarter. They popped into shops and took their time enjoying the scenery. They found a quirky coffee shop where they sat for an hour while Kit got her fill of caffeine and Declan talked about the concert nonstop.

"You haven't stopped smiling since you found the tickets."

His smile widened when he looked at her. "I just..." He trailed off and laughed, running his hands through his hair. "You really out-did yourself."

She smiled at him, and he had to fight the urge not to lean over the table and kiss her again. Last night was a mistake. He hadn't been lying when he told her he got caught up in the moment, but it was one thing to kiss her when others were around. It was a completely different thing to kiss her in the privacy of their own room. The lines were blurring already. He didn't need to go blurring them anymore than they already were.

"I'm just glad you're happy, Declan."

They both agreed that having an early night was needed for them to rest up before they headed back home the next day. Which was why they found themselves huddled on the bed, an empty pizza box discarded at their feet, and Declan's laptop resting on his knees while they watched a movie.

As the movie came to an end, Declan moved the laptop over to Kit. "Here, hold this for a second."

He could feel her watching him as he leaned off the bed and grabbed something from his backpack. When he found what he was looking for, he took the laptop back from Kit, and put the book he had grabbed into her lap.

They were both quiet as she lifted it. She glanced at him curiously. "What's this?"

Smirking, he said, "Open it and find out."

She did, flipping through the pages, and then gasped when she saw all the Polaroid pictures.

"We didn't have a photographer for the wedding, and to be honest, even if we did, they wouldn't have been able to hold a light next to your talent. But I gave Nat and Harry a camera and asked them to take photos." He took a breath. "Even if we are going to eventually divorce, I want you to be able to remember this day."

She stopped at a picture of Wesley drinking from a champagne bottle and beside it was another of Patty in the middle of Cupid's Shuffle. When she turned the page, there were pictures of the two of them. She was looking up at him smiling, he was laughing at her dancing, and the two of them were whispering to each other while everyone else looked on.

"Declan this is…" She ran her hands over the pictures. "When did you even have time to put this together?"

He shrugged. "You're a heavy sleeper *and* you sleep in late."

She looked at him for a moment and then back down at the photobook resting in her lap. When she closed it and put it at the end of the bed by the empty pizza box, he watched her every movement. She moved closer to him, her movements sure, but her eyes told him a different story. He could see the wheels in her head spinning as she seemed to ponder her next move. He didn't move a muscle when she leaned over to place a kiss on his cheek.

"Thank you for this, Declan." And with that, she slid off the bed and went to the bathroom.

After she disappeared, Declan closed his eyes and banged the back of his head against the headboard with a groan.

22

The first night Kit and Declan were on their honeymoon, Nat found herself at Harry's with a very excited Fox sniffing her head to toe. Harry had bribed her to come over with the promise of leftover wedding food.

While he prepared their plates, she stayed on the floor petting Fox. "I can take her tomorrow night if you want me to."

Harry walked in with two plates and wine glasses. "Nah. It's fine. I work late, though. So if you can come by after you get off shift to walk her?"

Nat took a glass from him. "Yeah, I can come by around 3:30."

He raised his eyebrows. "That's early."

"I'm a teacher, Harry."

"Oh, yeah." He took a sip. "I knew that. What grade?"

"Kindergarten."

Harry nearly spat out the champagne. "What? Seriously?" When she nodded, he laughed.

"What?" She looked offended, "What's so funny about that?"

"I just can't imagine you with little kids. Is it a bootcamp?"

She slapped his arm. "I'm great with kids, thank you very much. I got teacher of the year two years in a row."

"Wow, impressive."

The second night Declan and Kit were on their honeymoon, Harry came home to find Nat cooking dinner and feeding scraps to Fox.

When he shot her a questioning look, she shrugged. "I usually spend the evenings either at Hattie's Cafe *with* Kit or at home *with* Kit. Who isn't here."

"So I'm your stand-in."

She smirked. "Exactly. Now come taste this and tell me if it needs anything else."

On the third and last day of their friends' honeymoon, Harry called and asked if she wanted to order out. Nat arrived at his place with worksheets to go over in one hand and the food he'd ordered for them in the other. She sat on his floor, and his coffee table became her desk. They were both only half-watching whatever was on his TV.

Eventually, the silence got to him. "Why hasn't Kit dated much?"

Still focused on the papers in front of her, Nat said, "She really changed after the breakup between her and Jonah."

"How so?"

"She closed herself off. Didn't really let anyone know her anymore." She looked up then and tapped the purple flair pen she'd been using against her chin.

"You're worried?"

"She's always been different with Declan, but I think the lines are getting blurred for both of them. I don't want to see her get hurt again. I don't know if she can handle another heartbreak like that, especially if it's with him."

Harry couldn't help sounding defensive when he asked, "You think Declan would hurt her?"

"Not on purpose."

"Yeah." He let out a sigh. "I don't think Kit would hurt him on purpose either. But I also think it's inevitable."

She put the pen down and turned to look at him. "You think we should've tried harder to talk them out of it?"

"We've been over this, Nat. All we can do now is be the friends they need us to be."

Sixth Commandment: Thou (Kit this time—Ha) Shalt Accompany Declan To All Work Events

"Your work events are so dry and boring. I don't want to."

Declan nibbled on the end of the pen. After a moment, he said, "You could always come join me for lunch once a week at the office."

"Ew. No. Gross." She grimaced. "I'll go to the dumb events."

He smirked. "That's what I thought."

23

Declan grabbed the spare key that rested beneath the dying cactus by his friend's door, not bothering to knock or warn Harry of his arrival. Harry was sitting on the back of the couch on his phone. He waved when Declan walked in, but that didn't stop Declan from blurting out, "I'm in love with Kit."

Harry's eyes went wide, and Declan collapsed onto the floor and pinched the bridge of his nose.

Harry's voice turned a bit sharper. "Uh, yeah, I'm going to have to call you back. Yes, I'm sure everything is fine. Declan is just... having a crisis. Okay, I'll see you tonight."

A small part of Declan was curious as to who Harry was seeing tonight, but the larger, more selfish part of Declan only cared about his recent self-discovery.

Now without his phone, Harry peered at him from his perch on the

219

couch. "You're in love with your wife? Wow. Shocker."

Anna Katherine walked into Nat's apartment as she was ending a phone call. "Is everything alright? Well, keep me updated. We're still on for tonight? Alright, see you then."

When Nat hung up, Anna Katherine went to the kitchen in search of food. "Who was that?"

"No one important." Nat followed her. "How was the honeymoon?"

"Declan kissed me."

Nat's eyes went wide. "He *what*?"

Declan could feel Harry's eyes on him, and when Declan didn't say anything else, Harry prodded, "I think we should start at the beginning, mate."

"It all started during our vows."

"When you looked constipated?"

"I was nervous! When I had to repeat the words back to the preacher, I realized I really do mean them, and that's when it hit me. I love her."

"I still don't see why it's a bad thing that you love your wife."

"I lied to the government, H. We told them this was legit. I made an oath to *God*! I wouldn't be surprised if He smites me down at any moment."

"This is what you wanted. This was your entire plan."

"But then I kissed her!"

"That," Harry said, trying to hold in a cough, "was not part of the plan."

"And then she goes and gets me Fleetwood Mac tickets. I had no choice but to kiss her!"

"That one is on you, mate."

"And you know those Polaroids? I gave them to her last night, and she had the audacity to kiss me on the cheek looking as beautiful as ever and then just walk away!" Declan sat up. "And now I have to live with the fact that I married my best friend, that I am in love with her, and that I am going to have to divorce her."

When Harry remained silent, Declan turned to see him texting. "Who could you possibly be texting right now in the middle of my crisis?"

"Sorry, mate. I'm all ears now." Harry pocketed the phone once more.

"Yeah, he kissed me after I gave him the concert tickets."

Nat's phone buzzed, and when she checked it, she coughed. "So, he kissed you? Nothing else happened?"

"Nope."

"Interesting."

Anna Katherine shot Nat a glance as she grabbed a bag of grapes, "What?"

"Oh, nothing. I was just wondering if you kissed him back."

She popped a grape in her mouth and lied. "Nope."

Declan felt Harry watching him yet again. He sighed, "What, H?"

"I just need to point out that I saw this coming from the beginning."

"So, are you going to rub that in my face or be helpful?"

"I don't see why I can't do both." Harry shrugged. "So was the trip completely awful?"

Declan slid down the wall with a *thud* as his head hit the floor. "Not at all. It was great. She was great. I mean, yeah, she yelled at me the entire way there for not going her way. And she has a bladder the size of a pea. Every morning I would wake up to her clothes and towels all over the bathroom, and she just leaves her coffee cups all over the place." He groaned. "But none of those things bothered me as much as I thought they would."

"Declan, mate..."

Declan let out another groan. "She bought me Fleetwood Mac tickets. Do you know how good those seats were? And I just made her a dumb photo album. While we were there, I don't know... Walking around New Orleans and all, it felt like we were a proper couple. I had to keep reminding myself that we weren't. This entire situation is so complicated."

Harry joined him on the floor. "You ever think you should just be honest with her?"

"What? No way. I can't tell her that during our wedding I realized I was in love with her!"

"Oh right." Harry's voice dripped with sarcasm. "What was I thinking? Being in love with your wife on the day of your wedding. And then, a complete idiot I am for thinking you should tell her. Your wife."

"It's not real."

"I don't think it can get much more real than it already is. According to the government and God, you sealed the deal."

Declan buried his face in his hands. "How am I supposed to hide the fact that I'm in love with her?"

Harry was quiet for a moment before he said, "Can I be honest with you?"

Declan nodded.

"You've been acting like you are in love with her for nearly as long as you've known her. Ah-ah, don't argue. I've seen it first hand, Declan. I don't know if you have been in love with her that long and just didn't realize it, or if that's just how you are with her. It honestly doesn't matter. The point is, don't try to change it. Don't hide it. That's when she'll notice something is up. Which, as I've made very clear, I don't think it's a bad idea if she knows, but if you want to keep your feelings from her... just keep acting how you have been."

"I'm so screwed."

Harry nodded solemnly in agreement. "Yeah, you are."

Anna Katherine was in the kitchen cooking dinner that evening when she heard Declan come home. She called out to him, and he and Fox joined her.

She paused cutting up the vegetables she was planning to roast to look over her shoulder at him. "How was Harry?"

Declan sat at the table and watched her, giving her a small shrug. "The same."

Finished cutting, she turned around, leaning against the counter to really look at him. "You okay? You were quiet all the way home, and you ran out of here as soon as we dropped our bags."

Declan scratched his jaw, then stood up and walked over to her. His eyes roamed over her face, and there was a brief moment when she was sure he was about to kiss her again. When he instead reached around her to pop a bite of the vegetables she had been working on into his mouth, she didn't want to analyze the feeling of disappointment that coiled up in her stomach.

"I'm fine." He gave her one of his endearing and soft smiles. "Promise."

She shoved that strange emotion deep down and nodded. "Well, if you want to talk, you know I'm here."

He reached over and gave her hip a gentle squeeze toward him in a side hug. "Thanks."

"Also, Patricia called. Alex is hosting a family dinner tomorrow night." She turned around so she could focus on the food and not him. "I had to rearrange my shifts, but I figured it out. Does that work for you?"

"Yep. I can go straight there from work."

"Great. Perfect."

Later while they watched a show, they started off on separate ends of the couch. It was only a matter of time before Kit slowly but surely stretched out and made her way over to him. By the end of it, her head was in his lap and she was sound asleep.

Declan checked the time. It was late. He would regret staying up even longer when he had to get up early for work the next day, but he couldn't convince himself to get up. Reluctantly, he allowed himself a few more minutes watching Kit sleep.

He brushed her hair out of her face and smiled when she let out a long breath. His smile disappeared when an intrusive thought bombarded his mind.

You've ruined her life.

He yanked his hand away, glaring at it as if it were to be blamed for all of his problems. He stood up, careful not to disturb or wake her, and pulled a blanket over her before disappearing into his own room and his empty bed.

24

Despite living a short ten minute drive away from her brother, Anna Katherine hadn't been able to spend one-on-one time with him since she had first told him about marrying Declan. Between wedding planning, wedding activities, work, and his studying, there were few chances where their schedules matched up to hang out. So when Alex texted her saying she could come over early, she took him up on his offer.

Alex didn't have any roommates, but he still managed to somehow have a nice, one bedroom apartment that he could afford. It wasn't as nice as hers and Declan's, but it held up against Patricia's critical eye. He lived on the fifth floor, which was a pain since the complex didn't have an elevator, and there was a fire escape by his bedroom window that he sat out on when he was stressed.

When Anna Katherine walked in, slightly out of breath, she was greeted with the sight of her older brother dancing to Hanson while doing some last-minute cleaning. With a laugh, she immediately joined in and started singing along.

When the song ended, they both collapsed on the couch. Alex nudged her with his foot and wiggled his eyebrows. "So, how was the honeymoon?"

"It was fine." She checked her fingernails. "We went to the zoo and aquarium. I had my fill of beignets and live music. I gave Declan those concert tickets I told you about, and he gave me this really sweet and beautiful photobook from the wedding."

"With the pictures Nat and Harry were taking all night?"

She nodded. "Yep."

He gave her a piercing look. "You're hiding something."

She slid lower into the couch. "He kissed me when I gave him the tickets."

There was a beat. "And?"

She fiddled with an unraveled thread on the couch cushion. "Nothing."

"Two things. One, maybe you should talk to Nat about this and not me. Two, I don't believe you when you say 'nothing'."

Anna Katherine sat up then. "It's just frustrating, ya know? I've been friends with him for five years, and during that entire time I have never once felt attracted to him! Not even once! Then he goes and kisses me like that, and now it's all I can think about!" She blows out a breath. "Yesterday I thought he was going to kiss me again. I *wanted* him to kiss me again, but instead he was just reaching over to grab a sweet potato!"

"Right." Alex nodded to himself.

"He's my best friend. This is weird, right?"

Alex snorted. "It's been weird since the beginning."

"But I shouldn't be wanting to kiss him!" She stared up at the ceiling.

"You did marry him, Kit. The lines were sure to get blurry."

"They've never gotten blurred before."

"I think you're in denial."

And then, as if summoned, Declan walked through the door.

"Hey, guys. Sorry for getting here early. It didn't take as long to get here from the office as I thought it would." He gave Anna Katherine a piercing look. "Why do you look like you've just seen a ghost?"

While she spluttered for a response, Alex stood up. Panicked, she turned to her brother. "Where are you going?"

"Gotta order the food."

"You're supposed to be cooking!"

"I ran out of time. Just don't tell Mom, and it'll all be dandy."

Before Anna Katherine could argue further, Declan sat down next to her and patted her knee. "You good?"

She snapped her head back to Declan. "Uh..." She thought back to her conversation with Alex and immediately pushed it out of her mind. "Yeah, I'm good."

When he smiled and her stomach did a somersault, she wondered how right her brother actually was.

Alex ordered from an Italian restaurant, and when the food arrived, Anna Katherine sat on the couch with her legs and arms crossed as she glared at her older brother.

"I cannot believe you are getting out of cooking family dinner and lying to Mom about it."

Alex started taking the food out of the bags. "You're just mad that you never thought to do this before."

"No, I'm annoyed because we all know Mom isn't going to say a word to you about it, even if she does realize it's takeout, but," Anna Katherine huffed, "if I would even think about doing something like this, she'd somehow know even before she got to the door."

Declan stayed quiet, which was probably wise on his part when the two Tran siblings were bickering, but he reached over and gave her shoulder a gentle squeeze.

She sighed and turned her focus on Declan. "Just watch. Patty isn't going to say a word about it."

He laughed, "Whatever you say, love."

"Where is my handsome son-in-law?"

Anna Katherine, Declan, and Alex all looked up from their phones when Timothy and Patricia walked in, looking as put together and preppy as ever.

Anna Katherine stared at her mom. "What am I? Chopped liver?"

Patricia looked right over her. "I just saw you on Saturday. Don't be needy, Anna Katherine."

"You saw Declan, too!"

Thankfully, her dad at least seemed to love her more than Declan. "Kit, you are definitely not chopped liver in my eyes."

She stood up to go give him a hug. "Thanks, Dad."

"Now let me have a look at you. Where's that honeymoon glow?"

Her eyes went wide, and her face immediately grew hot. "*Dad!*"

She heard Alex snort behind her, and she spun around to glare at him. Her entire family was a bunch of traitors.

Patricia was pulling away from hugging Declan, "Honey, you look exhausted." She felt his forehead with the back of her hand. "You're not sick are you? Where's that post-honeymoon glow? Anna Katherine did something, didn't she? I bet she had to pee five times just on the way home."

Anna Katherine shot daggers at Declan. She knew she wasn't going to like how he responded by the way his lips curled into a smirk. "Oh, Patty—"

"No, no. Call me Mom now."

"*Mom,* she peed four times on the way there and then proceeded to get us stuck in traffic."

Anna Katherine went still and squinted her eyes in a glare at Declan. He winced when he saw, and turned back to her mom to say, "But in all seriousness, your daughter was the perfect road trip partner over these past few days, *Mom.*"

She maintained her glare as he walked over to her and kissed her cheek. She didn't hesitate shoving him away. "You're the absolute worst."

"You love me. I'm your husband."

"Don't remind me."

Her dad chuckled behind them. "Oh, young love."

Her three family members walked to the kitchen, and when left alone, she leaned against Declan. "Honeymoon glow?"

He snorted. "How do we even fake that?"

She could feel her face becoming hot again. "I don't think I want to."

He chuckled, placed his hand on her lower back, and led her to the kitchen where the others were waiting.

Anna Katherine was pushing her food around on her plate. Declan nudged her. "Not hungry?"

She shot him a look. "I lost my appetite. Wonder why," she muttered under her breath.

"What was that, Anna Katherine?"

She turned to look at Patty. "What? Nothing. What have you been up to since the wedding, Mom?"

"Well," Patty placed the cloth napkin in her lap, "your father and I have been planning our family Thanksgiving, but we realized we didn't know what your plans were."

She looked up, surprised. "My plans?"

Patricia nodded. "Of course. You're married now. I didn't know if any of Declan's plans would interfere with ours."

"Oh..." She glanced at Declan who was leaning back in his chair smiling.

Thankfully, he had a better response than she did. "We don't have much of a plan, Mrs. Patty. We have our Friendsgiving dinner, but that'll be the Wednesday night before. Whatever you and Timmy have planned will work for us, I'm sure."

Patricia nodded, pleased with the news, "Wonderful. Family will start arriving fairly early, so I would appreciate it if you all came to help out around nine." Anna Katherine nearly spat out her drink when her mom gave a pointed look at Alex. "That means you, too, dear."

Alex looked offended. "When have I ever been late?"

Timothy laughed, and Patricia just gave him another carefully pointed look with raised eyebrows. "Punctuality is not your strong suite. That is one area your sister has you beat."

"I feel like I should be offended, but that was also a compliment so I'm not really sure how to respond."

"No response is necessary, sweetie."

Anna Katherine snapped her mouth closed, and Declan chuckled beside her.

Declan watched as Kit took another bite of her cheesecake, and then swooped in with his own fork, stealing a bite. When she frowned at him, he looked away and did his best to act innocent.

Timmy took his final bite before he asked, "So, how was the honeymoon for the newlyweds?"

Kit choked, and Declan took a moment to rub and pat her back before answering the question. "It was fine. New Orleans in November is much better than the summer months. The humidity was nearly non-existent."

"That's wonderful to hear," Patty said. "How was the bed and breakfast? Was the room up to par?"

He and Kit looked at each other, both of them trying to hide a smile when he remembered the bed situation.

"It was really nice, Mom." Anna Katherine looked down at her plate.

"We can't thank you enough for giving us such a special honeymoon," Declan gave Patty the charming smile he knew she loved.

"Oh, it was nothing, Declan. It was the least we could do for the two of you. A wedding is such a special and important moment in a person's life." Patty took her last bite of cheesecake and placed her utensils and napkin on her plate. "You all will never guess what happened." She barely gave anyone time to guess before she went on. "I was catching up with Susan, and she was telling me this tragic news about her children."

Timmy already looked both enthralled and confused. "Who now?"

"Susan, you know, the new friend I made at the country club."

Timmy nodded, but he still looked unsure. "Oh, right."

"Anyway, her children. She recently found out that they have been laundering money through their four generation family business. Poor Susan has no idea whether to keep acting as if she knows nothing or to go to the authorities."

Declan felt Kit's eyes on him, and he refused to look her way. "Really? That's terrible."

Kit kicked him under the table, and he swatted her leg with his napkin.

"I know, Declan! I'm just so glad that I have you three who would never lie to me about partaking in something illegal. Especially with something that can be so life-altering. You three are too good to me, really."

Declan heard someone kick Kit, and when he looked around, he saw Alex watching the two of them with wide eyes.

Timmy, who was still looking at his wife, took a sip of his wine. "Which family is this again? Do we know the business?"

Patty waved him off, "Oh, I don't know. I don't care about the details, but the *children*."

"Right, right." Timmy nodded. "Those awful children."

Kit straightened up. "Well, Mom, you'll never have to worry about us laundering money since we don't have a family business."

"Right." Patty gave her a thin smile. "Lucky for us."

25

When Declan parked his car beside hers, Anna Katherine jumped out, slamming the door behind her, and pounced on him, desperation lacing her voice. "Declan! She *knows*."

Declan, much to her dismay, took his time gathering their things out of the car and locking it. He finally glanced her way. "What?"

"Patricia knows, Declan!"

"I have no idea what you're going on about."

"Susan! Susan doesn't exist, Declan! My mom doesn't have friends. and she certainly doesn't make *new* friends! She *is* Susan! We're the illegally-laundering, awful children!"

Declan sighed and ran his hand through his hair. "You're overreacting, Kit."

"You're *underthinking* this! What if she goes to..." Anna Katherine trailed off, and then, "Who would she even go to to report an illegal marriage?"

Declan started herding her out of the parking garage and to the elevator. "I don't know. The same people we've been sending all of our documents to, I guess."

"Right. Well, for all we know she has a meeting set up with them tomorrow! Soon you'll be kicked out of the land of the free and I'll be incarcerated. I will literally be living in the land of the free with absolutely no freedom. I can't go to prison, Declan! I'm not cut out for it! I could barely handle timeout as a child!"

He ushered her into the elevator, pressed their button, and waited for the doors to close before turning to face her. "Anna Katherine?"

"What if they're listening right now? What if she already went to them, and that was her second-guessing herself and giving us a clue! What if we just gave them all the information they needed to haul me off?"

The elevator opened with a *ding!* And, once again, Declan was ushering her through the doors, down the hall, and to their door. "Kit?"

"This is it. This is our last night of freedom, and I had to spend it with a mother who turned me in to the Feds."

Declan placed the backpack he had been carrying gently on the floor, and moved so he was facing her. He placed his hands on her shoulders. "Kit?"

She finally looked at him with wide, panicked eyes. "What?"

"Patricia would never turn you in to the Feds, and even if she would, she'd never do that to me."

"This isn't a joke, Declan!"

He smirked. "I know. I wasn't joking. Listen, your mom does not know. Our marriage is perfectly legal and sanctioned as far as she is concerned. Now, take a deep breath."

She followed his directions, and then took another, and another until he nodded. "That's good, love. Now, on the off chance your mother does think that this is a fake and illegal marriage, she has no proof. We've been friends long enough to make anyone think this is legitimate. I'm not going to let anything bad happen to you."

Anna Katherine sucked in a breath. She let her eyes roam over his face and let the familiarities wash over and relax her. Declan brushed her hair out of her face and asked, "Do you trust me?"

She nodded.

"Good. Then trust me when I say everything is going to end up okay for both of us."

She nodded again. "You're right."

And then there was that stupid, cocky smirk of his. "Of course I am, Kit-Kat."

Declan gave her one more reassuring smile, booped her nose, then turned the lock, pushing the door open. As soon as they walked through the doorway, all the serenity that enveloped her while listening to Declan evaporated.

"What the heck?"

Anna Katherine stepped past Declan and looked around their apartment. Shredded trash and rotten food covered nearly every square inch. She spun around to point her finger at Declan. "Your dog did this."

"My dog? She's our dog!"

"You're the one who adopted her without my permission."

He groaned. "Not this again. I thought we had moved past this."

The culprit, Fox Tran-Mullins herself, chose that moment to prance out of Declan's bedroom with an empty paper coffee cup dangling from her mouth.

"Looks like she's picked up your caffeine addiction, Kit."

"This isn't funny. Nothing about tonight has been funny. Where's your phone? This is all Harry's fault."

"Why do you need my phone?" But he was already pulling his phone out of his pocket and handing it to her. "And how is this Harry's fault?"

She snatched the phone out of his hand. "Well, she definitely did not do any of this before you thought it was a good idea for her to stay with *Uncle Harry*." She typed in his passcode and went to his contacts to FaceTime Harry.

Harry picked up almost immediately, "Maaate. How did the—" He stopped. "Oh. Hello, Angry Kit."

"You ruined my dog."

"Oh, now she's your dog." Declan muttered from behind her.

"Declan, what is your wife on about?"

"Don't talk like I'm not right here, Harry! You've completely ruined Fox!"

"How? We had a great time together. I even spoiled her by feeding her some of my leftover steak."

"You gave her *human food*?"

"What's wrong with human food? It's meat. It's not like it's chocolate."

"Oh, Harry." Declan sighed and shook his head as he walked toward the kitchen.

"Harold—"

"Not my name."

"I will never forgive you for this. You are losing custody rights of your god-dog."

Someone giggled, and Harry turned his head around to smile at whoever it was. Anna Katherine stopped what she was about to say, "Wait, who was that?"

Harry turned back to his phone. "Oh, uh, no one."

"No, no. That wasn't no one. I recognized that laugh."

Declan came back into the room then and peered around at the phone. "Does our Harry have a lady friend over?"

"I certainly hope not because that sounded like—"

Another giggle.

"Natalie Thompson!" Anna Katherine was shocked.

"Hey, Nat." Declan waved and then started cleaning.

"Harry, hand the phone to my friend right now." Surprisingly, Harry did as she asked. When Anna Katherine finally saw Nat's face on her screen, she gasped, "It is you!"

"Of course it's me. You've abandoned me to spend all your free time with your husband like a good little wife or something equally ridiculous. What did you expect me to do? Not have any friends?"

"But this is Harry! You hate Harry!"

"Heyy!" Harry protested from off screen.

"Hate might be a strong word. We found common ground in co-parenting you two."

"Co-parenting?" Declan called from where he was digging trash out of the couch cushions. "We're doing just fine on our own!"

Nat rolled her eyes. "Sure, Declan."

Harry snatched his phone back. "Our friendship is none of your concern."

"I wouldn't call it a friendship. More like a... an acquaintance-ship."

"You're not helping, Nat."

"Right. Sorry, sorry. Please go on, H."

"As I was saying, it's none of your business. However, your fake marriage is very much our business."

"You know what?" Anna Katherine scowled at the screen. "I can't deal with either of you right now. I'm hanging up, but I just need you to know that you're both on visitation probation with Fox."

She ended the call, marched up behind Declan, and slid the phone into his back pocket. "I don't like them."

"You love them."

She sighed and sat on the couch. "Maybe, but they're annoying."

"They probably feel the same about us."

She noticed the half full trashbag. "Here. I'll finish. You can go wash up. Patricia wasn't lying when she said you looked exhausted."

Declan rolled his eyes. "Gee, thanks, Kit."

He handed her the bag, and once he had disappeared into the bathroom, Anna Katherine stood up with a long drawn out sigh and began cleaning up Fox's mess.

26

Last night, Anna Katherine had slept in the very crowded spare bedroom. Her boxes of belongings were stacked along the walls and the Christmas tree was still sitting in the corner, looking quite depressing with a sheet over it to keep it from gathering dust. It wasn't really a welcoming bedroom all-in-all. She could take some time to organize it, or there was another option.

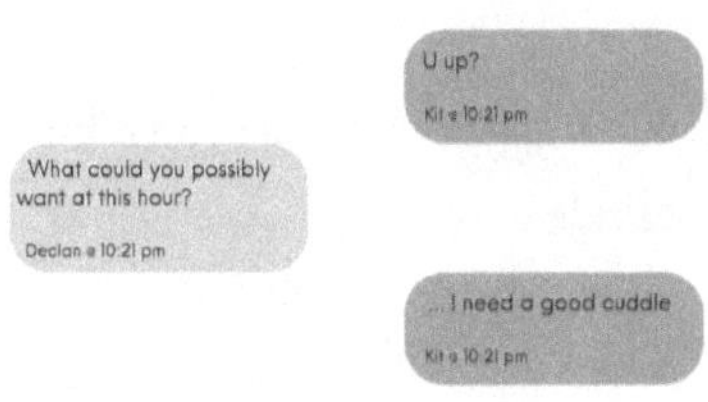

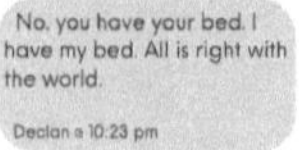

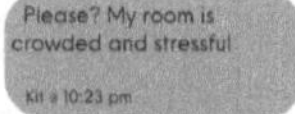

Declan knew that when he didn't immediately reply, she'd eventually show up. She did just that moments later with what he knew to be her favorite pillow. He sighed but patted the bed beside him.

"Do we have to cuddle?"

"I gave you the possibility of citizenship. The least you can do is cuddle me. C for C, Declan."

"Ugh, fine. Just get over here."

She smiled again and shimmied next to him. She was still and quiet for a moment until...

"No, this isn't going to work."

He felt more than saw Kit sit up. He closed his eyes. Maybe if he stayed still, she'd go back to being quiet, but his eyes shot open when she began crawling over him.

"Anna Katherine! What in the world are you doing?"

"I can't sleep on that side of the bed. It feels weird." She crawled the rest of the way over and pushed at his side. "Scoot over. I don't have enough room."

"You had plenty of room before you decided to invade my space."

"Declan!" She slapped his arm.

"Ow! Okay, I'm going! Sheesh."

He scooted over, and she wiggled and squirmed, until, finally, she was still.

"Better?"

"Yes." She wiggled over to him and got as close as she could, resting her head in the crook of his arm and slipping her feet between his legs.

"Are you wearing socks?"

"My feet get cold."

"Do you ever stop being weird?"

"Leave me alone and go to sleep, Declan."

Eventually, with her curled against his side and Fox curled up at the end of the bed, they all fell asleep.

Anna Katherine woke up when the first of Declan's many alarms went off. She squeezed her eyes shut and tightened her grip on Declan.

"Kit."

"No."

"If you want me to turn the alarm off, you're going to have to let me go."

"M'comfortable."

She could feel the vibrations in his chest when he chuckled. Reluctantly, she loosened her grip on him, and he rolled over to press snooze. When he rolled back and wrapped his arms around her, she hummed happily.

The second time Anna Katherine woke up, she kept patting Declan. "Turn that thing off."

"I would, but it's yours this time, love."

She groaned and pulled away from his warmth to blindly pat around the bed for her phone.

"What?" She held the phone to her ear, not bothering to look at who was calling.

"I see you're still not a morning person."

Her eyes flew open at the sound of the voice, and when she pulled the phone away to look at the number, she fully woke up. "Jonah?"

He laughed. "The one and only. I didn't wake you up did I?"

Declan gave her a curious look, but she shook her head as she slid out of the bed and slipped from the room.

"No, uh, we were already getting up."

"We? Oh, yeah. I'm guessing the wedding went well?"

"Of course." She leaned against the wall in the hallway and rested her hand against her forehead. "Why are you calling, Jonah?"

"Right. I have a client who hired me to revamp their site. They're in desperate need of some updated photos for it. You were the first one to come to mind."

Anna Katherine didn't know if she was speechless because of how early it was, because her ex was calling her for the first time since they parted ways two and a half years ago, *or* if it was because he was offering her a job.

Or, maybe she was still processing the fact that she forced herself into Declan's bed last night like a maniac.

She swallowed, and she was really wishing she had time to drink a cup of coffee before this conversation. "You want to hire me?"

"Yeah." And then as if second-guessing himself. "Unless it would be too weird for us to work together."

"Even if it was, I'd do it for the money."

He chuckled. "Figured. So you'll do it?"

She squeezed her eyes shut. She couldn't believe she was about to agree to work with Jonah. "Yeah."

"Awesome. I'll send you an email with all the details, and we can set up a time for a meeting. Is your email still the same?"

She nodded before remembering he couldn't see her. "Yeah, it's the same."

"Alright, I'll send it to you today. I'll let you get back to sleep now. Bye, Anna Katherine."

Before she could respond, the line went dead.

She was resting her hands against the counter while watching the coffee drip into the pot when Declan came up behind her, resting his hand on the small of her back as he reached around her to get a mug of his own.

"You're not going back to bed?"

She shook her head. "Jonah offered me a job."

When she turned around, she reveled in the feeling of his hand trailing over her back. Looking up at him, she was caught off guard by how tender he looked with his bedhead and half-asleep smile.

"You gonna take it?"

She shrugged and nodded. "Can't say no to a job."

When he just hummed, she asked, "What?"

He took a step away from her and shrugged himself. "You don't think it's interesting that he comes begging you to take a job weeks after he found out we were getting married?"

She pulled herself up to sit on the counter. "Are you jealous, Declan Mullins?"

He laughed, "No." He poured her a cup of the brew before pouring himself some. "I might be a little overprotective, though."

She just stared at him.

He sighed, wrapping his hands around his mug. "I don't want him to hurt you again, Kit."

"He doesn't have that kind of power over me anymore." She reached her leg out to poke him with her toes. "You don't have to worry about me."

"Maybe not." He shrugged. "But I'm going to anyway."

Anna Katherine watched as he walked back to his bedroom. And she definitely was not intrigued by the way his muscles moved beneath his thin white shirt.

27

The week of Thanksgiving came with a rush of fall decorations, festivals, and pumpkin pie.

"If I see another pumpkin pie, it'll be too soon." Declan went face down on the table with a groan.

Anna Katherine paused while whipping meringue for her lemon pie "You know you don't have to eat a slice every time you see one, right?"

"That," Declan said, lifting his head slightly, "is where you are mistaken. I must eat all the pumpkin."

"Then I don't want to hear you complaining."

"I get absolutely no sympathy? I'm hurt." He stood up and on his way toward her, he eyed the other three pies that were already finished. "Why are you baking so many pies anyway?"

"We have a standing mixer now, Declan. This is our contribution as a married couple. Plus—" She turned and pointed the whisk at him, "—this is how I show my love."

He stuck out his bottom lip. "Why don't you make more pies for me then?"

"Because I obviously don't love you," she teased.

He poked her in retaliation, and while she was distracted, he stuck his finger in the meringue for a taste.

"Declan!" she screeched, and he laughed, wiping some of the meringue onto her cheek. "You're about to be banished from the kitchen," she fumed.

He went for another swipe, and she waved the whisk at him, splattering him with meringue. He tried to duck out the way, but reached around, grabbing her by the waist and spinning her around.

"Declan Mullins! Put me down!"

"Not until you tell me you love me."

"You're ruining my meringue!"

"You're ruining my heart."

She hit his shoulder. "I refuse to say it."

He lifted her up again and carried her to their couch, dumping her onto it and staring down at her in an attempt to look menacing. He ended up just looking adorable.

"Tell me you love me or I'll tickle you until you pee yourself again."

"That was one time and you promised to never bring it up, ever."

He started to tickle her, but she squealed and wiggled out of his way. "Fine! I love you, I love you, I love you!"

When he pulled away with a smirk, she glared at him. "Happy?"

"More than you know," he said as he walked away. He wondered what it meant that his heart constricted at the thought of being able to hear those three words from her every day. He shook his head, ridding himself of that troublesome thought.

Anna Katherine unbuckled her seatbelt when Declan parked the car. He glanced at the backseat with a raised eyebrow. "You don't think you went overboard with the pies?"

"We've already talked about this."

As she stepped from the car, Nat pulled up beside them. "I have the deviled eggs and potato salad!" she called out as she closed her door, her hands already full of covered dishes.

"I don't think you needed to bring anything, Nat." Declan waved her off. "This woman here apparently thinks we're feeding an army with pies."

Nat peered through the window and saw all the pies stacked in the backseat. "Nice. I'm guessing the standing mixer works well?"

"Like a dream!" Anna Katherine grinned proudly.

Declan snorted. "Kit, stop being obsessed about kitchen appliances and come help me carry these."

Anna Katherine, after making a show of rolling her eyes to Nat, did as he asked. She stacked four pies up in his arms, and took the last one for herself.

Declan raised an eyebrow. "Really?"

She shrugged "You seem to be handling the others just fine."

Together the three of them took the elevator to Harry's apartment, and Nat grabbed the key he had hidden beneath a dead cactus to unlock the door.

Anna Katherine watched curiously. "You've really been making yourself at home here, haven't you?"

"I'm going to be dropping these pies if we don't get that door open."

Nat, ignoring Anna Katherine's comment, pushed the door open, and when she saw Harry wearing an apron in the kitchen she said, "I still don't understand why you're the one hosting Friendsgiving. You're not even American."

Harry looked utterly ridiculous in the apron with his hands on his hips. "I can still love this country, Natalie"

"Don't use my full name against me, Halford."

"Not my name." He gave her a questioning look. "Also, that name is new and came out of nowhere."

When she simply shrugged, he smirked. "You've been Googling names to call me, haven't you?"

"It means nothing if I did."

Harry chuckled and shook his head. "Sure. Keep telling yourself that."

Anna Katherine looked between the two of them. "It's the same bickering, but the underlying hate is missing," she remarked to her husband. "Look, Nat is even smiling. It's so weird."

"Anna Katherine Marie, come grab these pies or so help me…"

"Oh, right." She placed her one pie on the counter and then rushed to grab two more from Declan. "Sorry."

Harry's eyes widened at all the pies. "Geez, Kit."

Nat swatted his arm. "She has a standing mixer now. You should've seen this coming."

Harry looked over at Declan, who just shrugged. "Don't look at me, mate. It's just as baffling to me as it is to you."

"Right, well let's try to find room for all these pies then."

Harry had to rearrange his fall decorations, but eventually they had room for all of her pies. Once the food was all settled and he checked the turkey in the oven, they all gathered in his living room. Nat was in one of his overstuffed chairs with a blanket, looking completely comfortable in Harry's space.

He sat beside her on the arm of the chair, and without looking up from her phone, she shoved him off.

"Fine, I'll just sit on the floor then."

"Good."

"See if I ever buy you tacos again."

Nat didn't pay any attention to Harry or his comment, but looked up at Anna Katherine and Declan. "Hey, Kit. What time should I get to your parent's place tomorrow?"

Harry looked up too. "Oh, yeah! My first Tran family Thanksgiving!"

Confused, Anna Katherine asked, "What? Who said you two were coming?"

"Your mom!" Nat stated like it was obvious. "I think she still thinks I'm dating Alex, but I don't know why she invited Harry."

"Because I'm delightful as, mate."

Nat grimaced. "Sure, H."

"I can't believe she invited the two of you and didn't tell me."

"We're getting there at nine, so anytime after that I'm sure will be fine," Declan added helpfully.

"Thank you, *Declan*."

Anna Katherine stuck her tongue out at all of them.

Mack was the next to arrive with her famous creamed corn. William and Wesley showed up together with William's homemade sourdough bread, courtesy of his grandmother's recipe, and Wesley's store bought ham with a large can of green beans under his arm.

"We were supposed to bring homemade items, Wes," Harry scolded when he saw what Wesley had brought.

He quoted what had been his response for the last four Friendsgivings. "Unless the lot of you want to leave here with food poisoning, you will never ask me to cook ever again."

Once the turkey was ready, they all sat around Harry's table which had an overflowing cornucopia of leaves, squash, and pine cones for decor. Declan made sure he was seated by Kit.

"You really went over the top this year, didn't you, H?" Mack commented, giving the table's centerpiece a cautious eye.

"It's our last year all together and my first year hosting. Of course I did!"

Everyone looked around the table. William was the one to ask, "Wait, which one of us is leaving?"

Wesley, for possibly the first time in his entire life, looked sheepish. "I was going to tell you all after dinner, but Harry and his big mouth..."

Declan looked ecstatic. "You took the job in Dublin?!"

"Of course I did. I love it here, but I've been missing home a little more lately. Dublin will be just a hop and a skip away from Manchester."

There was a chorus of congratulations from everyone. Wesley seemed genuinely happy when he smiled and said, "Thanks, guys."

Harry clapped his hands. "Alright, this is a perfect segue for my favorite part of the holiday."

Everyone around the table groaned. "Not again, Harry!"

"We will now go around the table and say one thing we are all thankful for before we are allowed to eat."

Nat gave him a deadpan look. "I'm thankful for the day you finally stop talking."

Harry ignored her. "Wesley, you can go first."

"I'm thankful I can buy canned food so I don't have to cook."

"Amen to that."

"Guys!" Harry looked genuinely upset. "I'm serious about this."

Mack gave him sympathy. "Fine, I'll go. I'm thankful that Martin hired me and my job allowed me to meet Kit and the rest of you."

"Aw." Harry looked more than pleased. "There we go. We're off to a wonderful start."

Wesley rolled his eyes but was a good sport. "I guess I'm thankful that I got the job."

"And I'm thankful for Harry taking his hosting job so seriously," William added.

"I recognize that this is you kissing butt, but I will allow it."

"Alright." Wesley looked at Declan and Kit. "What about the happy couple?"

Declan was about to say his, but Kit beat him to it. "I'm just really thankful for Declan." When she looked at him and he saw genuineness instead of her typical mocking, his stomach dropped. "I always thought that whoever would marry him would be lucky, I just never thought that it would be me."

Over the ridiculous cornucopia, Declan noticed Harry and Nat sharing a look, but he couldn't find it in himself to care. All his attention was on Kit.

He was partially aware of the table verbally reacting as he leaned over to kiss her. He told himself it was for the act, but he knew he wouldn't have been able to resist kissing her if he had tried.

When she sighed and leaned into him, he once again thought that this woman was going to ruin him for anyone else.

He pulled away, and he couldn't look at her soft smile for one second more. He turned his attention to Nat, who was going on about how she was thankful for her kids or some other aspect of her job, but his mind was elsewhere.

Later that night, after eating too much dressing and turkey and laughing so hard their stomachs ached, Anna Katherine found herself on the couch with Declan watching *Married at First Sight* yet again.

When Declan put his arm around her and pulled her close, Anna Katherine happily obliged and snuggled into his side.

"Well, we did it," he said after a moment. "One Thanksgiving dinner down, one to go."

She chuckled. "Maybe we'll survive this after all."

"All while convincing people we're a happily married, in-love couple who definitely did not get married just to get one of them a green card."

This time, she full out laughed, gripping her sides. Once she calmed down, she tilted her head up to look at him. "You know, I meant what I said."

When he looked confused, she went on. "About what I was thankful for.

All of it. I really meant it."

There was a brief moment when Anna Katherine could have sworn he must have been thinking about kissing her again, but instead he just whispered, his voice a little husky, "For once you weren't mocking our marriage."

"Well," she said, trying not to giggle, "It's usually very mockable."

He smiled and turned his attention back to the screen.

She poked his side. "You never said what you were thankful for."

Declan cut his eyes at her. "I feel like you covered all our bases."

"Declan."

"Anna Katherine."

"Tell me." When he still only looked at her, she smiled. "You're thankful that your wife is drop-dead gorgeous, right?"

He laughed and ruffled her hair. "Yeah, something like that."

She gave him an encouraging look, and he sighed, "I'm thankful that you know me well enough and cared enough to get us the Fleetwood Mac tickets." He rubbed the back of his neck. "Made my gift look like crap."

Anna Katherine pulled away and stared at him. "What?"

"What, what?"

"Your gift isn't crap, Declan!" She took his hand in hers. "It means so much. You know how much our friends and our memories mean to me. To know someone sees me like you do is both terrifying and something I never thought I'd want."

He pulled her against him, and when she leaned in, he kissed the top of her head. "Good to know all that late-night and early-morning work paid off."

Anna Katherine hid her smile against his sweater. She was happy and more content than she could ever remember being. She didn't want to be anywhere else except here, next to Declan, watching one of the most ridiculous shows.

28

"**I** cannot believe there are three pies leftover," Anna Katherine grumbled.

"This is what happens when you make five pies for a dinner of seven people."

She shoved a pie at Declan's chest. "Shut up and take these pies."

"Why am I carrying all three of them? What are you carrying?"

"I've been carrying this entire relationship on my shoulders. It's time you put in some effort."

"Oh," Declan scoffed. "Is that how you see it?"

She nodded, already headed up the driveway and toward her childhood home. "Yep."

She heard him mutter behind her, but she smiled when he still followed closely behind her.

Patricia was already at the door ready to take their coats when they arrived on the front porch. "Oh my goodness, look at the two of you, matching and everything!"

Declan and Anna Katherine looked at each other, not realizing they were coordinating till Patricia had pointed it out. "Oh, yeah. Oops."

They were both wearing black pants and white shoes, and where Declan was wearing a black shirt and a burnt orange cardigan, Anna Katherine was also wearing a black shirt but with a flannel over top in a very similar coloring to Declan's sweater.

"This is not an 'oops.' This is adorable," Patricia waved them in. "Timothy! Get the camera. We need to document their first Thanksgiving as a married couple."

"We've had plenty of Thanksgivings together, Mom. Did you forget that he's been coming to these things for the last four years?"

"As a married couple, I said."

"Whatever." She shrugged out of her coat and took the pies from Declan so he could do the same.

Patricia eyed the pies, "I didn't know you were contributing this year, dear."

Declan laughed. "She didn't mean to. She just went overboard with the pies for our Friendsgiving."

"Ah," Patricia nodded. "I take it you're enjoying the new standing mixer, Anna Katherine?"

"Of course I am. I don't know why people find this surprising. I've been talking about owning one long before we even got it."

She ignored Declan's eye roll.

"Right. Just don't forget to send out your thank you cards in a timely manner."

Anna Katherine sighed, "Yes, Mother."

Striding through the foyer, Anna Katherine spotted her brother in the kitchen and dramatically checked her phone for the time. "Are we late?"

"Ha. Ha." Alex stuck his tongue out at her. "Since I was so rudely called out at family dinner, I got here a half hour early."

"Ignore your brother," Patricia sighed. "He's in one of his moods. He got all grouchy when I told him Nat was coming. Are they fighting?"

Anna Katherine laughed, enjoying this small moment when she wasn't the one under her mom's scrutiny. "I don't thi—"

"I'm not grouchy, Mom!" Alex called from the kitchen. "I just wish you would have asked me before you invited my *girlfriend*."

With Patty's back to him, Alex's eyes widened. And just like that, Anna Katherine understood. Thankfully, their dad saved any further conversation about Alex and Nat 'dating.'

Her dad bumped his shoulder with hers, a wide smile on his face, "I heard a camera was needed?"

Without being asked, Declan took the pies back from her so she could hug her dad.

While wrapped in his arms, she heard her mom say, "Oh, dear. Let me take those from you, Declan. You must be so tired from holding them."

Anna Katherine just grumbled. "I'm going to need another cup of coffee."

Once again, without being asked, Declan appeared with a steaming fresh mug of coffee moments later. She smiled at him in thanks. Then they were kicked out of the kitchen by Patricia who told them to watch the Macy's Day Parade.

As the morning went on, aunts, uncles, and cousins slowly started to trickle in. Eventually, she and Declan were pulled away from each other to be bombarded with questions about their wedding and honeymoon by over-nosey relatives.

Her Great Aunt Jeannie was sipping on a glass of wine, despite it being only ten in the morning. "Kitty, I have been so worried that you would never find a husband."

Anna Katherine watched her Aunt Jeannie with careful eyes. "I am only twenty-five, Aunt Jeannie. Even if I wasn't married to Declan, I would still have plenty of time."

"Yes, but your eggs!"

Anna Katherine choked on her coffee. She caught Declan's gaze from where he was sitting with the other men. "Uh, what about them?"

"If you don't start having children soon, they'll shrivel up and die."

"I don't think that's exactly scientific." She purposefully turned her back to Declan so she couldn't see him laughing at her.

"Maybe not, but the point still holds."

"And what's that point?" Patty appeared out of nowhere.

"Aunt Jeannie," Anna Katherine started, "is telling me about her worries that my eggs will shrivel up and die."

Jeannie turned to her Patty. "Aren't you ready for grandchildren from these two, Pat?"

"Of course I am, especially since Alex doesn't seem concerned with providing me with that ultimate joy of life."

Anna Katherine gave her mom a pointed look.

"But, as much as I would love to see little Declan and Anna Katherines running around, we need to let them get to that on their own time."

"Thanks, Mom."

Patty patted her shoulder. "No need for a thanks, sweetie."

Before Anna Katherine could get another comment in, Harry and Nat come waltzing through the door. She stared at them for a moment, taking in Harry's attire: an obnoxiously orange sweater with a giant turkey on the front paired with the tightest black jeans she'd ever seen.

"Harry, what are you wearing?"

He looked down at his clothes. "Nat got it for me! Isn't it great?"

Nat looked like she could kill him. "As a joke. I didn't think he would actually wear it."

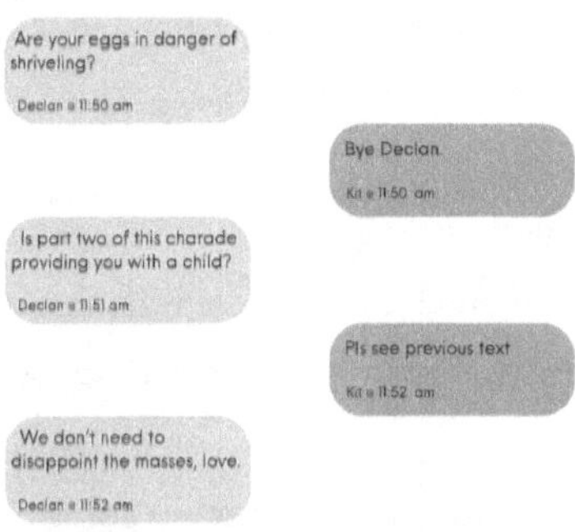

"Why are you smiling like that, Anna Katherine?"

She quickly turned her screen off so her mom wouldn't be able to see her texts with Declan. "Oh, nothing. Just, uh, Mack catching me up on her holiday family drama."

Patricia didn't look convinced. "Hm, okay."

Anna Katherine retreated to the kitchen to see what Harry and Nat had brought in the Crockpot they had carried in.

"You have to try my apple cider!" Harry immediately forced her to take a cup.

Nat laughed, her own cup in hand. "He even brought his own cinnamon sticks."

"Of course he did," Anna Katherine laughed and took a sip. "Surprisingly good, H."

He preened. "Thank you. Couldn't come empty handed to my first Tran family Thanksgiving."

"I came empty handed, but that was because my hands were too full making sure you behaved yourself."

"Yes, but Nat, this isn't your first Tran family Thanksgiving."

"Actually, it is."

"What? How?"

"Patricia and this so-called friend of ours never invited me. Plus, I usually have my own family dinner to go to, but this year my troublesome parents abandoned me to go on a cruise."

"But Declan is invited every year."

"I know, and you have no idea how much that has irked me, Harry."

Anna Katherine startled when someone came up behind her and placed their hand on her hip.

Declan leaned in close to whisper, "Are we going to give Aunt Jeannie what she wants?"

"Shut up before my mom hears you!" she hissed, spinning around to glare at him. "Or our friends. They'd be even more impossible than normal."

He shrugged, not appearing sorry in the least. "Just trying to give the people what they want, *Kitty*."

She groaned, "I don't want that. No one wants that."

He smirked. "Aunt Jeannie wants it."

"Aunt Jeannie is senile. We don't pay attention to anything she says."

Harry poked his head between them. "Who is senile? What do we want?"

"Kit wants children." Declan and that stupid smirk of his.

"Shut up, Declan! I do not!"

"It's okay, Kit." Nat came and put a hand on her shoulder. "Wanting to create a beautiful life with your husband is nothing to be ashamed of. It's the obvious next step."

Kit felt the heat radiating off her cheeks. "I strongly dislike all three of you right now."

Before she could walk away, Declan grabbed her arm and pulled her back. Her eyes went wide when he put a loud, wet kiss on her cheek. "We all know you'll want to see me tonight for a good cuddle."

Harry looked ecstatic, Nat, concerned. Harry was all too gleeful when he asked, "I'm sorry, has there been nightly cuddling we weren't made aware of?"

"Why on earth would we tell you guys if there were?"

"Because," Harry said, taking a sip of his apple cider, "We're the managers of this relationship."

Anna Katherine yanked her arm out of Declan's hand with a loud groan and stormed out of the kitchen.

After wandering around the house for a moment, she finally found refuge outside with a few of her cousins. She stayed out there enjoying the fresh air and quiet away from her friends for as long as everyone allowed her. When her six-year-old cousin climbed into her lap, Anna Katherine held her close.

"Kitty?"

"Hm?"

"What is it like being married to Declan?"

Anna Katherine chuckled. "Well, he gives me cuddles whenever I want them, and he takes the trash out without being asked. And, the best part is, whenever he knows I feel down, he buys me mint chocolate chip ice cream."

Olivia sighed. "That sounds amazing. Are you ever going to break up with him?"

Anna Katherine choked on nothing. "What? Why would you ask that?"

"I think I'm in love with him."

Her eyes went wide, and then she let out a loud laugh. "Well, if I ever get tired of him, I'll send him your way. Deal?"

Olivia beamed, "Deal!" before she slid off Anna Katherine's lap.

More aunts and uncles came out into the yard, invading her peace, and Anna Katherine went back inside. It didn't take her long to spot Declan on the couch watching the parade with one little cousin sound asleep against him and another sitting in his lap talking about the balloons appearing on the screen.

She leaned against the wall and watched as Declan nodded and gave her little cousins his undivided attention. Eventually, he noticed her watching and gave her a soft smile and wave. He lifted little Miles off of his lap, and stood up, careful not to wake Lyla who was still sound asleep. He leaned against the wall facing her. "Missed me?"

She shrugged. "Your company is better than anyone else's here."

He smirked, but they were interrupted by Harry running and frantically sliding to a stop beside them, his eyes wide. "I think Patricia is drunk."

Declan stood in the middle of the kitchen next to Kit while she watched her mom spoon another cup of Harry's *spiked* apple cider into her mug. "Harry, what have you done to my mother?"

"I thought everyone knew it was spiked!" he hissed back.

Declan placed his hand on her arm, sensing she was about to go off on their friend. He did his best to sound more concerned than annoyed. "How were we supposed to know if you didn't tell us, H?"

Nat, who was sitting on the counter top, said, "In his defense, he didn't know that you guys usually don't put alcohol in your cider."

"We make it all the time back home! And it's always spiked!"

Patricia came over to their small huddle. "Kit, I don't know why you're so stressed. Maybe you should have some more of Harry's apple cider. It's to die for!"

Kit tried to take the mug away from her. "I think you've had enough, Mom."

Patricia slapped her hand away. "I'm a grown adult. I know full well when I have had enough, and I have certainly not reached that point yet."

Declan fought to hold in a laugh.

Finally, all the food was ready and everyone was sitting at the table. Even with the younger cousins sitting at the kid's table, the dining room table was as full as Anna Katherine had ever seen it. Timothy led them in a prayer before they all dug in.

Uncle Sherman looked over at her and Declan. "I'm devastated you all wanted a small wedding and we couldn't attend, Kit. I was so looking forward to it. How was it?"

Anna Katherine opened her mouth to respond, but Patricia beat her to it. "Oh, Sherman. It was *wonderful.* I have been waiting for this day ever since I saw that picture of the two of them at the football game all those years ago. I tried to convince Anna Katherine to break up with Jonah then and there." She leaned across the table as if to tell a secret, "We all knew he was bad news."

Declan eyed Anna Katherine. "Did she really?"

She nodded, too shocked to say anything else.

When Aunt Jeannie spoke, Anna Katherine knew none of this would end well for her. "How long have they been dating?"

"Oh, just a few months according to them. But if you ask me, which you did, I'd say they've been dating for years. They just didn't know it."

"Mom!"

Patricia ignored her. "Kitty has been in love with this boy for so long. I was getting tired of waiting for either of them to make a move. I was about ready to do something about it myself."

Anna Katherine looked on in horror, but she couldn't help but ask, "What could you have possibly done?"

Her mom leaned back in her chair and shrugged, taking another sip of Harry's life-ruining apple cider. "I had a few plans up my sleeve. I just love looking at the pictures from your wedding. You looked so in love. It truly makes my mother's heart soar."

"Mom!"

"What? I know you don't like people knowing you, but there's nothing wrong with being in love with your husband."

Declan squeezed her knee and whispered in her ear, "Yeah, I'm your husband. You're supposed to be in love with me."

Anna Katherine glared at him, and then stuffed a bite of turkey in her mouth. She did her best to ignore Patricia narrating her apparent love for

Declan, but it was more difficult than she would have liked.

Once everyone had eaten their fill of food, Anna Katherine marched over to Harry. "This is all your fault!"

"Kit, I—"

Nat walked over to join them, "Aw, c'mon, Kit. Get off his back. It was an innocent mistake, and we all know Patricia would've made some kind of ridiculous comment with or without the help of liquor."

Anna Katherine was so surprised that her best friend defended Harry, that she forgot her annoyance. Anna Katherine blinked, and when Harry winked at Nat, she was truly caught off guard.

"I..." She looked between the two of them. "You know what? I'm going to go find my husband." And she walked off without another word.

On the night of Black Friday, Nat once again found herself on Harry's couch. When he handed her a plate of leftover turkey and dressing, he asked, "Did we realize that when our best friends committed their whole lives together that we were also committing ourselves to this friendship?"

"Definitely not." Nat stabbed the turkey with her plastic fork. "And I'm only here because you invited me."

"And I only invited you because you called to ask what I was doing tonight."

"And I only called because I am panicked over Kit and Declan!"

"Can I just say that I don't believe you, and I think you came over here because you actually enjoy my company?"

"No."

"Hm. Okay." He slowly chewed his food before pointing his fork at Nat. "Patricia."

"What about her?"

"Was she spitting out some truth, or was that the cider talking? Was Kit really in love with Declan this whole time?"

"I don't know. I don't think Kit even knows." Nat pulled her legs up to her chest. "There's a lot Kit isn't even admitting to herself right now."

"Like?"

"Like being attracted to Declan. She didn't even tell me she kissed his cheek as thanks for the gift, which is something so miniscule. If I didn't know her well enough, I'd think she was embarrassed. But she's not. She's scared. Proof number one she is hiding something."

"What is proof number two?"

Nat shrugged. "Dunno, but I'm sure it exists. Now, tell me about Declan and how he's in love with my best friend."

"I refuse to gossip about him."

"This isn't a gossip sesh. This is two friends being concerned about their other friends."

"Ha! You just said we were friends"

Nat rolled her eyes. "Fine, we're friends. Now was Declan being serious?"

"I've never seen him more gone over a girl before."

"Well, crap."

"You can say that again."

"Crap."

29

Declan rarely received calls at work. Mostly because all of his friends had the typical 9-5 job as well, and if Kit ever needed anything, she texted him. So when she did call that morning, his heart rate almost sky-rocketed as his mind raced with possible scenarios, each one more horrible than the last.

He answered it on the second ring. "Kit? You okay?"

"No, I'm not okay!"

"What's wrong?"

"I have the meeting with Jonah today. It's going to be so awkward. I mean, these meetings always are, but this time I'm meeting with my *ex*, Declan!"

As dramatic as she was being, Declan was just glad it wasn't anything more serious. "See, I knew I needed to be worried."

"Declan!" she whined. "Help me!"

"And what do you want me to do?"

"I don't know! But anything would be better than this."

"Kit." He twirled around in his chair so he was looking out his small window. "Just take some deep breaths, take Fox for a walk, and don't overthink this."

"I already am overthinking this."

"You're ridiculous, and I need to get back to work."

"But I'm—"

"Nope. Bye, Kit. I love you."

"Love you too, you jerk," she mumbled right before he ended the call.

A coworker looked on in sympathy. "Is the wife being difficult today?"

Declan laughed, "When is she not?"

The café Jonah told her to meet him at was completely decked out for Christmas. At her work, they had a miniature tree sitting in the corner of the counter beside the espresso machine, and she and Declan had put up their own tree last night. Still, somehow Christmas felt so far off despite it being only a little over a week away. She thought it probably had a lot to do with how it had still been in the high sixties until this morning. Now the wind finally had a bite to it, her nose felt raw, and that combined with the decorations of the restaurant made it feel a little bit more like the Christmas season.

She was about to order her coffee when her phone vibrated in her pocket.

You're one of the best photographers I know You're insanely good at what you do Dont be worried about anyone not liking your work Bc theyd be insane not to I believe in you and you've got this. Also, dont forget to breathe

Declan @ 10:58 am

She smiled as she sent him back a heart emoji. With a deep breath, she pocketed her phone and walked toward the one and only man who had ever broken her heart, feeling much more at ease than she did before Declan's text.

As she sat across from Jonah, it felt like she was thrown back in time before she was married to Declan, before Jonah broke her, and before the college tossed her out into adulthood with nothing more than a flimsy sheet of paper telling her the lie that she was ready.

"So," Jonah started. "How have you been?"

There was a paper snowflake dangling above Jonah's head. She was staring at it, but when Jonah asked that question, she lazily flicked her eyes to him. "We're not doing the small talk, Jonah."

"Alright. You're in one of your moods then."

"I'm not in a mood, but if I was, it would be because I have to be here sitting across from you." She was proud of herself for saying that with an even tone. Her voice might have sounded controlled, but at least her true emotions didn't leak through.

"So much hostility toward the person who is offering you a job."

"I mean..." she went to grab her things. "I could just leave."

He reached out to grab her hand. "No. I'm sorry. We can keep this professional."

She sat back down. "Good." She reached for her bag. "I brought my portfolio like you asked."

"Perfect." He smiled in a disarming fashion, and Anna Katherine wasn't phased by it like she might have once been. "I'll be sure to bring this to the next meeting we have with the client."

"Who is?"

"The city."

For a moment—a brief moment—Anna Katherine was speechless, "And you didn't think I should have known who our client was from the beginning?"

"I might've forgotten to mention it."

"*Might've*, he says." She rolled her eyes.

"I thought you'd love this opportunity."

"Obviously I do, but I just don't like being surprised," she bit back. "Which, with our history, you should've known about me."

"Sorry?"

Anna Katherine took a deep breath. She reminded herself that this job was a great opportunity for herself, and she would be an immature idiot to allow Jonah to ruin it for her. "Okay, tell me more about this project."

"They want to revamp the city's website and social media. Really highlight the areas in town and family-friendly activities that would bring in a new wave of the younger generation."

As he went on, Anna Katherine nodded as she took notes.

Anna Katherine waved at Mike, the security guard for Declan's building, on her way to his office. When Mike saw her, he smiled and waved back. "Good afternoon, Miss Anna. I haven't seen you in a while."

She dug around in her purse to find the container of mints she always brought him. "Been busy with the wedding and the holidays, you know. And, as always, here you go."

"Such an angel. I suppose it's Mrs. Anna now. Declan is one lucky fella."

She smiled again and stepped toward the elevator. "Thank you, Mike. I'll be sure to stop by on my way out to say good-bye."

"You better!"

Declan surprised her when he was waiting for her as the elevator doors opened. She eyed him up and down, appreciating how the cardigan he was wearing hugged his shoulders.

As she leaned in for a hug, she asked, "How did you know?"

She could hear the smile in Declan's voice when he responded. "Mike gave me a ring on the intercom. I've never seen that man care about someone as much as he does you."

"I buy his love with the good mints and better lattes."

"Ah. The secret finally comes out."

When he stepped beside her onto the elevator, she gave him a questioning glance.

"Thought you wouldn't want my nosey coworkers hearing all about your messy ex."

"Ah, always the perfect husband."

He laughed. "I try."

Declan led them back to the first floor and out the back of the building, where she was surprised to find tables, chairs, and umbrellas with even a grassy area.

"Why have we never eaten out here before?" She picked a random table and put down their food and drinks.

Declan shrugged. "It's not like you come here that often."

"I come here enough for Mike to love me."

"Okay, fine. It's not like you stay long enough for me to show you anything."

"Yeah, that's fair."

Anna Katherine began to unpack their food, handing Declan his rolls and extra spicy mayo. "I don't know how you can eat that stuff. It gives me heartburn." She frowned at his smirk. "Yes, I recognize how old that makes me sound. Let's not dwell on it."

"Whatever you say, dear." He popped a bite in his mouth, "Alright, so tell me about Jonah."

She immediately launched into the story of her meeting with her ex. She got so into it that she nearly forgot to eat until Declan motioned for her to take a bite before continuing. She was at the part where she threatened to leave the café, when Declan stood up, shrugged out of the gray cardigan he was wearing, and placed it on her shoulders.

She stopped mid-sentence, and he shrugged. "You were shivering."

"I was not."

"You were. Now keep going. I don't have much longer on my break."

"But now you're going to get cold."

"I'm fine, Kit."

She gave him a wary glance, but pulled his soft cardigan closer around her before continuing her story. After she finished telling him about the revamping the city wanted to do and how the rest of the meeting went, they lulled into a comfortable silence.

It was only when Declan kept glancing at her that she spoke up again. "What is it?"

"You're not going to like it."

She took a sip of her drink. "Tell me anyway."

He looked up at her, and a slow smile crept across his face, "So, there's this thing..."

"No." She shook her head, already knowing where he was going with this. "I will not."

"It's not like the typical quarterly get together. It'll be for the holidays and New Years, too."

She tried whining, "I don't want to, Declan."

It didn't seem to work on him this time. "It's in our marriage contract, and I need you to make me look good."

"Declan..."

"C'mon, please. You always look so beautiful when you come with me to these things, and my boss's wife adores you." He reached across the table and took her hand in both of his. "Come on. Come with me. You always say you make it worse in your head than it actually is."

"They're just always so dry and boring."

"There's going to be music and food and awards given out this time. Plus, William will be there."

"Free food?"

He nodded. "And dessert."

She tried one more time. "But you said the alternative to coming to your work events was coming to lunch with you at the office. And look—" She motioned to herself, "—here I am!"

"First, this is the first time you've been here in the month we've been married, and the alternative was coming weekly. Second, if I recall correctly, you declined that option because you thought coming here was gross." He squeezed her hand. "You here now is just an extra topping for me."

Anna Katherine let out a sigh in defeat. "Fine. When is it?"

"The 24th."

"That's Christmas Eve and the night before we leave for Ireland."

"Yeah, so?"

"You don't think we'll be busy packing?"

"You know good and well I'll already be packed."

"Fine, I will be panic packing."

"I'll help you." Another hand squeeze. "Promise."

"Yeah, whatever." She pulled her hand away from him. "Just know I'm not happy about tit"

"Oh," Declan said with a chuckle, "I am quite aware."

30

Declan was sitting on the couch, dressed, ready to go, and waiting for Kit to finish getting ready. He would never be able to understand what took her so long. She had taken forever to primp and preen for as long as he had known her. Even if they were simply going to the movies or the grocery store, Declan was always waiting for her to finish up.

He checked his watch for the third time, and when he saw how close they were to being late, he heaved himself off the couch and marched to Kit's door. He was about to knock, when it swung open.

"Oh. Hi. I'm ready."

Declan looked her over. He told himself he wasn't paying attention to how the dress hugged her body, or how the green complimented her eyes or how silky her dark hair looked, or how he wanted to take her into his arms and never leave the apartment.

And he was very obviously lying to himself.

He let out a long breath, and once he saw that she was in fact completely ready, he nodded. "It's about time." He found himself giving her another once over, and tried not to react when Kit smirked at him.

"Perfection takes time, Mr. Mullins."

Declan couldn't argue with that. The dress she had bought earlier that week was conservative enough that even Patricia would love it, but somehow Kit still managed to put him on edge with how stunning she looked. He was amazed he could speak.

He thought about snarking back, but instead he found himself saying, "You look beautiful, Mrs. Mullins. It was well worth the wait."

Anna Katherine never enjoyed attending Declan's work gatherings, and she doubted she ever would. The only plus side that ever came with being dragged to these things was seeing Declan in a suit. They might just be best friends, but she wasn't above admitting that Declan looked exceptionally good in a suit. Tonight was no different as he wore his charcoal, grid-pattern suit. Plus, he wore his glasses instead of his contacts. And there was something about him when he wore his glasses...

She was still struggling with the entire "being physically attracted to your best friend after five years of nothing" conundrum, and tonight wasn't helping, but that didn't stop her from appreciating him as he walked a few steps ahead of her.

She watched as his friends and coworkers came up to greet him. He addressed them all by name and always made sure to ask about a family member or some other personal aspect of their lives. She was perfectly content standing at his side with her arm hooked in his, smiling and only saying a brief hello here or there while he caught up with the people around him. That was until someone all but pulled him out of her grasp.

"Declan!" The woman was all but drooling over him. "I thought you weren't coming."

In his defense, Declan looked just as surprised as Anna Katherine felt. "Oh. Hey, Kelly."

When Anna Katherine saw the woman—Kelly—place her hand on Declan's upper arm, she found herself stepping back into Declan's side and asking, "Who's this, honey?"

She didn't give the curious glance he sent her any mind.

"Uh..." He startled when Anna Katherine wrapped her arm around his waist. "This is Kelly. We were in the same pod for a few months, but when we both got promoted, she was moved."

Anna Katherine gave Kelly a saccharine smile. "It's so nice to meet you, Kelly. I'm Anna Katherine. Declan's wife."

Kelly gave her a once over, "Oh. I remember Declan talking about you. Weren't you two just friends?"

Declan went to respond, but she pinched his side to stop him. Thankfully, he did a good job of hiding his yelp. "Well, I wouldn't say we were ever *just* friends."

This time, he spoke up before she could stop him, "Oh? Is that so, Kit?"

She shot him a quick glare, hoping Kelly didn't see, "Yes. We've always teetered on the edge of, well, something *more*." The look Declan gave her—baffled and a little in awe—made her want to take it all back. Instead, she added, "At least, that's what our mothers say, isn't it?"

Kelly looked between the two of them. "I see."

Declan seemed to tear his gaze away from Anna Katherine to give Kelly a friendly smile and to answer her previous question. "I convinced Kit here to come with me, so I decided to come after all. How are those nephews of yours?"

Anna Katherine leaned into him again while listening to their conversation taper off until Kelly finally walked away.

Once the woman was out of earshot, Anna Katherine made every effort not to look at Declan, despite feeling his stare.

"Kit."

"Nope."

"You were jealous." She could hear the smile in his voice, and she hated it.

"I was not. I just didn't like her."

"And why didn't you like her?"

She shrugged and finally looked up at him. "She was being very touchy for someone who could very clearly see you are a married man. I mean your wedding ring is right there!"

"Is this the moment that I point out the circumstances of our marriage?"

"No, because it's the moral of the thing, Declan."

"Ah." He smirked, clearly pleased with whatever just happened. "Whatever you say, Kit-Kat."

After a few more moments of catching up with his coworkers, they found their way to one of the tables. It didn't take long for Declan to spot William and weave them through the chairs and people to grab the two seats next to him.

When William spotted them, he stood up to hug Anna Katherine. "You look beautiful, Kit."

"Thanks, William. You clean up pretty well, too." She pulled out of the hug and took the seat where she would be sitting between William and Declan. After finishing up whatever conversation they were having, Declan came to sit next to her, resting his palm on her thigh. She worked very hard not to react.

They were all still sitting at the tables and sipping their wine when someone whom she assumed was the head of the company walked to the center of the makeshift stage positioned in the front of the room. Anna Katherine tuned him out while he waxed eloquent about something or another regarding the company and his employees. She was daydreaming about finally getting home and taking her shoes and bra off when she heard, "And this year's Thought Leader of the Year Award goes to one of our beloved analysts, Declan Mullins!"

She straightened up when she heard his name and spun around to look at him with wide eyes. "That's you!"

He chuckled, "I'm aware, love."

Anna Katherine was pretty sure everyone in the building could feel her amazement as she watched Declan walk up to accept the award. He took the plaque and shook the man's hand, and when everyone in the room cheered for him, he gave a little wave.

Her chest felt like it could burst with pride, and as he walked back to his seat beside her, she couldn't help but beam up at him. "Let me see, let me see!"

He laughed as he handed the award over. "I think you're more excited about this than I am."

"This is amazing!" She read the plaque. "Wait, what is this for?"

"It's just a leadership award." He shrugged. "I guess I impressed the CEO."

"You obviously impressed someone!" She handed the plaque back to him, and as they settled to listen to more awards being given out, Declan squeezed her hand.

She smiled brightly when she caught him watching her.

After the awards were handed out and the CEO finished his speech, Declan took Kit to find food. As they made their way through the throngs of people, he kept his hand on the small of her back. When people stopped to congratulate him on his award, he'd wrap his arm around her while he thanked them and introduced her as his wife.

It was still weird for him at times to call Kit his wife, but in moments like these with her at his side, a proud smile on her lips, and eyes beaming, it all felt as natural as breathing. They were once again on their way to the buffet when he interlaced their hands.

"You're definitely helping me get my touch quota in for the day."

He gave her a puzzled look. "I haven't touched you that much."

She laughed, "You haven't stopped since we parked the car, Declan."

"What?"

"I wish I was exaggerating." She paused. "Actually, I don't. I love this."

"I didn't realize I was doing it so often."

"Don't overthink it." She patted his arm. "Just keep doing what you're doing. I'm living for all this physical contact."

He gave her a smile. "Your wish is my command."

"Wait." She stopped walking so suddenly, he tripped. "What's *your* love language?"

He blinked down at her. "What?"

"Your love language. We both know mine, but I've never thought to ask yours!"

He shrugged. "Dunno."

She stared at him. "What do you mean you don't know?"

"Why should I know?"

"It helps you understand yourself better!" She hit his arm. "And it helps others love you better!"

"I think people are loving me just fine on their own." He started walking again, but she pulled him back.

"Declan!"

"Kit!" Declan mock screeched back.

"You're taking the test."

"Not tonight I'm not."

"I will win. Just wait. Maybe not tonight but soon." She strutted away toward the buffet with a huff.

He scratched his head while he watched her walk away. "Wasn't aware this was a competition."

Somehow between reveling in all of Declan's touches and just wanting to get another glass of wine, Declan convinced Anna Katherine to dance.

She was still complaining as he led her out to the dance floor. "I don't like to dance, Declan."

"We've danced plenty of times together." He pulled her to him so they could sway to the music.

"We have danced exactly once, and that was because Patricia would have killed me if I had refused to dance with you at our own wedding."

Declan tutted. "I think you forget about the night you were crying over John Mayer and his broken heart."

She snapped her head up to look at him. "You remember that?"

"Of course I do."

She wasn't sure if what they were doing constituted as dancing since they were simply swaying side to side, but she felt herself begin to relax into it. "You just haven't brought it up since it happened."

Anna Katherine leaned into him, reveling in the firmness of his chest and the feeling of his arms wrapped around her. She found herself amazed at how Declan could make something she despised so much even the slightest bit more comfortable for her. It wasn't the first time it had happened. It happened all the time. He calmed her down and helped her feel comfortable at their wedding, when she had gotten too far into her own head and couldn't get out. He even helped her feel comfortable and confident as she walked into her meeting with Jonah.

"Neither have you," he pointed out.

She tilted her head back to look at him, and he was already watching her. She took a moment to take him in. The way his lips turned slightly upwards. The day old scruff since he hadn't shaved this morning. The way his eyes stayed on her, watching her, taking her in. The pressure of his hand on her hip. She moved her hand to the back of his neck and tried to focus on how soft his hair was there as she ran her fingers through it in an effort to escape the rush that seemed to happen wherever he touched her. She wondered what it meant that she could feel her own heart beating in her ears.

She wanted to kiss him, but she pushed that urge deep down. She knew it wasn't because they needed to convince the people around them that they were in love, but because he was Declan and she was Kit, and they simply fit. Her mind wandered to their time in New Orleans and how he had kissed her. How *she* had kissed *him*. The way he felt against her. How he let her be in control. How even though she had probably been confusing the heck out of him—because she had certainly been confusing the heck out of herself—he let her. And she had felt how badly he wanted it just as much as she had, and how he had been holding himself back. How she had to calm herself down when she went to hide in the bathroom.

Her skin felt hot when she said, "There's a lot of things we don't bring up after they happen."

Declan hummed. "Communication has never been one of our strong points."

"Why do you think that is?"

She watched as he thought it over. "I think maybe it's because we're both cowards."

Anna Katherine couldn't find the words to argue.

Seventh Commandment: Thou Shalt Split The Bills 60/40

"You have to pay for sixty percent of the bills."
"Kit. Why?"
"I'm a lowly barista. You have a big boy job." She shrugged. "Makes sense."
"You're lucky I love you."
She beamed at him.

31

"You have to call me as soon as you land." Anna Katherine sighed. This was the fifth time her mother had called her since she had woken up that morning.

It was already far too early for such a conversation between Anna Katherine and her mother. Thankfully, Declan had answered the second, the third, and even the fourth time she had called. From what Anna Katherine could gather, Patricia didn't even seem to mind that her daughter was avoiding her calls, but now while they waited to board their second and last flight of the day, the phone sat on Anna Katherine's knee while on speaker.

It was the first time Anna Katherine wasn't waking up in her childhood bedroom and joining her chaotic family for another whirlwind of a Christmas. Their mornings were usually filled with rushing to get ready and piling all into one car for the Christmas service at church. They came home to stockings stuffed full of logical presents, a Christmas lunch cooked by her dad, and then a visit to her grandparent's house for the extended family dinner and presents. She was missing it, sure, but she wasn't heartbroken over it, either. This year, her Christmas began in the airport with her best friend with repeated phone calls from her overbearing mother. It wasn't exactly putting her in the Christmas spirit.

"We won't have service right away, Patty. But as soon as we get WiFi, I'll remind Kit to call you."

She rolled her eyes at Declan. "We're about to board, Mom."

"I just can't believe I won't see you this Christmas!"

Anna Katherine really wasn't missing her mom at all at the moment. "You saw me two days ago."

"But it's Christmas! We're about to leave for the service, and it just doesn't feel right with just Alexander and Nat. Your father and I are missing the two of you."

Anna Katherine almost missed the mention of Nat. She picked up the phone and held it closer to her ear. "Did you say Nat?"

"Yes, your father and I thought it would be nice for Nat to come with us since she's dating Alexander. Besides, you know how her parents can be..."

For a split second, Anna Katherine forgot about the little white lie that her brother and best friend were living. Compared to the lie of her marriage, it was nothing. "That was really sweet of you, Mom."

"Well, I'm not the Wicked Witch of the East, dear."

Declan took the phone, clicking off of speaker when he brought it up to his ear. "We miss you all, too. Remember that I promised you we'd make it up to you, Patty."

She could hear her mom's long-winded response, but couldn't understand what was being said.

"I know, Patty. I'll take good care of our girl. Don't worry about a thing. We'll be back with presents for all. You just take care of your grand-dog. And don't let Harry come to steal her."

Another pause and then, "Yes, I know you love Harry. We all love Harry, but you know Kit banned him from watching over Fox."

She was dying to know what Patty had said to make Declan's eyes light up the way they did. "She does have a tendency to be overbearing. I haven't the slightest idea where she gets that from. Right. We'll talk soon. Happy Christmas!"

As soon as the call ended, Anna Katherine snatched her phone up. "What did she say? I'm not overbearing!"

"Of course you aren't. She was just saying she thought you had too high of expectations for your friends and you should just let your dog be a dog."

She slouched in the airport chair and crossed her arms over her chest. "Even when I'm about to be an ocean away, she's still finding ways to be unbearable."

"Quite unlike you when you Skyped me the first time I flew home after graduation and woke me up at three in the morning just because the smoke alarm in your new apartment wouldn't stop beeping and you were mad about it."

"In my defense, you promised you were going to change the batteries before you left."

"Yeah, so you say." He gave a look that edged on worry, and it didn't seem to add up with their light-hearted bickering.

She reached out and placed her hand on his arm. "What's wrong?"

He glanced around the airport before he looked back at her. "I'm sorry you're spending your Christmas in an airport and traveling for twelve hours."

Anna Katherine looped her arm through his and rested her head against his shoulder. "I honestly don't mind. I'm with my best friend. I'm about to go to Ireland, which you know I've been dying to do."

"Yeah, but you're missing family breakfast and all the presents and—"

"Declan."

"What?"

"Shut up. I'm here because I want to be and not anything you did. Don't give yourself that much credit."

He laughed. "Of course. No one could make the great Anna Katherine Marie Tran do anything she didn't want to do."

"Mullins," Anna Katherine said.

"Hm?"

She elbowed him so he'd look at her. "My last name. It's Mullins now, not Tran."

He smiled, "Yeah. I guess I should get used to that."

"Also, I want to be here with you."

Declan was mindlessly scrolling on his phone when Kit asked him, "If you were having a bad day, which would you prefer? Me comforting you or lazy Netflix night?"

He lifted his head so he could look at her. Kit's long, black hair was braided and hanging lazily over one shoulder. Her baby-hairs were sticking out around her temples, and while her indifferent tone of voice would lead people to believe she wasn't bothered by the question, the pink on her otherwise ivory cheeks told him differently. Declan smiled, both because she was beautiful and because he knew she was up to something mischievous. "What're you doing?"

"Just answer, Declan." Her eyes remained focused on her phone screen as she refused to make eye-contact with him.

"Lazy Netflix, I guess."

"Okay, that's what I thought. Now, do you hate it most when I criticize you or always think about other things?"

This time, he placed his phone down and leaned over to see what she was doing. "What—" He snatched her phone away from her. "What is this? Is this a dumb love quiz?"

"It's not dumb! I need to learn how to love you better." She huffed out the last part.

"You only gave me two options out of the five."

"I knew the other two weren't you."

"If you're making me do this, I'm doing it myself." He refreshed the page so he could start over. "Wait. This is for couples."

Kit rolled her eyes. "Duh."

He gave her an amused look. "Okay." He clicked to start the quiz, and when Kit leaned over to see, he positioned himself away so she couldn't see the phone screen. "This is a dumb question."

"Which one is it?" She tried again to peer over to get a look. "Declan, let me see!"

"Would you survive a world where no one verbally complimented you?"

"I think you would choose..."

"No!" Declan stood up to get away from her. *"I prefer spending one on one time together rather than receiving compliments.* This is the most accurate, I guess. But I don't like it."

Kit stood up next to him. He held his hand out to keep her from getting any closer. "Just choose the one that you relate to the most!"

"And what if I don't relate to any of them?"

"You're being impossible."

"Sounds like someone else I know." When she stopped trying to get to the phone, Declan went to the next question. After reading the question and options aloud for her, he said. "I think I'd choose the first one."

"No!" She stomped over to him, "That's not right. You'd for sure prefer staying in together!"

"That sounds like every night we spend together."

"Exactly."

Declan rolled his eyes, but in the end he chose the second option. They sat back down and went through the next few options. Declan reluctantly allowed her to lean on him so she could see the screen. He answered a few of them with ease, but when he got stuck on one, he tilted the screen toward Kit. She quickly picked the third option.

When she noticed him looking at her, she shrugged. "I know you."

He hummed in response, but kept going. After a few more, he got to another that stumped him. "*How would you show your significant other that you love them? Two, take some time out to spend together* or *four, cuddle and spoil them*? Is this what I would rather do or what I would do because I know what you would prefer?"

She turned to look at him. "What do you mean?"

"Well, for most people, I would spend time with them to show them I care, but with you, I give you the cuddles you so greedily demand from me."

Instead of the snarky comment he expected, he noticed her cheeks go pink again. "Um, it is supposed to be about you and your significant other, so, uh. I don't know."

He glanced back down at the phone, and after a moment of hesitation, he clicked the last option. He was on a roll after that, easily choosing which answer best fit him, while Kit watched over his shoulder and offered her own little comments about the quiz and his answers. It was all going fine until they got to the last question. Declan could feel his neck and face turning a bright shade of pink. .

"What?" Kit reached over and took the phone. *You're most likely to make love to your partner when…"* She scrunched up her face. "Well, I wasn't expecting that one."

"I thought you took the quiz."

"It was a while ago, and this probably isn't the same one. I just clicked on a random one."

Declan took the phone back and read the options. "One, *whispers into your ear how desirable you are.* You would never be able to do that with a straight face. Two, *has been really attentive to you throughout the day.* Three, *shows off the sexy nightwear they've bought for you.*" He laughed. "As if you have any."

"Actually," she said, while leaning even further over his shoulder to see the last option, "your mom and I went lingerie shopping when she came for the wedding."

Declan whipped his head around so quickly his neck popped. "What?"

"It's what women do before a wedding, Declan."

"So there's just… lingerie sitting around in our apartment? That you and my mum picked out together? For me?"

"Yes. Keep up. Why is that weird?"

"Why wouldn't it be weird?!" He nearly squeaked as he leaned away from her so he could see her more easily. "My mum went with you to pick

out lingerie! She was assuming I would see it. She was thinking about us...
you know..."

"Yes... And?"

"She's my mum! And you're... you're..."

"Your wife." Her cheeks began to turn pink again.

"Yeah, but it's—"

"Not real, I know. But everyone else thinks it is. Should I have told her
this was all a marriage of convenience?"

"Well, no..."

"Then I don't know what the problem is. I have lingerie. Big deal. You'll
never see it. You don't have to worry about it. It's fine."

Declan still didn't think it was fine, but Kit made it clear she wanted the
conversation to end. He cleared his throat. "Fine."

"Now pick an answer and finish so we can finally see what your love
language is."

Declan clicked the second option, and then clicked the button to finish
the quiz. He read the results out loud. "Quality time and words of affir-
mation."

"I knew it!"

"If you knew it then why did you force me to take this quiz?"

"You know what they say about assuming, Declan." She patted his
shoulder, "Now read the description, please. I need to know everything."

Begrudgingly, he did as he was told.

On the flight, Anna Katherine had the window seat after Declan all but demanded she sit there, and even though she had the window to lean and sleep on, she ended up passing out on Declan's shoulder. She ended up waking up halfway through his movie. He offered her the food he had grabbed for her when the stewardess came by while she had been sleeping. "Hungry?"

"Starved."

She dug into the airplane meal, and when Declan spotted her watching the movie on his screen, he took an earbud out and handed it to her. "It will probably be better with sound."

With a mouth full of instant mashed potatoes, she smiled wide. "Thank you very much."

Anna Katherine felt as though she were half asleep as they went to baggage claim and walked through customs. Declan led her through the airport with his hand firmly on her back, and it stayed there even once they were away from the crowds and could see Móirín waving at them.

Anna Katherine stepped away from Declan to give Móirín a hug, and she didn't like how she was immediately so aware of the lack of his touch.

"Móirín!" She stepped into her mother-in-law's arms. "I've missed you."

After a long moment, Móirín pulled away and patted Anna Kathereine's cheeks. "Oh, I've missed you, too. Tell me everything I've missed."

"Well, Harry ruined my dog."

She looked amused, "Yes, Declan told me about that mishap."

"Speaking of Declan, Declan is right here waiting to hug his dear mum." Declan was standing off to the side, his bottom lip excessively sticking out in his attempt to look like a petulant child.

She and Móirín both made an exasperated face at each other, but Anna

Katherine stepped away so Declan could embrace his mother.

"Happy Christmas to the both of you. I feel so terrible that you two had to travel during the holiday."

Anna Katherine saw the guilt come back on Declan's face. Before he let it eat him up too much, she reassured them both. "It's fine. You Mullins worry too much. It truly didn't bother me."

"Still, let's get the two of you home so we can start our Christmas celebrations. I'm sure both of you are hungry, too. I've been cooking for the past two days."

When they arrived at the house, Declan took their bags up to his room, and when he came back to the kitchen, he wrapped his arms around Kit to hug her from behind. She leaned against him, and tilted her head back to look at him. "Hi, there."

He smiled. "Want a tour of my childhood home?"

When she nodded, he untangled their arms from each other, took her hand, and started leading her through the house. It wasn't particularly large, just big enough for him and Móirín, but it was cozy in a way that he hoped helped Kit feel at home. He took them through the kitchen and front room, pointing out the corner where he had done most of his assignments when he was still in school, and then led them up the stairs.

"And this—" he waved her in "—is my bedroom."

She walked over to his dresser and picked up a picture. "Oh my gosh. Is this baby Declan?"

Declan came and snatched the photo away from her. "Give that!"

"Heyy." She pouted and tried to grab it back, but he lifted it over their heads.

"No, because you're about to make fun of me."

"I would never." When he gave her a very disbelieving look, she said, "I would only say how cute you were and then ask what happened."

"That was mean."

She jumped to grab it, but he stepped back. "Ah-ah. You called me ugly."

"You're twisting my words."

"You heavily implied it."

"Declan."

"Kit."

"You know you're not ugly."

He smirked. "Oh, do I?"

She went to grab the picture again, but he ducked around her. She spun around as he went behind her. "I've already told you that I think your accent is sexy, isn't that enough?"

"Nope."

"Well, that's too bad."

She sat on his bed and seemed surprised when he followed her. "Don't be a party pooper."

When she refused to look at him, he reached out to poke her. "Kit-Kat."

She squealed and moved out of his reach. She was trying to hold in a laugh when he lunged toward her and tackled her onto the bed. The photo slid off the bed and landed on the carpeted floor with a dull *thump*.

As he began to tickle her, between gasps, she managed to get out, "Let me go, Declan!"

"Not until you validate my charming good looks."

"Declan Anthony, let. Me. Go."

He let her go, but kept his hands ready for another tickle attack. "You know what you have to do."

She glared at him, and when she realized he meant it, she relented. "You're a very beautiful man."

He tilted his head to the side. "Beautiful?"

She struggled to get out, but his grip was too strong for her. "Yes, beautiful. Your stupid, stupid blue eyes and that soft, ridiculous smile you do and your perfect hair. Don't get me started on that chin dimple or your stupidly cute nose or your freakin' hands."

Declan looked taken aback. "That was, uh, my hands?"

She refused to look him in the eye when she shrugged. "Hands are a thing."

"For who?"

"Plenty of people."

"Like who?"

"Me! You just have really good hands, okay?"

He turned his hands around, looking at them. "Huh. Really?" He looked at her again, but she refused to look back.

She wiggled further away from him. "Can you stop being a validation hog?"

She was still glaring at him when he reached out and traced his thumb against her cheek. "Would it make you feel better if I told you all the things I find attractive about you?"

She squinted her eyes at him. "Maybe."

"The first time I saw you, it was your legs." She swatted him, and he laughed. "Now your eyes get me. They light up when you start on one of your passionate rants. And how you scrunch up your face when you think something is gross. That's really adorable, and I think you know it."

She was still glaring, but there was a smirk hiding behind it.

"I'm really into your ears."

"Ears?"

"Mhm."

"Declan, that's weird."

"You're the one with a hand fetish."

"I feel like that's more normal than ears."

He went to tickle her again, but she leapt off the bed away from his reach. She picked up the photo, and it was only when Declan reached for her again that she looked up.

"Hey."

All the fight left her when she heard his tone. "Hi, Declan."

"I'm really glad you're here."

She gave him a bright smile that caused his heart to stutter and gave him a quick kiss on the cheek. "It's what any wife would do. Now c'mon so I can get food."

She was out the door before he could find a response.

As Anna Katherine walked to the kitchen, Móirín gave her a knowing look. "The tour of the house took a bit."

She felt her cheeks heat up. "We, uh, got distracted."

"No need to be embarrassed."

Declan came in behind her and rested his elbow on her shoulder, "Why are we not embarrassed?"

"The two of you took an awfully long time in your bedroom."

"It wasn't that long, but also, gross." Declan walked toward her. "I could go without my mum insinuating certain things about my life."

"Love making is a natural and beautiful part of marriage, Declan."

"Yeah, Declan." Anna Katherine came up behind Declan and swatted his rear. "It's a beautiful experience. No need to be so shy."

Declan startled and glared at her. "Anna Katherine."

"Hm?"

He looked from her to his mom and then, "Ma, is it normal for someone to have a hand fetish? Because Kit here—"

"Declan!"

She tried to slap him, but he ducked out of the way laughing and ran out of the kitchen.

Loud enough that she knew he could still hear her, she asked Móirín, "And what about an ear fetish?"

"Anna Katherine!"

"You started it."

Móirín smiled. "You two are really something else."

32

They sat around the small kitchen table with Anna Katherine sitting across from Declan for their Christmas dinner. Móirín had really outdone herself. They all helped clean up once they had stuffed themselves to the brim, and then made their way to the front room to sit around the tree and open presents. Móirín had knitted them both Christmas sweaters which Anna Katherine immediately pulled on over her head before opening the next present from Móirín, which was a new wallet, something she had told Declan in passing that she needed just weeks before. When she looked over at him, he was already smiling at her.

"Móirín, I love these." She turned the wallet over in her hands. "Thank you."

Móirín opened her present from them both, which was her very own standing mixer. She laughed when she saw what it was. "Kit's idea, I'm assuming?"

"It was the best thing that ever happened to me."

"Other than marrying me," Declan piped up.

She ignored him. "I figured you would love it just as much as I do."

"Well, thank you. Both of you."

That night, Móirín headed up before the two of them, and on her way to her bedroom, she turned to look over her shoulder with the same mischievous glint that Declan got in his eyes when he was about to drive Anna Katherine crazy.

"You two be sure to lock up before you head to bed, and…" She looked at Declan. "Try not to make me a grandma yet. I'm not quite ready for that."

"Ma!"

"Don't worry, Móirín." Anna Katherine laughed. "I don't think we're ready for that, either."

She laughed all the way up the stairs.

Anna Katherine moved so her head was in Declan's lap. "Today was good."

He brushed her hair out of her face. "Yeah. It's been long, though. Aren't you tired?"

"Extremely." She stretched out and cuddled further into him.

"Kit."

"Hm?"

"If you fall asleep on me, I'm not carrying you up the stairs."

"You'd probably drop me anyway." She yawned. "Besides, I won't fall asleep."

They both ended up falling asleep, and it wasn't until Declan woke up in the middle of the night with a crick in his neck that they both stumbled to bed with half-closed eyes.

Anna Katherine woke up to Declan pulling her to him. She kept her eyes closed as she curled up into his chest.

"Móirín made us breakfast."

"No."

"No, she didn't or no, you don't want any?"

"No."

"She has coffee."

"Mm. Yes."

"Do you want me to bring you a cup?"

She nodded her head, but when he started to move his arms away from her, she tightened her grip on them.

"Kit, if you want me to get you coffee, you're going to have to let me go."

She groaned, but when he went to move her hands away, she let him.

When Declan came back, Kit had stolen his pillow and was holding it to her chest. "Did the pillow replace me?"

She cracked an eye open. When Kit saw the two mugs of steaming coffee, she sat up and grabbed one. Before she took a sip, she mumbled, "No one could replace you, Dec."

"I want that in writing."

"Shh. No more talking until at least three sips."

He sat back down on the bed beside her with a chuckle, and she immediately scooted over to lean against his side.

"I feel like you're being more touchy than usual."

She elbowed him. "No talking."

"Oh, right."

He draped his arm over her shoulders, and in the time it took for Kit to down four sips, he was still working on his second.

"So." He ran his fingers over her arms. "Why so touchy?"

"I'm not."

He drummed his fingers. "I strongly disagree."

She took another sip of her coffee. "If I am, which I'm not, it's probably the holidays."

"Are you a big softie, Kit?"

She wrapped her fingers around her mug and held it close to her chest. When Kit leaned her head against his shoulder, she said, "No. Especially when people are annoying, which you are this morning."

"I have been nothing but a doting husband."

She snorted. "Who won't shut up."

"I will never understand why you're so cranky in the mornings."

"Most mornings I have to get up before the sun to go to work. I would think people who rarely are able to sleep in *are* cranky."

"I'm not."

"I know." She pulled away from him, shoving her cup at his chest so he was forced to take it, and climbed over him.

"Where are you going?"

"Gotta pee, gotta pee, gotta pee."

He laughed as she ran down the hall to the toilet.

They finally made it to the kitchen, and while Kit was stuffing her face, she asked, "What's the plan for today?"

Declan shrugged. "There's not much of one."

"Oh, Declan, you should take her around town. Let her see where you grew up," Móirín suggested.

Kit immediately smiled. "Oh, sign me up."

Declan told her a dozen times to bring warm clothes, yet somehow he wasn't surprised when she immediately started complaining about the cold. He was lounging on his bed while she dug through her suitcase looking for something cozy to wear.

"You brought a jacket at least, right?"

She shot a glare at him over her shoulder. "Yes, but it's not thick enough to keep the wind out."

"I told you to pack—"

"It's not my fault! I'm from the *south*, Declan. We have warm Christmases."

"The temperatures aren't *that* different."

"But the wind!"

He slid off the bed. "You're hopeless."

He dug into his closet, all too aware of her eyes on him, until he found an old Derby jumper of his. "Here." He tossed it to her. "Wear that underneath your jacket and you should be fine."

She jumped up, and the next thing he knew, she was pecking his cheek. "Thank you!" And then she darted off to change. Again.

He took her downtown first, and it was after they went to a few shops and he pointed out a few things that she said, "I don't want The Boring Tour. I want the Baby Declan Tour."

Declan gave her a flat look. "The what?"

"The Baby Declan Tour. You know, the one that shows me everything about you. Show me where you scraped your knee or made a fool out of yourself in front of all your mates or where you first fell in love!"

"Really?"

Her smile widened. "Yes!"

Declan wasn't thrilled about it, but he could feel himself relenting to her wishes anyway. He took her by the pub where he first got drunk, the shop where he had his first job, and where he and his mates went when they skipped class.

As they walked by a beautiful stone building he said, "And this is where I went to church."

Kit took the building in, and then she turned to him smirking, "You were an altar boy, weren't you? Oh my goodness. I bet you were the cutest altar boy to have ever altar boy'ed."

He gave her a shove. "Why must you always mock me?"

"You usually find it endearing," she laughed. "Ooh. Wait. You're Catholic, and I'm Protestant. This makes us like Romeo and Juliet or something."

"I hope not." He snorted. "They both died."

Kit wrinkled her nose. "Good point. Never mind."

He draped his arm over her shoulder, "It might be a classic, but I'd rather not think about your death to be honest."

Next, he took her to his school, another beautiful stone building. "And this is my secondary school."

"Why is every building in Ireland so beautiful?"

"Your home has beauty, too."

She shook her head. "Not like this. My high school had cinder blocks for walls and awful laminate flooring."

"The inside isn't that great. Trust me."

"You're biased, therefore I don't trust you. Even if it isn't as beautiful as the outside, this makes up for it. I bet it's gorgeous when it snows."

He shrugged. "I guess. I've never really thought about it."

"All of this beauty is wasted on you, I swear."

"Well, it's a good thing I have you to point it all out to me then."

"Yes. Lucky you." She took his hand and pulled him along, "Alright, so tell me about Baby Declan. What was he like? Did he have any girlfriends? Did he get in trouble a lot?"

"Uh..." He scratched his neck. "Not many girls. I did have my first kiss behind this building though."

"Oooh. Scandalous. Who was the lucky girl?"

He cut his eyes at her. "Vivian, actually."

She stopped. "Really? Your first love was also your first kiss?"

He nodded.

"When was that?"

He thought for a moment. "I was either fourteen or fifteen."

Her eyes went wide. "So you two dated for what? Five or six years?"

Silently, he nodded.

"Wow." Kit looked at him, but then kept walking, her hand firm in his. "No wonder you were so torn up about her when she ended things."

"Yeah, but I don't regret it. I don't think Jonah and I would have become as close without that heartbreak, so who knows if you and I would be friends today without Vivian completely crushing me."

"No." Kit shook her head adamantly. "I don't like that thought process. I like to think that in every alternate universe, we always find our way to each other."

He smiled down at her. "Yeah?"

"You're my person, Declan. I refuse to have it any other way."

His smile only grew.

He took her to a few more places like where he got in a fight and nearly got expelled from school, and the field where he tore his ACL playing a footie match. The last place he took her was his favorite place in all the world. They climbed up a hill on the outskirts of town where an old abandoned cottage sat long forgotten by most of the town. The view from the top was beautiful, but it was the peace from being away from the hustle and bustle that drew Declan in.

Once they reached the top, he spread his arms out. "And this is my favorite place."

Kit turned in a circle, taking it all in. And then there was that infamous Kit smirk. "I bet you take all the girls up here, don't you?"

"Actually," Declan cocked his head to the side, a little surprised himself. "You're the only person I've ever brought up here."

Even though Kit tried to hide it, Declan could see that little fact pleased her. She wrapped her arms around his middle, tilting her head back to look at him. "I'm just that special, huh?"

He brushed her windblown hair out of her face. "Yeah. You really are, Kit-Kat."

33

"M orning."

"Good morning, sleepy head." Anna Katherine's eyes were still closed, but she heard the smile in Declan's voice. "I have coffee for you."

"Mm." She blindly grabbed for him and pulled herself close. "My hero."

He started running his fingers through her hair. "You don't want it now?"

"Not yet. Just hold me."

She smiled into his side when he did just that. She relished in his warmth as he scrolled through his phone, and even though she knew she needed to get up, she couldn't find the motivation to do so. Eventually, she patted Declan's stomach, and despite her not saying a word, he knew what she wanted. He handed her the coffee as she sat up, and after her third sip, he spoke up.

"Wesley wants us to go see him while we're here."

"I feel like that was a given."

"Yeah, but now we have to figure out when."

"Ugh. That sounds awful. I'll leave that to you."

Declan chuckled. "Gee, thanks."

"Anytime."

"Don't forget I'm going to see some friends today."

"Yep. Don't worry. Móirín and I will have a wonderful day."

"Just don't buy any more lingerie."

She slapped his arm, and he laughed.

Móirín showed Anna Katherine some more of the town. They grabbed lunch where everyone in the building seemed to know Móirín and Declan, and after they finished shopping, they went to see one of her friends for afternoon tea.

On the way back to the house, they walked through the park. Anna Katherine was enjoying the scenery when Móirín said, "You love my son well."

Anna Katherine looked at her mother-in-law, a little surprised by her comment. "What do you mean?"

"I see the way the two of you are with each other. You balance each other out." Móirín looped their arms together. "Declan told me how you helped him out of that slump when he was in between jobs and how he came close to accepting that job in New York City, but it was your influence that stopped him."

Anna Katherine tried to brush it off. "Oh, but that was selfish of me. I didn't want to see him leave."

"It might've started that way, or that might have been a large reason, but I also think you saw his worth well before he did. He wouldn't have been able to work his way up the way he has at the company he's working for now. You were the one that told him he needed room to grow, and he has that now. He received that leadership award because of that—because of you."

She shook her head. "No. That was all Declan. He would be successful no matter where he is."

"That is true." Móirín patted her arm. "But you help him just as much as I'm sure he helps you."

Anna Katherine stayed quiet, unsure of how to respond.

"It's not just that, though," Móirín continued. "Declan has always loved deeply. He's very observant and thoughtful, and he expects people to have the same intentions he does, which causes him a lot of heartbreak. But you do. You're intentional with him, and I want to thank you for that."

Panic began to rise in her throat. She did her best to swallow it down. "I don't deserve him."

She wasn't sure where those words came from, but she felt the truth behind them. Declan had been there for her through thick and thin since he first came into her life. He had loved her, and Anna Katherine was self aware enough to know that wasn't an easy task. She was cranky and demanding and difficult. But Declan never lost his temper with her; he never belittled her. He called her out on her crap, but he was always there afterward to pick her back up. He saw her in a way many people couldn't, and how did she repay him? With sarcasm and sass and enough attitude to last anyone the rest of their lives.

"Oh, no. Don't think like that, dear." Móirín gave her another pat. "Life isn't about what anyone deserves. If any of us actually got what we deserved, we'd all be doomed. Isn't that the real story of Christmas?" She waved a hand around them. "Our lives are about our choices and what we decide to fight for and believe in. You and him? You chose to believe in each other, and that's enough. I love you so much more for how you choose him."

The panic had now made itself at home in her throat, and it made it difficult to breathe. Nothing Móirín had said wasn't true, and that was the scariest part. Maybe Móirín saw Anna Katherine better than she could even see herself. And then a more horrifying thought invaded her space.

What if she finds out this is a sham?

Her blood ran cold, and panic gripped her heart.

Anna Katherine did her best not to be obvious about it, but as soon as they got back to the house, she ran upstairs to Declan's room, hoping he was already home. When she saw him on the bed reading a book, she collapsed on the bed and hid her face in one of the pillows.

"Uh, hello."

"We're going to crush and shatter and *destroy* your mom, Dec."

Declan closed his book. "What are you on about now?"

She scooted up and propped her chin on the pillow. "On the way home today, she kept going on about…" She almost told him how Móirín had gone on about how well she loved him. But that felt too raw to tell Declan, which was a strange place for her to be. She typically told him everything.

"About what?"

"Just." She heaved out a sigh. "The two of us and how we're perfect for each other and—and if she finds out we're not doing this for love, it's going to shatter her!"

He brushed her hair behind her ear and gave it a tug. "I need you to look at me, Kit."

She did as she was told, reluctantly.

"She's not going to find out. Just like your mom isn't going to find out or anyone else for that matter. You say you trust me, so trust me on this."

"I just…" Another sigh. "I love her. I don't want to hurt her."

"And you won't. Even if she does find out, that pain she'll feel is on me, not you."

"No. We're in this together."

"Fine, but the point still stands. She won't find out."

Anna Katherine went back to hiding her face. She was surprised Declan could still understand her when she muttered into the pillow, "I won't be able to stand it if she does."

He gave her arm a rub. "I know, but it'll all work out. Promise."

"She's going to be devastated when we get a divorce," she couldn't help but add. And her stomach dropped at the thought, because she'd be devastated, too.

"We'll cross that bridge when we get there. Breathe, Kit."

She did, turning onto her side and wrapping her arms around herself. When Declan gave her a reassuring smile, she tried her best to return it.

34

Declan and Kit borrowed Móirín's car to drive to Dublin where they met Wesley at his new flat and spent the day walking around the city. When they walked through St. Stephen's Green, Declan could tell Kit immediately fell in love with it by the look of awe and excitement on her face. They bought sandwiches and coffees at a small shop and had their own picnic outside. Wesley surprised both of them by cooking dinner that night.

The next day they lazed around until Wesley forced them to get up and head over to a coworker's place who was throwing a New Year's Eve party.

Knowing Wesley and the type of people he typically attracted, it wasn't surprising to see that the party was reminiscent of their college years—filled with too much drinking and loose morals. It wasn't a scene that Declan nor Kit necessarily wanted to be in, but this was their best chance to visit Wesley and some of Declan's local friends.

More people continued to arrive throughout the night, and soon the bass of the music was thumping through the walls, everyone had a drink in their hand, and there were two tables of beer pong set up.

Kit stood on her tiptoes, leaning against Declan's shoulder to whisper, "I feel like we're in college again."

"We haven't been to one of these in a while, have we?"

"Must be because we're that old married couple who stays in watching reality television."

"Must be that." He wrapped an arm around her and pulled her close. "Let me know if it gets to be too much and we can head home."

She seemed thoughtful for a moment, and Declan briefly wondered if she'd ask to go home now, but instead, she simply nodded.

Declan found Kit in the kitchen, perched atop the counter, sipping a glass of water and munching away on chips that sat in a bowl in her lap. When she smiled at him, it was as if she were a magnet pulling him in. He couldn't have stopped himself even if he tried. Once he was close enough, he lifted the bowl of chips off her lap and set it to the side. "You disappeared."

"I wanted a snack," she said with a shrug.

His eyes left hers to glance at the bowl of chips beside her. "I see that."

He took another step toward her, and suddenly he didn't know what to do with his hands. After hesitating, he placed them on the counter on either side of her legs.

"Did ya miss me?"

He chuckled because it was such a Kit question to ask after being gone for only a few minutes, but also because, yeah. He did.

"What do you think, Kit?"

They were close enough that he could feel her breath against his cheek.

"I think you miss me every time I leave a room."

He thought she was being sarcastic, but the near perfect accuracy of her words felt like a blow to his chest. His neck began to feel too tired to hold up his head, and he let it fall and rest against her shoulder, sighing when her hands went to his hair, running her fingers through it and massaging his scalp. They both stayed there for a moment, tangled and taking each other in with each breath.

He didn't know if it was the late hour or the endless possibilities that the new year promised, but whatever it was, he found his courage.

With his head still resting against her shoulder, he mumbled, "I wanna kiss you."

He heard her sharp intake of breath, but she still felt relaxed in his arms. "What's stopping you?"

He heard the classic Anna Katherine snark in her voice, but when he pulled back to look at her, he saw a myriad of emotions on her face and the vulnerability in her eyes.

He didn't say anything. He couldn't. The ability to form words had left him. He took in her features, stared at her lips, and then she was pulling him forward.

As they began to kiss, tucked away from prying eyes in the deserted kitchen, Declan's entire world fell away. There was only Kit. Her hands in his hair. His hands against her back. He couldn't think of anything other than her. He didn't want to think of anything else. All he wanted was her and whatever she was willing to give him.

They pulled away to breathe, and he leaned his forehead against hers. Her eyes were closed, but she was smiling. "Anna Katherine, I..."

But she cut him off when she surged back for another kiss, this one somehow more intense than the first. She tugged at his hair, and in response he gripped her sides.

"Well, well, well."

They jumped apart and turned to look at the source of the voice.

"Guess that honeymoon feeling hasn't left yet," Wesley smirked as he took the two of them in. He grabbed another beer from the counter and shook his head at them. "But on a kitchen counter that's not even yours? Don't be animals!"

They watched as he left the kitchen, and then Declan slowly turned back to her. He was relieved to see she was still smiling. He intertwined their fingers and helped her off the counter. "C'mon. Let's go join the others."

That night, they stayed at Wesley's, and Anna Katherine was quiet as Declan drove them home the next morning. The drive was comfortable, and every once in a while Anna Katherine would catch herself staring at Declan as he focused on the road ahead. There was greenery and beauty right outside her window, but Declan was the one that kept stealing her attention.

More often than not, she found herself thinking back to their kiss in the kitchen. It hadn't been like any of their others. It wasn't Declan getting caught up in the moment or them putting on a show for anyone else. It had been raw and honest, and it had shaken her to her core.

As they parked the car in front of the house, Kit stumbled upon the horrifying realization that she was quite possibly in love with Declan Mullins.

Well, crap.

35

Anna Katherine and Declan didn't talk about their kiss in the kitchen. The morning after it happened, her stomach was coiled in fear of how it would change their dynamic, but Declan still brought her coffee, still held her close, and still snarked back when she complained about having to wake up so early. Nothing changed between them when they arrived back at Móirín's or flew back home a few days later.

The only thing that changed once they were back in Serenity Grove was how busy they were. Hattie's Cafe was shorthanded, which meant Anna Katherine suddenly had to begin working more doubles than she was used to. For the first three weeks of the year, she barely saw any of her friends. And that included Declan.

The other thing that changed was that she had grown confident that she was falling for her best friend. She thought she was handling it well, but she still wanted to talk about it with Nat. Unfortunately their schedules never matched up. Before Anna Katherine knew it, January began to fade into February, and weeks had passed since she had last laid eyes on Nat. When she finally had an evening off, she texted Nat on her way home, asking to meet at Declan's place.

Nat, who had made herself at home on Anna Katherine's bed, looked up from her phone. "Geez, you look like you've been run over."

"Thanks. Working doubles for three weeks will do that to you." She plopped herself at the end of the bed with a groan. "Can we go back to the holidays?"

"Sorry. Seems we have to wait another eleven months."

"That's just unrealistic."

"Alright." Nat sat up and crossed her legs. "Enough stalling. Why am I here?"

"Can't I just miss my best friend?"

"Yes, but your text screamed crisis."

"I was very careful about it *not* screaming crisis."

"Which is why I could tell it was, in fact, still screaming crisis."

Anna Katherine let out another groan.

"Out with it."

Anna Katherine twisted over on her side so she was facing Nat, but when she opened her mouth to say what was on her mind, her eyes flicked to her comforter, and she picked at a loose thread. "It's nothing, really. It's just that…" She rolled onto her back. "I think I might be falling for Declan."

Nat was silent, which honestly surprised Anna Katherine. She turned back to face Nat only to find her staring.

"No comment?"

Nat shrugged. "I'm not sure what you want me to say. It's not like this is a surprise to anyone but you." She thought for a moment. "And probably

Declan. You're both idiots."

She glared. "I get it. We're idiots. Now, will you help me?"

"Help?" she asked, incredulous. "How in the world am I supposed to help right now?"

Anna Katherine sat up, swinging her legs around and pulling her knees up to her chest. "I don't know! Just... help!"

Nat sighed. "He's your husband, Kit."

"That's the exact problem. Thank you for pointing that out."

"Having feelings for your husband is normal!"

"Did you forget that our situation is not normal?"

"Doesn't mean you can't just ride this out." At the appalled look Anna Katherine sent her, Nat kept going. "Let's start at the beginning. When did you start to feel this way?"

She told Nat about her conversation with Móirín and the kiss in the kitchen and her terribly horrific realization on the drive back to Declan's childhood home.

"Wait, wait, wait." Nat waved her hands. "You're telling me that all those things Móirín said is what sparked this?"

She nodded.

"I've been saying those things for years!"

She shrugged. "But you're not Móirín."

This time the groan came from Nat.

By the time Nat and Anna Katherine emerged from the bedroom, the sun was setting, their nails were freshly painted, and Declan was home and cooking in the kitchen. Anna Katherine was still mid-crisis, but it didn't feel quite as overwhelming as it had before she had talked to Nat.

When Declan heard them come into the kitchen, he greeted them with a smile. "Hi."

Anna Katherine came up behind him, wrapping her arms around his middle and looked over his shoulder. "Whatcha cookin'?"

"Nothing special. Just a simple pasta."

"Well, it smells delicious."

Declan squeezed the hand that she rested against his stomach. "Thanks."

She untangled herself from him and went to the table where Nat was watching them. "What?" she hissed to her friend.

Nat shook her head. "Nothing."

"You staying for dinner, Nat?" Declan asked.

"If you have enough food, sure."

"We always have enough for our Nat." Declan spooned them all a serving into bowls and joined them at the table. "Have you seen Harry lately?"

Nat stopped twirling the pasta with her fork. "No. Why would I?"

Declan shrugged. "Just that you two have that new blossoming-friendship thing going on."

Anna Katherine huffed. "Which I still find so strange. You hated him."

Nat took a bite and carefully chewed. "I never *hated* him. He just rubbed me the wrong way. He still does, actually."

"He seems to do that to a lot of people. But once you get to know him, he's just..." Declan trailed off trying to find the right words.

Nat stabbed at her pasta. "A bundle of joy that somehow still makes you irate but also makes you fall in love with the world and all of humanity again?"

Declan and Anna Katherine stared at her in stunned silence.

"Uh..."

Declan began to smirk. "Yeah. Something like that."

After Nat left, Declan and Kit didn't waste any time getting ready for bed. They both squeezed into the bathroom. Declan brushed his teeth while she washed her face. Once she used the towel to dry off her face, he hung it up for her. She followed him into his room as she braided her hair and watched him pull back the covers of his bed.

"What're your plans for tomorrow?"

"Just going for drinks with William after work. He's been a bit lonely since Wesley moved."

"Aw. Poor guy."

"I know. What about you? Working?"

"Yeah, but not a double, thankfully. I have that follow-up meeting with Jonah, and then my shift starts at five."

"What time is your meeting with him?"

"Ten."

"Wanna get lunch together after?"

"Sure. I can just come to the office if you want."

Declan seemed surprised. "It's not cringe?"

Kit shrugged. "It might not be as bad as I always made it out to be."

He threw his head back in laughter. "I knew it!"

"Yeah, yeah." She finished her braid and flicked it over her shoulder.

He watched as she pulled a blanket from the foot of the bed to wrap herself in and laid across the bed.

"Kit?"

"Yes?"

"What are you doing?"

"What does it look like?"

"It looks like you're about to fall asleep on my bed."

"Mm." She yawned. "I think I could sleep for a week straight."

"Pretty sure I've seen you do that before, so I wouldn't be surprised."

Her response was to wrap herself tighter in the blanket.

"Go to your own bed if you're so tired."

"But I'm already so comfortable here."

"There is no way you are sleeping in my bed tonight."

"I won't. I'm just resting my eyes for a little bit."

"We both know that is a lie." He sat down on his bed, plugged in his phone, and got settled. "But I'm too tired to fight you on it tonight. The least you can do is lay on it the right way."

She huffed and puffed but rearranged herself so she was laying parallel to Declan.

"Goodnight, Dec."

"Night, menace."

Anna Katherine arrived at the coffee shop before Jonah, which gave her plenty of time to order her drink and find them a table. She ended up outside, and despite the fact that it was February, found it comfortably warm. The barista brought out her coffee around the same time Jonah showed up with the same canvas backpack he had used in college.

He smiled when he saw her. "Hi, there. You good if I go grab a coffee?"

"Yeah." She nodded. "Take your time. No rush."

He placed the backpack in the chair across from her and then ducked inside the building. It didn't take him long to come back with his classic black coffee and two chocolate croissants. She raised an eyebrow. "Two?"

He slid one over to her. "Knew this was your favorite. Figured we could both have a snack during this meeting."

Hesitantly, she grabbed the plate. "Uh, thanks."

He watched her over the brim of the mug as he took a sip. "I feel like I should apologize."

Anna Katherine thought he should probably be apologizing for a lot of things, but all she said was, "Oh?"

"I wasn't very professional last meeting, and no matter what's taken place between us in the past, I shouldn't have acted the way I did."

She squinted at him, suspicious. "Really?"

He laughed. "Yes. I'm not a complete monster all of the time, Anna Kay."

Hearing his nickname for her was a punch in the gut with a rush of memories flooding her mind. She did her best to look unaffected, though. "Well, thanks."

Jonah pulled out his computer and her portfolio. "The team and client went over your stuff, and they were all as impressed as they should've been."

When he smiled again, she found herself smiling back this time. "That's good to hear."

"Between you and I, anyone who isn't blown away by your work is an idiot."

She surprised both of them by laughing, and when she calmed, he said, "I mean it."

"Yeah, I know."

Jonah went on to show her the vision board for the project, and while he talked, she ate her chocolate croissant. Anna Katherine nodded along and gave her input on a few ideas. At one point, she was moving her hands around so much that she nearly spilled her coffee everywhere, and would have too if Jonah hadn't caught it. They had a good laugh about it before getting back to work.

"Anna Kay."

She looked up from tearing a bite off of the croissant. "Yeah?"

"Do you remember that night after the team miraculously won the bowl game our junior year and—"

She lit up. "And we went to the mural downtown?"

"Yes! And we took all those ridiculous photos, and it was just the best night ever?"

"You want me to recapture that night?"

He pointed his finger at her. "Still able to read my mind."

They shared another smile and talked a few more minutes before wrapping things up. They started to pack their things away and were headed their separate ways when Jonah went in for a hug. For a moment, she froze, completely unsure how she felt or whether or not this was okay. In the end, she hugged him back with a snarky, "Oh, we're back to hugging?"

When they pulled away, he said. "A handshake didn't feel like us."

She chuckled. "Yeah, I suppose."

They said their final goodbyes, and then Anna Katherine was off to pick up her and Declan's lunch.

Declan was once again waiting for her when the elevator doors opened. She laughed. "Mike?"

"Of course." He took the food from her. "C'mon, we can eat in my office today."

He made sure Kit was following him before taking her past the front desk and walking through all the cubicles.

"Where are we going?"

He looked over his shoulder. "My office, silly."

When he opened the door to his office, Kit stood in the doorway giving him a disbelieving look. "This isn't your office."

"Uh…" Declan looked around as he sat the food on his desk. "Pretty sure it is."

"Last time I came up here to meet you, you were in a cubicle!" She stepped the rest of the way in, letting the door slam behind her, and spun around.

Chuckling, he scratched his jaw. "Yeah, well, I've had a promotion since we've eaten in the office last."

"Declan!"

"Kit!" When she gave him an irritated look, he laughed and shrugged. "I thought we were just screaming each other's names."

"I would say I hate you, but I'm too proud of you right now. This is amazing! Why didn't you tell me?"

He motioned with his head for her to come over to his desk so they could start eating. "It just didn't come up."

She rolled her eyes. "Right. Well, you're not getting out of a celebration that easily. I'll go buy a cookie cake and invite Harry and Nat over tonight."

"Fine. How was the meeting with Jonah?"

"It was better than the first."

He watched as she popped a fry in her mouth. "Yeah?"

She nodded. "He started it off with what I assume was a peace offering in the form of a chocolate croissant because—" she deepened her voice to mock him, "—*I know it was your favorite.*"

"But that's not your favorite. It's banana bread."

She seemed amused. "Yes, Declan. My favorite pastry is now banana bread."

"So he doesn't actually know your favorite."

She laughed. "Why are you so stuck on this? Of course you know my favorite things better than him. You live with me."

Declan didn't really want to dissect why Jonah's attempt to get into her good graces bothered him so much, so he took a sip of his drink and motioned for Kit to go on with her story.

"He went over the vision board and we came up with a plan. I'm actually really excited about it. You remember that mural we went to that one night where we took all those pictures?"

Declan's stomach twisted. "Uh, yeah."

"Jonah wants me to recreate that night since it was such a memorable one."

That night wasn't necessarily one of his favorites to remember. His breakup with Vivian had still been fresh, and it was a night that truly reiterated how in love Jonah and Kit had been. Something he thought he had with Vivian for all those years, and then he was left with nothing. The pictures were good, though. He had used one as his profile picture until they graduated.

"Those pictures were really good."

"Right?" She smiled. "And then at the end, he hugged me, and it wasn't nearly as awful as I thought it would be."

That, out of it all, surprised him the most. "Did you want to be hugged?"

She shrugged, seeming oblivious to how the need to protect her consumed him. "Not necessarily, but once it happened, it's not like I minded."

Declan didn't say anything in response, but his silence drew her attention, and she looked up at him.

"What?"

He took her in, trying to find answers when he wasn't even sure what the questions were. "You know I just worry."

She gave him a soft, lopsided smile. "And you know you don't have to. I'm a big girl. He won't hurt me again."

"And you know, regardless of whatever else is going on, I'm always going to worry about you."

"Which is truly ridiculous."

"Not on my end."

"Good thing I love you, huh?"

He forced a chuckle. "Yeah, lucky me."

"Oh!" She poked his leg. "Don't forget we have that family dinner coming up."

"It's at our place this time, right?"

"Yep."

"Hopefully it goes better than the last one we hosted."

She snorted. "One can only hope."

36

Anna Katherine was surprised by how smoothly family dinner had started off. Patricia wasn't being over the top. Her dad and Declan were having a nice conversation about something she was not paying attention to, and Alex was, well, being himself. She should've known that as soon as she started to relax, things would go awry.

She was getting the food out of the oven when she heard her mother ask, "Alex, did you invite your girlfriend to family dinner tonight?"

Anna Katherine froze. She immediately started wondering who Patty was talking about. Alexander hadn't dated anyone in a while.

"Uh, who?"

"Natalie! Who else?"

She peeked her head around the corner to watch Alex stumble over his response. "Oh, right. Yes. My girlfriend. Natalie. No, I did not invite her. We're taking things slow."

"I see." Patricia sounded amused. "Well, it's a good thing I did."

Alex choked. "You did what now?"

"Honestly Alex, you're acting like your sister. Try to pull yourself to-gether." Patricia rolled her eyes. "She's your girlfriend. I don't see the problem."

"The problem," Anna Katherine said as she walked to the table with the food, "is that you place yourself in the middle of all of our relationships and don't even consider our side of it."

"And there she is. My loving daughter who would never be over dra-matic."

She dropped the dish in the middle of the table. "I wonder who I got it from."

"If you're implying you got it from me...."

"Well, I certainly didn't get it from Dad!"

She heard Declan snicker, and then her dad turned his attention to them. "What? What didn't you get from me?"

"Her dramatics, apparently," Patricia answered.

There was a knock on the door, and then Nat slunk in, looking more shy than Anna Katherine had ever seen her.

"Hello there."

Alex waved. "And there she is. My girlfriend."

Natalie grimaced but tried to cover it with a smile. "That's me."

Anna Katherine watched her mom watch her brother and best friend. There was a mischievous glint in Patricia's eye that was usually reserved for dealings with her daughter. It made Anna Katherine a little nervous for the other two.

Patricia motioned toward Alex and Nat. "Well, don't be shy! Just be-cause you're with family doesn't mean you two can't act like you normally would."

And, in another twist, the door flew open again and Harry pranced in. "Hello, my lovely family."

Anna Katherine tried not to laugh as he hooked his arm through Nat's and dragged her toward Alexander.

"I'm sure you are all wondering what I'm doing here."

Declan snorted. "Not in the slightest."

Harry, to his credit, ignored him. "So there I was minding my own business. Well, actually. I was minding Nat's business. One of her chairs broke, and she had called me over to fix it."

Patricia nodded like she understood, but then she said, "Why wouldn't she call Alex?"

"I live closer to her, and we never want to take Alex away from his work." Harry winked. Anna Katherine wasn't entirely sure who he was winking at or why. "Anyway, that's why I was there when good ol' Patty FaceTimed our Nat to see if she was coming to family dinner. When she saw me, she pity invited me."

Patricia waved the comment off. "It was not a pity invite, dear. We love having you at our gatherings. You bring a sense of... well, humor, that is usually lacking."

Timmy looked around the room and seemed equal parts confused and amused. "Well, I think it is high time we start to eat."

As they all gathered around the table, Anna Katherine heard her dad say, "With all the wedding excitement, I didn't get a chance to ask. How did the two of you start dating?"

Patricia found that to be an excellent topic. "Oh! What a wonderful question. Yes, Nat and Alex, please tell us."

They all sat around the table, and Anna Katherine didn't miss the way

Harry nudged Nat so she would sit by Alex.

"You know..." Alex cleared his throat. "It wasn't anything special. We just... you know. And now we're..."

"Wow," Harry chuckled. "You really have a way with words, don't you, Alex?"

Nat coughed and placed a tentative hand on Alex's shoulder. "Don't worry. I'll tell it. We all know I'm the better storyteller anyway. It comes with the territory."

Patricia leaned over to Timmy and loudly whispered, "She's a teacher, dear."

"Yes, I recall, Patty."

Nat went on. "I had just had a really bad night. Truth be told, Kit and I had just gotten into an argument. I was feeling a little abandoned from her spending so much time with Declan. You know, it was an adjustment. Anyway, I didn't really have anyone to go to who understood the situation. So I called Alex but just ended up going over to his place."

Anna Katherine rested her chin on Declan's shoulder so he could hear her when she whispered, "She's good at coming up with a story on the spot."

He hummed in response.

"When I went over there, he listened to me rant about the situation. He gave me a glass of water and cooked me dinner. Really took care of me. I didn't realize it until I went home later, but it really dawned on me at that moment how much he cared for me."

"Aw..." Patty smiled at Alex. "Our son has such a big heart. Of course he fell for you first."

Harry was watching Nat intently, and Anna Katherine couldn't read his face. But his usual playful smirk was missing.

"Anyway, I was still too chicken to do anything about it, but thankfully your son felt the change between us. He asked me out the next day, and here we are."

Alex popped a bite of bread in his mouth. "Now that the story is out of the way, can we please eat?"

The rest of the table nodded in agreement, and finally, the food was served, and Anna Katherine spooned a large portion of asparagus onto her plate.

"I see you're eating asparagus." Patricia felt the need to point out.

She glanced at her plate and then up at her mother, "Yes?"

"Is that because it helps boost your fertility?"

"Mother!"

"Mom! I don't want to hear about my sister's fertility!"

Declan swooped in. "You know we're waiting, Patty."

Anna Katherine leaned against the table as she sent a disbelieving glare in her mother's direction. "And weren't you just on my side about the baby thing at Thanksgiving?"

Patricia scoffed. "That was months ago—"

"Barely three."

"Times have changed."

Anna Katherine tossed her hands up in the air. "What could have possibly changed in three months!"

"I have found the name I want my grandchildren to call me."

"What in the world?"

"Mom, that's..."

Harry leaned in curiously. "And what name is that?"

"Gigi! And Timmy here will be Pops."

Alex and Anna Katherine groaned.

Harry completely ignored them. "Oh, Gigi and Pops! I love it."

"Thank you, Harry."

Timmy hummed. "Good to know I had a say in this, dear."

Patricia waved him off. "You would've told me you didn't care anyway."

"Don't worry, Dr. Timmy. I think it's a great name."

Anna Katherine glared. "Hayden—"

"Not my name."

"—stop encouraging her."

Declan gripped his wife's knee. "As much as we're thrilled that you decided on what you want to be called, I still think Kit and I have a few things we want to do before we pop one out."

That sent her into a coughing fit. Somehow, between coughs, she managed to croak, "Pop one out?"

"I'm on your side, don't nitpick my word choices," he whispered to her. Then to her parents, "But as soon as we decide to try, everyone at this table will be the first to know."

Anna Katherine tried to hide her annoyance toward Declan.

Harry perked up. "Even me?"

"No," Anna Kathereine spit out.

"Yes," Declan agreed at the same time

"Thanks, *Declan*." Harry glared at Anna Katherine. "I have nothing to say to you."

"Good."

"Fine."

"Okay, then."

"Well." Timmy cleared his throat. "On that lovely note, we need to start planning our family trip to the mountains."

Anna Katherine had never been more thankful for her father than in that moment.

Declan was brushing his teeth when Kit showed up in the bathroom door-way with arms crossed over her chest. "Why would you say that?"

The toothbrush dangled from his mouth. "Huh?"

"That we'd tell them when we'd start trying! I don't want my entire family to know when I'm in my fertile window or when we're having sex to try to create a small and tiny human!"

He spat in the sink and wiped his mouth with the back of his hand. "What?"

"Declan!"

"What!"

Kit took a deep breath. "You told my parents, Alex, his fake girlfriend, and *Harry* that we would tell them when we were trying for a baby!"

He gave her an incredulous look.

"Just how far are we taking this sham of a marriage!"

Declan followed her as she stormed off to his bedroom. "I still don't understand what the problem is."

She got in the bed and grabbed a pillow to scream into.

"Uh, that's my pillow."

She threw it at him with a glare. "I am so mad at you right now."

"I still don't know why."

There was another sigh from Kit. "It's the principle of the thing, Declan. You promised my parents something we both know will never happen."

Thinking it was safe, he got in bed next to her. "What do you mean? I'm sure we can make Aunt Jeannie and your mom's dreams come true."

She slapped his arm and screeched, "Declan!"

He threw his head back laughing, and when he looked at her again her cheeks were tinted pink. "Kit, are you *blushing?*"

"I hate you, Declan Mullins." She huffed as she plopped down and turned her back to him.

"I know you, and I know when you say that you actually mean love."

"Leave."

Her back stayed facing him as he slid underneath the covers. "Did you forget this was my bed?"

She ignored him.

"I guess we're sleeping together tonight then."

"In your dreams." She huffed again and got up to storm across the hall to her room.

He laughed again and called, "Love you too, Kit!"

Fox, who had been in her kennel during the dinner, now watched the two of them with a bored expression while she laid curled up at the end of Declan's bed. She made absolutely no move to follow Kit to her bedroom, and he was sure that just fueled her irritation.

Declan settled himself in bed with a smile. Little did Kit know, having a forever family with her was exactly what he dreamed of. He was still smiling when he finally went to sleep.

37

Declan woke up once again by Kit bouncing on his bed and patting his leg.

He groaned and covered his face with a pillow. "I thought you hated mornings?"

"I've been awake for hours. I had an opening shift this morning."

"It's only ten."

"Exactly! Time's a wastin'!"

He groaned again and she laughed, hopping off of him. "C'mon. You're coming with me today."

He kept his eyes closed. "Where are we going?"

"Taking pictures for the Jonah job."

He opened his eyes then, only to find that she had slipped on one of his shirts. "You're ruining me."

She smirked at him over her shoulder, looking a little too proud of herself for his liking. "Feeling's mutual, Dec."

Declan didn't think it was mutual at all. At least, not to the extent that he meant it. He was in love with his best friend, only he couldn't tell her because he asked her to marry him in order not to get deported. Their situation was so confusing that he no longer knew what was a facade and what was real. For the most part, he knew the parts he was faking, which were limited and few. Kit, though. She was a different story. She was playful and teasing, and where Declan used to be able to see through the many masks she wore, he was suddenly having trouble understanding the reasons behind most of her actions.

What was simply Kit? What was an act for Kit? What was the heart she hid so well from the world?

"I'll go start the coffee." She tied her hair back and grabbed one of his hats to wear, "Don't take too long. I want to get going before it gets too warm."

It didn't take him long to get dressed, and when he went to the kitchen where Kit was eating dry cereal, he asked, "Why do you always take my Saturdays away from me?"

She looked smug, "You married me. This is what you get."

He thought back to all the other weekends she had dragged him across the city for one reason or another even before he was being threatened to be deported. "I feel like this was already part of my life before the marriage."

"Fine." She huffed. "You chose to be my friend five and some years ago. This is what you get."

He poured himself coffee in the to-go mug she had gotten out for him and took a sip before saying, "Can I get a refund?"

She laughed and slid off the counter, "As if I'd ever let that happen. You're stuck with me, pal."

Declan couldn't help but hope that would actually be true.

They went to the mural first, and when Kit shoved him in front of it and told him to pose, he glared at her. "You never said I'd be forced to be in your pictures."

"You're my muse, Declan. Now suck it up and look pretty."

He, of course, did as she wanted, and after a few minutes they were both laughing and doing one ridiculous pose after another. Eventually, Kit set the timer on her camera, and Declan pulled her in front of the mural with him. He lifted her up and spun her around, and his stomach swooped when gravity pulled her toward his body. There was a moment where she was still flush against him, standing on her toes, looking up at him and he thought he could see the same emotions he felt mirrored in her features. But when they disappeared, Declan knew he must have imagined it all.

Anna Katherine began editing the photos as soon as they got back to the apartment after grabbing lunch together. The mural pictures were as wonderful as she had expected, and after clicking through them a few times, she went and found the original mural pictures in one of her old folders. She found them easily enough, and looking back at them made her crave for the simplicity life had possessed during those days. They were in college, carefree, and their worries only stretched to the end of each term. She had been in love. She clicked on what had once been one of her favorite photos of her and Jonah, and the longing she expected to feel for something that could have been never surged to the surface

She zoomed in on her own face, staring for a moment. She had once thought that she had looked completely and utterly in love at that moment, but now she wasn't so sure. She had definitely been enamored, but she didn't see the love she had been so certain was there.

Her heart began to beat faster as she pulled up her favorite picture of her and Declan from earlier that day. She was leaning against him, gazing up at him, and...

Her throat felt tight. She slammed her laptop shut, stuffed it in her bag, and ran out the door.

"Where are you off to in such a hurry?" Declan called after her as she ran to put on her shoes and grab her keys.

"Uh, Nat's." And then she was slamming the door shut and racing off to see her best friend.

As soon as she was in Nat's living room, she took her computer back out, opened it, and shoved it in Nat's face.

"What do you see?"

Nat looked at Anna Katherine like she was insane. Probably because her heart was beating too frantically for her to concentrate on that at the moment.

"Uh, I see you and Declan?"

She shook the computer. "What else?"

"The mural we all went to that one time?"

"And?"

Nat was exasperated. "I don't know what I'm supposed to be seeing, Kit. All I see is you and Declan being you and Declan!"

Anna Katherine zoomed in on her face and placed the computer on Nat's lap before falling on the couch. "What do you see now?"

Nat eyes her wearily before looking back at the photo. "I see you looking at Declan like you always do."

"I look like I'm in love with him, Nat."

Anna Katherine was staring at the ceiling, but she could feel Nat's eyes on her. "I thought we'd already been over this?"

"No." She shook her head, "I *thought* I was in love with him. There was no certainty. But this—" she pointed to the picture, "—is the look of someone completely and utterly in love with the person they are looking at. That girl is completely in love with that boy."

"Right."

"Declan doesn't do relationships. His only long-lasting relationship was with Vivian who he dated for five years or something, and she completely shattered him. Ruined him. Broke him. *Destroyed* him. He's never had a relationship since."

"That also happened five years ago. He's probably over it for all you know."

"I know everything about him. He hasn't even attempted to enter into a relationship."

"That might be because he's now married." Nat gave her a careful look. "To you."

"But even before then. He's never even talked about wanting to settle down."

"Ever thought that's because he had you?"

"We're friends, Natalie." She took the computer back from her. "And now I'm ruining it all with these stupid emotions."

"Kit—"

She cut Nat off. "You know what? It's probably just because of the wedding, you know? All the acting and pretending and lying. It's just making me confused. This entire situation is making me think that I'm in love with him, but really he's just Declan and I'm just Kit, and that's all we'll ever be."

"I don't know what I'm supposed to say here."

"Just tell me I'm right."

"You know I'd never lie to you."

Anna Katherine scowled. "Why do you have to be such a good friend?"

Nat smiled, but it didn't reach her eyes. "Look, you know I have my issues with trust and relationships, thanks to my parents, so I'm probably not the best person to give advice. However, don't let whatever this is ruin the good thing you and Declan have. Whatever happens, just be careful."

Anna Katherine didn't have a response for that.

Anna Katherine was lying with Declan on the floor. Declan was resting his head on Fox's bed, and Anna Katherine was using one of their pet's toys as a pillow. He was reading over the possible questions that the immigration interviewer might ask them while she scrolled through Facebook.

"I really think we know most of these answers." She heard him rustle the papers, probably turning the page.

"Like what?"

"One is 'how did we meet', which we're sticking to our original story as closely as possible, so easy. College."

"More specifically, my ex-boyfriend."

He laughed. "Right. There are also questions about our wedding, which we were both there for. Again, easy. And then questions about our daily life."

"Daily life?"

"Yeah, like..." More rustling of pages. "How we start our day."

"I wake up hours before you to open Hattie's Cafe. On the days that I'm off, you wake up, and make us coffee before going to work. Unless it's a weekend. In that case..."

"If it's a Saturday, and then you rudely wake me up and refuse to allow me to sleep in."

She gave him a side-eye. "Only if there is something exciting happening, otherwise I love a good sleep-in. And on Sundays, we're lazy. Unless Patty demands a family church gathering."

"And you make the coffee."

She smiled. "Have we always been so predictable?"

"Haven't a clue. How often do we talk when we're not together?"

"Like not together during the day or when you go home to Ireland?"

"Dunno. Both?"

"We text pretty constantly throughout the day, don't we?"

"Yeah, you're almost always at the top of my messages."

"But do we talk on the phone?"

He hesitated. "I think we only really FaceTime when I go to Ireland. So, no. Not often. Who cooks and who cleans?"

"You do both."

Declan chuckled. "I'm starting to realize you bring very little to this relationship."

"I bring you freedom."

"Sure. Alright, there could potentially be several about kids."

"Kids?"

"Yeah. Do we have any? No."

"Excuse you, do not forget about Fox, our lovely first born."

At the sound of her name, Fox's ears perked up from where she was chewing on a bone from her seat on the couch.

He snorted. "Fine. We'll mention her. How many kids do we want?"

"I—"

"—You change your mind depending on your mood. You either want to adopt a hoard of children or you only want two."

She huffed and turned so she could look at him. "How do you even know that?"

He shrugged. "I pay attention."

"Well, how many do you want?"

"At most, three. But I don't want a middle child with all that 'middle child drama', ya know? So I would prefer one or two."

"That's at odds with my apparent want of a hoard."

He laughed. "I'm sure our love is strong enough to endure our difference of opinions."

Declan reached down and ran his fingers through her hair. Anna Katherine closed her eyes, enjoying the feeling of it. "Surely there are tough questions they might ask us."

"They might ask about our finances. Don't worry, I'll do that math and figure it all out."

"Thank you very much."

His fingers caught on a tangle, and he took his time smoothing it out. "In our independent interviews, they'll ask us physical questions... like what we look like. Tattoos. All those types of things."

"Independent interviews?"

"Yeah, they'll separate us for one part of it to see if our questions line up."

She groaned. "This is going to be the worst."

He intertwined their fingers. "It's going to be fine, Kit-Kat."

Eighth Commandment: Thou (Kit) Shalt Do My (Declan's) Laundry

"*That's not fair. I hate doing my own laundry.*"

"*I'm paying over half of the bills, Kit.*"

"*And I'm marrying you to prevent you from being deported.*"

He ignored her. "This includes ironing my work clothes."

She collapsed on the floor, her legs and arms flailed out dramatically. "You're killing me, Dec," she groaned.

He didn't pay her any mind, his focus on the paper in front of him as he wrote out the most recent rule.

38

Declan rubbed Kit's arm. "Your phone is ringing."

She snuggled against his side. "No."

"Kit."

"You answer it."

With a sigh, he reached over her and grabbed her phone where it sat on the bedside table. "Hello?"

"Uh, Anna Kay?"

Declan pulled the phone away to look at the name on the screen. A groan escaped before he could stop it. "Mate, do you have any idea what time it is?"

Jonah chuckled. "It's eight. Plenty of people are up this early."

"But it's a Saturday. People don't work on Saturday."

There was a pause, and Declan didn't like the feeling of it. He liked what Jonah said next even less. "I, uh, I'm not calling for work. Is she there?"

He looked down at Kit who was still cuddled against him with her eyes squeezed shut. "She's trying to sleep."

"C'mon. We both know she's faking it right now. She's too nosey for her own good."

Declan didn't bother whispering when he asked Kit, "Do you want to speak to your jerk of an ex who cheated on you about something not work related or would you like me to hang up on him?"

Jonah snorted. "Real nice, Declan."

Kit blindly reached for the phone, and Declan placed it in her hand.

"What? Of course I sound annoyed, you woke me up."

He was watching when her eyes flew open. "What? Why?"

He sent her a questioning look, but she ignored him and sat up against their headboard. "Fine. But I'm busy the next two weeks. Yeah, fine. That works. Okay. Bye."

She flung her phone to the end of the bed and slid down so she was lying against him again. He traced patterns on her back where her shirt had scrunched up. "What did he want?"

"He wanted to get dinner together. Like, without work."

He froze. "So, a date?"

"No." She almost laughed. "Two friends catching up. At least, that's what he said."

"You two were never friends."

"He also said something about closure." She patted his stomach in an attempt to comfort him. "Don't overthink this, Declan. I'm still half asleep and don't have it in me to ease your worries."

His fingers started up the patterns on her back again.

"Let's just go back to sleep."

He held her close against him. "Whatever you want, Kit-Kat."

Declan and Harry were on their way to Nat's when Declan found the courage to ask, "So, hypothetically, if another man were to ask a married woman out to dinner just to catch up, how should the husband feel?"

Harry shot him a glance. "Is the other man Jonah?"

"How'd you know?"

"It's not hard to figure out, man." Harry turned on his blinker to switch lanes. "When did this happen?"

"Yesterday morning. Woke us both up like an idiot."

"I'm sorry—" Harry sounded surprised and risked another glance at him "—both?"

"Yeah, we've been sleeping in my bed."

Harry merged into the turning lane. "Mate."

"What?"

"You said you weren't going to do that anymore after the honeymoon."

Declan ignored him. "Can we get back to the topic at hand?"

"You're an idiot. But sure. Jonah. What about him?"

"Am I crazy for being..." He trailed off, unsure how to articulate his feelings.

"Jealous?"

"I'm not jealous. I'm just... uneasy."

"Right," Harry snorted as he turned onto Nat's street. "Jonah is her ex, so in a normal situation I feel like the husband has a right to be jealous or uneasy. Whatever you want to call it. But you guys aren't in a normal situation."

"But isn't it sketchy that he asked a married woman out to dinner?"

"Not necessarily. For all we know, he really does just want to catch up with her."

"Yeah, if catching up means—"

Harry cut him off. "Declan."

"What?"

"Jealousy does not suit you."

He huffed. "I just don't understand why she agreed to it. What if she decides she wants to get back together with him? What if marrying me has completely derailed her future? I've ruined everything."

Harry pulled into the spot beside Nat's car. Once the car was in park, he turned to face Declan. "You didn't force her to marry you. Kit does what Kit wants. You know this."

"Yeah, but she also changes her mind every thirty seconds. Just the other day she told me she wanted to have Thai food for dinner, but by the time we got in the car to go, she wanted hamburgers instead. What if she regrets getting married?"

"I have it on good authority that she has no regrets regarding this marriage."

Declan glared at him. "How?"

"Her best friend."

"I don't like how much you and Nat talk about us."

"You two are our common ground. Deal with it."

"What else have you and Nat said?"

Harry smiled. "Sorry. I've been sworn to secrecy."

Unbuckling, they got out of the car, but before they headed up to Nat's door, Harry stopped them. "Is this about you still being upset that Jonah slept with Rachel while dating Kit, or is this about you loving Anna Katherine?"

Declan thought for a moment before answering. "The two are one in the same. I'm over him using the girl I was with to cheat on Kit. What I'm not over is him hurting her."

"I think you need to tell her that, Declan."

He shook his head and started up the sidewalk that led to Nat's apartment. "No way. We've been over this."

"And I still don't understand why you're being stubborn about it."

Declan spun around to look at Harry. "Because, both of our emotions are all over the place. It's hard to pretend to be married and in love with someone you're not actually married to or in love with. Feelings get messy. If I tell her I love her, how would she know I meant it? And if by some God-given miracle she says it back, how am I to know if she means it? If one of us messes this up, our entire friendship is gone." He took a deep breath, "If she tells me she loves me, and then takes it back... I couldn't handle that. I wouldn't be able to go back to how we were before."

"I don't think you're giving Kit enough credit here."

Declan shook his head. "She means too much to me, H. I can't risk it."

"I, for one, think love is worth all the risks."

"Hey, Harry?"

"Yeah?"

"Shut up or I'll punch you."

Harry laughed. "I think I'm going to start interviewing for a new best friend."

"I'm sure Alex will jump on this opportunity."

"I don't like grouchy Declan."

"I don't like *you*."

"Yeah, I get that a lot."

The food was already delivered when they walked through the door, and as Harry and Declan unpacked the food, Harry smirked. "Our girls know us so well, Declan."

Nat looked up at the use of *our girls*, but Kit didn't seem to notice, too engrossed in whatever she was doing on her phone. Nat greeted Harry with a soft smile, and then turned her attention back to her phone.

Declan, watching this all unfold, gave Harry a questioning look, but didn't ask. "Yeah, we're lucky." When he pulled Kit to his side, she let him. He didn't think he would ever get tired of the feeling of how well they fit together.

39

I want to die.
Kit a 5:21 pm

I'd rather you didn't.
Declan a 5:21 pm

I'm hiding in the storage room I cant do this anymore Id rather have a slow bleed out From someone stabbing me in the gut.
Kit a 5:22 pm

Why are you hiding in the storage room?
Declan a 5:25 pm

The customers.
Kit a 5:25 pm

And?
Declan a 5:26 pm

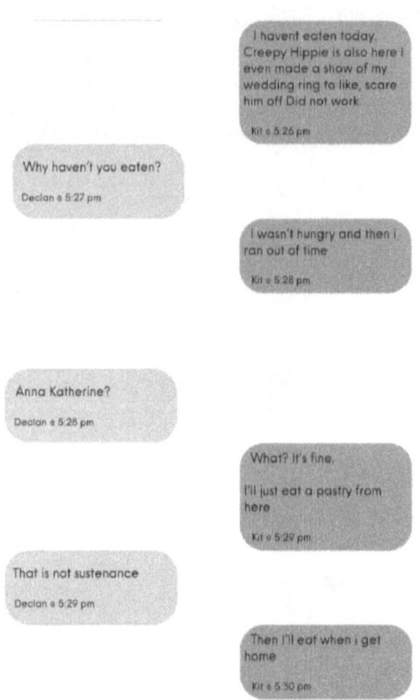

Anna Katherine pocketed her phone when Declan didn't immediately text back and braced herself to go back to work. It wasn't that this was the worst shift she'd ever worked. She was just in a terrible mood and had been since she woke up that morning. Her mood got even worse when Declan was supposed to come home for lunch but couldn't because of a project at work. Then, he had to work late, so she wasn't able to see him before she left for her shift, either. It was raining when she took Fox for her walk, which just added to her dreary mood, and traffic was horrible on her way to work. Work was busier than usual for a Wednesday night, and this guy wouldn't stop staring at her cleavage, not that she had much, but it was the moral of the thing.

There was also a small chance she was hangry, but it was too late for her to do anything about that now. She would just have to settle for a muffin once she got her break. That is, if things ever slowed down enough for her to take one.

"Tips are basically nonexistent tonight," Mack told her as soon as she emerged from her hiding spot.

"One day we will have better jobs and won't have to do this. My feet can rest. My hair won't smell like old coffee. I won't have to rely on tips to survive. It'll be great."

Mack laughed, "Yeah, but you're married to Declan. You'd be fine even if you quit now and only had your photography job."

Anna Katherine scoffed. "I think 'fine' is over-selling it. Besides, I don't like the idea of stealing Declan's money."

"Seriously?" Mack looked at her like she was crazy. "You're married to the guy. What's his is yours and yours is his."

She froze. Hiding her sham of a wedding from Mack had been mostly easy, but there were times—like just now—where she forgot that Mack didn't know the truth. "Right. But, you know me, I just like my independence."

"Well Miss Independence, why don't you go take Creepy Hippie's order. He's been staring at you ever since you came back out."

Anna Katherine shot Mack a glare. "We both know what he wants isn't on the menu. Whenever I take his order, he just flirts in the most awful of ways."

Mack shrugged. "Too bad. I took his order last time. It's your turn"

Creepy Hippie was the nickname the staff at Hattie's Cafe gave him. He had long hair that was thinning out on top and was usually tied back with a string. He had a mustache that seemed to have a mind of its own with the way it moved when he talked. Overall, he was harmless in the sense that he never actively did anything to put their lives in danger, but he was creepy in the way that he continued to stare at whichever girl was working that night.

Creepy in the way he smirked and winked, and in the way he sat there nearly all night long. Anna Katherine wasn't necessarily scared of him, but he did put her on edge. On the nights when he showed up, she never walked to her car alone if he left right at closing.

She braced herself as she walked toward him. "What can I get for you tonight?"

He smirked. "Just the usual."

The wink is what really made her shiver.

"And that is?" She knew what it was, but she would never give him that satisfaction.

His cocky, creepy smirk faltered. "Oh, uh, just a decaf with whole milk."

"Right," she said. "It'll be right out."

Anna Katherine might've taken longer than necessary to get him his drink, but he didn't seem to mind, judging by the wink he gave her when she handed it to him.

Anna Katherine was in the middle of two mocha frappes, also known as the bane of her existence, when she heard Mack shout to her over the noise, "Husband is here!"

She spun around, nearly dropping the blender that was still in her hand when she saw Declan leaning against the counter, smiling at her. He swung a bag in front of him. "C'mon. Time for your break."

She gaped at him. "I can't just leave Mack here by herself."

"Sure you can. Right, Mack?"

Mack smirked, "He texted me earlier. I told him I could manage. Now get out of here before I change my mind!"

Anna Katherine was still trying to catch up on what was going on as she finished up the drinks and led Declan out back to the rotting picnic table out back. It creaked as they both sat down facing each other.

She took a moment to study Declan. "What are you doing here?"

He motioned to the bag sitting between them. "Thought it was obvious."

"Yeah, but..." She trailed off as he started pulling food out of the bag. Her mouth watered when she saw the cheeseburgers and sweet potato fries from her favorite restaurant. "You didn't say anything."

He shrugged. "Didn't think I had to." He passed her one of the drinks, and she immediately knew it was a rootbeer float. "I didn't want you closing tonight on an empty stomach."

"I would've gotten something once I got home."

He gave her an unimpressed look. "Sure."

There was a beat of silence that was interrupted by her stomach growling, causing them both to laugh.

"Thanks for this, Declan."

He smiled around a bite.

"You didn't have to do this, you know. It's late and you have work in the morning."

He reached across the table and rubbed his thumb across her knuckles. "When are you going to learn that I'd do anything for you? Bringing you food is nothing."

The light out back flickered, and the shadows danced across his face. She turned her hand over and laced their fingers together. She was struck by how different he was than Jonah. Where Jonah was all sharp angles and piercing stares, Declan was gentle smiles and soft glances. She wondered when she started preferring Declan's smoothness to Jonah's roughness. She didn't think she actually wanted to know.

"I'm really glad you're my friend."

He pulled his hand away, swallowing before saying, "Wouldn't have it any other way, Kit-Kat."

They didn't take long eating, and soon they were headed back inside. Anna Katherine expected Declan to leave and was surprised when she saw him sitting on a stool a few feet down from Creepy Hippie.

Declan widened his eyes and nodded toward the guy. Anna Katherine rolled her eyes but nodded. She tried not to be obvious about watching as he slid to the next stool and started talking to their annoying guest. She did her best to ignore their conversation, but glances in their direction told her it at least seemed friendly.

When she walked by she couldn't help but overhear what Declan said, "You come here by yourself? I'm only here to see the wife."

She took the next order and helped Mack restock the milks when things started to slow down. She made Declan's half-caf breve and walked back over to them. "Here you go."

Declan looked at her with a blinding smile. "And there she is. The woman who stole my heart."

Anna Katherine rolled her eyes. "Shut up and drink your coffee, Mullins."

"Always such a charmer," he laughed.

She chanced a look at Creepy Hippie who was watching them carefully. "Didn't know you were married."

She flashed the ring at him. "Thought this was a clear sign."

"How long has it been now, love? Five months?" Declan oozed adoration.

"It was exactly four months last week."

"See?" Declan pointed his thumb at her. "I'd be lost without her."

Creepy Hippie just nodded. "Lucky fella."

"Tell me about it. What about you? You got a special someone?"

Anna Katherine left them to their conversation and went to shut down and clean half of the espresso machine. Midway through, she noticed Creepy Hippie walking out. She went straight to Declan. "You got him to leave!"

He took a sip of his drink and shrugged. "Wasn't hard. Just kept telling him how in love we are."

"Well, thanks. He's a menace here."

He flicked the mug that Creepy Hippie had been drinking out of. "I better get going. I need to take Fox out and finish a load of laundry before bed."

She grimaced. "Sorry. I hate that you have to pick up the slack."

"Don't worry about it." He quickly dismissed her concern. "Text me as you're leaving, yeah?"

"Oh, now you're going to be playing the overprotective husband bit?"

He smiled, but there was sadness, almost regret in his eyes. "Not playing anything, Kit."

"If this is about Creepy Hippie, he's been here since the beginning of time. He never bothers us once we close up."

"Just save me from an anxiety attack and keep me updated. Please."

It was the 'please' that really did her in. "Yeah, okay. I will." Then she smiled, "Only if you give me a goodbye kiss."

"You'll get in trouble. No PDA at work, remember?"

She waved him off. "The boss isn't here. It's just Mack."

When he leaned over the counter, she met him halfway. It was their most innocent kiss to date—just a peck on the lips. It was barely even a kiss, but it still left her smiling for the rest of the night.

40

Mack created a group chat
Mack added William, and two others to chat
Guess who has next saturday off?
Mack • 9:12 am
Im going to take a wild guess here You?
William • 9:12 am
U?
Nat • 9:12 am
Yes but most importantly....
Kit and I both are off Which means everyone is off this Saturday
Nat • 9:12 am
You dont know my life
Harry • 9:14 am

Harry shut up

Nat @ 9:14 am

And...?

William @ 9:15 am

It's getting hot. We have the weekend off. We are just an hour and a few minutes from the beach...

Mack @ 9:15 am

Are you saying what I think youre saying?

Harry @ 9:15 am

Beach trip!!!

Mack @ 9:17 am

What is going on Why is my phone going off?

Declan @ 9:17 am

Are you incapable of reading the texts?

Harry @ 9:20 am

Im at work and unlike SOME ppl im trying to do my job

Declan @ 9:20 am

Yeah, yeah. Rub it in our faces wont ya

Harry @ 9:21 am

Guyssssss

Mack @ 9:22 am

I'm down for a day trip if everyone else is And i'll be sure H is there

Nat @ 9:22 am

What Nat said

William @ 9:24 am

Yeah, that should work for us

Declan @ 9:24 am

Where is kit?

Mack @ 9:25 am

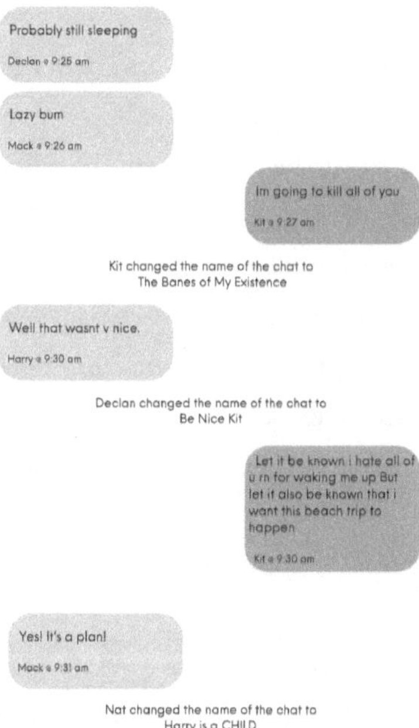

T he plan was to be on the road by six. This meant waking up at the most ungodly hour of five, but Anna Katherine woke up as soon as the first alarm went off and quickly turned off all the others. She felt bad for Declan. Even though he definitely needed this one-day vacation, work had truly been horrendous for him the past week, and she could tell how exhausted he was. He told her he would wake up and make their lunch for them, and Anna Katherine hadn't argued because she knew he wouldn't agree to anything less. But that didn't mean she couldn't wake up before him, turn off her alarms as well as his, get everything ready, and *then* wake him up at the last possible minute.

And she did just that. She made them both PB&J's—two for Declan and one for her—put the drinks he had bought on his way home last night in the cooler along with the frozen waters, and she cut up the fruit, making them a fruit salad. Packing their beach blanket and portable chargers, towels, sunscreen, and a change of clothes for the both of them, she shoved it all into a beach bag. Lastly, she put on a pot of coffee and threw two bagels into the toaster oven. Once she changed into her clothes for the day, she went to get Declan up.

Seeing him sleeping, she didn't want to wake him, but knew she had to if they wanted to go to the beach with their friends. Running her fingers through his hair, she whispered, "Declan, it's time to wake up."

He groaned and buried his face in the pillow.

She gave his scalp a scratch. "C'mon. You need to get dressed. The others will be here soon."

He peeked an eye at her. "You turned off my alarms didn't you?"

She smiled. "Maybe."

He turned over on his back, and the way he stared up at her was a little unsettling. She stayed still when he lifted his hand and traced his fingers across her cheek. His eyes went to her mouth, and when his thumb ran across her lips, she felt her heart flutter.

She thought he was about to say something, but Fox barked, and his hand fell to the mattress. "Thanks for letting me sleep."

She thought she nodded, but she wasn't completely sure. "Yeah. I'll go take Fox out. There's coffee and a bagel ready for you."

Before he could respond, she was off the bed and out of the room.

On the way back from walking Fox, Anna Katherine ran into Nat. Almost literally.

"Hey!" She was all smiles and much too perky for how early it was. She took in Anna Katherine's face. "Whoa. What's that look for?"

"What look?"

"You look like you're trying to solve world hunger."

She thought back to Declan's thumb grazing her lips, the pad of his fingers trailing her skin. "Uh, nothing. Just.." She knew she probably looked desperate, but she couldn't find it in herself to care. "What car am I riding in? Can you make sure Declan and I aren't in the same car?"

Nat immediately looked concerned, and Anna Katherine was thankful that her friend knew her well enough not to ask any more questions. "You and Declan were going to ride with Mack, but I'm sure they'll all agree if I say all the girls can be in one car and the guys in the other."

"Yes. Please." She looked down at Fox and then back at Nat. "You have no idea how much you'd be helping me if you did that."

"Of course." Nat took her in. "If you need to talk about it…"

"Yeah, yeah." She nodded. "I know. And you'll be the first I go to when I'm ready. Promise."

The drive to the beach was what every road trip with friends should be. They blasted music from their childhood, only to turn it down mid-song to reminisce on sleepovers and late night conversations and that feeling every girl felt when she unburdened her heart to her closest friend while they shared a blanket and their heads rested on the pillow. There had been an odd sense of security during those nights with the lights off and all adults sound asleep in the other room.

They sang off key and laughed when they sang the wrong words. When the boys tried to pass them, they sped up and laughed when Harry playfully flipped them off. They all stopped at the fruit stand to buy fresh boiled peanuts, homemade jellies, and more fruit than any of them could possibly eat in a day. For a moment, Anna Katherine forgot she married Declan just to keep him in the states. She forgot that she was in love with him but had no idea how he felt about her. She forgot all about this morning when his gentle touch and soul-piercing eyes spooked her like a deer caught in headlights.

They were some of the first people at the public beach, which is what they wanted and why they'd left so early. They parked side by side, and when Declan got out of William's car, he walked straight to her.

He pulled on her braid. "I can't believe you made me ride in the car with those fools."

"Don't pretend you didn't enjoy it."

"Yeah, but I missed you."

She laughed and shoved his chest. "You just saw me at the fruit stand an hour ago."

He grabbed her arm and pulled her to him. "You don't seem to understand that there is no minimum amount of time that can pass for a husband to start missing his wife."

She propped her chin on his chest to look up at him and rolled her eyes. "You were one of those kids that had separation anxiety from their parents weren't you?"

He laughed. "Actually, no." He brushed a loose strand of hair behind her ear, "Just prefer when we're together. Nothing wrong with that."

Something stirred in her stomach, and she was pretty sure her heart was doing cartwheels in her chest. Not for the first time, his words had made her speechless.

"Hey, lovebirds!" They looked up to find Harry staring at them. "Cut the romance short, will you? We gotta load up and find the perfect spot on the beach."

As they were walking down the beach, Nat nudged her with her elbow. "I thought we were avoiding Declan?"

Anna Katherine let out a quiet groan. "I don't even know anymore, Nat. I've never been so confused and conflicted in my entire life."

"Conflicted?"

"He's my best friend."

"I don't see how him being your best friend is a problem."

"I can't lose him."

Nat hummed and linked their arms together. It made it a little more difficult to walk in the sand while carrying everything, but Anna Katherine appreciated the comfort it brought.

Nat gave her an encouraging smile. "C'mon. Let's catch up with the others."

Mack finally deemed a spot perfect for their group, and the guys put up the two umbrellas, while the girls set out the chairs and turned on the speaker. Once everything was set up, they lathered on the sunscreen.

Harry jumped on the balls of his feet. "You guys ready to go in?"

"Yeah!" Anna Katerine started taking off her coverup.

"You're supposed to wait thirty minutes to get in water after applying sunscreen, guys."

She and Harry ignored Nat. He stripped off his shirt and smirked at Anna Katherine. "Race ya to the sandbar."

"Oh, you're on."

As she slammed against the first wave, she heard Declan yell, "The sandbar is where the sharks are!"

Much to her annoyance, Harry beat her to the sandbar, and much to the annoyance of their friends, they stayed out there until her hair was caked with salt and their fingers turned to prunes. They took their time swimming back, and when they were halfway back to the beach, everyone else joined them in the water.

Nat got on Harry's back, her arms resting comfortably over his shoulders. Mack and William jumped the waves, and their laughter could be heard over the sound of them crashing. Anna Katherine smiled when Declan came over to her. He was still an arm's length away when a wave caught her by surprise and drew her into the water as it tumbled over her. She couldn't tell up from down or whether she was going forward or backward. It wasn't until a hand grabbed her wrist and yanked her up that she began to gather her senses once more.

"Have I ever told you that you and Harry are going to be the death of me?" His thumbs rubbed circles over the soft skin of her wrist.

Anna Katherine coughed as she brushed her hair out of her face. She was sure it looked like a stringy, tangled rat's nest from the salt and the whirl the waves just took her on. "It's usually just me that you mention, but yeah. You have."

"It obviously hasn't sunk in for you."

She scrunched up her face. "Might need to say it one more time. You know, for it to really sink in."

Another wave came, and Declan placed himself between it and her so he would take the brunt of the force. The push of it caused him to stumble closer to Anna Katherine. He tugged her the rest of the way to him until she was close enough for him to rest his forehead against hers. "Hey, Kit?"

The butterflies erupted at the softness of his tone, but she managed to smile and ask, "Yeah?"

He leaned back just enough for him to be able to flick her nose with his fingers. "You're going to be the death of me."

"Just me? No more Harry?" She jumped as a wave came and started swimming backward away from him, but she didn't get far before he reached out and grabbed her wrist again. He gently pulled her to him and watched her for a breath of a moment. Anna Katherine could have sworn that even her butterflies had butterflies.

Declan pressed a soft kiss to her cheek. "Just you, Kit-Kat."

For a sweet moment, it was just the two of them. They were in their own bubble, but it popped when a wave came crashing on them, shaking them out of their reverie and pulling them apart.

They locked eyes, and Declan once again looked like he was about to say something. Nat beat him to it when she grabbed Anna Katherine's arm saying, "Mack and I are about to go walk the shoreline. Wanna come?"

She looked past Nat's knowing look to Declan who was watching her carefully. Nat gave her arm a gentle squeeze, and she tore her gaze away from Declan and looked at her friend. "Uh, yeah. Sure."

Nat gave her a reassuring smile. "Good." She tugged on Anna Katherine's arm, "Let's go."

As the world crashed back down around her, Anna Katherine wondered how much more of this she could take, and then, with her heart hammering in her chest, she wondered how much of this their friendship could take before it was too late for them to turn back.

When they arrived back at their spot from their walk about an hour later, Declan was sitting in one of the chairs, laughing at something William had said. She was nervous until he gave her a smile, and it was only then that she felt herself start to relax for the first time since the moment they had had together in the water.

She took the seat next to him, and when he nudged her knee with his own, she felt herself smile.

"Had a good walk?"

She nodded.

"Good." He passed her his water. "Don't forget to drink plenty of water."

She rolled her eyes. "So bossy."

"Just looking out for my girl."

She ignored the feeling in the pit of her stomach and took a long gulp of water to appease Declan.

The day went by as any day at the beach does—slow and steady with a sense of contentment that only the lapping of waves and the warm, white sand can create. They all sat or laid in a circle, listening to William's beach playlist and running into the water whenever they began to feel too hot. All of their lunches consisted of sandwiches that the seagulls tried to steal, chips, and fruit. By the time the sun started to set, they were all properly sunkissed.

Anna Katherine wasn't entirely sure who started it—her money was on either William or Harry—but somehow a sandball fight began. At first, Anna Katherine was just watching, but then Declan threw sand at her. It was an all out war at that point. William and Harry eventually ran to the water for cover, but Nat and Declan chased them and dumped a pile of wet sand on the top of their heads. Eventually, a truce was called, and the six of them spent the last few moments of daylight enjoying their time in the water. When the sky turned orange and pink, they got out and started packing up. It was fully dark by the time they had the last of their things packed away and all of them had changed into more comfortable clothes.

Anna Katherine and Nat walked back to the cars together after changing, and while they were still alone, Nat reached out and touched her arm. "Wanna stay with me tonight?"

She gave Nat a questioning look. Nat read the question in her eyes. "I've been thinking about what you said earlier about how you feel conflicted. Maybe having a night away from him will help you clear your head."

There was a loud voice in Anna Katherine's head that screamed against this, but she listened to the softer voice of her friend instead. She nodded.

"Yeah, probably a good idea."

When she told Declan their plan, he looked concerned. "Are you okay?"

She nodded, and he changed the question, this time whispering so only she could hear. "Are *we* okay?"

Her heart plummeted. "Of course we are, Declan." She rocked forward onto her toes to kiss his cheek. "There's nothing for you to worry about."

When she pulled back, he still didn't look convinced, but he smiled anyway. "Alright, well, I'll see you tomorrow then." He cupped her cheek and gave her hand a squeeze. "Hope you two have fun."

"We will. Give Fox lots of cuddles for me."

"Of course."

She gave him one more smile before slipping into the car with Mack and Nat.

Anna Katherine was facing Natalie in the dark bedroom, their heads resting on Nat's pillows.

Despite no one else being in the room, they still whispered.

"Remember when we were younger and stayed up all night talking?"

Anna Katherine smiled at the memories. "We would be stressing over tests and who was dating who and whether or not our parents were going to let us go to a concert."

Nat giggled. "We thought our lives were so stressful back then."

"If only our younger selves could see the mess I'm in now."

"Being in a marriage of convenience definitely wasn't in our ten-year plan."

Anna Katherine turned over on her back. It was too dark to see the ceiling, but she could hear the fan as it spun around. "Things were simpler back then."

Nat was quiet for a moment. Then, with a sigh, she said, "I wouldn't want to go back to it, though."

Anna Katherine surprised herself by saying, "Neither would I."

Declan told himself repeatedly that Kit hadn't been acting weird because of what he said at the beach, but every time she pulled away from his touch, he couldn't help but question it again. It had been days, and she was still choosing to snuggle against the closest pillow rather than him. She took Fox on walks without inviting him. She left for her shifts before he got home from the office. The only time they felt like Kit and Declan was when they went to bed, and even then she seemed not to be her usual self.

By Thursday, he was desperate for things to go back to how they had been. She told him she thought they should hang out with Harry and Nat rather than spend the evening on their normal date night. He had agreed, but only because he didn't want to start bickering with her.

Also, he might have been a little bit of a chicken.

That day, he left work early and hurried to beat the rush hour traffic. He made it home an hour before Nat or Harry were scheduled to show up, and he had every intention of using that time to figure out what was going on with Kit.

Fox was sleeping on her bed in the living room and lazily lifted her head when he walked in. Other than that, she didn't pay him much attention. He noticed that Kit wasn't in the kitchen or bathroom. He dropped his bag at the foot of his bed, then walked across the hall to the spare room.

They had slowly been unpacking her belongings, and now there were only a few boxes stacked in the closet they still had yet to go through. He was glad the room no longer made him feel like he was suffocating whenever he walked in.

Kit was sitting propped up on the bed wearing one of his old college shirts with a book resting on her knees. He closed the door behind him and leaned against it, crossing his arms and legs.

Her eyes went wide when she saw him. "What're you doing home? Why did you close the door?"

"We need to talk."

She closed her book and sat up. "About what?"

He nodded toward her. "You. Why have you been acting weird?"

She blinked. "I haven't."

"Oh, come off it, Kit," he scoffed. "This is me and you we're talking about. I know you better than anyone else."

"It's *nothing*, Declan. I promise."

"If it was nothing, you wouldn't recoil every time I touch you."

She slid off the bed. "I don't!"

He pushed himself off the door and threw his hands up. "Yes! You do!"

She was quiet and refused to look at him.

He softened his voice. "Kit..."

She looked at him then, but it was more of a glare. "Don't. I don't want to talk about it."

"Which is it? Nothing, or nothing you want to admit?"

Anger flashed in her eyes, and she marched over to him and tried to get to the door. He blocked her path, and no matter how much she shoved and pushed, he refused to move.

"Neither of us is leaving until you talk to me."

She set her jaw and crossed her arms. "Then we're never leaving this room."

They stared at each other, both of them with their chests heaving in anger. After a moment, Declan decided to change tactics. His hands dropped to his side, and he took a step toward her. Kit squinted, suspicious of what he was about to do.

When he reached out and started tickling her, she let out a high-pitched squeal and pushed away from him. She jumped on the bed and sat up on her knees, pointing a finger in his direction. "Declan. Don't."

He smirked and gave a quick shrug. "You know how to stop this."

He started walking toward the bed, and she slowly moved backward. When she was in the middle of the bed, he ran and tackled her, tickling her sides and underneath her knees—all the places he knew she hated being tickled.

She was squealing and laughing, and soon he was laughing too. But then he tickled behind her knee again, and her other leg jerked up and kneed him in the crotch. He immediately stopped and rolled off the bed with a loud thump.

He let out a groan and squeezed his eyes shut. Once he was able to open them, he saw Kit peeking over the edge of the bed. She at least had enough decency to look a little apologetic.

"You okay?" She was holding back a smile.

With another groan, he reached up and pulled her off the bed, making her join him on the floor with a thump of her own. He rolled his body on top of hers, propping himself up on an elbow. "That wasn't very nice."

She shrugged, all hints of being sorry seemingly gone. "What you get for tickling me and locking me in my room."

His eyes roamed across her face, resting on her lips before flicking back to her eyes. "Did you hit your head? I didn't hurt you, did I?"

She shook her head, and his hand caressed her cheek. Her voice was the softest he'd ever heard when she said, "I'm fine, Declan."

He rubbed his thumb across her cheek, and she leaned into his touch. "Talk to me, Kit."

He felt her body tense, and he was scared she wouldn't say anything. It would be a very Kit thing to refuse to talk to him after everything that had just happened.

She reached up and interlocked her fingers behind his neck, her thumbs rubbing against his jaw. He didn't think he would ever tire of that feeling.

"I want to kiss you."

His heart thumped against his chest. That hadn't been what he was expecting. He swallowed and then, "What's stopping you?"

Her eyes went wide in surprise. Then, in the blink of an eye, she was surging up and kissing him, and his hand was tangled in her hair.

As much as he should, he didn't care if this was only Kit trying to take the attention off of her odd behavior and avoid talking about whatever was going on with her. He'd give her whatever part of him she craved, even if it was only this.

Then they heard a door slam shut.

"Guys?"

It was Nat.

Declan's head fell onto her shoulder with a groan.

Her hands found their way into his hair. "She's going to come in here soon if we don't go out there."

"We could just—" He looked up at her, his playful smirk a stark contrast to how he was looking at her earlier, "—barricade the door and be quiet."

"Declan, mate, we know you're here! We saw your car."

And that was Harry.

"C'mon, let's go." If it was both of them, their time alone together had officially ended. He offered a hand to help her up, and she gladly took it. They went to the door and opened it, and Nat was standing directly in front of them.

"Nat—"

"Come here." Before anything else could be said, Nat pulled Kit further into the bedroom, shoved Declan out, and slammed the door shut.

Through the door, he heard Nat say, "Tell me everything!"

Harry smirked at Declan.

"What?"

"It took you a while to come out. What were the two of you up to in there?"

Declan avoided looking at him. "We were just hanging out."

"Mhm." Harry chuckled. "Sure."

"Yeah, well, you're one to talk. What have you and Nat been up to? Don't think I missed all that flirting at the beach."

Harry was suddenly very interested in the kitchen cabinets. "You know what? Don't turn this on me. I know good makeout session hair when I see it."

Declan halfheartedly tried to smooth down his hair. "Look, it's nothing.

We're just—"

Harry suddenly had an Irish accent when he cut Declan off. "*Oh, we're just platonically married best friends who just sometimes makeout now. It's fine.* You're a full-fledged dingbat, Mullins."

"That was a terrible Irish accent."

"Just tell her before it's too late."

The girls came back out then, and Declan shot Harry a look to make sure he shut up.

That night, when Kit turned the lights off, hurried to the bed, and huddled under the covers, there was a softness that surrounded them. Declan moved to her and held her close. Her hair was still damp from her shower, and when he breathed in, he realized she smelled like his shampoo.

"Did you use my shampoo again?"

Her answer was muffled in his shirt. "I ran out."

"I'm going to start charging you."

"You would never." He could hear the smile in her voice, and she was right.

They were quiet and allowed the comfort of the night to envelop them.

Declan took a deep breath and tried to find his courage from earlier. "We still need to have that talk."

She slid her foot between his legs. "Do we, though?"

"*Kit.*"

"Fine." She gave his chest a pat. "But can we do it at a more reasonable time? I just want to sleep."

It wasn't the answer Declan wanted, but it was more than he had before today. "Yeah. Of course."

Anna Katherine didn't purposefully make plans that weekend just to avoid talking to Declan. She could see how one may have come to that conclusion, but it truly started off as an innocent lunch with her dad. She had work and other commitments, and then she had the dinner with Jonah that she had genuinely, completely forgotten about until he texted her confirming the time and place. She wasn't upset about not having time to talk to Declan, but she hadn't planned it this way.

The problem was, she didn't even know what she would say to him. She knew the questions he needed answers to—knew he wanted to talk about what he said at the beach and what happened in her bedroom. She had enjoyed it all and loved every second of it, but her fears haunted her. She hadn't loved anyone since Jonah. He had shown her that all of her fears were logical. She was too much, and people would always leave. She didn't want Declan to leave.

So while a part of her wanted to have that conversation with him, a more primal part of her told her not to. She had always been more of a runner than a fighter. Apparently that was true for matters of her heart as well.

Jonah was waiting for her outside the restaurant, and even she couldn't deny how handsome he looked in his crisp button-down and slacks with the street lights shining down on him.

"Anna Kay." He smiled when he saw her. "A part of me thought you'd stand me up."

She chuckled and leaned into his one arm hug. "You'd deserve it, but I'm not that cruel."

"Well, I appreciate it." He held the door open for her, and she smiled in thanks as she walked in.

The hostess brought them to a booth, and after a moment of scanning the menu, Anna Katherine laid hers down. "I was surprised you wanted to go to dinner."

Jonah looked at her over his menu. "How come?"

"Well." She fiddled with her napkin. "We were never friends. Not really. And after our breakup, there isn't much to catch up on."

"You don't think we were friends?"

She shrugged. "I mean, we knew each other, but we jumped straight from classmates into a relationship. There was never any middle ground."

He eyed her. "Unlike you and Declan."

"I mean, yeah." She cleared her throat. "And I thought this was purely a professional relationship."

"I don't think it's hard to imagine that I miss having you in my life, Anna."

His words caught her off guard, mainly because she hadn't missed having him in hers. Not for a while, anyway. The thought that she missed Declan even after being away from him for just a day came in uninvited, but it wasn't a surprise to her. Declan had become so much more to her than whatever Jonah had ever been.

She locked eyes with him. "You're the one who left and never looked back."

After a moment of tense silence, Jonah nodded. "Point taken."

And so they talked about his life and her photography business. She told him about Fox and about Alex's studies. He told her how his parents were doing and what his next plans were. And for a moment, things were easy between them.

They went back to looking at the menu after that, and when the waiter came, they were both ready to order. They made small talk while they waited for their appetizers and meals.

Jonah was cutting his steak when he spoke up again. "You know, I bought a ring."

Anna Katherine choked on her noodles. "What?"

He nodded. "Yeah. I was going to propose that weekend."

Her blood ran cold. "You mean the weekend you cheated on me?"

He reached out for her hand, but she pulled it back. "You have to understand..."

"No." She sat up straight and glared at him. "I don't have to understand anything. You lost that when you weren't man enough to tell me yourself."

"Declan should have minded his own business." His voice had turned hard and unforgiving.

Hers matched his tone. "It *was* his business. Not including everything else, we're best friends. He did the right thing. Don't try to pin your mistakes on him."

There was a pause, and when Jonah spoke again, his voice was soft. "Do you think we would have ever gotten back together if you weren't married to him?"

Kit looked up from her plate, surprised by Jonah's question, but the answer was easy. "No."

He seemed shocked at her answer. "How come?"

"Our history." She twirled the noodles onto her fork. "You cheated on me, Jonah. Not only that, but you cheated on me with the girl my best friend was dating."

Regret and desperation filled his eyes. "I thought you were sleeping with Declan."

Her fork dropped with a clatter, and she leaned forward, resting her elbows on the table. "Look. I don't know why everyone thinks that I was dating or sleeping with Declan before I actually was. Especially *you*! You knew my stance and that I wanted to wait until I was married!" She took a breath, and shoved her hair behind her ear. "We didn't start dating until two months before our wedding, and I wasn't even sure I loved him until after the wedding."

"See!" He pointed a finger at her. "That's why people think that. He asked you to marry him, and you said yes without even knowing how you felt! You would do anything for him. You trust him. You never trusted me."

"With good reason, apparently."

She could feel the tension between them. And when his eyes flashed with anger, she knew she had hit the mark.

"I was sorry. Almost immediately."

"Yeah, but that's the thing." She leaned back in her seat, trying to control her voice. "You messed up. And that was actually your second mess up. The first being when you decided to move across state lines without even telling me you were thinking about it. One day we were talking about getting engaged, and the next you were moving. And then a few months later, Declan catches you in his bed with someone he was dating. And instead of talking any of that out with me, you drive off to your new home after the colossal mess blew up in your face. And you never called me again. I genuinely do not care if you were or are sorry. You shouldn't have done any of that. Declan would never do that."

Jonah was silent and then, "Maybe this dinner was a mistake."

"Yeah, maybe so." She put her napkin on the table. "Just finish up so we can get the ticket and leave."

Once they were finished and the bill was settled, they walked outside.

Before Anna Katherine could walk away, he stopped her.

"Do you love him now?"

It was the easiest thing in the world to say. "Yes. More than I've ever loved anyone."

The hurt in his eyes didn't hurt her as much as it probably should have.

Anna Katherine went to Alex's after the dinner and ended up staying later than she had planned when they started a movie. By the time she got home, Declan was already asleep. The next morning, she woke up earlier than him to open the coffee shop. After her shift, she went straight to Nat's for girls' night, and it was only when she came home after that she finally saw Declan.

He was on their couch with a drink, watching a documentary with Zac Efron in it.

She dropped her purse by the door and made her way to the couch to join him. "How were William and Harry?"

He watched her walk toward him, and when she went to sit beside him, he lifted his arm so she could lean against him. "Fine. William couldn't stop talking about that girl he's been seeing. How were the girls?"

She shrugged and reached out to take his beer from him. She took a sip before answering. "Fine. Mack talked nonstop, and I'm pretty sure Nat is seeing someone but isn't telling me."

He smirked. "Why do you think that?"

"Call it friend intuition."

He chuckled, "Gotcha."

There was a beat of silence and then, "You're not avoiding me again, are you?"

She groaned. "Declan. I am here. Sitting on the couch with you. Not 'recoiling from your touch' as you so eloquently phrased it on Thursday.

Would I be doing that if I was avoiding you?"

He scratched her shoulder. "Well, you have been MIA all weekend."

She rolled her head back to look at him. "I've been *busy*, Declan. That's a thing that happens in people's lives."

"Fair enough." He gave her another scratch. "I'm guessing you're too tired to talk tonight?"

"Will you think I'm avoiding it if I say yes?"

"I'll give you the benefit of the doubt for now."

"Then, yes. I'm too tired. Raincheck?"

He took his beer back and chuckled, "Raincheck. Hey, you have Thursday off, right?"

She tried to remember her schedule. "I think so. Why?"

"I need you to double check. That's our interview."

"We should probably practice again."

"Wouldn't hurt. Especially since my citizenship is riding on this."

She ignored how her heart picked up the pace. "Tomorrow at lunch?"

"Sure, I can come home. Pizza?"

"No. I want tacos."

He laughed. "Fine. Tacos it is."

The next morning, Anna Katherine woke up to Declan kissing her shoulder. "G'morning."

She cracked an eye open. "Why am I awake?"

He smirked. "I'm about to leave for work."

"You've never woken me up before you left. I liked that routine. Let's go back to that."

He chuckled and brushed her hair out of her face. "I just wanted to check in."

"Ugh."

"This is a big week for us. I know you're not ready to talk, but I just want to make sure you're good."

"The only way I could possibly be better is if you hadn't woken me up."

He laughed. "Right. Well, let's not forget that if we screw this up, at minimum, we could both be fined."

"So reassuring and encouraging. Thanks."

He kissed her cheek. "Anytime, Kit-Kat. I'll see you at lunch."

She waved him off and then went back to sleep. When she woke up again, she felt like her heart was in her throat, and Declan's words were playing on loop in her head.

His citizenship was on the line. They could go to jail. He could be shipped off. Her future could be ruined.

This will all be fine.

Declan came home with Kit's favorite tacos and her favorite brand of sweet tea, only to find her on the floor with her legs propped up on the wall and her head resting on Fox. The papers with the interview questions were scattered around her, and he wasn't sure if she was asleep or just dead to the world around her.

"I hope you're not dead. That would really mess up my plan to stay in the states."

She rolled over and propped herself on her elbows. Judging from the way her eyebrows were angrily knitted together, she was in a foul mood. "Oh, yeah. How dare I inconvenience you with my death. I forgot you only care about me as a way to become an American."

He shot her an unamused glance and tossed her a drink. "Just get over here and eat your tacos, Kit."

"What if I don't want to eat?"

"Did you eat breakfast?"

"Does coffee count?"

"Geez, Kit. Just come eat the tacos."

She was still glowering, but she got off the floor and joined him at the table. Fox followed and climbed up into one of the empty chairs. He eyed the dog. "She thinks she's human."

"As she should."

Declan slid the three tacos to Anna Katherine and then unwrapped his own. He was on his third bite when he noticed Kit still hadn't started eating. "Are you really not hungry?"

She shrugged. "My stomach has felt uneasy all day."

"You should've told me. I could've gotten you soup or something instead. I'll pick some up on my way home this evening."

"Declan. You don't have to do that."

He scoffed. "It's not about having to. It's about wanting to."

She tried to protest again, but he ignored her and made a mental note to stop by the store on the way home.

When he was on his second taco, he grabbed the questions from where Kit had left them on the floor and scanned over them. "So, they're going to do a group interview with the two of us together, but they're also going to do individual ones."

When he saw her tense up, he tried to calm her down by saying, "It's not a big deal. It's going to be fine."

"This is your future we're talking about."

"And it's in your hands." He gave her a reassuring smile. "There isn't a safer place for it to be."

She snatched the papers out of his hand and read the first question. "Where did we meet?"

"Easy. On the green while tailgating for the homecoming game. You were wearing that gold dress and complained the entire time because the wind wouldn't stop blowing it up."

He felt her eyes on him, but he continued looking at his taco when she asked, "How do you remember that?"

"There's a picture."

"Don't think I've seen that one of us." Her focus went back to the paper. "Alright, what did the two of us have in common?"

Declan thought back to their time in college. "Did we have anything in common besides Jonah and going out with our friends?"

"We did have a shared hatred of that one professor."

"Yes! The public speaking one. What was her name?"

Kit laughed. "All I remember is her black, rotting teeth."

"She was the worst."

"She really was. When did we meet each other's parents?"

"Easy. I met Patty and Timmy a week after meeting you, and you crashed a Skype call with my mum the week I got back from the winter hols."

She scoffed. "I did not crash anything. Móirín wanted to meet me!"

Declan laughed, "Yeah, okay."

"Do we spend a lot of time together?"

"Always, unless you're avoiding me."

She tossed a chip at him. "When did we begin to have romantic feelings for each other?"

"That night we danced in the kitchen." "What?"

He looked up to see her staring at him. He cleared his throat. "It's the most believable time it could've happened for me."

"But that was years ago. The interviewer is going to ask you why you didn't ask me out until years later."

"Easy. I didn't think you were over Jonah, and then I didn't want to ruin our friendship."

She kept staring at him, but she eventually nodded. "Yeah, that works."

"What about you?"

"I, uh, don't know."

He scratched his neck. "You could say you didn't realize it until I asked you out."

She nodded. "Yep. Okay. That works."

They continued going through the questions while Declan ate and Kit fiddled with her tacos. Once he finished eating, he cleaned the table and put her tacos in the fridge for her to eat later.

"I better get back to work."

The scowl on her face was back in full force. "Yeah."

He walked over to her and brushed her hair out of her face. "You sure you're okay?"

She was still scowling, but her eyes softened slightly. "I promise I'm fine."

His thumb traced the freckles that had popped up on her cheeks after their day at the beach. "Alright. Take it easy before your shift this afternoon, yeah?"

"Yes, Declan." She rolled her eyes.

He leaned down to kiss her forehead. "I'll see you tonight."

He heard her sigh and smiled at the sound. Pulling himself away from her, he forced himself out the door before he allowed himself to do something truly stupid like kiss her.

42

Anna Katherine was pretty sure that when Declan told her to take it easy, her panicking about the interview was not what he had in mind. But the more she tried not to panic, the more panicked and anxious she felt. When two o'clock rolled around, she found herself packing up her things and heading toward one of the three people that knew the truth, outside of her and Declan.

She didn't see Harry's Jeep when she parked at his apartment complex, and when she knocked, there wasn't an answer. She knew the key was hiding under the dead cactus, but she felt weird about intruding into his personal space. She sat down on his welcome mat and leaned against the door, waiting for him to come home.

She was fiddling on her phone when he finally walked up. "Anna Katherine?"

She looked up and smiled when she saw him. "Hey!"

His keys dangled from his fingers, and he repositioned his bag that was slung over his shoulder. "What are you doing here? Is everything okay?"

She stood up and dusted herself off. "Yeah, uh. Can we talk?"

He eyed her curiously. "Of course. Let's go inside, yeah?"

She moved aside so he could unlock the door and then followed him inside. She sat on the couch while he put all of his things away, and when he came back he asked, "Why aren't you going to Nat about whatever is going on?"

"Nat is acting weird."

He seemed surprised by that. "How so?"

"I think she's seeing someone and isn't telling me about it. Either that or she's like, dying."

Harry had a coughing fit.

"And I tried to call Alex, but..." She trailed off and glared at him when the coughing continued. "Pull yourself together, Hardin. I'm having a crisis over here!"

In between coughs he said, "Not my name."

"Whatever. I tried calling Alex but his phone is off."

Harry finally stopped coughing. "Why can't you go to Declan?" "Because it's about him."

He started coughing again.

"Honestly, Harry. Go get a cough drop or something."

Finally he pulled himself together. "Declan?"

She nodded. "Our interview is this week for the whole citizen, no-being-deported-or-fined thing."

"Oh, yeah. That has to be exciting, right?"

"Exciting?" She scoffed. "I was fine until Declan reminded me that our entire lives depend on this interview. What if I mess it up?"

Harry joined her on the couch. "You sure you shouldn't be talking to Declan about all of this?"

She shook her head. "It's bad enough that I'm a nervous wreck. He doesn't need to be as well."

He watched her for a moment before sighing. "What's his favorite color?"

"Green." She looked at him like he was an idiot, but the response was immediate.

"And what does he order from your favorite Thai restaurant?"

"Yellow chicken curry."

"How does he take his coffee?" "Black with two sugars or a breve, which is disgusting, with two sugars."

"How often does he get a haircut?"

"Every two months. Harry, what does this have to do with anything?"

"You *know* him, Kit." He said it as if it were the most obvious thing in the world. "You know what makes him tick and how he thinks things through. Big and small, you know him."

"But—"

"Ah-ah. *But,* nothing. You know him, and because of that, this entirely ridiculous scheme had a possibility of working in the first place. Have I ever lied to you before?"

She gave him a flat look.

"Okay, fine. Have I ever lied to you about something important?"

"No."

"Then trust me when I say that you have nothing to worry about. The interview is going to be fine."

She let out a long breath. "Okay. Yeah, you're right."

He smirked. "I know I am." He stood up and pulled her off the couch.

"Now, as much as I love having you around, I need you to leave."

"What? Why?"

He herded her toward the door. "I have a date coming over, and I don't need you ruining the mood."

She lit up. "A date? What's her name?"

He opened the door. "None of your business. Now get out before I call your husband to come and fetch you."

"You're no fun."

"Bye, Kit."

She turned on her heel. "Bye, Hunterton."

"Not my name!" he called after her. She laughed.

Her talk with Harry helped keep her calm the rest of the day, but when she woke up Wednesday morning, the panic was back, and somehow it was worse than before. When she got back from her opening shift, she laid in bed, staring at the ceiling, trying to ease the tension in her chest. When that didn't work and the pressure felt like it was about to crush her, she jumped out of bed and took a shower. She sat on the fluffy rug she had convinced Declan to buy last year while she dried off, and then she got dressed and grabbed her computer and the interview questions. She was going to type out a detailed answer to every single possible question the interviewer could ask. She wasn't about to ruin this for him.

She turned her phone off and only took breaks to refill her coffee. She was so concentrated on the questions and the answers she was carefully typing that when Declan walked through the door, she nearly jumped out of her skin.

"Crap, what time is it?" She checked the time on the computer and realized she should've left for work five minutes ago. "*Crap.*"

She slammed the computer shut and ran to her bedroom to change.

Declan called after her. "What were you doing?"

There was a pile of her and Declan's laundry on her bed, which was a shocking reminder of how little she had used her own bed in the last few weeks. She dug through the piles until she found a fresh, but wrinkled, work shirt and a faded pair of jeans. "Preparing for the interview."

He appeared in her doorway, and she stepped behind the closet door to quickly change. Just because they were husband and wife didn't mean that she wanted him to see her in her unmentionables.

"Speaking of which," Declan started, but there was a pause. Anna Katherine was certain that if she was able to see him, Declan would be rubbing the back of his neck, "I think we really need to have that conversation before the interview. It's going to be a stressful situation, and it'll be best if we didn't go in with any unresolved baggage."

"I'm late for work, Declan." She shimmied into her jeans, which were almost too tight since she forgot to air dry them. She had to lay on the bed to fasten them. "I had to open this morning, and when I came home, I started going over the questions and completely lost track of time. I can't be late for my second shift."

"I get that, but this is important—"

"*Declan.*" She leapt off the bed and pulled her shirt over her head. "I can't do this right now."

She shoved past him to get to the bathroom to run a brush through her hair. Her skin itched all over, and when the brush hit a tangle, she felt like her chest was going to explode from anger. She knew these were her signs of an anxiety attack, but she couldn't take the time to calm down or explain any of it to Declan. She just wanted to get out and sit in her car in silence while driving to work.

"I get that you think that, but—"

Anna Katherine felt out of control. She couldn't control the interview or how the interviewer perceived them. She couldn't control her mother meddling in her life. She barely even had control of her *own* life.

She spun around and glared at him, *"It was a mistake!"*

The words were out of her mouth before she could stop them. They weren't even a full thought at the time, but with being late to work and stressing over the interview, they somehow slipped out. Declan looked as surprised as she felt by her words, but it was too late to take them back now.

"Is that what you want to hear? It was a mistake. All of it. The kiss on New Year's, the beach, my bedroom." She waved her hands around. "If I could take it all back, I would!"

She could see the hurt on his face, and it was worse than any tension felt that morning. She swallowed back her tears and tried to ignore what it meant for him to be so hurt by her words.

She masked her own heartbreak with a softer voice. "This is why I told you I didn't want to have this conversation, Declan."

She pulled her hair back in a ponytail and squeezed between Declan and the door. "I gotta get to work." She couldn't look at him. The pain in his eyes was too much. "I'll see you tonight."

As soon as she got in her car, Anna Katherine let her tears fall. She hadn't been lying when she told Declan it had been a mistake. It had been, but she hadn't told him why she felt that way. She had only hurt him and run out of the apartment. And, for that, she hated herself.

That night when she arrived home from work, she cracked the door to Declan's room open. He was sound asleep, huddled on his side of the bed. Her side was completely untouched and empty. She watched him sleep for a moment before carefully closing the door and going to her own room, quickly falling asleep amongst the piles of laundry.

43

She woke up the next morning to the smell of coffee and fresh bacon. Her face felt puffy, and she had one of the worst headaches she'd had in a while. She felt like she had a hangover, but instead of it being caused by too much alcohol, this one was caused by an overwhelming amount of emotions she didn't want to deal with. She slid out of bed, one pile of clothes falling to the floor as she did, and got dressed for the day before heading to the kitchen.

Declan was standing by the stove with only a pair of running shorts on. His hair was slick with sweat, and Anna Katherine wanted to walk up to him and wrap her arms around him. But she couldn't do that to either of them—not after what she had said yesterday.

Without turning around, he went to the coffee pot and poured her a mug. He gave her a half smile when he handed it to her. "We only need to get through today."

She wasn't sure she could survive the day without her heart crumbling to ruins. "Yeah. Easy peasy." There was no life in her voice.

She went to the table, and he wasn't long behind her with two plates of eggs and bacon and a bowl of biscuits. The only sounds were their utensils scraping against the plates. She wordlessly cleaned up once she was finished, and Declan disappeared into his room. It seemed to be a silent agreement that they stayed in separate parts of the apartment until the interview. When Declan knocked on her bedroom door, she waited for him to open it himself, but when it stayed closed, she got up to do it herself.

His face was void of all emotion when he said, "Time to go. You'll need a coat. It's raining."

"Right." She nodded and went to grab her things before following him out the door.

The ride was completely silent except for the music on the radio. Neither of them bothered to connect their phones to Bluetooth to listen to a playlist. Declan gave her a look when they had parked and gotten out of the car. "Don't forget we need to act in love."

"Yep."

She trailed behind him as they walked up to the building, but once they started up the steps, she hurried to get beside him and take his hand. He gave it a squeeze, and she was thankful that despite the awkward tension separating them, she at least had the comforting weight of his hand in hers.

The individual interviews were longer and more intensive than she had thought they'd be, and when they were over, she only felt relieved when she was able to go and sit by Declan again.

He leaned over to whisper, "How'd it go?"

"Nerve shattering, but it was fine."

He patted her knee. "Told ya that you'd do fine."

After a few moments, they were called back together for the joint interview. She was a lot less nervous for this one with Declan by her side. Most of the questions were easy enough, and they only had to bend the truth on a few of them. She was glad that they had practiced, though, since it assured her their answers lined up.

The woman who had been interviewing them smiled. "You two seem to really know each other. Declan, what is the weirdest thing Anna Katherine has ever asked of you?"

She perked up, curious as to how Declan would answer. This hadn't been one of the questions they had practiced.

He chuckled, a little self conscious. "Well, it would have to be that time—and this was a few weeks after we met—that she interrupted my studying to say, 'If we're still friends when we're old, I need you to die second, because you have to take my brain out.' She had been reading this book and apparently had just learned that your brain leaks out once you start to decompose, and that, out of everything else, was what stuck with her. At the time, she had been very adamant about that not happening to her."

Anna Katherine stared at him in shock. "How in the world do you remember that?"

She had almost forgotten about it, but hearing Declan describe it brought the memory rushing back. She remembered how Jonah had later mocked her for it when she brought it up to him weeks later, but Declan had just nodded very solemnly and told her that of course he'd do that for her.

He smiled at her, and for a moment, she forgot that there was anything amiss in their friendship. "There are very few things you've said that I don't remember, love."

The woman asked a few more questions that they answered flawlessly, and they even laughed at a few of the answers, like if she ever handled the finances.

She scoffed. "He had full access to all my accounts even before we were dating. He's the number guy. I just do as he tells me."

Declan laughed. "It's the only time she doesn't put up a fuss about being told what to do."

"Numbers scare me." She shrugged.

When the woman told them they only had one more question, Anna Katherine let out a relieved sigh, thankful this nightmare was almost over.

"How did he propose?"

Her heart stopped, and all thoughts left her brain when she realized the question was directed at her. "Uh…"

Declan squeezed her hand. "She gets embarrassed telling the story. Mainly because she's a horrible story-teller. Can I tell?"

The woman motioned for him to go on.

"Kit, as we've mentioned, is a photographer. She takes proposal photos all the time, and she always comes home gushing about these elaborate and romantic proposals. Some people probably think that because of all the proposals she's seen and documented that she'd want something grand and out of this world."

She stared at Declan, trying her best to hide her interest and surprise. He winked at her when he noticed her staring.

"But I've known this woman for five years, and I know that even though she goes on and on about how beautiful and romantic those types of proposals are, those aren't the kind she wants. Which, before I met her and before I knew I was going to marry her, I'd always imagined myself doing one of those big proposals." He chuckled. "I like to think of myself as a romantic."

Anna Katherine swallowed.

"So, as hard as it was, I had to reign that in for my girl here. I got a mate of mine to help me, and we took some goofy Polaroid pictures of me with these poster boards, and each one of the posters had a single word on it."

Her heart was hammering against her chest.

"We took the pictures and then placed them in an envelope, and I taped it to her bathroom mirror where I knew she'd see them. When she laid out all the pictures—it took some rearranging at first— the pictures spelled out the question, *Will You Marry Me?*"

She finally found her voice. "And how could I say no after a proposal like that?"

They locked eyes. "Exactly."

Declan tore his gaze away from her. "Anyway, I was at the door already on a knee when she turned around."

Once the interviews were over, they thanked the woman for her time and walked out of the building into the pouring rain. The ride home was just as quiet as the ride earlier had been, only this time, even the radio was off.

Harry laid on the floor at Nat's feet, his hands interlocked underneath his head as he stared up at her.

Nat nudged his elbow with her foot. "What are you looking at?"

His smile looked like he held all the secrets of the world, and for all Nat knew, he did. "Just you."

"Sounds boring."

He clumsily shook his head. "It's not. I was just thinking—" Harry's eyes roamed over her face, "—we both need to eat."

She smiled. "Yeah."

"And we typically eat dinner together when I come over."

"This is also true."

"So, and I'm just throwing out crazy ideas here, what if we both go out to eat. At the same restaurant. At the same time. And if we're feeling really crazy, maybe even sit at the same table."

"Like a date?"

"If you want to call it that."

She laughed. "I don't think that's too crazy of an idea."

His eyes widened, "Really? Is that a yes?"

"Yes, Herschel—"

"Not my name."

"—That's a yes."

His smile was contagious. "I thought I'd have to convince you."

She shrugged, for once not trying to hide how happy he made her. "You're growing on me, Whitlock."

Ninth Commandment: Thou Shalt Not Have Any Sexual Relations With Each Other

*D*eclan scratched his neck. "If we want to keep the image of a happily married couple, we can't be caught cheating.

Kit nodded. "No dating during our marriage."

"Shouldn't be too hard. Haven't really dated since Vivian."

She chuckled. But then her face turned serious. "What about, you know..."

And somehow, he followed her train of thought. "We can't blur the lines. Even though we're married, no sex."

"Easy peasy."

44

Anna Katherine closed the apartment door behind her and turned her back to Declan, while she shrugged off her raincoat and hung it on the hook. She stood there a moment, still processing the interview.

"You okay, Kit? You've been quiet." She could feel his presence close behind her, and her body hummed.

She crossed her arms over her chest and whispered, "You know me."

She heard him scoff and felt the breath of it against her neck. "Of course I do. I've known you for years."

He placed his hand on her shoulder, encouraging her to turn around. And she let him.

"What's going on in that head of yours, Kit-Kat?"

He was right there, but she craved to be even closer to him. His hair was damp and flat from the rain, and somehow his eyes were more blue than usual. Or maybe Anna Katherine was just paying more attention to them.

He needed a shave, and his lips were still chapped from when they went to the beach and he had been sunburned. He was her best friend in the entire world, and he was beautiful.

Before she could overthink it and talk herself out of it, she stretched up on her toes, placed her hands on his shoulders, and kissed him.

And he let her.

When she pulled back, he was watching her carefully, and she noticed the uncertainty in his eyes. He brushed a strand of hair behind her ear and said, "What was that?"

He was her best friend, yet she couldn't find the courage to say the truth behind it. She loved him. She loved him so much it hurt, and having to pretend to not be in love with him while acting like she married him for all the right reasons was making her heart hurt even more.

"Declan, I..." She let out a breath. Her heart was hammering against her chest as her eyes darted across his face, and they landed on his lips again. She thought back to the other night and the hurt that was in his eyes when she told him it was a mistake.

"It wasn't a mistake." She bit her lip, and watched as Declan's face went from cautious to confused. "Yesterday. I was wrong. It wasn't a mistake. I had been stressed and anxious—"

The words were barely out of her mouth before she got her wish, and his lips were crashing against hers, one hand cradling the back of her head, and the other resting on her hip. Her body melded with his.

His fingers brushed against her cheek and down her neck.

"Anna Katherine..."

She looked up at him and saw the adoration in his eyes. "I know, Declan. I know."

Anna Katherine woke up before Declan, and she took a moment to take him in. His hair was pressed down on one side and sticking up in the front from the chaotic way he slept on his pillow. He looked peaceful, but more than that, she was once again caught off guard by how beautiful he was. She allowed herself to stare at him for another moment before sliding out of bed.

When she came back to the bedroom, she had two cups of coffee for her and Declan. He stretched when she sat back on the bed.

She smiled at him when he cracked an eye open. "You have a really bad case of bedhead."

"Thanks," he snorted. He nodded toward the extra mug. "Are one of those for me?"

She nodded and handed it to him. He sat up, careful not to spill it, and after he took a sip, he glanced at her. "I'm surprised you're still here."

"Why?"

"You have a tendency to run when things or people make you feel uncomfortable."

Something twisted in her gut. "You don't make me feel uncomfortable, Declan."

"The last few weeks say otherwise."

"It's not you. It's the way you make me feel."

A smirk slowly spread across his face. "And how's that?"

She placed her cup of coffee on the nightstand and attempted to smooth down his hair, but it was a hopeless cause. "I think you know how I feel about you."

His face softened into a smile, and then turned mischievous. "Kiss me."

"I don't just do as you—"

Her comment was cut short when he rolled his eyes and leaned up to kiss her.

Their coffee was forgotten. When they finally remembered it, it had gone cold, and Declan had to rush to be to work on time.

Anna Katherine was washing their coffee cups when Declan came home with their lunch. Fox greeted him with vigorous tail wagging and barking until he finally gave her what she considered to be adequate attention. Anna Katherine turned around to lean against the sink when she heard him come her way. He crowded against her so much that she had to tilt her head back to look at him.

"I think you lost your sense of personal space."

He smirked. "As if you don't love it."

She fought to keep her smile hidden. "I mean, I do get tired of you from time to time."

He laughed, obviously not believing her for a second. "I'm sure you do." He pinched her side. "C'mon. The food'll get cold."

She tried to peer into the bag. "Whatcha get?"

He stepped out of her space. "You know I hate it when you tell me to surprise you with food."

She waved him off. "You always pick something that I like."

"Yeah, but it's nerve-racking every time. You get so grouchy when you have to eat something you're not craving."

"You truly make me sound like a miserable person to live with sometimes." She followed him to the table and sat across from him.

He raised his eyebrows at her.

"Don't be a turd, Declan," she pouted.

"I got you crawfish baked potatoes."

She gasped and grinned. "Crawfish season! The season of Heaven itself."

"Have you always been this dramatic or just since I've known you?"

"Don't act like you don't love it."

"I mean..." He smirked. "I do get tired of it from time to time."

"Jerk."

"Brat."

She smiled. "Can't argue with that one. Thanks for picking up the food by the way."

"No problem. Work was providing lunch for us today, but it wasn't anything I was interested in."

"Well, I'd rather have you here anyway." She immediately stuffed a bite in her mouth after her admission. And her stomach swooped from the honesty of it.

Declan watched as Kit shoved a crawfish into her mouth and avoided looking at him. Not for the first time that day, he wondered what was going on in her head. He was able to see so much, but there were things that she kept under lock and key, even from him. Though, he did like to think he was better at picking her mental locks than anyone else. She'd just been more difficult lately than she has been in the past.

"Why do you do that?"

Sometimes, the best way to get answers was to call her out.

She almost looked scared, but he only felt a little guilty. "Do what?"

"Say something and then get all embarrassed about it."

She bit her lip. "I don't do that."

He gave her a flat look. "Really, Kit?"

"Sometimes it's just…" She let out a frustrated sigh. "It's hard for me to be completely open with people. It's hard for me to process my emotions and then voice them. You know that, Declan."

He wanted to hug her, but he stayed where he was. "Yeah, I do. But that doesn't mean I understand why, especially when it's with me. Since when do we hide things from each other or get embarrassed in front of the other?"

Declan's mind very unhelpfully pointed out that he'd been hiding the fact that he was in love with her for months now. He did his best to shove that thought to the back.

"Doesn't it count for something that I'm more open with you than I am with others?"

He wanted her to be completely open, not just more than normal. "Yeah, it does." He took a bite and chewed before adding. "You know I'd never intentionally hurt you, right?"

Her smile made his heart soar. "I don't think you'd ever intentionally hurt anyone."

"But especially you."

If possible, her smile widened. "Yeah. I know."

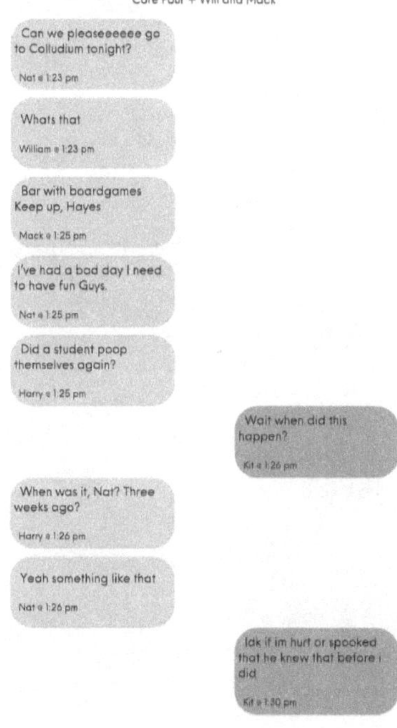

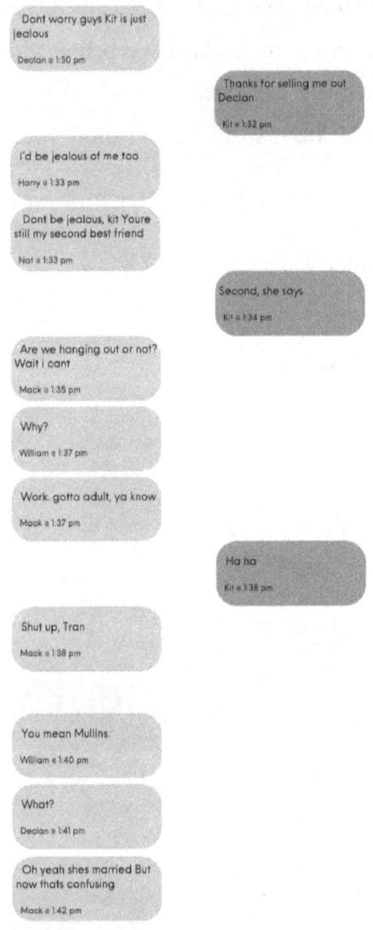
Dont worry guys Kit is just jealous
Declan @ 1:30 pm
Thanks for selling me out Declan
Kit @ 1:32 pm
I'd be jealous of me too
Harry @ 1:33 pm
Dont be jealous, kit Youre still my second best friend
Nat @ 1:33 pm
Second, she says
Kit @ 1:34 pm
Are we hanging out or not? Wait i cant
Mack @ 1:35 pm
Why?
William @ 1:37 pm
Work. gotta adult, ya know
Mack @ 1:37 pm
Ha ha
Kit @ 1:38 pm
Shut up, Tran
Mack @ 1:38 pm
You mean Mullins.
William @ 1:40 pm
What?
Declan @ 1:41 pm
Oh yeah shes married But now thats confusing
Mack @ 1:42 pm

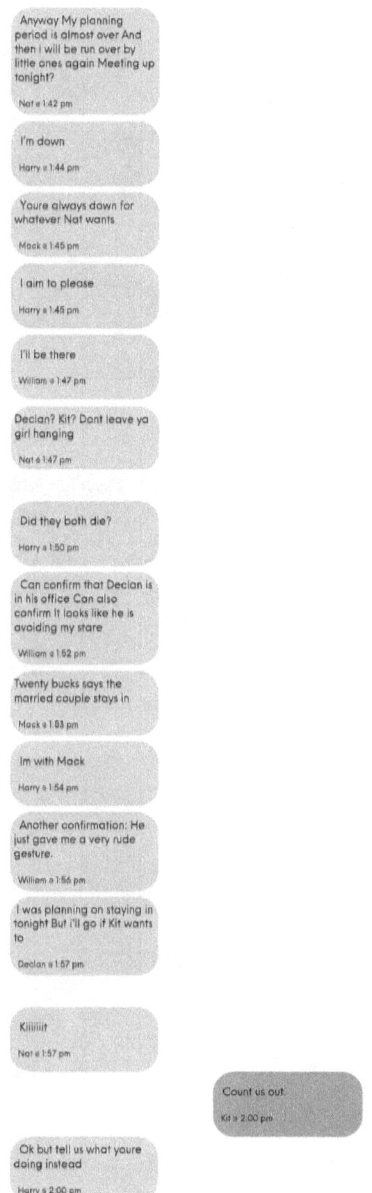
Anyway My planning period is almost over And then i will be run over by little ones again Meeting up tonight?
Nat a 1:42 pm

I'm down
Harry a 1:44 pm

Youre always down for whatever Nat wants
Mack a 1:45 pm

I aim to please
Harry a 1:46 pm

I'll be there
William a 1:47 pm

Declan? Kit? Dont leave ya girl hanging
Nat a 1:47 pm

Did they both die?
Harry a 1:50 pm

Can confirm that Declan is in his office Can also confirm It looks like he is avoiding my stare
William a 1:52 pm

Twenty bucks says the married couple stays in
Mack a 1:53 pm

Im with Mack
Harry a 1:54 pm

Another confirmation: He just gave me a very rude gesture.
William a 1:56 pm

I was planning on staying in tonight But i'll go if Kit wants to
Declan a 1:57 pm

Kiiiiiiit
Nat a 1:57 pm

Count us out.
Kit a 2:00 pm

Ok but tell us what youre doing instead
Harry a 2:00 pm

I dont kiss and tell

Declan @ 2:01 pm

Can confirm that's false

Harry @ 2:03 pm

Can also confirm thats false

Nat @ 2:03 pm

I cannot confirm

William @ 2:04 pm

Declan.
what have you been saying

Kit @ 2:05 pm

Declan Left Core Four + Will and Mack
William Added Declan to Core Four + Will and Mack

Hey, Kit Just remember that our friends are liars

Declan @ 2:10 pm

Hahahha

Kit @ 2:10 pm

Heyyyy

Harry @ 2:11 pm

Not cool.

Nat @ 2:11 pm

45

Declan came home to find Kit sitting at the table with her computer. "Whatcha doing?"

"Last minute things for the Jonah project."

He went to stand next to her. "When is that going to be finished?"

She looked up at him. "Our last meeting is tomorrow, and after that, if anything else needs to be done, emails exist."

His hand found her shoulder and gave it a squeeze. "You've worked hard on this one."

"Thanks." She smiled. "I'm glad we decided not to go with the others tonight."

"Me too."

"Once I finish up, wanna go with me to walk Fox? We can pick up some dinner, too."

"Yeah, sounds good." He gave her shoulder another squeeze before going to his room to change out of his work clothes.

Putting the harness on Fox was always an ordeal, and this time was no different. It took Kit straddling her while Declan bribed her with a treat to finally get it secured.

"We probably should've trained her better."

Declan cut his eyes at Kit. "Our dog is perfect just the way she is."

"Sure, and I'm my mother's pride and joy."

"You are."

"No, that would be Alex."

Declan shook his head. "Whatever you say, Kit."

The weather had done a complete turnaround since yesterday. The sun was out with barely a cloud in the sky, and the birds were chirping and enjoying the few weeks of spring weather they had. They walked Fox the normal route—around the block and then to the dog park—and while they were leaning against the fence watching Fox run around with the other dogs, Declan asked Kit where she wanted to eat.

She thought for a moment. "I'm honestly just craving a good sandwich."

"How about we stop by the deli? It's near the park, and we can just eat at one of the picnic tables there."

He wrapped his arm around her when she leaned into his side. "Sounds good to me. I'll buy it since you bought lunch."

"Did you even bring your wallet?"

"Uh..."

He laughed. "I don't mind buying again."

"I'll pay you back."

He gave her a gentle squeeze. "Since when do we worry about paying each other back? Besides, we're married, remember?"

Kit smiled into his shoulder. "How could I forget?"

She took his hand as they walked to the deli and smiled at him as she swung their hands back and forth. He shook his head at her when she let go of him only to swing around a light pole, twirling and skipping her way back to him before taking his hand again. Once they got to the deli, he stayed outside with Fox while she went inside with his wallet and ordered their food. She came back out all smiles and nearly gave Declan a heart attack when she ran across the road to the park without much care whether there was traffic or not.

Declan and Fox took the crosswalk only after he pressed the button and waited for the light to change. Kit was waiting for them on the other side, a smirk plastered on her face.

"You're lame, Declan Mullins."

"At least I don't purposefully try to give you anxiety."

She laughed. "I don't *purposefully* do it."

He reached out for her, and she linked her hand in his. "For some reason, I don't believe you."

"Probably because you've known me for too long. Which is a real shame if you ask me."

"Good thing I didn't."

She made a point to roll her eyes at him before heading toward the picnic tables. When they reached them, all the tables were taken. It seemed like they weren't the only ones taking advantage of the spring weather. They ended up sitting on the grass on the hillside overlooking most of the park while Fox ran around close by, miraculously not wandering off too far. They ate their sandwiches in silence, and when Kit finished hers, she propped her head in his lap while he kept eating. He didn't bother stopping her when she started stealing his chips.

"Why didn't you buy some for yourself?"

"I didn't want any then."

"You always end up wanting some."

"Well," she said as she grabbed his free hand and pressed their palms together, "I really thought I didn't want any."

He watched as she traced the lines on his hands and the calluses on his fingers. He stayed quiet for a moment, letting her continue exploring his hand before he smirked and said, "Hands, huh?"

She laughed and dropped her hand from his. "Are you searching for a compliment?"

"Would I ever?"

She kissed his palm. "Your hands *really* do it for me."

A surprised laugh erupted out of him. and nearly made him choke on his sandwich. "Geez. Kit."

She smiled, a little too proud for his liking. She pressed her palm against his again and slid her fingers between his. "Since you didn't want to hang out with our friends and texted me, making me take the fall for it, what are we doing tonight?"

He finished his sandwich and moved his bags of chips out of her reach. "What do we normally do when we stay in?"

She pouted when she realized he'd moved the chips, but he ignored her. "We always do boring stuff. Watch something. Stuff our faces."

"And you don't want to do that?"

She shook her head and moved so she wasn't lying in his lap anymore.

"I want to do something different."

"Like?"

She shrugged.

It was moments like these when Kit drove him crazy. It was obvious to the world that she wanted something, but she wasn't willing to voice it. He rolled over on his side and looked at her. "You could just kiss me. That would pass the time and give us something to do."

She stared at him. "I really want to find something in that statement to argue with."

"But?"

"But…" She rolled over on her side, mirroring him. "I think I want to kiss you more."

He reached out and trailed his thumb across her jaw, resting his hand on her neck. "Then why aren't you?"

He thought she was about to argue or roll her eyes again, but she surprised him by leaning toward him and kissing him. He couldn't help but smile into it.

They ended up in bed watching Netflix anyway, with Kit curled around Declan while he played with her hair.

They woke up to Fox barking, announcing to their entire apartment complex that she was ready for her morning walk. Anna Katherine's back was to Declan and his arm was draped over her waist. She giggled when he moaned into the back of her neck.

"Whose idea was it to get a dog?"

"One hundred and ten percent yours."

"What was I thinking?"

"That's exactly what I asked myself when you came home with her."

"I'm sure I had good intentions at the time."

"You had nothing but idiocy."

He kissed her shoulder. "That was rude."

She turned around to face him, and her heart fluttered when he rested his forehead against hers. "Good morning."

He pressed a kiss to her nose. "Morning, Kit-Kat."

"Want me to take her out?"

He shook his head. "I'll do it. I need to go for a run anyway." He went to get up. "Are you going to be here when I get back?"

Anna Katherine rolled onto her stomach and watched as he dug through his dresser and changed clothes. "Depends on how long your run is. I need to get ready and go meet Jonah."

He turned around after he pulled on his running shorts. "Oh, yeah. That's today."

She nodded. "That's today."

"You excited?"

"Yeah." Then she paused to think about it. "Excited for it to be over."

Declan's easy smile faltered for a moment but was back before she could question it. He walked toward her, pulling on his shirt as he went, and kissed the top of her head. "Well, I'll either see you when I get back from the run or when you get back from seeing Jonah."

She smiled up at him. "Sounds good." She paused and wrinkled her nose. "Please brush your teeth before you go."

He laughed. "You're one to talk. Your breath could kill a plant."

When she threw the pillow at him, he was already running out the door.

Anna Katherine stretched out in the bed and watched the sun cast shadows on their floor and bed for much longer than she should have. Eventually, she got up to get ready for her day. When she stepped out of the shower, she had a text from Nat that bordered on an interrogation about the night before. The thought of texting exhausted her, so she opted to call Nat instead.

"Wow, a phone call," Nat said as a greeting. "I feel so honored."

"Shut up before I decide to hang up on you and find a new best friend."

Nat laughed. "Fine. I'll behave. Are you going to tell me why you and your husband decided to stay in instead of gracing us with your presence last night?"

Before she knew it, she was saying, "We had sex."

There was silence, and then Nat coughed. "I'm sorry. Can you repeat that?"

"It happened after the interview."

"And you're just now telling me?!"

Nat's screeching hurt her ears. Anna Katherine held the phone away from her and glanced at it briefly before responding. "I wasn't aware I needed to update you on my sexual adventures."

Nat scoffed. "When it comes to this complicated relationship you do." Nat sighed. "So does this mean you've told him you love him?"

"No, not in so many words, but I'm going to." She took a deep breath. "Soon."

"I'm not sure if I believe you."

Anna Katherine dropped her towel and grabbed clothes from the pile on her bed. She had the thought that she really needed to fold them. "Look, I'm going to go meet up with Jonah, so I don't have all the time in the world to convince you, but it is going to happen."

Nat sounded shocked. "You're serious about this."

"I love him, Nat. And I'm finally able to admit that to myself and anyone else, really. Declan deserves to know that."

"I'm a little surprised. This has been going on for so long, I didn't think you'd ever get to this point."

She snorted. "Thanks for the vote of confidence, Nat."

"Anytime." Before Anna Katheirne could get a word in, Nat said, "When are you going to tell him?"

"Not today. I'm not there yet. It's terrifying and exciting, and..." She stopped talking when she realized she was smiling. "I love him, Nat."

Her best friend laughed. "Took you long enough to get here."

"Yeah, well I'm about to leave to meet up with Jonah, but I'll call you later?"

"You better. I want to know every detail of you two idiots finally admitting your feelings."

That caused Anna Katherine to pause, and that pause allowed doubt to creep in. "You don't know if he feels the same. He hasn't really dated since college."

"Neither have you."

She let out a relieved sigh. "That's a good point."

They hung up after saying their goodbyes, and Anna Katherine walked back into the hallway only to see Declan standing in the entry, staring in her direction.

Declan never meant to overhear Kit's conversation with Nat. It just happened, and when he heard her say that she was going to meet up with Jonah and tell him that she *loved him*, he was so caught off guard, he couldn't breathe, much less move. He was a deer caught in headlights when she walked out and spotted him.

He tried to act like the world hadn't just been ripped right out from under him, but neither him or Kit had ever been great at hiding anything from the other. "I got back from my run."

Her eyes had gone wide, and they stayed like that when she said, "I can see that."

"Was that Nat?"

She nodded. "Yeah, uh, how much of that did you hear?"

Enough, he thought to himself. "Not much. You headed out?"

"Yeah." She nodded again. "I'll see you when I get back?"

"Yep." He took a few steps to his room and closed the door behind him.

He heard Kit tell him bye and the door click shut, and then he was by himself, reeling with the information that the woman he loved was in love with Jonah, the guy who stabbed them both in the back.

Anna Katherine's heart was still racing when she got in her car and pulled out of the car park. She had been wracking her brain to try to remember what she had said out loud, what Declan could have possibly heard. He said he hadn't heard much, but something was off with him. She tried to think if she had said anything that would make him act like that—shutting himself in his room without saying bye to her— and couldn't think of anything. Unless he heard her tell Nat that she loved him, or somehow pieced it together and didn't feel the same way.

She tried to tell herself that she was overreacting, but her heart kept racing and her brain kept coming up with scenarios, the next always worse than the previous.

She let out a sigh and did the best she could to stuff all the what-if's and worries out of her mind. She needed to focus on this last meeting with Jonah, and then she could worry about Declan. Until then, she needed to suck it up.

Declan was sitting on the couch when Kit walked through the door and he stood once the door closed behind her.

"We need to talk."

She made her way to him and sat down on the other end of the couch. He wanted to reach out to her, but there was an entire cushion separating them. Something told him that she put that space between them on purpose. He cleared his throat, trying to find the words he desperately needed to say.

"So," he said, and mentally kicked himself. What a lame start to this conversation. "I heard you talking to Nat."

The blood drained from her face and her eyes went wide.

"And, Kit... I..." He ran his hand through his hair. Why was this so difficult? "I need to know.... Who were you talking about? I heard you say you love him, and if you're in love with Jonah then just—"

She held her hand up, something fierce and angry in her eyes. "I'm sorry, *what*?"

At first, Anna Katherine was simply terrified and distraught that Declan found out she loved him before she was ready to say those words, but then she realized that somehow in his twisted brain he thought she had been talking about Jonah. As if she would ever cheat on anyone, much less on Declan.

Not that they were in an official relationship, but in a way they were. They were *married*. And their ten commandments clearly stated no outside relationships with anyone.

After everything Jonah put them both through, Declan should have known that she would never cheat, even emotionally, on anyone.

She tried to calm herself down with a deep breath. "What are you saying?"

He looked startled by her question, "Just that if you are in love with Jonah—"

Anna Katherine interrupted him. "You have got to be kidding me! Do you really not know me? After everything, do you really think I would still be in love with my ex?"

"Kit, just take a moment and—"

"I will not *take a moment*, Declan Mullins! You're accusing me of something you of all people should know better! Why would I be in love with him?! Why would I cheat?"

Declan had apparently had enough of her interrupting him if his glare was anything to go by. "It's not cheating if it's a fake relationship, Anna Katherine."

She laughed, but it was filled with bitterness and not an ounce of humor. "Right. Because it's not like we didn't make our vows in front of the people we care about most and God or that we signed legal papers proving our marriage."

"So real, in fact, that you wouldn't let me voice how I felt before we had sex."

She seethed. "That has nothing to do with this."

"It has everything to do with this!" He stood up, his hands waving wildly before they landed on top of his head. He turned around as if he couldn't look at her and took a deep breath.

She ignored the pang in her chest at him turning away from her. "I don't understand how."

Slowly, he turned around. When he finally looked at her again, she saw a myriad of emotions warring across his face. "Of course you don't."

She wanted him to sit back down, but he continued to stand. She wasn't about to offer him the seat next to her.

"You're so angry with me right now because you thought I was accusing you of being like Jonah, but you don't even realize you're constantly accusing me of being like him, of not being worthy of your heart. You're saying I'm untrustworthy by comparing me to him when you refuse to let me through your carefully built walls and allow me to love you." His voice had started off hard, but softened as he went on. What he said next was barely more than a whisper, yet held so much truth and emotion in it. "Truly and authentically love you."

And there it was. The four letter word that Anna Katherine thought she had been ready to say, but hearing it from Declan made her throat go dry. But the truth and weight of it hung between the two of them.

It was her move, and she was paralyzed with fear.

She had told Nat she loved Declan. She had told herself in Ireland. But there was a deeper layer of vulnerability in voicing that to the man who held her heart in the palm of his hand. The choice of *when* and *how* to tell him was taken from her, and now she was frozen. Did she actually trust him as much as she always claimed?

Tears sprang to her eyes, and when she sniffed them back, Declan deflated.

Declan took a step back, his heart beating erratically in his chest. He went into this conversation thinking that she was in love with Jonah, but halfway through it had clicked. She wasn't in love with Jonah. Hadn't been in a long time. She was, however, in love with *him*. If she wasn't, she never would have become as angry as she did when she thought he was accusing her of still being in love with her ex. As much as that thrilled him, it terrified her.

The conversation he had overheard came flooding back to him. Her voice flooded his mind as if she were saying it all again right in front of him.

"Not today. I'm not there yet. It's terrifying and exciting, and I love him, Nat."

She loved him. Him, as in Declan himself, not some idiot from their college days. But she was scared and knew herself well enough to know she wasn't there yet. Her freedom of choice was ripped away from her, whether he intentionally had taken it from her or not, by eavesdropping on her conversation.

"Kit..." He so desperately wanted to say those words. To tell her how much he loved her, and that he would wait until she was ready. "You're clearly not ready for this conversation."

If at all possible, she turned even more pale, but she remained quiet.

"I'm going to go see Harry," he said as he grabbed his phone from where it had fallen on the couch. When he stood back up, he made sure she was looking at him before he went on. "When you're ready to talk, that's where I'll be."

She didn't say a word as he grabbed his keys and left.

46

The drive to her childhood home was a silent one. Anna Katherine didn't bother turning on music or talking to herself as she sometimes did. Even Fox, who sat in the passenger's seat, didn't talk or whine like she almost always did when she was in the car with her and Declan. It was almost as if she could feel the heaviness, too.

Anna Katherine had sat in silence once Declan had walked out of their apartment. Her heart had pounded in her chest and her hands had been slick with sweat. She hadn't moved until Fox came up and butted her knee with her nose. It had only been then that Anna Katherine had taken a deep breath, trying to calm her racing heart, and started petting the dog.

"What—" But she couldn't even get the question out before she began crying. She had angrily grabbed the tissue box and wiped her tears away. She hadn't been sure what she was about to ask the dog sitting at her feet, but whatever it was came second to the pressure in her chest.

When she pulled into the long driveway and saw her mom tending to her flowers in the side yard, some of that pressure lifted. Declan was her safe place, but coming home to her parents would always be a close second, no matter how ridiculous Patty could be.

When Patricia spotted her, she stood up from where she had been kneeling by a bush sprinkled with blossoming flowers. She smiled and dusted her hands off, but that smile morphed into concern when she saw Anna Katherine getting out of the car.

Fox immediately started running around the yard and sniffing every inch of the place. Patty ignored the pup and started toward Anna Katherine. She was halfway to her when she asked, "What's wrong?"

The tears sprang up again, just as unwanted as before. She shrugged and wiped the tears away. "I've messed up, Mama. Really, really messed up."

Patty sat Anna Katherine down on one of the barstools at the counter and slid a plate of cookies and a glass of milk toward her. Patty was kind enough to allow her to nibble on the cookie and take a sip before the questioning began.

"Tell me more about this mess. What happened?"

Her stomach twisted, and she dropped the cookie back on the plate. She somehow managed to look her mom in the eye when she said, "You're going to be so mad."

Patty placed her hand gently on top of Anna Katherine's, her voice gentle and reassuring. "Maybe, but that just means I have yet another chance to show you forgiveness and grace."

That made Anna Katherine's throat feel tight. As ridiculous as her mother was, she was her mom, and she was a good one. Was she really about to confess to her that her marriage with Declan was a sham? And, on top of that, she might've ruined whatever chance she had with her best friend.

She tried to swallow, but it hurt. She looked around the kitchen. First at the pile of cookies in front of her, then at the glass of milk, and then at the sink that was as spotless as it was when it first been installed.

Patty lifted her hand off of hers and snapped her fingers. "Stop that. Out with it."

Anna Katherine groaned and covered her face with her hands. "Declan and I only got married to help each other out."

Patty, shocking Anna Katherine to her core, giggled. Her mother actually *giggled*. Anna Katherine dropped her hands and stared at her mother in pure shock.

"Oh, honey. If you're thinking that you hid that from me, you are sadly mistaken."

When Anna Katherine continued to sit and gawk at her mother, Patty chuckled. "Don't be so surprised. Besides, I need to know more about this mess. Surely it's more than just that."

Her world seemed to tilt at that moment. Her high strung mother who wanted everything perfect was okay with Anna Katherine's not-so-perfect and not-so-traditional start to her marriage. She went back to staring at the cookies, taking a moment to process that realization before sharing the rest with her mom.

"Do you remember Jonah?"

If Patty thought it was an odd question for the topic, she didn't show it. "Of course I do."

"He told me he loved me." When Patty's eyes went wide, Anna Katherine quickly added, "Not recently. While we were dating. He told me, and I believed him. Yet somehow, he left me so easily."

Patty seemed to realize where she was going with this. She reached out and placed her hand on top of Anna Katherine's. "My sweet girl, Declan is not Jonah."

"I know that." Anna Katherine took a deep breath. "But what if…"

When she trailed off, unable to continue the thought, Patty gave her hand a squeeze. "What if what, honey?"

"Jonah got tired of me. When I lived with Nat before the wedding, she got tired of me. You and dad get tired of me—"

"We do not!"

Anna Katherine rolled her eyes and continued. "When we go on family vacations, you two always say you'll need a break from me halfway through it." Patty went to interrupt her again, but Anna Katherine lifted her hand to stop her. "It's okay. I get tired of you two, too. The point of it is, if you guys get tired of me, what hope is there that Declan won't grow tired of me?"

"Oh, honey," Patty said in what was probably her most motherly voice. "There is no hope. He is going to get tired of you."

Anna Katherine gawked at her again. This was not the encouraging conversation she thought she was about to receive.

Patty went on. "And you're going to get tired of him. That's what happens when you live with and do life with someone. That's what love is for."

"I don't understand."

"You love Declan, and I have no doubt in my heart that he loves you just as much. The thing is, and this is so important to remember in all relationships, that love isn't always this happy, butterfly, giddy feeling in your stomach. Love is so much more than an emotion. It's an *action*."

Anna Katherine sat there mulling it over in her head for a moment. Then she said, "Deciding I'm too much is also an action."

"Do you trust him?"

"Of course I do."

"Then you need to trust him with this. Trust him to keep choosing you, while he trusts you to do the same with him. And when life gets too hard, and marriage seems impossible, trust God. He, more than anything else, fills in our cracks." Patty took a cookie for herself and broke it in half before continuing. "The Kit I know and love never allowed fear to dictate her life."

Nat tried not to work on weekends. It wasn't like she would get paid for it, but sometimes the quietness and stillness of being alone in her classroom on a Saturday was worth it. It was also nice because her phone didn't get service in the school building, so any annoying messages from her friends wouldn't come through to distract her.

The downside to that was all the missed calls and messages flooded her phone as soon as she walked outside to her car. And to her horror, she had seven missed calls and thirteen texts from Harry.

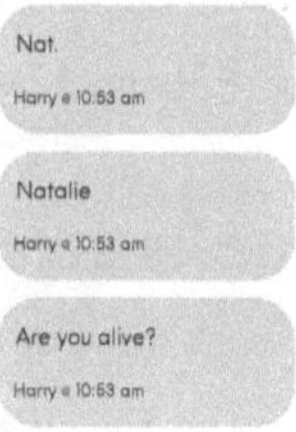

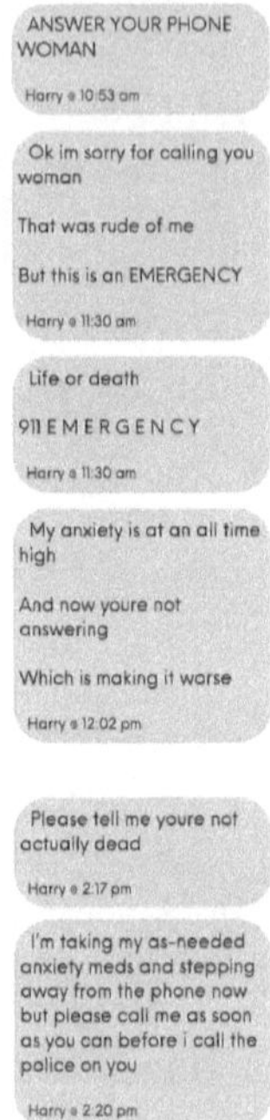

Nat was torn between smiling and allowing her own anxiety to skyrocket. What was going on with Harry? She called him as soon as she read the last text, and he answered on the first ring.

"Where have you been?" he whispered instead of greeting her.

Without thinking about it, she whispered back, "I've been at work!"

"It's a Saturday!"

She slid into her car when she whispered-yelled back, "So?!"

He was still whispering. "We need to work on your work boundaries."

"Are you going to tell me why you were having an anxiety attack?" She realized then that she was whispering and cleared her throat. "Why are we whispering?"

"I'm whispering because Declan is in the other room. I have no idea why you're whispering."

"Why does Declan determine whether or not you whisper?"

In a very loud whisper that she was sure Declan could hear from wherever Harry was hiding in his apartment Harry said, quite frantically, "*They broke up!*"

Nat had been about to start her car, but when Harry dropped that bomb, she dropped her keys onto the floorboard.

Her mind was reeling. "What do you mean they broke up? We're talking about Declan and Kit, right? She called me this morning and told me she was about to tell him she loved him!"

"Well, apparently it didn't go as planned because he's currently on my floor crying."

She gasped. "*No.*"

"I'm going to deal with Declan. You find Kit and figure out what the heck happened!"

They said their goodbyes, and then Nat found her keys and hurried to Kit and Declan's apartment to interrogate her friend.

The only problem was when she arrived at the apartment, Kit and Fox were nowhere to be found.

Declan had his arm over his eyes when he heard Harry step back from around the bookcase he had been hiding behind.

"How was your conversation with Nat?"

"You weren't supposed to hear any of it."

Declan peeked at him from underneath his arm. "Mate. You live in a loft and you are absolutely terrible at whispering. Also, I'm not crying. And we didn't break up."

"You were. I saw the tears." Harry went and sat on the couch. "Are you ready to tell me what happened?"

"Kit loves me."

Harry had been about to cross his legs, but he froze with one leg hovering over the other. It would have been funny if it weren't for the situation.

After a moment, he relaxed again, crossed his legs, and leaned forward. "Am I supposed to be shocked?"

"No, but—"

"Wait!" Harry jumped up. "Kit loves you! Why are we upset about this?!"

Declan groaned as he sat up so he could properly look at Harry. "It's the way I found out. And," he sighed, running a hand through his hair, "the fact that she isn't ready to admit it."

Harry sat back down, a frown taking the place of the excited smile that was just there. "I'm confused."

Declan stood up and started pacing the room. "We, uh…" He paused, trying to find the words. "We consummated our marriage, and I was going to tell her that I loved her right before things became too heated. But she stopped me. She wasn't ready to hear it yet, I don't think. She's scared, and I just don't know why."

"Okay, but that doesn't explain how you found out she loves you. I mean, it's been as clear as day this whole time, but something had to have caused this crisis."

"I overheard her on the phone with Nat. She said she loved someone, and at first I thought it was Jonah, and we got into a little tiff about it. It wasn't until then that I realized she had been talking about me. I took away her control of when to tell me, and she completely froze."

"So." Harry studied him for a moment. "You're telling me that you found out she loved you. And you love her. And then you just... left her?"

Declan shot him a glare. "When you phrase it like that, it sounds ridiculous!"

"Because it is ridiculous!" Harry jumped up again and was suddenly directly in front of Declan. Declan froze when he put his hands on Declan's shoulder. *"Mate."*

"What?"

"She's scared."

"I know!"

"And you left her."

"Obviously."

Harry waited a beat before groaning out another mate and throwing his hands up in the air. "Have you always been this daft?! You know the issue! And instead of being there and helping her through it, you left her to deal with it on her own!"

"I don't want to force her to do anything she doesn't want to do!"

Harry shot him a disbelieving look. "She *married* you, Declan! Do you think she would've married me had I messed up my visa?"

Declan's stomach churned at the thought of her marrying Harry. He ignored the rare bout of jealousy and shrugged. "She'd do anything to help a friend."

"No. She'd do *almost* anything to help a friend. She'd do *anything* for *you.*" Harry was back in his face again and poked his chest with a finger. "You two idiots have been in love long before now. You're both just too stubborn and scared to do anything about it."

Declan was about to say something—what, he wasn't sure—but thankfully Harry's phone ringing saved him.

When Harry glanced at the phone, his entire body softened. "Hey, Nat. Did you find Kit?"

Whatever Nat said, Declan couldn't hear. But by the glare Harry was giving him, he doubted he wanted to hear it anyway. And then, several things happened all at once.

The first was the door to Harry's apartment swinging open, slamming against the wall. The second was Fox running full speed toward him, only to bypass him to lick-attack Harry, knocking him back into the couch. The third was that the door hit the wall so forcefully that it bounced off and hit whoever was standing in the doorway. And if Fox wasn't enough to clue him in on who was there, the sound of Kit's yelp certainly was.

47

Anna Katherine stood in Harry's doorway, her eyes closed, holding her forehead and nose with both hands. She hadn't meant to open the door so aggressively, but now her nose was throbbing in pain thanks to her mistake.

Declan was at her side before she opened her eyes. She only knew it was him by the frantic, "Kit!" as he made his way to her and the feel of his hands on hers as he gently pulled them away from her face. "Kit, are you okay?"

She sniffed, which caused her nose to hurt even more, and she let out a soft whine.

"Kit!" Declan sounded frantic again. "You're bleeding!"

That made her eyes snap open, and sure enough, her hand was covered in blood. She reached up to gently touch her nose with her clean hand, and when she pulled it away, there was blood on her fingertips. She let out a groan. "Great."

Before she could do anything, Declan ushered her inside and led her to the kitchen. He all but shoved her onto a stool, told her to stay put, and rummaged around Harry's kitchen until he found a cloth that he soaked in water.

Harry's voice tore her attention away from Declan. "No, Nat. You do not need to call 9-1-1."

"Nat? Why are you on the phone with Nat?"

Harry waved her question away. "It did not sound like we were being murdered. Okay, fine. But it was just Fox and Kit." He paused and rubbed Fox's ear. "Yes, Kit. I don't know what she's doing here! If you would let me get off the phone, I could find out!"

Declan appeared in front of her with an ice pack and the wet cloth. "Here. Let me help you."

She took the ice from him and held it to her head, while he cleaned up the blood that made its way down her chin, then gently held the cloth beneath her nose to stop the bleeding.

After a moment, they managed to look at each other.

Declan was the first to speak up. "What was that?"

She shrugged. "Nothing went according to plan."

He was quiet and looked at her carefully. "And what was the plan?"

"I—" But she stopped and glanced at Harry. "What's going on between him and Nat?"

He let out a breathy chuckle. "Pretty sure they're dating."

"What! Ow!" In her excitement, she bumped her nose. "That hurt."

His face turned sympathetic. "I'm sorry, Kit."

Anna Katherine looked up at him again. His hair was still messy from his run and probably him stressing and running his hands through it. But his eyes were just as kind as always, and his smile was her favorite thing.

Without allowing herself to overthink her actions, she reached up and placed her hand on his cheek, her thumb tracing over his freckles. Her heart melted when he leaned into her.

Anna Katherine couldn't stop the smile from spreading across her face as she finally said, "I love you."

There were gasps behind them, but they both ignored Harry and Nat and only focused on each other. In the moment, Declan was the only one that mattered.

A smile inched its way onto his face. His blue eyes twinkled, and happiness radiated off of him in waves. "What was that?"

She smiled back and moved her hand to where she could run her fingers through his hair. "You were right. I was comparing you to Jonah and assuming you would treat me the same way he did. The thing is, you're my best friend, and I just needed a reminder that you haven't stopped standing by my side since the day I met you. I love you, Declan Anthony Mullins."

His smile was full-fledged now. "Yeah? No one forced you to say that?"

"I mean, Patty did have some choice words, but since when do I listen to her?"

Declan tucked a strand of hair behind her ear. "I don't care who you listened to as long as you mean it."

"With my entire heart."

He was so close. She could feel his breath on her skin, but she wanted him even closer. "I love you back."

He leaned closer. She was ready for his kiss, but then from behind her she heard, "Turn the camera around, Hector!"

Harry's face twisted in disgust at the name. "That is—"

"Now is not the time!"

Declan threw the bloody towel at Harry—thankfully her nose had stopped bleeding—and Harry dodged it. "Do you mind?"

Harry tried to look innocent, but his cheeky grin couldn't hide for long. The phone pointed in their direction also didn't help any. "Nat just wanted to be a part of this moment."

Declan shot him a downright dirty glare that made Anna Katherine giggle before he pulled her off the stool and behind Harry's bookshelf. It was only then, behind their false sense of privacy, that he finally leaned down and kissed her. His hands stayed on her waist, a firm, physical reminder that he wasn't going anywhere.

Declan broke away, ending the kiss a little too early for Anna Katherine's liking. His hands left her waist, but she wasn't without his touch for long because he quickly intertwined his fingers with hers. He brushed a soft kiss on her forehead before resting his against hers.

"Ow." Anna Katherine winced but didn't pull away from him. No matter how much pain she was in, she didn't think her smile could disappear.

"Sorry." He moved so he wasn't resting on the fresh bruise. "There had to be an easier way to get to this point."

She laughed. "Yeah, but where would the fun have been in that?"

He made a disbelieving sound that was a mix between a snort and a laugh and pulled her closer to wrap her in a hug. "We need to work on your definition of fun, Kit-Kat."

Growing up, all of her friends talked about how they wanted someone tall, dark, and handsome. Declan possessed one out of the three characteristics. He had the handsome down to a fault. He wasn't dark. He was sunshine on an autumn day with golden brown hair that always looked soft to the touch, and he was only a few inches taller than her. But, oh, was he perfect for her. She would choose him over and over again, and if there were alternate universes like in the movies, she'd choose him in those, too.

He knew her weaknesses. He knew that she would leave mugs out long enough and with just enough coffee left in them that mold would grow. He knew that she wouldn't clean her hair out of the shower and it would clog the drain. He would set her alarms for her when she forgot. He would buy her favorite foods. He would be annoyed at her when they went on road trips and she'd have to stop every hour to use the bathroom…

But that wouldn't stop him from loving her.

48

The Core Four

Ladies and gents I hope
we are all having a fabulous
day But more importantly...

Harry @ 10:32 am

Why are we here?

Kit @ 10:33 am

I just wanted to point out...
That i have officially won
Patty over

Harry @ 10:33 am

It doesn't take much. Just
be a guy with a foreign
accent apparently

Kit @ 10:34 am

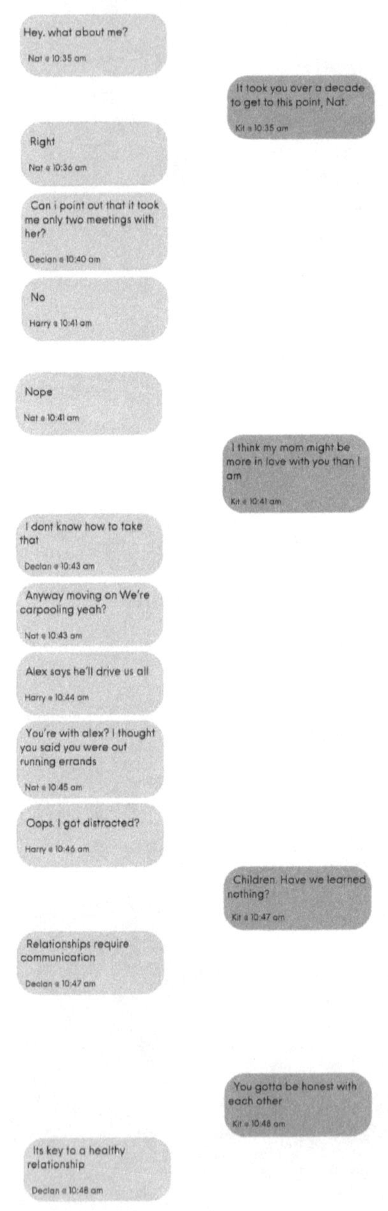
Hey. what about me?
Nat @ 10:35 am

It took you over a decade
to get to this point, Nat.
Kit @ 10:35 am

Right
Nat @ 10:36 am

Can i point out that it took
me only two meetings with
her?
Declan @ 10:40 am

No
Harry @ 10:41 am

Nope
Nat @ 10:41 am

I think my mom might be
more in love with you than I
am
Kit @ 10:41 am

I dont know how to take
that
Declan @ 10:43 am

Anyway moving on We're
carpooling yeah?
Nat @ 10:43 am

Alex says he'll drive us all
Harry @ 10:44 am

You're with alex? I thought
you said you were out
running errands
Nat @ 10:45 am

Oops. I got distracted?
Harry @ 10:46 am

Children. Have we learned
nothing?
Kit @ 10:47 am

Relationships require
communication
Declan @ 10:47 am

You gotta be honest with
each other
Kit @ 10:48 am

Its key to a healthy
relationship
Declan @ 10:48 am

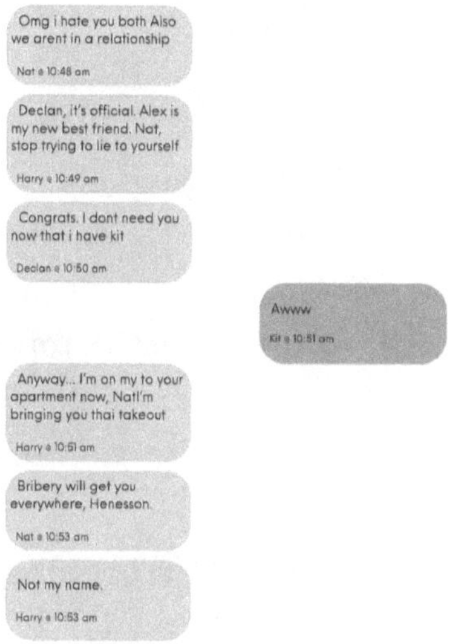

Patricia met them at the door with smiles and greetings and more compliments than Anna Katherine had ever heard in her life. She had cooked her award-winning lasagna with homemade sourdough bread, and Timothy had supplied the salad.

"It's the best part of the meal," he told them with a wink.

Patricia whacked him with a dishcloth before shooing them all out of the kitchen while she finished up.

The six of them were in the living room waiting for Patricia to tell them that the food was ready when Timothy glanced toward Harry and Nat, only to do a double-take.

"I thought Nat was dating Alex."

All of them glanced at each other.

"Well, you see..." Alex trailed off.

Kit groaned. "They were never dating, Dad."

Patricia walked in then, and one look at everyone's face, she asked, "What's happening now?"

Timothy looked at his wife. "Apparently, Alex and Nat were never dating."

"Oh, I know."

He seemed to be shocked by that. "You knew?"

She scoffed. "Of course I knew, dear. These are my children. I'm more perceptive than you all seem to believe."

"Well, someone needs to catch me up because I'm still quite confused."

Patricia sighed. "Fine. Alex and Nat were being a wonderful brother and friend by taking the spotlight off of Declan and Kit—"

"Mother!"

"—during their fake engagement announcement."

"Their announcement was fake?"

"No, the engagement was."

Timothy blinked. "But we saw them get married."

"Yes, but they did it to get Declan citizenship. Keep up, Timothy."

Timothy shot up from his chair. "They *what*?!"

Kit shrunk back against the couch, doing her best to hide. When her father's glare turned to her and Declan, she was sure she would die on the spot.

"Honestly, you're being a tad dramatic." Patricia waved his concern and outrage away, "They're happily in love and married now. That's all that matters."

Timothy was seething. He turned back to Patricia. "Why are you so accepting of this?"

Patricia grabbed his arm and pulled him to the dining room. "Because this was bound to happen eventually. It was just a little messy and a little illegal this way, but they're fine now."

"A *little* illegal?"

"Timothy."

"What?"

"Relax. You and I will discuss this later. Right now, let's just enjoy having all of our children together tonight."

Once Patricia led Timothy out of the room, the rest of them stared at each other.

"Well," Nat said as she stood up, "he took that fairly well, wouldn't you all agree?"

Declan stood up and offered his hand to Kit to help her to her feet. "I'm pretty sure he wants me dead."

Alex nodded. "And I'm pretty sure Kit and I are grounded for the rest of our lives."

"Does this mean I won't be invited to the next Tran family Thanksgiving?" Harry asked.

Nat swatted his arm. "Harry."

"What?"

"Now is not the time."

They all walked in a single file behind Nat and quietly sat around the table. While Patricia brought out the food, Timothy cleared his throat.

"I was threatened and told not to bring up the situation apparently everyone but me knew about."

Patricia shot him a glare when she placed the baskets of bread at either end of the table.

"Since that's the case, who would like to distract us all from my lying children and tell me about their day?"

Nat raised her hand. "Oh! Let me tell you all about the frog and the hand dryer."

Harry scrunched up his face. "Right before we eat might not be the best time, babe."

She slouched back in her chair. "Ugh, fine."

Patricia finally joined them at the table. "If no one else has news to share, I'll update you all on Susan and her money-laundering children."

"Wait." Anna Katherine leaned across the table to stare at her mom. "Susan is a real person?"

Patricia looked at her daughter like she had gone insane. "Of course she is. Why wouldn't she be?"

"I thought you made her up to make us feel guilty about lying to you about our marriage."

"I definitely used her story to my advantage, but I didn't *lie*." She gave her and Alex a piercing glance and then went on. "She called me just yesterday to tell me she ended up turning them in. I can't imagine the kind of drama that is going on in that household right now."

Timothy scoffed. "I can."

When Patricia gave him a similar glare, he sighed. "Right. Sorry."

The rest of dinner went by without a hiccup, though it was slightly awkward. Declan was thankful once Alex dropped him and Kit back home and they were able to shut the door to the prying eyes of their friends and family.

Kit draped her purse on a chair before turning to look at him. "Well, that was fun."

A surprised laugh came out of Declan. "I think we need to look up the meaning of the word 'fun' for you."

"Ha-ha, very funny. At least my dad didn't try to kill you."

He took the few steps toward her and rested his hands on her hips. "Give him time."

She tilted her head back to look up at him. "What now?"

"What'd you mean?"

The smile she gave him was almost shy. "How do we date while married?"

"We take it one day at a time." And then, he kissed her.

Tenth Commandment: Thou Shalt Divorce in Two Years.

"We obviously can't stay married forever."

Declan nodded, still snacking on the cookies. "Obviously."

"When should we end this charade?"

"Two years?"

Kit shrugged. "Sounds good."

Epilogue:

Kit was, as always, running late. Her therapy session had run long, so she was claiming that it wasn't her fault this time. Thankfully, she had cleaned up the kitchen while Declan took Fox for a walk earlier that morning, so she at least didn't have to worry about that today.

Running from the elevator to their apartment door, she slipped out of her shoes as soon as she made it across the threshold and flung her keys toward the bowl on the table.

From somewhere in their bedroom, she heard Declan yell, "You're late, Kit-Kat!"

"It's not my fault, my session ran long!" she called back.

For the past year, Kit had been seeing a counselor that both someone from church and Harry had recommended. At first it had been hard opening up and being vulnerable to a complete stranger, but the more she went, the more naturally it came. And the more her therapist was helping her learn how to trust again and how to be a better wife.

Rummaging through the cupboards to grab a granola bar, she heard a ruckus from the other room. Within seconds, Fox was at her side, sitting like a good girl at her feet and wagging her tail.

"You only came because you heard me open the cupboard, didn't you?" she asked the dog, smiling as she broke off a piece of her snack bar and tossed it for Fox to catch mid-air.

Declan poked his head out of their bedroom. "What was that?"

"I was talking to Fox."

He grinned at her. "How was your session?"

"Perfect. I made her laugh, so I think I won."

The grin morphed into a full fledged smile as he laughed and said, "I don't think that's how therapy works, love."

"Of course it is." She broke off another two pieces of granola, one for her and one for Fox.

He walked out of their bedroom holding at least four mugs—she was never going to be perfect, okay? Once he placed them in the sink, he made his way toward her as he put something in one of his pockets. "C'mon, how did it go?"

She offered him a bite of her granola bar which was not going as far as she had hoped thanks to Fox, then shrugged and ate the rest when he shook his head no. "It went well enough. We talked about my childhood and my ADHD and how awful I am and how perfect you are."

He laughed again as he wrapped his arms around her in a tight hug. "Yeah, sounds about right."

She rested her head on his shoulder and sighed. After a minute of her body fully relaxing into his, she went on to say, "It really was good, though."

"Not too tired? We can postpone family lunch if we need to."

"Absolutely not." She pulled away from him so she could look him in the eye. "Patty would have a fit."

"Anna Katherine." His smile turned more serious. "Answer the question."

She rolled her eyes. "No. I am not too tired. And, as you stated, I'm late. Which means you're late. Which means we're late. Which means...."

Together they both nodded. "Patty."

Pulling apart, Kit quickly changed, and Declan put the harness on Fox. Within a few moments, the three of them were getting into Declan's car and heading to Kit's childhood home.

Everyone sat around the patio table that Harry had helped Timmy build last summer as Declan continued to succeed in wiggling his way into the Tran family. The weather was cooling off, finally, as they reached the end of the year and began to prepare for the holidays. Patty already had her fall decor leaves wrapped around the railing of the porch and a giant turkey and cornucopia that looked to have seen better days.

Harry poked the head of the ceramic turkey with a curious look. "And what, uh, happened to our decoration?"

He was sitting between Patty and Alex, and they both glanced at Kit when they heard the question.

Declan glanced around the table. In previous years he had never paid much attention to the turkey or the cornucopia. "What did Kit do to the poor turkey?"

Timmy was trying to hide a smile. "She *claims* she wanted to have a tea party and on her way upstairs, dropped the turkey and the cornucopia and failed to catch them as they tumbled back down the stairs."

"It's the truth!" Kit threw her hands up and looked down-right offended at the possibility of people not believing her.

No one around the table looked like they did believe her, with the exception of Nat who had been at her side when the incident had occurred.

"It was my grandmother's," Patty said. "So it was a sad day, but thankfully, we were able to piece it back together."

No one mentioned the giant missing tail feather or the chipped and crooked wattle.

Timmy cleared his throat. "Before we dig into this delicious meal that everyone pitched in to help prepare, let's go around and list a struggle and a blessing from this week."

Alex started them off, and as the thanksgivings rounded the table, Kit leaned over to whisper to Declan, "My struggle was definitely getting up early every morning this week, and my blessing would be you."

He chuckled and draped his arm over her shoulders. "You know they're not going to let you use that. You try that every family dinner."

She scrunched up her nose. "It's not my fault if it's the truth."

He smiled as he shook his head and then pressed a kiss atop hers.

As the rounds continued, the struggle ranged from something small like having to wait in line at the store, to Nat's students throwing furniture around the room. The blessings were just as diverse but even more genuine. Her mom's was the same as it was every week. She was thankful that all of her children, both biological and bonus, were willing to have weekly meals with them. And every week, Harry and Nat smiled ear-to-ear hearing it.

When it was Declan's turn, he positioned himself so he was facing Kit. She raised an eyebrow curiously but didn't voice her questions.

"My struggle this week was, without a doubt, keeping this from my best friend." He pulled out an envelope from his back pocket and handed it to Kit.

She took it hesitantly. "What's this?"

Everyone around the table fell silent. Declan smiled. "Just open it, Kit-Kat."

She looked unsure as she slid a finger under the sealed flap. She looked even more unsure as five Polaroid pictures came tumbling out. Again she asked, "What is this?"

But Declan didn't answer, and by the light blush on her cheeks, she was already guessing what was on the Polaroids.

She spread them out on the table, her hands unsteady as she attempted to put them in order.

Just like he had said in their interview, he had taken Polaroids of himself and Fox holding—or chewing in Fox's case—poster boards with words that asked a very important question.

"Will you renew our vows?"

Her head snapped around to stare at him, and he was already holding the same velvet box he had handed her in the car what seemed like a lifetime ago.

Her eyes crinkled into a smile. "Really?"

He nodded. "Really, really."

She looked back at the pictures and then glanced around the table. "You guys helped with this, didn't you? I recognize your handwriting, Nat."

Harry and Nat nodded, but it was Timmy who spoke up. "We know you two had an unorthodox start to your marriage, but the love you two share is genuine. Your mom and I were thrilled when Declan came to us with this."

"Also, I was still upset that you never got a proper proposal." Nat eyed Declan critically. "Though, he still hasn't gotten down on one knee."

Declan grabbed her hand and placed the velvet box in her palm. "So, what do you say?"

Her smile was one of the most beautiful sights he'd ever seen, and when she nodded and said yes, his heart soared.

Opening the box, she frowned when it was empty. "Um, Declan?"

He laughed. "The ring you have on belongs in there. It was my Gram's."

Her eyebrows shot up in surprise. "What! Declan Anthony, you told me you'd found it and that it was worthless!"

He took her hand in his, rubbing his thumb across the ring. "Which is technically true. I had forgotten Gram had given it to me, and I found it the week before I gave it to you."

"But—"

"Oh, just kiss him already!" Patty sent her daughter a bemused look.

Declan and Kit glanced at each other, and then with a giggle, Kit did exactly what her mother demanded.

THE NEW COMMANDMENTS OF OUR ACTUAL MARRIAGE:

1. *Both shall know, respect, and show the other love through their love language.*

2. *Kit will do the dishes as long as Declan doesn't drink from the carton.*

3. *Every Thanksgiving will be spent with the Tran family, and every Christmas and New Years will be spent with the Mullinses.*

4. *Thursday night date night will never stop being a thing.*

5. *We will choose to love each other even when it's hard.*

6. *~~We will share Fox Bath Duty. Kit will bathe Fox every Monday.~~ Declan will bathe Fox every Monday since he's the idiot who adopted her.*

7. *We will both be honest about how we are feeling, even if it seems impossible.*

8. *Listen. Apologize. Forgive.*

9. *Grow with each other. (adapt as we both change)*

10. *I love you. - AKMI love you back. - DAM*

ACKNOWLEDGEMENTS

This book never would have made it out into the world without heaps and heaps of people. Writing this, my biggest fear is leaving someone out, but I'll do my best to include everyone who has helped make this dream of mine come true. I can't do that without first acknowledging that the only way any of this was even possible was because of my Lord, without whom I wouldn't have the gift of creativity.

Now, on to the others.

To the OGOQ Squad, who I first met in Vermont, but who have poured into me and my writing since that summer only a few short years ago. Thank you Jeff for creating a space where creative minds can come together, feed into one another, and be lifted up. Thank you for giving us a voice, guiding us, showing us the publishing process, and praying alongside us.

To Ari and Rebecca who have a heart for fictional worlds and traveling, and who I love dearly. Thank you both for always taking time to listen to my stories, help flesh out characters, and share your own worlds with me. Thank you for our long talks both on the phone and as we explore new cities. Our friendship was unexpected, but I will be forever grateful for both of you.

To my editors, cover designer, and all of the Glory Writers team, I wouldn't have been able to follow through on this without you. Megan, thank you for creating a cover that captured Kit and Declan so well. Thank you for being patient and working to make this dream of mine become a reality. Abigayle, thank you for not only reading and helping me become a better writer, but encouraging me along the way. Victoria, you have mentored me, coached me, and edited my book. You have been such a pivotal piece in this journey, and I truly believe I'd be lost without you. You have become a dear friend, someone I can go to with worries that go beyond writing, and know that you will be on your knees in prayer alongside me. Thank you for always being willing to talk with me for hours on end. I do not take your time or your friendship for granted.

To my beta readers, Molly, Chelsea, Ayaa, Stevi, Morgan, Jessica, Robin, and Georganna, thank you for the time spent reading, critiquing, and encouraging this little book of mine. Molly, a short acknowledgement is not enough space to thank you for everything, but know that I am so thankful our paths eventually crossed, even if our time in the Green House didn't overlap. Chelsea, thank you for being my cheerleader. You always have been, and you continued to be just that as you read and fell in love with my characters. Thank you for loving them as much as I love them. Ayaa and Stevi, you two have been with me since my fanfiction days, and it means the world to me that you both would want to be a part of this next step. Boybands brought us together, but you're both stuck with me now. Morgan, Jessica, and Robin, thank you for not only sharing the parts of TTCOFM that you loved, but also the parts that needed more attention or help. You three have made me a better writer. And Georganna, thank you for being a great example of what it means to be a follower of Christ and thank you for helping me on this journey.

To my chosen and my God-given family, thank you for dealing with me as I ventured out to make this happen. I know it wasn't always easy and that I definitely wasn't always fun to be around, but I love you all and am so thankful for each of you. To my Cave people, thank you for loving me, feeding me, and making me feel comfortable enough to take pictures. To my mom and dad, thank you for helping me financially so I could achieve my dream. To my big sister, thank you for always reading my newsletter and being one of my biggest fans. To Kayla, thank you for being such an amazing friend, going on endless adventures with me, and showing me what true friendship is. You have given me more than enough inspiration for these characters and more. To Kassie, who was there when I wrote my first story and has cheered me on every step of the way since, this story wouldn't exist without you – literally. Thank you for sitting on the phone with me for hours on end while I figured out who Kit, Declan, Harry, and Nat were. Thank you for loving Patty and Tommy as much as I do. Thank you for your one liners that somehow ignited entire scenes, and perhaps most of all, thank you for listening to Macklemore with me in the most dire of moments. You're a real one.

Thank you to each and every one of you who have helped me along the way. I appreciate you and realize I couldn't have done this alone.

Finally, to any reader who picked up this book and took a chance on a first time author, thank you. I hope these characters made you laugh and smile. Thank you.

About the Author

J. M. Brinson is a Mississippi native and lover of the Deep South, home of all of her favorite nostalgic adventures with the family and friends she holds so near and dear. With a servant heart and a love for God's creation, she takes every opportunity to travel to all of the wonderful places of the world, creating relationships that make every new place a home and every new relationship a family.

With a deep love for literature, J. M. has always yearned to find the love and adventure she seeks in life within the pages of a book. Finding this unique combination hard to come by, she began writing her own stories in her bedroom as a young teenager. Satisfying not only her own craving for real heart, relationships of all sorts, and the adventures of everyday life but those of her best friends, she has never stopped writing the stories that bear the deepest truth of life. You can follow J. M. Brinson on Instagram @authorjmbrinson.